ALL THE PIECES

— ✦ —

by Rebecca Davis

For my husband, the real Elijah Garrison.
The boy who survived the fire and still chose to love me
through all the chaos.
The man who wrangled gators by hand and flies just to feel
free.
You taught me that broken things can still be beautiful, and
healing isn't soft; it's survival, and it's ours.
And for my daughters, who remind me every damn day that
love is the bravest choice we can make, and the only one worth
fighting for.
These four saved me.
And now that our story is finally written,
I want them to know they are the reason.

Content Warning

This book contains mature themes and subject matter that may be triggering or disturbing to some readers.

Please read responsibly.

Potential Triggers Include:

- Suicidal ideation and self-harm references

- Depression, anger issues, and mental health struggles

- Parental neglect and emotional abuse

- Substance abuse (alcohol)

- Physical violence and fighting

- Sexual content (consensual, explicit, not fade-to-black)

- Themes of trauma, healing, and obsession

This is a work of fiction intended for adult readers only (18+).

Reader discretion is advised.

If you choose to continue, please take care of yourself while reading.

He was the wound and the cure, the sin, and the salvation.

I was never meant to survive him, only to feel him in every part of me.

— Rebecca Davis, All the Pieces

Table of Contents

PART I

THE SPARK THAT BURNED US

CHAPTER ONE

I kicked at the sand, staring out at the ocean, hair whipping across my face in the thick Florida breeze. Salt burned my nose. Seagulls screamed, probably celebrating my slow mental breakdown. Distant voices drifted down the beach, but they were too faint to matter. Six p.m., and it was still ninety-two degrees in Treasure Island. I wondered how far I'd have to swim before something with teeth decided to do me a favor. I could already see the headline: Depressed teen flees Washington, eaten by shark in dramatic beach debut.

I skipped helping my family unpack. My mom didn't even fight me after I chucked a snow boot at my sister's head, a snow boot that never should have been packed in the first place. No one needs snow boots in Treasure. Freaking. Island. Florida.

Thanks to my dad's old high school buddy offering him a pity job at a funeral, I wouldn't be graduating from Bellingham High. In two weeks, I'd be starting my senior year at Boca Ciega High School. Home of the Pirates.

So yeah. Thanks, Dad. I don't want to be a goddamn pirate.

We gave up four acres for a beachfront condo smaller than my old bedroom. Now I get to share a room with my ten-year-old sister, who lives in a Barbie war zone. Waking up in a twin bed and stepping on tiny plastic stilettos every morning is Groundhog Day from hell.

A seagull dive-bombed the water and came up clean. I hated how free it looked. How much it belonged here. How much I didn't.

Sweat slid down my spine, gluing my shirt to my back. The air was heavy and wet. The heat crawled under my skin and stayed there. Even the sun felt like it wanted to burn me out of spite. My shoes squished from stepping too close to the tide, every step sounding like a sarcastic laugh. This whole place felt like a setup, too shiny to be real, like someone painted paradise over rot.

The ocean was a wall of color, deeper and louder than anything back home. It didn't just look endless; it sounded alive. The crash, the hiss, the pull. Like something breathing, waiting. I walked in until the waves hit my thighs, the water so warm it felt wrong, like bathwater left too long. Tiny shells scraped my ankles. Seaweed brushed my legs like fingers. I kept walking until the water was up to my waist, until my shorts clung to me like second skin. The salt smell was stronger now, sharp enough to sting.

The ocean pressed against me, not gentle, curious. Testing. Every step took effort, like it was deciding if it wanted to let me in or spit me back out.

A wave hit, harder than I expected, slapping my face. Salt burned my eyes. I wiped it away, but it came back with the next one. My breath stuttered, the air sticking in my lungs. The world shrank to sound and pressure, waves crashing, seagulls shrieking, my heartbeat pounding out of sync with everything else.

Another wave rose caught me in the ribs, and I ducked beneath it. The water swallowed me whole. Everything went blue and muffled and endless. I opened my eyes and saw nothing but a storm of light and motion. For a second, it was almost peaceful. Silent. Weightless. My hair floated around me like ink.

Then my feet couldn't find the ground. I kicked harder. The current tugged at my legs, pulling me sideways. My pulse jumped.

The burn in my arms turned sharp. The sun above warped into a smear of gold and white, too far away to touch. The panic came slowly, slippery, until it wasn't small anymore. It was everywhere, clawing up my chest.

I turned back toward the beach, but it looked farther now. The ocean felt thicker, heavier, like it had made up its mind.

I laughed once, a broken sound that vanished in the waves. I wasn't scared, not exactly. Just tired. Tired enough to stop fighting for a second. To see what would happen if I did nothing.

So, I did.

I stopped kicking. Stopped moving. Just floated. Let the water lift me like a careless hand. The sun blurred into white heat above me. The ache in my chest spread until it felt calm.

And right when I thought the sea might actually let me go, something slammed into me.

A blur of color. Pressure on my arm. A hand. I sucked in water, choking and flailing, thinking this was it, the shark finally came.

Except it wasn't a shark. It was a boy.

He had one arm locked around my ribs and the other dragging a board through the water, his mouth set tight, eyes locked ahead. The thing that hit me, a kite, snapped in the wind, strings everywhere, wrapping around us like spiderwebs.

"Get off me!" I yelled, thrashing him. "Let me go."

"Would you shut up," he snapped, voice low and rough. "You're making it worse."

13

"Because you tackled me, asshole."

He didn't answer. He kept kicking until my feet scraped sand. I stumbled, still half tangled in his lines, my hair plastered to my face, chest heaving.

Everything smelled like metal and ocean.

When we hit shallow water, he yanked at the cords, jerking them so hard one snapped. The broken string sliced across his palm. He swore, blood spilling bright against the salt water, then ripped the rest free. His kite lay twisted down the beach, fabric torn, the wind dragging it like something dying.

"What the hell were you doing out there."

"Swimming. What the hell were you doing attacking me with your flying circus tent."

He gave a short, angry laugh. "It's a kite, genius. You almost drowned."

"I didn't almost anything. You blindsided me."

He looked me up and down, water dripping from his jaw, blood still streaking his hand. His expression wasn't calm. It was the kind of pissed that simmers quietly, all heat and control.

"You were halfway to Cuba."

"So."

"So maybe next time you try self-destruction, pick somewhere without rip currents."

I folded my arms. "You always this charming or do you save it for girls you nearly decapitate."

That got a small smirk. It was mean, sharp, the kind of smile that said he'd like to make me regret every word I'd said. "Guess I have a type."

He wiped his cut on his thigh, crimson mixing with the saltwater. The muscles in his arm flexed, and for some reason my stomach flipped.

The accent hit me then. Slight. Lazy. Southern. I hated that it sounded good. His voice was smoke and salt, and when he pushed his wet hair back, I saw the sharp angles of his face. Tan skin kissed darker from the sun. Jawline like he'd been carved from something unkind. Water dripped from his lashes, tracing down a mouth that shouldn't have looked that soft when he was glaring.

And those eyes. Green, hard, unblinking, the kind that could slice you open and still look bored about it.

He was beautiful in a way that hurt to look at. Dangerous in a way I didn't know what to do with.

I hated the way my stomach twisted under his stare.

"You always swim in clothes, or was today just special," he asked, voice low. It wasn't teasing. It was accusation.

I looked down at my soaked clothes clinging to my body, then back up. "Maybe I was hoping a shark would take me out before fashion could."

He snorted. "Good luck. Sharks don't bother with crazy."

15

"I'm not crazy."

He tilted his head. "Sure, about that."

We stood there, the tide washing over our feet, his stupid kite lines still tangled around my ankle. The silence buzzed between us, hot and uncomfortable. He smelled like salt and sunscreen and blood. The copper mixed with ocean air, sharp enough to taste. His eyes tracked every breath I took, like he was deciding if I was worth hating or saving again.

"Thanks for the save," I started, then stopped. "And... sorry. For your hand. And your kite. I wasn't exactly trying to." The words tripped over themselves and died in my throat.

He stared at me, water dripping from his hair, blood curling down his wrist. His jaw flexed once.

"I don't fucking care."

And with that, he turns and walks away.

CHAPTER TWO

I groan when the first beam of sunlight hits my face. Rolling over, I squint at the alarm clock. Barely 7 a.m. SpongeBob SquarePants blares at full blast. Of course, my little sister is already up, bouncing on her bed like we're at a sleepover instead of hell.

"Why so early?" I grumble, chucking a pillow across the room. It lands near her feet. She doesn't even flinch.

Thanks to our new floor-to-ceiling windows with the "gorgeous beach view," there's no hiding from the light. Blackout curtains stayed behind with our old life. Here, it's all sunlight and cheerfulness and overpriced decor with seashells glued to it. I'd trade it all for a single moment of peace. Or blackout blinds and some goddamn quiet.

Dragging myself out of bed, I shuffle into the kitchen. Two pills from the orange bottle on the counter. A gulp of water. No eye contact. Just routine.

Mom appears behind me like a ghost. "Oh, good, you're up already. Did you take your medication?"

I shoot her a look. She literally watched me take them. I snag a piece of bacon off the plate and bite into it like it owes me money. Crunchy, salty, greasy, perfect. One of the only things here that doesn't suck.

"I think we should go shopping before school starts," I mumble through the salt and grease. "I need new clothes. I do not want to stand out like a sore thumb here."

"I'll have Vanessa take you this weekend. You know your father and I must work."

"Obviously," I snort, maybe too loud.

Mom ignores my tone and walks over, brushing her fingers through my hair. Her palm lands soft against my cheek like she's trying to soothe a wild animal. Like I might bite if handled wrong. Maybe I will.

"I want you to be happy here, Vic. This can be a fresh start. No one has to know how things were before."

Ah, the speech. We're already there.

"Before" means back home. Where I had zero friends and enough teenage trauma to write a memoir. It wasn't always like that. I had Lisa and Angela. Then they moved, and I was left alone to navigate hallways full of assholes and teachers who smiled too wide when I passed because they'd read my file.

I never really fit anywhere. Too weird for the cool kids. Too average for the nerds. Couldn't play instruments, couldn't run track. A ghost in the system. Alone in my head, which, let's be honest, was a dangerous place to be.

The more isolated I got, the angrier I became. Or maybe I was always angry, and no one noticed until it exploded. Until they had to.

I still remember the blood.

Not a knife. A pencil. Straight through the top of her hand. The way she screamed.

My stomach flips. I push the memory down like I've been trained to do. Pills. Therapy. Repeat. I'm good now. Better. Almost.

"I'd really appreciate a room change," I say, pushing bacon around my plate. "Vanessa's nineteen. I'm seventeen. Why are we not sharing a room?"

"Vanessa's working. I don't want her late-night schedule affecting your sleep."

I roll my eyes. "My sleep patterns. Got it. Because I'm some alien experiment."

"You know what I mean."

"No, I don't. You want me to be normal," I say, air-quoting the word just to get under her skin. "But I'm seventeen with no car, no phone, and now I get to share a pastel prison with a child. I've done everything you and Dr. Feldman asked. Straight A's, GPA perfection, meds, therapy. Hell, I haven't flipped out in forever."

Mom crosses her arms. "Forever? You slapped a girl a few months ago. Let's not even mention—"

"Right, let's not mention the skeletons in the closet. We don't dare talk about the pencil incident. Anyway, I don't plan on hurting anyone here. If they leave me alone."

Mom exhales like she's holding the weight of the world. "If you do better here, you can have those things. A phone. More freedom. But you must earn them."

I raise my hands in mock surrender. "Can I please go down to the beach to read? I can't think with cartoons on blast."

She nods, probably just relieved the conversation's over.

Ten minutes later, I'm in a bikini and a cover-up, novel in hand, slipping out the door before she can change her mind.

The sand is already warm beneath my feet. The salt hangs thick in the air. I walk, trying to shake off the weight of the morning, but it clings to me like static. Even the ocean breeze feels like it's judging me. Like it's whispering, damaged girl, table for one.

That boy's face flashes behind my eyes. Green eyes. Sharp jaw. That serious stare. The universe doesn't need to say it out loud. I can already feel it.

You've met your match.

I don't even know his name, and yet something in me recognizes him.

It's the look. That calm confidence. It reminds me of Dylan Kramer, sixth-grade tormentor and certified little shit. He used to pull my hoodie strings until they choked me, whispering cruel things in my ear just loud enough for no one else to hear. One time, I tripped over my own shoelace in front of the whole bus stop, and he said, "Even the ground doesn't want you."

I laughed. Because if you laugh first, it doesn't sting as bad. Because if you act like it doesn't matter, maybe one day it won't.

But it always did.

The beach is much more crowded at this time of morning. The sun is burning down on me like it has a personal vendetta, close to a hundred degrees. I make my way to the same spot where I'd humiliated myself yesterday, determined to reclaim it like some salty little queen. I don't want to be near anyone.

I pull off my cover-up, toss it to the side, and lay out my towel. The waves crash in front of me, loud and rhythmic, but I find myself wishing it were pouring down rain instead. That the noise from the ocean was really a waterfall high on a mountain somewhere, fogged in so thick you couldn't even see the sky.

I open my copy of Frankenstein and sink into Mary Shelley's pages, letting the words drown everything else out.

Until a thud jerks me back to reality.

To my left, a wakeboard and a massive gear bag slam into the sand like they're trying to make an entrance. Of course, a human body follows. My stomach drops.

It's him.

Same boy from yesterday. Hair wet and wild. Body sun-drenched and smug. He looks like he hasn't stopped thinking about his own greatness since the moment he woke up.

He locks eyes with me and gives me that smirk.

I stare back, my voice flat as Florida sand. "Do you need something?"

He shakes his wet hair like a dog, sending a spray of saltwater too close to my towel for comfort.

"I thought it was you, Ariel," he says.

"That's not my name," I snap, though my voice wavers when his eyes pin me in place like I'm a shell stuck under glass.

21

"I see you do own a swimsuit," he teases, glancing me over.

I shrug like I don't give a single damn. "You've got eyes. Congratulations."

"I've never seen you around here before."

"There are hundreds of people who live here."

"So… you do live here?"

"Unfortunately."

He grins. "Ah, I can see how thrilled you are. Welcome to paradise."

"You really circling back to this again?" I ask, dry as the sand between my toes. "Do you need something, or are you just bored and annoying?"

He tilts his head like I amuse him. "What's your name?"

"Victoria."

"How old are you, Victoria?"

I sigh, loud and dramatic. "Old enough."

He doesn't even blink. "So, you moved here with your parents?"

"Do you always ask a hundred questions of strangers?"

"Only the interesting ones," he says, pulling open his gear bag.

I watch as he unfolds a massive kite and begins working on a tangle of wires. I glance at the board, then back at him. He's fidgeting with the pieces like a scientist who moonlights as a lifeguard.

"What is that stupid thing, anyway?"

He doesn't look up. "This 'stupid thing' is not stupid at all. If your memory works, you broke my wires yesterday. Had to go get new ones this morning."

"I didn't break anything. The dumb boy who wiped out into the ocean broke his own stuff."

"The very brilliant man," he corrects, raising a finger, "who saved the dumb girl. And who now has to replace two-hundred-dollar kite wires? You owe me."

I blink. "Wait. Two hundred dollars? For string? Sounds like it's not the kite that's stupid. It's the boy who paid two hundred bucks to fly one."

He laughs. "You must not have had much fun where you came from."

"No, not boring at all, actually."

I set my book down and stand up next to him. "So let me get this straight, you're surfing and flying a kite at the same time, like it's some macho multitasking stunt to impress beach girls?"

He chuckles. "Not quite. It's called kitesurfing. Doing both at once is the whole point. You've seriously never seen this before?"

I shake my head.

23

"You must've lived under a rock."

I sigh. "Something like that. So what else is there to do around here besides try to break the Guinness World Record for beach showboating?"

"Anything you want," he says. "Depends on what kind of stuff you're into."

I hesitate, biting my lip. I'm not even sure how to answer that.

"What's your name?" I ask instead.

"Elijah. Eli."

I try it out on my tongue. "Eli, the kite-wrangling surfer boy."

That makes him smirk. "I wrangle more than just kites," he says, giving me a wink before sprinting toward the water like he's escaping a rom-com scene on purpose.

I sat back down on my towel, watching him out of the corner of my eye. The kite soars and dips above him like it has its own pulse, and he moves through the water with ease, like someone born for it.

He probably has the easiest life. Beautiful people always do. But I keep watching.

And maybe I don't hate it.

CHAPTER THREE

I woke up earlier than everyone else, like usual. It's easier that way. No one in my face. No fake smiles. No hovering. I scarfed down a bowl of cereal, dry, because God forbid, we have milk that isn't expired. Then I packed a bag from my closet: book, notebook, pen, MP3 player, water, towel. I tossed on a black one-piece and jean shorts, slipped on my Vans, and left without a word.

No one noticed. No one ever does.

The condo was too loud last night. Mom and Dad argued over the bills again. My little sister threw a tantrum at dinner, and Vanessa tried too hard to play peacemaker, like she always does. She has this exhausting optimism that makes me want to scream.

I don't scream, though. I just disappear.

Outside, the air hits me like warm soup. Humid and sticky, thick with salt. The faint hiss of waves carries across the street. Somewhere nearby, someone's frying bacon, the smell clinging to the breeze. I shove my earbuds in, pretending I'm somewhere else.

I walked the boardwalk along Sunset Beach for what felt like miles. I get why people think it's beautiful. The waves, the breeze, the pastel buildings. It's cute, sure, but it's not my home. It's not rainy Washington. It's not cliffs and evergreens and a sky that always looks like it's on the verge of crying.

I wandered past the crowded sand and climbed out onto the rock formations. They were slick and uneven, but I found a flat one and sat down. It wasn't sunny today. In fact, it looked like it might rain, even better.

I clicked on Lifehouse's "You and Me" and pulled out my notebook. NYU's early admissions essay wasn't going to write itself. If France didn't work out, New York was the plan. It was the only place loud enough to match the noise in my head.

I tried to focus, pen in hand, when a group of teenagers ran into the water nearby. Loud, laughing, tanned within an inch of their lives. And of course, Eli. The kite-wrangler. He was with them, laughing like he didn't have a single thought in his beautiful, smug head.

The girls in their group wore bikinis that might as well have been made of dental floss. I glanced down at my one-piece and pale legs and sighed.

This is going to be rough, Victoria.

Maybe if I lived outside and survived on air and lettuce, I'd fit in. But probably not.

I looked back down at my notebook when something hard smacked me on the side of the head.

"Seriously?" I muttered.

A blonde boy jogged over, grinning like he just invented the Frisbee. "Hey! Sorry about that. You, okay?"

Why is he yelling? My music isn't even that loud.

I gave him a tight smile and a thumbs-up. He ran off, and sure enough, Eli followed. He grabbed the Frisbee from him, launched it in the opposite direction, then said something to me.

I pulled out one earbud, confused. "What?"

He grinned. "I said, if you want swimming lessons, I'm available later."

"And I told you, I know how to swim."

He leaned slightly closer, that teasing spark in his eyes. "I didn't say they'd be free."

Before I could respond, a voice called out behind me. "There you are!" Vanessa. Of course.

She trotted over and plopped down beside me. "Mom wanted me to make sure you had sunscreen, but it doesn't look like you need it anymore."

We both looked up at the sky. Thick gray clouds. Rain incoming.

"Looks like we're about to get poured on," she said.

Eli didn't move. "You brought a friend, Ariel."

Vanessa looked at me, confused. "Ariel?"

I sighed. "He's an idiot. Ignore him."

"Wait, how do you know him?"

"I don't. He just threw a Frisbee at my head."

"Technically, it was Jonah," he said, strolling closer.

Vanessa smiled way too big. "I'm Vanessa."

27

"Elijah," he said, extending a hand. "Nice to meet you. Glad Victoria has a friend already."

I turned to her, glaring. You sound like Mom.

"He's not my friend," I said sharply. "I told you, I don't know him." They ignored me entirely.

"Did you just move here?" he asked her.

"We did. From Upstate Washington. Total culture shock." She was glowing. Charming. Perfect.

"Hurricane season's about to pick up," Eli said. "If you want sun, you've gotta get out early. The weather flips fast here."

Good, I thought. Maybe I'll get sucked up like Dorothy and land back home.

"That's how the snowstorms are in Washington," Vanessa said. "Instant chaos."

"I have an aunt in Seattle," Eli added. "Bipolar weather, right?"

I zoned out while they chatted. Their voices got softer, like white noise. Until—

"If you want, Victoria, I could show you around sometime. You should give me your number."

I looked up, confused. He was asking me.

I hesitated. "I don't have a phone right now. We just switched companies."

"She can use mine," Vanessa jumped in. "I'll give you my number so she can call you."

He handed her his phone without missing a beat. Rain started to fall in light sprinkles.

We gathered our things. Eli waved as we left, and Vanessa waited until we were inside to say, "Second day here and already catching the eye of a local hottie. See? Things are looking up."

I snorted. "He probably likes you."

She looked at me like I had six heads. "He didn't ask for my number, did he? Don't be so hard on yourself. You're allowed to be liked, too, you know."

I didn't respond right away. The words scraped something in my chest.

"Why would he want to talk to me over you?" I asked quietly. "You're the pretty one. The friendly one. I'm just the weird sister."

Vanessa stopped in her tracks, grabbed my wrist. "Don't do that. Don't talk about yourself like that. You're amazing, Victoria. People see it. He saw it. You just don't let yourself believe it."

I looked away, heat rising up my neck.

"You should make friends," she said gently. "Real ones. Not just characters in books."

"Don't tell Mom."

"I'd never," she said, wrapping an arm around me. "Scout's honor."

We stood by the sliding glass door, watching the storm roll in. The sky cracked open like a secret. The air outside turned heavy and wild, rain streaking against the glass like a warning.

And for once, I was glad to be inside.

CHAPTER FOUR

I told Vanessa I was going for a walk. She didn't ask questions, just smirked and tossed me her tinted lip balm like this was a date and not me following some boy's half-baked invitation to "hang out." I didn't even ask where we were going. Elijah just said, "Stop by my place. 106. Ten sharp." So, I showed up. Of course I did.

I knocked before I could chicken out. The door opened more slowly than I expected.

He was shirtless. Barefoot. Plaid pajama pants hanging low. Hair a mess. Eyes barely open. Somehow, it was still annoyingly hot.

My breath caught. I'd never seen a boy like this up close. Raw and real and sleepy, without armor. Every magazine I'd ever read said guys don't wake up looking like that, but apparently, Elijah didn't get the memo. It wasn't just his body or his face or any of the things Vanessa would swoon over. It was that he wasn't trying. He was just there. Casual. Undone. Unbothered.

And for a girl who had never held hands so much as held hands with someone she liked that level of intimacy, being let in this early, this undone, felt like standing barefoot in front of a fire. Too close. Too fast. But I didn't back away. I let the heat crawl up my spine and settle somewhere I didn't have a name for yet.

"Hey," he said, voice thick and scratchy.

"Did I wake you?"

He shrugged. "Was already up." Total lie. He stepped back and motioned me in. "Give me two minutes to rinse off."

31

He cracked a soda open and disappeared into the back.

I stood there, alone in his place, taking in the disaster.

It was bare. Not modern and clean bare, just neglected. A couch that looked borrowed from Craigslist. A TV on the floor. A literal motorcycle in the corner, like it lived there. No decorations. No pictures. Just the kind of space that screamed temporary.

I wandered down the hall toward the open bedroom. Mattress on the floor. No comforter. One pillow. Dresser piled with chaos: military antiques, old knives, a busted trophy, a Trojan helmet, what looked like a bullet the size of my fist.

Nothing soft. Nothing sentimental.

And zero signs of a woman's touch.

He reappeared in swim trunks, towel around his neck.

"You always leave weapons out in case someone breaks in?" I asked, holding up a WWII bayonet.

He smirked. "That belonged to a Nazi officer. Found it in Indiana."

"Because that's normal."

He laughed. "I collect war stuff. My dad's a vet. Vietnam. He's big into history. His mom, my grandma, always collected things, so it rubbed off on both of us. Guess it runs in the family."

I raised a brow. "So, this dresser is like... your personality in objects?"

He picked up a massive bullet. "Fifty cal. Normandy. Recovered from the beach." He paused. "That one's my favorite."

It was weird. Dark. Specific. But I got it.

I didn't say anything. I just nodded.

"You ready to trespass?" he asked.

I snorted. "Always."

The Bilmar wasn't anything special, but Elijah talked about it like it was a landmark. He parked around the back like a pro, grabbed our towels, and jumped the gate like he'd done it a hundred times.

He probably had.

I stared at the fence, frozen.

"Come on," he said. "I'll boost you."

"You're not strong enough to lift me."

He gave me that stupid, cocky grin and patted his shoulder. "Try me."

I stepped into his hands, and he launched me over like I weighed nothing. Then he hopped up behind me like a cat burglar.

"Not your first crime," I muttered.

"Definitely not my last."

The pool area was full of hotel guests, families, tourists, and sunburned couples drinking out of coconuts. We slipped right in like we belonged.

I peeled off my shirt and stepped out of my shorts. His eyes immediately found me.

"Damn," he said, almost under his breath.

"It's my sister's suit," I muttered, instantly covering myself. "She's smaller than me."

His gaze didn't waver. "No. It's good. You look... yeah. It's good."

But I didn't believe him. Compliments made my skin itch. Especially from someone like him, confident, golden, the kind of boy who could talk to anyone. I wasn't used to being looked at like that, like I was worth noticing.

Everything in me screamed to hide. To pull the shirt back on and disappear. My body never felt like something to be proud of. It was just there, too pale, too awkward, too mine. I didn't know what to do with eyes on me. Especially his.

I crossed my arms and turned away, pretending it didn't matter. Like my heart wasn't thudding loud enough to drown out the pool music.

He didn't press. Didn't make a joke. Just gave me that lopsided grin and ran straight into the pool like a child on Red Bull.

I followed, because pretending I wasn't flustered was easier underwater.

34

We swam for maybe an hour. Floating. Splashing. Dunking each other like it wasn't weird that we barely knew each other.

But it was weird.

Weird that I felt safe. Lighter. Like I didn't have to say a single damn thing to be exactly where I needed to be.

Eventually, he dunked me one too many times, and I shoved him underwater, then swam to the edge, gasping and laughing.

He came up beside me, water dripping off his lashes.

"You hungry?" he asked, like it wasn't even a question.

We ended up walking the boardwalk at John's Pass, damp and sun soaked. Elijah pointed out places like he owned them.

"That place? That's where I get all my kites. The old man in there's been selling them since I was a kid. Doesn't even have a website, just knows what I like. Always puts the newest ones aside for me."

He didn't go inside, just paused like it mattered. That kind of small loyalty most people forget, but he carried it like it meant something. And somehow, I loved that about him, how he remembered people most wouldn't.

Then he flashed that crooked grin and kept walking like he hadn't just revealed a piece of his soul.

"Best pizza place on the beach. Never order the wings. You'll regret it."

"That store sells real alligator heads."

"Don't eat from the guy with the hot dog cart. He once tried to fight my dad."

I just listened. Half-smiling. Letting the rhythm of the day settle over me.

We stopped at a rickety photo booth between two souvenir shops. Elijah grabbed my hand without warning. "Come on. We need proof this happened."

Before I could argue, he pulled me inside, the curtain swishing closed. It smelled like vinyl and cotton candy. He shoved a couple of crumpled bills into the slot.

"You've done this before?" I asked.

"Only like a hundred times. But never with a girl as weird as you."

"Gee, thanks," I muttered, even as my pulse spiked.

The camera clicked.

I tried to smile. Awkward. Tooth-baring.

Click.

He made a ridiculous face and stuck out his tongue.

Click.

I laughed for real that time, and he turned toward me just as the flash went off.

Click.

The strip rolled out. Elijah yanked it from the slot, grinning like it was treasure.

"Here," he said, handing it to me. "You'll want to remember this place. Even if the shrimp gives you food poisoning."

I took it carefully, like it might crumble. For a second, I didn't feel like a tourist in someone else's story. I felt like I belonged.

We stopped outside Bubba Gump's.

"This is a real place?" I asked.

He blinked. "You don't like shrimp?"

I launched into a deadpan impression. "You can barbecue it, boil it, broil it…"

He cracked up like I was the funniest person alive.

"You're strange," he said, shaking his head.

"Not the worst thing I've been called."

We ate outside. Cheap baskets. Greasy food. Perfect breeze. He talked more than I expected. About his mom living in Indiana with her new family. About four younger siblings. About switching schools. About failing tenth grade, not because he was dumb, but because life was chaos.

"I moved up there three different times," he said. "Each time only lasted six months before I was sent somewhere else."

"Why?"

He took a slow sip. "My mom wanted better. Said I deserved stability, a clean slate. She didn't want me around my real dad anymore. Said it was toxic. Said I'd fall back into chaos.

And part of me understood it. I'd felt it too, that invisible tether to the mess you come from. I think I stayed longer than I should've because I felt guilty. None of my siblings picked my dad. None of them stayed. But I did. I felt like if I didn't, no one would. And that kind of weight can mess with your head. Make you think you owe your life to fixing someone else's."

He looked away. "Like a guest in my own life. Trapped."

I didn't say anything. I just let the silence be enough.

"You ever get the feeling," he said quietly, "like you're just visiting your own life?"

I looked at him. And yeah, something cracked inside me.

"All the time," I whispered.

He nodded. And we didn't say anything else.

By the time we pulled into the condo lot, the sun was setting.

"Thanks," I said, slipping out of his car. "For today."

"Yeah. Anytime."

He didn't push for more. Somehow, that made it worse.

Because what was this, really? A date? A fluke? A hangout?

The whole day replayed in my head. His laugh, the way he looked at me, the way he didn't. Was I pretty enough? Normal

38

enough? Worth enough? Nothing about this felt like the movies. No fireworks. Just quiet moments, just enough to keep me suspended in uncertainty.

And that's what got me. The not knowing. The second-guessing. The voice whispering: Don't get used to this. Don't trust it.

Maybe it was all a fluke. Maybe I was just a passing distraction in a summer he wouldn't remember. But what really haunted me was the way I couldn't stop replaying every glance, every laugh, wondering if I was too much or not enough. Wanting something more was terrifying. But scarier was the idea that maybe I wasn't enough for it to matter.

That kind of want made everything worse.

That night, Vanessa slipped quietly into my room and handed me her phone. No words. Just her unreadable look.

Elijah: Can you ask Victoria if she's busy tomorrow?

Me: What time?

Elijah: 10:00

Me: I'll be there.

Elijah: Meet me at my place again. Unit 106. I'll try to keep the illegal activity under control this time.

I stared at the message like it was dangerous.

Maybe it was.

But I wasn't saying no.

39

CHAPTER FIVE

When Elijah opened the door, he was wearing jeans and work boots. I immediately regretted my sundress and sandals.

"You don't look very... beachy," I said.

He smirked. "It's supposed to rain today. We've got to beat the weather."

"Where are we going?"

"You'll see."

He didn't give me a hint the entire drive. Just turned up the music and drummed the steering wheel like the world wasn't on fire. I stared out the window, quietly memorizing every street sign and building, trying to piece together a town that still felt like a rental life.

When we pulled into the lot, I blinked at the trailhead.

"Okay... where are we?"

"You said you liked history," he said, already hopping out. "Welcome to Fort DeSoto."

"I've never heard of it."

He just smiled and started walking.

As we hiked the path, Elijah transformed. Gone was the smirky beach boy. In his place there was someone who knew things. Who explained every building and pointed out relics like he'd grown up in them.

We stopped in front of two massive coastal mortars, and he launched into a story about Robert E. Lee, and the Union Army as it was common knowledge.

"Wow," I said honestly. "How do you even know all this?"

He shrugged. "What, you think I just surf and screw around all day? I paid attention in school." His smile faded slightly. "Wow. You just assume I'm an idiot?"

I blinked, caught off guard. "Oh, no. I didn't mean it like that," I said quickly, defensive. "I just… I like it. It's kind of unexpected. You know stuff. I like that."

We kept walking. Concrete bunkers. Cracked plaques. Weather-worn cannons. Everything smelled like rust and salt. I stayed quiet, watching him move through it all like it belonged to him.

Eventually, we stopped at a ledge overlooking the Sunshine Skyway Bridge.

"Tell me what you see," he said.

"Perfect paradise," I whispered.

And it was. It wasn't Washington, but it had its own kind of stillness. A beauty I hadn't let myself acknowledge until now.

We sat side by side, brushing our arms, just listening to the wind and waves. I glanced sideways at him, surprised by the calm on his face, like he belonged in this moment more than I did.

"I didn't expect Florida to have places like this," I said quietly. "I always thought it was just tourists and chaos. But this, this is kind of beautiful."

He turned to me then. His green eyes softened, like he was seeing more than just my face.

"It is beautiful," he said, voice low. "But not as much as you in it."

Before I could process that, thunder cracked somewhere overhead.

"Storm's rolling in," I said, watching dark clouds drag across the sky.

"Come on. We can wait it out under Battery Laidley."

Before I could ask what that even was, he grabbed my hand and took off running.

By the time we ducked under the concrete stairs, we were soaked. The rain had gone from laziness to anger in seconds. I wrung out my hair while Elijah pulled off his shirt and twisted it dry.

"I should've worn shorts," he muttered.

"I should've worn... anything else. This dress wasn't even mine. My sister picked it out."

"So why wear it if you hate it?"

I shrugged. "Girls like me don't get to wear what we want. We wear what we're supposed to."

He gave me a look. "You try too hard to be something you're not?"

"I try too hard to be… normal."

There was silence. Just rain hammering above us.

Then he asked it.

"The day I met you… were you trying to drown yourself?"

It wasn't accusing. Just soft. Honest.

I hesitated. "Wow. We're doing this already?"

He shrugged. "We've got nothing but time."

I slid down onto the concrete and stretched my legs in front of me. "Sometimes, I just get… overwhelmed. Like life is shouting in my face. And even in the quiet, it's still loud."

He nodded. "Yeah. I know that feeling."

"Other days, it's like I'm screaming, and no one can hear me."

"Yeah," he said again, quieter this time. "I get that too."

And just like that, the dam cracked.

"I hate that it's so hard to be okay. I know I should be grateful for a roof, for food, for parents who are alive, but I wake up and it's like the weight of existing is too much. I'm tired of pretending to be fine. Tired of my mom acting like a pill will fix everything, and my dad acting like I'm invisible. I'm tired of being the angry

43

girl, the broken one, the disappointment. I want friends. I want to be happy. I want a mom who hugs me instead of scheduling another appointment. I just… want to breathe without it hurting."

I wiped my face, but the tears kept coming.

Elijah didn't try to stop me. He just sat beside me, still. Silent.

"Yes," I said finally, my voice barely above the rain. "I was trying to kill myself. Because some days, being alive is too hard."

He didn't flinch. Didn't recoil. Just exhaled like he'd been holding that breath too.

"Yeah," he said. "I've thought about it too. But drowning? That would've been the worst way to go. Feels slow. Like your body's betraying you inch by inch."

I stared at him. "You sound like you know."

He nodded slowly. "I've been under too long before. The ocean doesn't forgive. And you don't forget."

Something about the way he said it shifted the weight in my chest. Not gone but moved.

"Sometimes," I said, choking back a breath, "I think I belong somewhere else. Like Paris. London maybe. Somewhere I could just read and sip tea and forget my worries."

He looked over. "Paris, huh?"

"Ernest Hemingway said it's the most beautiful place on earth."

He smiled. "Then why'd he move to the Florida Keys?"

God. Smarter than he let people think. That made me smile through the ache.

"Your turn," I said. "Tell me something real."

He leaned back against the wall, exhaled. "I don't have a person. Someone I could call if everything fell apart. Everyone thinks I'm chill, that I've got it handled. But it's just noise. No one really knows me. I don't have someone to lean on."

I nodded. "Same."

"I've had a million girlfriends. Hookups. Whatever. But I never let them see too much. Never told them anything real."

"You mean like this?"

"Exactly like this."

That silence was heavier than the storm.

"I've been to jail," he said suddenly.

I turned to him.

"For fighting. A couple of guys jumped me, and I snapped. I don't always know how to stop once I start."

I guess we've got that in common.

I laughed a little. "I stabbed a girl in the hand with scissors."

His eyebrows rose.

"I didn't get arrested. My parents spun it into a misunderstanding. Straight A's and a baby face go a long way."

45

"Must be nice."

Then, quieter: "I've got scars, you know. From when I didn't win the fight."

He lifted his shirt slightly, pointing to a faded purple mark near his ribs. Then another near his hip. One on his neck. His hand found mine, guiding it gently over the scar tissue. Not sexual. Not seductive. Just real.

"People messed with me. I used my fists. They used a knife."

I pulled my hand away, not because I was scared, but because it suddenly felt too big for this space.

"You think I'm a bad guy now?" he asked, voice low.

I shook my head. "No. I think everyone has a story."

We stared at each other, just a second too long. It knocked the breath out of me. Before I could think better of it, before my brain could stop me, I leaned in and kissed him.

At first, he didn't move. Then his lips parted, and everything shifted. His mouth was warm and soft, tasting faintly of rain and something unnamable, him. It wasn't rushed or clumsy. It was slow. Careful. New.

It was the kind of kiss you feel in your chest before your lips even understand what's happening. My whole body stilled like I was memorizing every second. My first kiss, and I'd always imagined it would be awkward or messy. But with Elijah, it felt like gravity. It felt like my body had finally stopped floating.

His hand cupped my face. My hand slid to his chest, fingers trembling. We kissed like we were trying to disappear into it, like something fragile and rare had just cracked open.

But just when it started to get heavy, just when I leaned closer, he gently pulled back.

"Whoa," he whispered, sitting up straighter. He adjusted his jeans and smiled like I'd knocked the wind out of him.

"Yeah," I said. "Whoa."

We didn't say anything else. Just sat side by side, waiting for the rain to stop.

I wrapped my arms around my knees and tried to breathe normally, but my mind was already spiraling. Had I done it wrong? Was it too fast? Too much? It was my first kiss, and even though I initiated it, I suddenly felt like I'd misread everything.

Maybe he hadn't liked it. Maybe I'd been stupid.

I kept my eyes on the concrete, trying to keep my hands from shaking. But then Elijah's pinky brushed mine, just a tiny nudge, intentional and grounding, and I felt a little less like I was unraveling.

When we pulled into the condo parking lot, he killed the engine but didn't move.

"I'd walk you up," he said.

"But then my parents would kill you. And me. And then we'd both be dead. So, maybe not."

He grinned. "Exactly."

I opened the door, but my hand lingered on it too long.

"Thanks," I said, glancing back. My voice came out too soft. Unsure.

He gave me a lazy salute, grin tugging at his lips. "Anytime."

I nodded like it was enough, like I hadn't just had my entire world rearranged, and shut the door a little too fast, heart thudding like I'd done something wrong.

Mom didn't look at me when I came into the kitchen.

She stood at the counter pouring coffee, slow and quiet, like she was trying not to spill her anger into it.

The radio was on again. Always was. Some talk show buzzing low in the background, filling the space between us.

"You've been out all day," she said finally. "You don't need to run back to that beach again tonight."

I leaned against the doorway. "I wasn't planning to."

"Good." She sipped her coffee. "You've barely been home since we got here."

I crossed my arms. "You wanted me to make friends."

"I wanted you to learn how to stay out of trouble."

My throat went tight. "I'm not in trouble."

Her shoulders stiffened. "That's what you said last time too."

"That was different," I said quietly.

"You stabbed a girl, Victoria."

"She wouldn't stop."

Mom turned then, setting her mug down on the counter. "You don't fix things by hurting people. You don't start over by pretending it didn't happen."

"I'm not pretending."

She stared at me for a long time. Her eyes looked tired, like every word between us cost something.

"You think moving here fixes everything. It doesn't. You still have to live with what you did."

I wanted to tell her I already did. Every day.

But she wouldn't believe me.

She rubbed the side of her face and exhaled like she'd been holding her breath since we arrived.

"I just need you to stop making me worry every time you walk out that door."

"I wasn't doing anything wrong."

"Maybe not," she said. "But something about you draws the wrong kind of people. You have to be careful who you let near you."

The words cut deeper than she meant them to. I looked away before she could see my face.

"Go get cleaned up," she said softly. "Dinner's on the stove."

When she left the kitchen, the air felt heavier.

The coffee pot kept sputtering behind me, dripping slow, steady, like it was counting the seconds until I broke again.

CHAPTER SIX

DAY ONE AFTER KISS

The beach was already humming when I stepped onto the sand, towel slung over my shoulder, and my heart doing that annoying flippy thing it did every time I thought I might run into Elijah. The sun was brutal today, already baking the sand by mid-morning, but I didn't mind. I found a spot near the dunes where I could people-watch without being totally visible.

It wasn't long before the usual group showed up. Elijah was among them. Shirtless. Bronze. Beautiful. Wakeboard under one arm, calling out to someone behind him. Three other guys and two girls, all laughing and carefree, dragging kitesurfing gear across the beach like they owned the place.

They staked out a spot nearby with towels and a cooler. One of the girls, blonde with legs for days, wrapped her arms around Elijah's waist. He didn't really hug her back, but he didn't push her away either. He just smiled. Tired. The kind of smile that didn't reach his eyes.

I buried myself in my book and pretended not to care. Useless.

"Hey, Ariel."

I looked up to see Elijah squatting beside me in the sand, sunglasses perched on his head, hair wind-blown.

"You stalking me?" he grinned.

I closed my book slowly, heart thudding. "This is a public beach. And don't call me Ariel."

51

I hated how sharp my voice came out. I had stupidly assumed he would do something, text my sister, wave, anything, after I kissed him. Instead, he let another girl drape herself on him and went right back to calling me Ariel like none of it mattered.

He smirked but didn't leave. "You good?"

"I'm great. Why?"

He glanced back at his group. "Because you're sitting over here like a ghost."

"I like my solitude."

"Even better," he said, offering his hand. "Come kite with us. Wind's perfect."

I stared at his hand like it was a trap. My stomach churned. I wasn't even sure why I was considering it. Maybe because I didn't want to look pathetic. Maybe because I didn't have anyone else.

"I've never done that before," I said, aiming for casual.

"I'll show you." His grin said it was the easiest thing in the world.

I hesitated again. He was acting like nothing happened. Like we hadn't kissed. Like I was just some random girl on the beach. But the truth was, I didn't have a friend group to fall back on. No one else had invited me.

So, I took his hand.

Suddenly, I was being pulled into his circle of sun-kissed daredevils.

Elijah helped me with the gear, explaining everything with too much patience and zero condescension. He didn't touch me unnecessarily, didn't show off, but he was watching me. I felt it.

Just as I was starting to get the hang of things, one of the other guys, a tall, sunburned kid named Logan, took over coaching duties. He cracked jokes and gave instructions like it was his job. Before I knew it, I was swept up in the group vibe, elbowed into conversations I didn't quite follow, half-listening while I tried to keep up.

Elijah drifted off to help someone else, and I was left figuring out where I fit in this loud, laughing circle of strangers. They seemed used to this, like they had been doing it forever. I was just a guest appearance.

I did okay. Not great. I face-planted once and swallowed a gallon of saltwater, but Logan just laughed and helped me up.

When the wind finally died down and everyone broke for rest, I flopped back on a towel, exhausted. Logan sat beside me, cracked open a water bottle, and handed it over.

"You did good," he said.

"You're lying."

"A little."

We both laughed. He smirked, took a swig, then nodded toward Elijah, who was walking up the beach, board under one arm, sun dripping off his shoulders like it belonged there.

"Careful," Logan called out, nudging Elijah as he passed. "Wouldn't want Sarah hearing about this one."

Elijah shot him a look that could've burned through bone. Logan just shrugged, grinning like it was worth it, and handed me back the bottle.

I frowned, confused, but before I could ask, a man's voice cut across the sand—loud, angry.

"Elijah!"

The whole group froze. Elijah's jaw clenched before he even turned. Elijah's shoulders went rigid, his whole body tightening like a storm about to break.

A man stood a few yards away, red-faced, bottle of clear liquid in his hand, vodka by the look of it. His clothes were disheveled, his eyes bloodshot.

"Come here. Now."

Elijah stood without a word. I watched him walk over, watched the man grab his arm and start yelling. I couldn't hear it all, but it didn't matter. The tone said enough.

The group awkwardly looked away, pretending not to notice. Like they had seen it before. Like this was just another scene in a long, uncomfortable play.

I didn't pretend. I watched.

When Elijah finally walked back, face tight and eyes distant, I didn't say anything.

Logan was on one side of me when Elijah dropped onto the other, stretching out like nothing had happened. His body language was casual, but his jaw stayed tight, and his eyes fixed on the horizon like he needed to anchor himself.

"Sorry about that. My dad's complicated."

I wanted to ask more. But I knew better.

Instead, I broke my protein bar in half and offered him a piece. He took it.

"Thanks, Ariel."

"I'm still not calling you Prince Eric."

He laughed. But he didn't go back to the group.

He stayed beside me for the rest of the afternoon, quietly. Like something had shifted, but he didn't have the words yet. Like he was trying to figure out what came next.

So was I.

Still, that name lingered small, insignificant at the time. Sarah. Just another word I didn't realize would matter.

I didn't realize it at the time, but that day left a mark I couldn't explain. Not a scar. Not yet. Just an ache that settled deep.

Why hadn't he acknowledged the kiss? Why didn't he text? Looked at me like it meant something? What was he hiding behind that perfect, unreadable smile?

He turned suddenly.

"Come on," he said.

I blinked. "Where?"

"Anywhere but here."

He didn't wait. He just started walking.

I glanced back at the group. Julie and the others were still half-wrestling over a volleyball, music buzzing from someone's speaker. They didn't even notice us leaving.

I followed him.

We walked forever, the sun melting into the horizon, smearing everything gold. The sounds of the beach faded. The voices, music, and laughter all replaced by the hush of waves and gulls crying high above.

By the time we reached the far stretch of sand near the dunes, the sky was threatening rain.

A breeze kicked up. Elijah glanced back at me.

"We can hide over there," he said, pointing to a patch of tall sea oats bowing in the wind. Behind them, low sand dunes provided just enough shelter for us to sit with our backs to the wind.

Not a word passed between us for the first few minutes. Just our breathing. The hum of the ocean. The wind brushing against my cheek.

Then the first drops fell. Light, misty at first, then heavier. Steady.

I tucked my knees into my chest.

"Did you ever think about being rich?" I asked, breaking the silence. "Like, stupid rich. Mansion. Staff. Parents who throw money at you instead of attention?"

He gave a half-smile. "We live on an island in Florida. We're not exactly struggling."

"I know. But..." I sighed. "This isn't it for me. I can feel it. There's something better. Somewhere people don't call me crazy or look at me like I'm about to explode."

He shifted to face me more fully. "You're not crazy."

"Yeah?" I said, bitterly, "Tell that to literally everyone else."

"You're misunderstood. Just like me."

I blinked at him. "Yeah, but you're misunderstood in the hot, mysterious way. I'm misunderstood in the she-might-snap-and-key-your-car kind of way."

He huffed a soft laugh, but I didn't. "I just wonder who decides that. Why one of us gets curiosity and the other gets caution tape."

That silenced him.

The rain softened again. We watched it flicker across the sand.

"Tell me something," I whispered. "Something no one else knows. Something you wish you could change."

He was quiet for so long, I didn't think he would answer.

Then, softly, "I wish I had a better dad."

I looked over.

"Someone who was there. Who rooted for me. Helped me. Even just stayed." He paused briefly before emitting a single, restrained laugh. Dry. Sad.

"He used to go to McDonald's and buy thirty cheeseburgers. Singles. No fries. He'd throw them in the freezer and say that it was dinner for the next few weeks. Then he'd leave. Wouldn't say where. Wouldn't say how long. I'd just be there. Alone. Rationing frozen burgers. At times, I waited while walking along the driveway. Hoping today was the day he'd come back."

My throat burned. A tear slipped before I could stop it.

He noticed. Wiped it away with his thumb.

"Don't do that," he said. "I don't want pity."

"It's not pity."

He didn't argue.

"Where would you go?" he asked, voice lower now. "If you could be anywhere."

I smiled, eyes still watery. "Paris."

"So, you said before. But why Paris?"

"I don't know, honestly. But I'd live in a tiny apartment with crooked walls and peeling paint. Eat croissants every morning.

Drink coffee with too much sugar. The old guy at the flower shop would know my name. Everyone would. They'd think I was beautiful. Smart. Not crazy. Just... worth something."

He looked at me like I was already there.

"You are," he said. "Worth something."

I swallowed hard. "What about you? Where would you go?"

He glanced at the water. "Somewhere up north. Not Indiana. Maybe Tennessee. Somewhere with land. Trees. A big cabin and a dozen animals. Somewhere no one could bother me."

I laughed, wiping my face. "You want to be a farmer now, kite boy?"

His smile cracked wide. "Don't mock the vision."

"I'm picturing you in overalls."

"Shirtless?"

I shoved him with my shoulder.

The laugh faded. His voice softened.

"I'm not good at this," he said.

"At what?"

"Letting people see me."

"You're doing fine."

He reached for my hand, threading our fingers together.

No fireworks. No sudden, world-ending kiss.

Just skin against skin.

Warmth in the rain.

Proof that maybe neither of us was as alone as we thought.

CHAPTER SEVEN

DAY TWO AFTER THE KISS

It had been two full days since Fort DeSoto, but my brain hadn't slowed down, especially after our conversation in the dunes.

After dinner, I lay on my bed staring at the ceiling. The fan spun lazy circles above me, mocking the stillness inside. When the clock hit eight, I knew sleep wasn't happening.

I pulled on a hoodie, slid into my sandals, and crept out to the beach. The night air had cooled, but it was the ache in my chest that made me cold.

The sky melted into twilight, deep purples and bruised pinks, the ocean stretching endlessly in every direction. I found a quiet patch of sand near the waterline and sat down, knees pulled to my chest. The sound of the waves was the only thing louder than the thoughts screaming in my head.

I thought about Lisa. Angela. About the ghost of the girl, I used to be. About the girls I thought were my friends.

Lisa, with her secret pen pal and soft-spoken guilt.

Angela, who turned invisible whenever a crowd showed up.

I remembered the rock I threw at Nathan's head. The scissors pressed Brandy's shoulder. The weight of being the girl who fought instead of cried.

And for once, I wasn't ashamed.

A thud beside me.

I didn't even have to look. Elijah.

He didn't speak at first, just lay down next to me in the sand, hands behind his head, letting the silence fill the blanks. Like he knew I needed space but wasn't going to let me disappear.

"There you are, sunshine," he said eventually, voice low and steady.

I didn't answer.

He sighed. "My dad's drunk again. Lost it because I didn't wash the dishes fast enough. He started yelling about respect and how useless I am. I had to get out before I said something I couldn't take back."

I stayed quiet.

He turned his head toward me, voice quieter now. "This beach is the only place I can breathe some nights. Then I saw you sitting here, like the universe was trying not to be a total asshole for once."

I looked at him, studying the shape of him in the darkness. His jaw was tense. His throat moved when he swallowed.

"Do you ever wonder what it would be like to wake up with someone else's life?" I asked quietly. "Wake up one morning in a house where nobody yells and nothing hurts. Just once."

His answer came after a long pause. "All the time. But I wouldn't know what to do with the silence."

I stood and peeled off my hoodie and jean shorts, tossing them onto the sand like I was shedding skin. Then I walked into the ocean.

He followed.

We waded in until the water reached our waists, the moonlight turning everything silver and unreal. He stayed quiet as I floated in front of him, staring up at the sky and trying to breathe around the weight in my chest.

"So," he finally said, "what's your deal, Victoria? Anger issues or something?"

"Or something."

He chuckled, low and genuine. "Come on, give me something real."

"You want real? Fine." I looked out over the water. "It's like carrying a bomb around in my chest that no one else can see. You don't need to ask. I know you get it. You wear it too."

He moved closer, slowly. Close enough that I could feel the heat radiating off his skin even through the water.

"What's the deep end for you?"

"It's when everything goes quiet," I said after a beat. "Not peaceful, just empty. When your brain forgets how to scream and all that's left is numbness. That's when I know I'm in trouble."

He didn't flinch. "Yeah. That's when I start doing reckless stuff just to feel something again."

"I don't want to talk about it anymore."

"Then don't."

I turned away, ready to swim back to shore and pretend none of this had happened. But then I felt his hand on my arm, gentle and unsure.

When I looked back, he was already moving closer, the space between us vanishing like it had never existed.

He kissed me.

It wasn't urgent. It wasn't desperate. It was careful.

Like he needed to make sure I didn't shatter from the touch.

His mouth brushed against mine once, then again, like he was relearning softness, like this kind of closeness scared him more than anything else.

The kind of kiss that didn't take. It offered.

The taste of salt lingered between us. The waves whispered against our skin, and the world felt too quiet for a heartbeat too long.

When we finally pulled apart, his hand lingered at my waist, grounding both of us in a moment that already felt like it might slip away.

"I have to go to Big Cypress tomorrow," he said, voice rough. "My aunt needs help with her alternator. You want to come?"

"What's Big Cypress?"

"A preservation. An hour from here. Swamps, gators, history. The real Florida. I could show you around."

I raised an eyebrow. "You're inviting me to the wilderness?"

He smirked. "Figure you might like to know where the bodies go."

I laughed before I could stop myself. "I'll think about it."

"Don't think too hard."

I was already thinking too much. About him. About what this was turning into. About how it terrified me and thrilled me in equal measure.

Eventually, we waded back to shore, soaked and shivering but lighter somehow.

He picked up my hoodie and helped me into it without a word, like it was something he had always done. Like it was normal now, this thing between us.

We sat on the sand for a long time, not touching, not talking. Just breathing.

And somehow, it felt like enough.

CHAPTER EIGHT

Of course, I was going to lie to my parents.

I scrutinized every piece of clothing in my closet like I was dressing for a red carpet. Except the carpet was mud, and the theme was "Don't Get Eaten Alive."

After what felt like an hour of intense decision paralysis, I walked into my parents' bedroom, where my mom was folding laundry.

"So," I started, trying to sound casual, "our neighbor, Ethelle... I met her the other day. Her family's going to the preservation today, and they invited me. Can I go?"

Ethelle. Who the hell was Ethelle?

My mom beamed. "Oh, you didn't tell me you made a friend already!"

"Didn't I? Could've sworn I did."

"How old is she?"

"Sixteen. Her family lives that way." I gestured vaguely to the left.

"What preservation?"

"Big Cypress. Not too far. I'll be back tonight. No camping."

"I'm glad you made a friend already. Does she go to your school?"

"Same school. She's great. Super nice. Goes to church and everything," I added for good measure.

"Sounds lovely. Take bug spray. The mosquitoes are awful at this time of year."

"They're campers, Mom. They'll have it."

I kissed her cheek and bolted before she could poke holes in my story.

I rushed downstairs and knocked on Elijah's door, trying to calm the adrenaline crash from my lie.

A tall, wiry man opened it. Long gray hair tied back, biker tee, Southern vibe. He looked like he could kill a gator with his bare hands. And had.

"Hi, I'm looking for Eli."

"Still sleepin', sweetheart. Come on in."

He vanished into the kitchen without another word.

I stood awkwardly in the living room, unsure if I was supposed to just go wake Elijah up myself.

Eventually, I tiptoed to his door and knocked lightly. No answer.

I cracked the door open.

Elijah was sprawled diagonally across the bed, snoring, in nothing but tight white boxers.

I stood in the doorway a moment longer than I probably should have. His back rose and fell with each breath, scars littered across his skin like a broken map. There was a softness to him in sleep, a vulnerability he never showed when awake. The cocky grin and swagger had melted into something quieter.

My eyes drifted down. I didn't mean to look, honestly. But my gaze lingered for a second on the way the sheet clung to his hipbone, the outline of muscle and skin and everything I wasn't supposed to notice.

I wasn't exactly swimming in experience here, but even I knew he was a lot.

Something inside me tilted, like gravity had shifted and I hadn't caught up yet. He wasn't supposed to look like this, unguarded and human. It made my chest ache in a way I didn't have words for yet.

I wanted to reach out and trace one of those scars or ask if any came from something that wasn't a fight, something deeper. But instead, I just sat beside him and whispered, "Wake up, Elijah."

He groaned and blinked awake. "What are you doing here?"

"Did you forget Big Cypress?"

"Shit!"

He bolted upright and stumbled into the bathroom.

He did not close the door.

I looked everywhere but at him, which was pointless because the only thing to look at was him.

"What time is it?"

"A little after eleven."

A few minutes later, he came out with a toothbrush in his mouth, water dripping down his chest. "Can you grab me some clean boxers?"

I played Russian roulette with his drawers until I found them. Navy blue. Safe bet.

I handed them over.

He grinned, shook himself like a damn dog, and said, "Wanna sample before I put it away?"

I rolled my eyes so hard I saw my soul.

But underneath the sarcasm, a flush crept up my neck. He had no idea. No clue how inexperienced I was. I had never seen a boy like this, half-naked, scared, and shameless. My brain short-circuited trying to decide if I wanted to run or stay and memorize every second.

It wasn't lust exactly. It was something heavier. Like my heart recognized him before my logic did. Like every red flag in the world couldn't stop me from wanting to understand what was behind those scars.

He put on jean shorts, a white tee, and Nike Shox. Then he finally looked me over.

Black tank top. Ripped jean shorts. Army-green rain boots up to my knees.

"I see you came prepared," he laughed.

"What? This is not swamp chic?"

"Let's go crazy," he said.

In the living room, his dad watched TV and ignored us.

"Heading to Mary Jean's to fix the alternator," Elijah called over. "Be back later."

He took my hand. No introductions. No goodbyes.

At the gas station, Elijah filled up and grabbed snacks. I sat in the passenger seat, wanting to ask about his dad but unsure how.

"He seemed calmer today," I said carefully, watching Elijah's profile. "Your dad, I mean."

"Yeah. Some days, he doesn't even recognize me until I talk. Makes introductions pointless."

"And Mary Jean, she's your aunt?"

"Kind of. She was married to one of my dad's ex-wives' friends. Just stuck around."

"How many wives has he had?"

"Six. Possibly seven. Lost count."

We talked for the rest of the ride until we hit dirt roads lined with endless trees. It felt like we'd left Earth and landed in some wild, backwoods dream.

Mary Jean's house was a giant log cabin on stilts. Airboats, four-wheelers, and taxidermy for days.

Mary Jean herself, tan, wiry, and vibrant, came down the stairs and hugged Elijah like a son.

"Didn't think you'd come around!"

"Been busy," he muttered. "Brought a friend."

He turned to me. "This is Victoria."

She smiled warmly, brushing her hands off on her cargo shorts before offering one to me. "Nice to meet you, sweetheart. I'm Mary Jean. I've heard more about you this week than I've heard about most girls Elijah meets in a year."

My eyebrows shot up. "Oh?"

"Don't let him fool you. He acts like the strong, silent type, but he's got tells. Mentioned you twice on the phone. That's a record."

Elijah groaned. "Mary Jean. Come on."

She laughed. "Don't get your boxers in a bunch. It's nice seeing you with someone who doesn't look like she'll bail the second the airboat hits a bump. You look like you've got grit."

Then she added, with a sly smile, "Not like that other girl. What was her name? Sarah? She screamed the whole time we took her out. Practically begged to turn around."

My stomach flipped. Sarah.

I tried not to let it show, but Elijah stiffened beside me.

"We're not really a thing anymore," he said quickly, like he didn't believe it himself. "It was complicated. Never serious."

71

Mary Jean shrugged. "Just saying. This one doesn't seem like the screaming type."

I smiled thinly, filing the name away like a splinter I knew I'd have to dig out later.

It shouldn't have mattered. But it did. The thought of him with someone else, someone who already had pieces of him, made something ugly twist in my chest.

"I've got boots," I offered.

"That's a start."

She glanced back at the house. "Alex got the boat running again, but he's working late. Y'all be safe out there, you hear? Water's high this week, and the gators are moving weirdly. Hormonal. Breeding season or something."

"Perfect," I muttered.

She stepped closer to Elijah. "You good, baby? Sleeping okay?"

He nodded too fast. "Fine. Just keeping busy."

She gave him a long, unreadable look, then smoothed her hand over his shoulder. "Alright. Y'all have fun. Don't do anything dumb. And bring back something fresh if you can."

"Gator it is," Elijah said with a half-smile.

"Lord help me," Mary Jean muttered as she turned back toward the house.

I followed Elijah down a dock, boots squelching.

He jumped into the airboat and held out his hand. "Coming?"

"I don't know if I can go in that water."

"What'd you wear the boots for then? Fashion week?"

"They're rain boots, not swamp boots."

"Same thing. Get in."

I hesitated, then climbed in. The water was coffee-colored and still. The air was thick and humming with mosquitoes. Mom was right. Again.

Elijah drove us out until we were alone with nothing but sky, moss, and murky water. Then he killed the engine.

"Are there alligators in here?"

"You haven't seen any yet?"

"What does that mean?" I scowled.

"It means you're in the swamp."

"Take me back."

"Relax. It's just like swimming with sharks."

"That does not help."

He laughed, jumped off the boat, and pulled out the biggest knife I'd ever seen.

I shrieked. "Are you insane?"

"You have no idea," he said.

73

Then he vanished underwater.

Seconds passed. Then minutes.

A gator surfaced.

"OH MY GOD, ELIJAH!" I screamed.

Suddenly, he popped up riding the damn thing like it was SeaWorld. Knife in hand, he flipped the gator, slit it clean, and hauled it onto the boat like it was a pool toy.

"Tape makes it friendlier," he said, binding its snout.

Then he did the one thing guaranteed to get him killed.

He ran at me with the taped gator.

"RAWRRR!"

He shoved me into the water.

I screamed, flailed, full panic mode. He hauled me back in, laughing his ass off.

"You're insane!" I yelled, hitting him.

"But strong, though, right?" he teased.

"Strong and crazy!"

We both started laughing, loud and unhinged. I collapsed into his lap, and he wrapped his arms around me.

"Relax. That's a baby. Five-foot, tops."

"You could've died!"

"Been wrangling since I was fifteen. Gatorama every summer."

"You do shows?"

"Feeding, wrangling, all of it."

"You're a lunatic."

He just smiled. "And that gators for Mary Jean. She cooks them."

"That's disgusting."

"So's cow. Avoid speciesism."

"You keep teasing like that, and the gators are gonna pick you off first," I warned, swatting a mosquito.

"Gators digest bone. So technically, no one would ever find us," he said with a wink.

I raised a brow, half-laughing. "That's your idea of flirting?"

"Might be," he said, brushing a strand of wet hair from my face. "But you're not on their menu. Gators are lazy. They want easy prey."

"Cool. So, I'll just lie here like a buffet with a death wish. That's comforting."

"Besides," he said with a grin, "if anything goes wrong, we'll blame the mosquitoes. Those bloodsuckers have a hit list anyway."

"You're deranged," I said, unable to keep from smiling.

He paused, grin fading slightly, eyes flicking to mine like he was fighting himself.

Then, like he couldn't stop it, he leaned in and kissed me.

Slow. Grounding.

His lips were soft, tasting faintly of salt and adrenaline. Then he turned my head toward the sunset.

The sky was bleeding gold and crimson through the cypress trees.

Something cracked wide open inside me. The kind of quiet realization that doesn't come with fireworks, just a shift in the air. The feeling that this, whatever it was, might actually matter. And that terrified me more than anything else ever had.

And in that moment, half-wet, mosquito-bitten, sitting on a gator corpse, I realized something terrifying.

I might fall for this chaos-incarnate boy.

CHAPTER NINE

I woke up with a belly full of butterflies and a chest full of confusion.

I hadn't seen Elijah since the swamp. From the moment he pulled me into him and the rest of the world had disappeared. It had been two days, and he hadn't called or stopped by. Not even a text. And now it is the first day of school.

I stared into the mirror, curling my hair with hands that would not stop shaking. I tried to ignore the memory of his mouth on mine, the way my heart had sprinted when he touched me. My makeup looked perfect.

I didn't.

Tight jeans, fitted top. I looked like a normal girl. Victoria Drayton. Seventeen. New student. Clean slate. Right?

My sister dropped me off and offered to walk me in. I rolled my eyes and told her I would survive. But inside, I was ready to vomit. The last time I walked into a school, I was the psycho girl from Washington. The one nobody liked. The one who stabbed a bully with scissors. The one who finally snapped.

Now I was the girl who kissed Elijah Garrison and hadn't heard from him since.

I made it through the main office, got my schedule, and a map that might as well have been written in hieroglyphics. The campus was massive, hot, and loud. I was seconds from melting into a puddle when I spotted a redhead in a Nirvana shirt dumping trash.

"Hey," I said, pasting on my friendliest fake smile. "I'm new. Any chance you can help me find English Lit before I cry in a bush?"

She looked up and grinned. "Mr. Creighton? I'm heading there now. I'm Julie. You can sit with me."

"Thank God. I was five seconds from becoming a cautionary tale."

"Don't worry," she said, looping her arm through mine like we were old friends. "I'm basically the unofficial welcome committee around here. Come on, let's get you educated."

"Does the welcome committee provide snacks?"

"If you play your cards right, I might share my gummy worms during third period."

Julie was the exact opposite of me. Chatty. Bold. Allergic to silence. She talked the entire way to class and didn't even seem to notice I only nodded.

"So, where are you from? You sound like you've seen some shit."

"Washington. And... you're not wrong."

"Ooh, mystery girl vibes. I like it. Don't worry, no one here is normal. Especially not our class. Mr. Creighton once made a kid cry with a poem. It was beautiful."

By lunch, I knew she hated a girl named Chelsea. She thinks lip gloss is a personality trait, loved a boy named Daniel. She thinks he has trauma eyes, it's fine, and she had enough siblings to form a cult.

She led me to a courtyard full of upperclassmen who looked too cool to breathe. Julie bought me a chicken sandwich and declared I was now adopted into her group.

"No takebacks," she added. "Even if you turn out to be a serial killer. Especially if you turn out to be a serial killer."

"Good to know," I said, trying not to smile too much. It was overwhelming but also a relief. Maybe I could survive here.

And then I saw him.

Elijah. Across the courtyard.

My heart flipped, and I smiled before I could stop it. The weight I had been carrying for two days lifted just enough to let hope slip through.

And then I saw her.

The blonde girl who walked right up to him like she had done it a hundred times. She hooked her arm through his, leaned in, and kissed the side of his face like she owned him. He didn't push her away. Didn't flinch. Didn't even blink.

My stomach dropped so fast I thought I might throw up. My throat closed so tight I couldn't even swallow. Like someone had shoved glass down my windpipe.

"Hey, Julie," I said, trying and failing to keep my voice light, "who are those people over there?"

Julie followed my gaze. "Oh boy. Those are the Treasure Island troublemakers. Logan Daniels, Jesse Lockwood, Elijah Garrison. Gorgeous but doomed."

I forced a laugh. "What's their deal? Doomed how?"

"Elijah's the broody, bad-boy hero of this cursed school. Logan's the stoner with daddy issues. Jesse's the wildcard who might end up in jail or become a famous DJ depending on the week."

My throat tightened. "And the girl?"

Julie rolled her eyes. "Sarah Brown. Elijah's on-again, off-again girlfriend. She's Treasure Island royalty. She's dated half the guys here, but Elijah's the one she keeps going back to. No one gets it. It's like she has him under a spell."

Of course. He belonged to the kind of girl who sparkled in the sun, not the one who looked like storm clouds.

"They look close," I said, my voice barely audible.

Julie looked at me for a beat. "Hey. You, okay?"

"Yeah. Just hot. Florida heat is next level."

"Well, don't dehydrate on my watch. And for what it's worth, Elijah and Sarah break up once a month. Sometimes twice. She causes a scene, he leaves, she flirts with someone else to get his attention, and then boom, they reunite."

She nudged my shoulder. "Honestly, if you're gonna crush on anyone in that group, make it Logan. His dad's some big-shot attorney, which means trust fund vibes and a Tesla by senior year."

I gave her a tight smile. I hoped it passed for casual. Inside, I was bleeding.

After school, I stuck to Julie like glue, avoiding every hallway Elijah might be in. It wasn't planned, but somewhere between third period and final bell, she decided I was hers to protect. When the last class let out, she slung an arm around my shoulders and said, "You riding with me? You'll never survive the parent pickup line. Plus, my car has A/C and snacks. Total no-brainer."

I hesitated. We hadn't even known each other this morning, but she was already unlocking her beat-up red Corolla like it was a done deal.

But luck ran out in the parking lot.

The courtyard was buzzing with noise and reunion energy as Jesse and Logan strolled up mid-joke, both laughing like they hadn't just broken half the female population's hearts by showing up.

Julie perked up immediately. "Okay, prepare to meet Treasure Island's golden trio."

Before I could process what she meant, Logan's eyes locked on mine. Recognition flared.

"Well, if it isn't Kite Girl," Logan grinned, nudging Jesse. "Didn't expect to see you here."

Julie's eyebrows shot up. "Wait, what? You two know each other?"

"Kinda," Logan said, still grinning. "Caught her at the beach a couple weeks ago trying to fly a kite in hurricane-level winds. It was… entertaining."

Julie turned to me, eyes wide with amusement. "Are you serious?"

"It's a long story," I muttered, cheeks heating.

Lea popped her gum and tilted her head. "That sounds like code for something scandalous. Should we be taking notes?"

Logan chuckled, sliding his sunglasses down just enough to wink at her. "Only if you're ready for the uncut version. I don't do PG."

Elijah showed up a beat later, slower than the others, hands in his pockets, eyes distant. Sarah clung to him like she was staking a claim, her arm wrapped around his bicep, her lips whispering something against his ear.

"Guys, this is Victoria," Julie said brightly. "She moved here recently. She's my lunch buddy now, so be nice."

Jesse gave me a lazy grin. "Nice to meet you. Anyone Julie claims can't be all bad."

"She lives by Elijah," Julie added innocently.

"Oh?" Sarah's voice tightened. She gave me a slow once-over. "That's convenient."

Elijah didn't speak. He just looked at me, his expression unreadable. I couldn't tell if he was surprised, annoyed, or didn't care at all.

"We should do something this weekend," Logan offered, stepping in with a charming smile. "Could be fun to stir up a little chaos."

"Tempting," I said quietly, shooting him a sideways glance that wasn't quite a yes and wasn't quite a no.

Sarah rolled her eyes. "Elijah's not really into group stuff unless it involves me, him, and a locked door. We've got better plans for the weekend, if you catch my drift."

Jesse snorted. "Didn't you say you liked it better when she was out of town?"

Sarah shot him a glare.

"Anyway," Logan cut in quickly, eyes still on me. "If you ever get tired of the drama, Victoria, you know where to find me."

That earned him a look from Elijah. Subtle. Cold. But it was there.

Julie's head swiveled like she was watching a tennis match. "What is even happening right now?"

I couldn't answer. Neither could Elijah.

He met my gaze for one heartbeat.

Then his eyes dropped. Like the moment meant nothing. Like I was just another stranger passing through.

He didn't even hesitate.

He turned away, walking with Sarah and the rest of them, leaving me anchored in place, burning with a thousand questions and zero answers.

Julie glanced at me, sensing the shift. "You good?"

No.

I lied. "Yeah. First day of chaos. I'm just ready to go home."

But my heart had already gone somewhere else. It was chasing someone who couldn't even look back.

Julie dropped me off at the curb like it was any other day. And for her, maybe it was. But for me? This was the day I fell apart.

"Want me to pick you up tomorrow?" she asked cheerfully, oblivious to the war going off in my chest.

"Yeah," I said, my voice more breath than sound. "That'd be great."

I waved. I smiled. I played the part.

The second her car disappeared, I didn't go upstairs. I didn't want to talk about school, or how I made a new friend, or how normal everything seemed for five hours. I didn't want my mom's hopefulness. I didn't want to lie about how good I felt.

I wanted the truth.

So, I walked to Unit 106 and leaned against the door like it could hold me up. It couldn't.

I debated knocking. Maybe he wasn't home.

Then his car pulled in. My heart leapt stupidly just before it detonated.

Because she was with him. Sarah.

Her blonde hair swung as she laughed and climbed out of the passenger seat like she belonged there. Like she had been there the whole time. Like the kiss in the swamp, the conversations, the way he looked at me like he saw all the ugly pieces and didn't flinch—none of it meant a thing.

She slid out of the passenger seat like she had practiced it. Like the car had always been hers.

Maybe it was. Maybe I was just the borrowed moment in between.

I froze. For a second, I didn't breathe.

Then I turned and stormed upstairs. I didn't even know how I got there. I threw open the condo door, slammed it behind me, and ignored my mom's voice asking how my day was.

I didn't speak. I couldn't.

I made it to my room. Locked the door. Dropped my bag.

Then I screamed into a pillow so loud my throat burned. I punched the mattress. The wall. My fist connected with the wood, and I welcomed the sharp sting that shot through my skin.

He made me feel like I was different. Like I wasn't broken.

Stupid girl.

I dug under my mattress and found the journal I stopped writing in months ago. I ripped out a blank page. Then another. I scribbled so hard the pen almost broke through the paper.

Liar. Fake. I hate you.

The words blurred. My eyes stung. I crumpled the pages and threw them across the room. They scattered like dead leaves.

I kicked the closet door shut. I shoved everything off my dresser. I grabbed the snow globe my mom bought me from our last family vacation and threw it across the room. It exploded against the wall in a rain of glitter and glass. Glitter and water streaked down the wall like the pieces of a world I thought I had. Broken. Spilled.

And in between the chaos, for one unbearable second, I saw him in my mind—his pinky brushing mine, the quiet way he had said my name.

Nothing to hold.

Still not enough.

I sank to the floor, knees to my chest, arms wrapped around them. My whole-body shook, and I let it.

I let it all out.

Because no one ever warned me what heartbreak felt like.

No one told me how much it burned when someone touched your soul and then acted like you were nothing.

I was stupid. Naive. I thought I could outrun my past and start over.

86

But I'm still the girl with the cracked voice and the clenched fists.

The girl who snaps.

The girl who breaks.

Maybe normalcy isn't possible for me. Maybe this is who I've always been.

The girl who ruins everything she touches.

Outside, thunder rolled in the distance. Fitting. Even the sky knew how to fall apart.

CHAPTER TEN

TWELVE DAYS WITHOUT HIM

It's strange how someone can disappear and still leave fingerprints on everything they touched.

Twelve days.

That's how long it's been since Elijah stopped existing in my world.

No knocks. No calls. No headlights flickering across the blinds. Just silence.

And the silence is louder than any goodbye.

At first, I made excuses. Maybe his dad was worse. Maybe his phone broke. Maybe he cared but didn't know how to show it.

By the fourth day, I stopped pretending.

He wasn't gone.

He just didn't want me.

The halls of this high school smell like bleach, perfume, and heartbreak. Julie's talking a mile a minute beside me about some guy who once set his locker on fire. I nod, smile, and try to look alive.

Then I see him.

Elijah.

Coming from the opposite end of the hall.

The world doesn't just go quiet. It stops.

Every sound folds inward. Every color dulls.

He's walking with Logan, laughing at something I can't hear, his head tilted just enough to show that perfect curve of his jaw. The sight of it hits me like a memory I didn't consent to relive.

Our eyes meet.

And everything in me locks up.

For a second, he stops walking. Just stops. The laughter dies on his lips. Logan keeps talking, oblivious, until he realizes Elijah isn't beside him anymore.

Elijah's stare finds mine across the chaos.

It's not cold.

It's not kind either.

It's something in between, like a storm that doesn't know whether to drown you or turn you clean.

The crowd swells between us, kids brushing shoulders, slamming lockers, filling the air with noise, but I still see him. I see the twitch in his jaw. The small exhale he tries to hide. The war flickered behind his eyes.

For a heartbeat, he looks like he might come closer.

He doesn't.

He just stands there, the space between us pulsing with everything we never said.

And then, slowly, his gaze drops.

He turns away.

That's it.

That's all.

One look. One heartbreak. One more scar I'll never stop tracing.

Julie tugs my sleeve. "You okay?"

"Yeah," I say, my voice paper-thin. "Just tired."

She doesn't see my hands shaking. Or the way I keep them hidden in my pockets, so I don't fall apart in the middle of the hallway.

That night, I walk the beach. The air's thick with salt and heat, and the waves hiss like they're mocking me. I sit in the sand and stare at the horizon until my eyes blur.

The silence drags up ghosts.

Washington ghosts.

Lisa's face. Angela's voice. The sound of my own heartbeat the day I snapped.

The scissors.

The blood.

The look on the teacher's face when she realized the quiet girl finally broke.

People talk about rock bottom like it's a single moment. They never mention the part where you start to belong there.

I thought moving here meant starting over. That maybe if I found new sun, I'd stop rotting in old soil. But it's still me under the skin. The same fuse. The same fire. Just waiting for the next spark.

By day nine, I stopped checking the window. Stop waiting for headlights. Stop pretending my heart is something that can heal with time.

Then, one afternoon, I saw his car parked by the seawall.

But he's not with her.

It's just Elijah and Logan, sitting on the hood, laughing about something.

He looks lighter.

And it makes me feel heavier.

I don't look away. Not this time.

I let the hurt sink in, slow and steady, like poison I'm learning to live with.

On day twelve, I sit on my balcony with my journal open on my knees. The one I ripped half apart during the last breakdown. The one that still smells faintly of salt and blood.

I write one line:

He doesn't get to break me twice.

Then I tear the page out, crumble it, and toss it into the wind. The breeze steals it, drags it toward the ocean, maybe toward him.

Maybe he'll find it.

Maybe he won't.

Either way, I'm done bleeding for ghosts.

When Julie honks outside for the Thunderbird party that night, I don't even hesitate.

I don't think about him.

I just grab my jacket, smear on red lipstick, and tell myself the oldest lie in the book, that I'm fine

CHAPTER ELEVEN

THE PARTY

By the time Julie picks me up, I've convinced myself I'm fine.

I tell my reflection that I don't care.

That I'm over it.

That I can breathe without him.

I'm a liar.

Her car smells like perfume and rebellion. The radio's too loud, the windows down, and she's singing like heartbreak doesn't exist. Her energy is electric, crackling through the air, and I let it pull me in like static.

I wear ripped jeans, a fitted red tee, and my favorite paint-splattered Converse. No crop tops. No cute. Just armor.

The Thunderbird Hotel is already pulsing when we arrive. The base hits my ribs like a heartbeat I can't control. Music, smoke, laughter, chaos—it all bleeds together until the world feels blurry at the edges.

The room smells like sweat, whiskey, and bad decisions.

Lea's on the bed, eyeliner smudged, shoes gone. Daniel's shouting some story about stealing a golf cart. Logan's here, which means Elijah might be too.

Of course he is.

Julie grabs a bottle of whiskey and shoves it toward me. "You drinking tonight?"

I hesitate. "I've never—"

"Perfect time to start."

She tilts the bottle closer. I take it. I don't sip.

I swallow.

It burns like betrayal.

I cough until my eyes water. Julie laughs. "That's the face of a girl who's about to make bad choices."

She's right.

I take another drink.

And another.

The music shifts to Disturbed's "Down with the Sickness." Chelsea jumps on the bed, screaming lyrics like she's exorcising demons. The room moves like one living thing. Bodies, light, chaos.

I start moving too.

Not dancing. Just moving.

Like if I stop, I'll feel again.

Michael catches my hand, spinning me once, laughing. I let him. The alcohol makes everything bright and stupid. The sound in my head drowns out the ache in my chest.

For a few seconds, I almost feel okay.

Then I see her.

Sarah.

Leaning against the wall with Logan, tossing her blonde hair, laughing like the universe owes her joy.

Elijah isn't there, but I feel him in the empty spaces.

My stomach twists.

"Whore," I mutter under my breath. No one hears.

I drank again. The world tilts. Lights smear. The bass pounds through my chest like a warning.

He kissed me.

He held me like I was gravity.

He made me believe I was something more than chaos.

And then he vanished.

And I hate him for it.

I hate myself more for still caring.

I want him to show up.

I want him to see me.

I want him to hurt.

And then—he does.

I didn't notice at first. The room is still spinning, still vibrating with noise and laughter. But Julie leans close, her breath hot against my ear. "Well, damn," she says, voice low. "Guess who finally showed."

I follow her gaze.

He's standing in the doorway.

Elijah.

Leaning against the frame, arms crossed, expression unreadable.

Eyes locked on me.

He's alone.

Sarah isn't with him.

The world goes silent again.

The air changes.

Every nerve in my body lights up like a fuse.

I should look away. Run. Do anything but stand there and unravel.

Instead, I turn to Michael.

He's still beside me, swaying, grinning.

"Kiss me," I say.

He blinks. "Wait, what?"

I don't repeat it. I just grab his shirt and pull him closer.

And kiss him.

It's not love.

It's not even like.

It's war.

His lips taste like whiskey and cheap gum. His hands hesitate at my waist, unsure, like he knows this isn't about him. I kiss harder anyway, because I want it to mean something to someone watching.

I open my eyes mid-kiss.

Elijah is still watching.

Still. Watching.

His jaw is tight. His chest rising and falling too fast. His stare burns through the crowd like a match looking for something to ignite.

Good.

Let it burn.

Nick stumbles into him, drunk, a Solo cup sloshing amber down his arm.

"Yo," Nick slurs, shoving Elijah's shoulder. "Didn't think you even partied anymore."

Elijah doesn't move. "Back off."

Nick smirks. "Oh, look at that. The silent soldier speaks. What's wrong, man? Lose your girlfriend again?"

The air shifts. Conversations stop. Even the music feels quieter.

Nick laughs louder, feeding on the attention. "Come on, hit me. Everyone knows you want to."

Elijah's voice drops, low and deadly. "Don't."

Nick shoves him again.

Bad idea.

Elijah moves before anyone can blink. He grabs Nick by the shirt and slams him against the wall so hard the frame above them crashes to the floor.

Gasps ripple through the room. Someone screams.

Nick swings wildly, but Elijah dodges it and hits him once, hard and clean. The sound is sickening. Nick folds, choking, but Elijah doesn't stop.

He hits him again.

And again.

The crowd scatters, people yelling, trying to pull him off. Elijah's face is twisted in fury, eyes blazing. His knuckles split open, blood blooming fast, and still, he doesn't stop until two guys grab his arms.

He thrashes once. Twice. Then goes still.

Not calm. Just contained.

His shoulders tremble. His chest heaves like he's breathing fire. And then his eyes find me.

The room stops breathing.

There's blood on his knuckles. Pain in his eyes.

And me—standing in the wreckage, holding someone else's hand.

He doesn't look at Nick.

He doesn't look at anyone else.

Just me.

That look is everything and nothing all at once.

Hate. Hurt. Want.

I caused this.

I lit the fuse.

Someone yells, "Get him out of here!" but it's all underwater now. The noise, the crowd, the chaos. None of it matters.

He wrenches himself free, stiff shoulders, jaw locked. Walks past the broken table, the blood, the shattered glass, and pushes open the door.

He doesn't look back.

And still, somehow, it feels like he took the air with him.

The door slams.

Silence.

Julie's voice cuts through it, distant. "Holy shit."

My stomach twists. My pulse is racing. My hands won't stop shaking.

But it's not fear anymore.

It's fire.

It's rage.

And this time, it's mine.

He didn't break me.

He just reminded me how easily I could shatter.

CHAPTER TWELVE

THE QUIET AFTER THE FIRE

Dinner was meatloaf. Again.

My mother's obsession with 1950s cuisine was honestly criminal.

I sat at the table in stiff silence, stabbing a green bean like it had personally wronged me. My parents chatted casually, like we were the Cleavers. Like they hadn't uprooted me from everything I knew and dumped me on some mosquito-infested, salt-crusted island that smelled like sunscreen and rot.

"Eat your vegetables, Victoria," my mom said, her tone sugary sweet and fake enough to rot teeth.

"I'm not hungry."

My voice came out flat. Detached. Like it belonged to someone else. I wasn't here. Not really. I was floating somewhere above my own body, watching myself pretend to care.

"You didn't eat lunch either," she said softly, the concern in her eyes too polished to be real. "You need to keep your strength up."

"I said I'm not hungry."

My dad cleared his throat, his favorite way of existing in a conversation without participating. "You've had a bad attitude lately."

I dropped my fork. "Sorry, I'm not doing cartwheels after being yanked from my life and dropped into this tropical hellhole like a Sims character on randomize mode."

"That's enough," he said, sharper now.

"Oh? Now you have something to say?" I shot back, heat flooding my face. "You ignore me ninety-five percent of the time, but the second I say something honest, suddenly I'm out of line?"

"Victoria," my mom warned, standing. "Go cool off."

I laughed, with an ugly, unsteady sound. "Cool off? I'm fine. Totally. I just chucked my phone into the Gulf last night like a rational human being. Bye-bye, iPhone. Hello, emotional instability."

Her mouth dropped. "You what?"

"I stood on the pier and hurled it into the waves. It made a nice splash."

"Victoria—"

"I don't want a lecture," I snapped, pushing back from the table so hard the chair screeched against the tile. "I don't want your concern. I don't want anything."

My dad stood too. "You don't get to talk to us like that."

"Why not? You talk at me, not to me. You make decisions without me. You tell me how to feel, how to act, but God forbid I act human for five seconds."

"You're being ridiculous," my mom said, crossing her arms.

"No," I said, my voice cracking for the first time. "I'm being real. Sorry, that's so damn inconvenient for everyone."

I left before they could say another word.

In my room, I slammed the door and locked it. The echo of it vibrated through me like a pulse I couldn't slow down. I collapsed onto the bed and stared at the ceiling. No tears. Just pressure. The kind that builds and builds until it feels like your bones might snap from the inside out.

This wasn't about one thing. This was everything.

Every time I'd bitten my tongue. Every time I'd smiled when I wanted to scream. Every time someone told me to calm down, to be better, to be less.

And nobody noticed.

Because I was good at pretending.

Because I wore eyeliner and straightened my hair and said "I'm fine" like it was a prayer I believed.

I wasn't fine.

I was unraveling.

That night, sleep refused me. My body was exhausted, but my mind was on repeat. I kept seeing Elijah, the blood on his knuckles, the fury in his eyes, the way he looked at me like he didn't know whether to hate me or run toward me.

I could still hear the fight echoing in my head, the way the crowd had gone silent, the way he'd left without a word.

The way he always left.

By morning, I was hollow.

I skipped breakfast. Skipped brushing my hair. Skipped pretending.

I threw on a hoodie and sat on the balcony, knees to my chest, staring at the ocean. It was loud and endless, waves crashing repeatedly like it was mocking me for thinking anything in life could stay still.

Julie texted: Wanna go thrifting?

I stared at it until the words blurred, then typed.

Me: Homework. Rain check.

Lie.

I couldn't fake sunshine today.

When the sun started bleeding pink across the horizon, my mom poked her head outside. "You okay, sweetie?"

I nodded. She didn't push. She never did. Not when it mattered.

When she closed the door, I finally stood up. My body moved before my brain caught up, and suddenly I was walking, down the stairs, across the boardwalk, until the sand swallowed my shoes.

The air was sharp with salt. The wind bit my skin. The horizon stretched forever.

I walked until the condos disappeared and the only sound left was the ocean and my heartbeat trying to remind me, I was still alive.

For the first time in weeks, I let myself go there.

Back to Washington.

Back to Brandy and the scissors.

Back to Lisa and the letters.

Back to the girl who snapped first and apologized later.

I hated her.

The girl who swung before she spoke. The one who turned silence into a weapon and shame into armor. The one who'd rather burn everything down than be forgotten.

I thought I buried her back there in the rain.

But she's still here.

She's always been here.

Waiting under my skin, breathing through my ribs, whispering: Let me out.

And for the first time in a long time, I wasn't sure if I wanted her gone or if I needed her.

Julie found me hours later, her flip-flops crunching through the sand. She held a massive 7-Eleven slushie like a peace offering.

"You've been ignoring me all day," she said, sitting beside me. "I brought sugar. And judgment. What the hell happened?"

I didn't answer. I couldn't.

So, she didn't press.

She just sat with me, shoulder to shoulder, watching the waves swallow the sky.

And maybe for the first time, I realized what it meant to be seen without having to perform.

No words. No pretending.

Just breathing beside someone who didn't ask me to explain the storm.

CHAPTER THIRTEEN

The First Word After Silence

I hadn't seen him since the party.

Since the fight with Nick.

Since he looked at me like I was both the storm and the shipwreck.

He'd been missing from school all week, and nobody seemed to know why. I pretended not to care, but I checked the halls. The lunch tables. The damn parking lot like some hopeless addict chasing a ghost.

That was a week ago.

A whole week of silence.

Until now.

I was walking home from school with my earbuds in and my head down, trying to disappear. Julie had gone with her new boyfriend today, all heart eyes and giggles, so I was alone. The Florida heat was muggy and thick, pressing against my skin like regret.

I had just passed the gate to our condo complex when I heard someone say my name.

Soft. But not soft enough to ignore.

"Victoria."

I froze.

I didn't want to turn around.

Didn't want to see him.

But I did.

Elijah was standing near the vending machines by the laundry building, one hand in his pocket, a dark bruise blooming beneath his left eye, ugly and raw. His lip was split and swollen, the kind of injury that hadn't been there after the fight with Nick. This was new.

My stomach twisted.

"What happened to your face?" I asked before I could stop myself.

He didn't answer right away. Just leaned against the wall like his body was made of tired bones.

"Wrong day to come home," he muttered. "He was already deep into the vodka."

Oh.

I didn't have to ask who he meant. It was always his dad.

We stood in silence. The air between us felt like a bruise that hadn't healed.

His sleeve was ripped. His knuckles busted again. His eyes avoided mine, but I could feel them. Like a storm hovering just out of sight.

"I'm sorry," I said quietly.

He let out a half-laugh that sounded like pain trying to escape. "For what?"

"I don't know. Everything?"

He nodded like he understood. Like maybe he was sorry too.

"This isn't how I wanted it to go," he said. "I didn't know how to tell you about Sarah. Every time I tried, the words got stuck."

"So, you said nothing."

"Because everything I wanted to say felt like too much. Or not enough."

I looked at him. Really looked. The bruises. The exhaustion. The way he held himself like he was afraid to unravel.

This wasn't the boy who smirked his way through every rule.

This was the one underneath, the one who never got to be safe.

And I hated how much I loved him for it.

"You look like hell," I said, because anything softer would've cracked me open.

He smirked. "Feel worse."

I moved closer, leaning beside him against the wall until our arms almost brushed. The silence was heavy. Not awkward. Just full.

"Sarah's been in and out of my life for years," he said finally. "One day she's gone, the next she's at my door acting like nothing changed. I didn't plan on you being more than a friend. I didn't expect you to matter. But you did. You do. And when she came back, I didn't know how to handle it. I didn't know how to walk away from something familiar when I'd already started falling for something real."

He rubbed the back of his neck, eyes on the pavement. "It's messed up. I know that. But when chaos is all you've ever known, peace feels suspicious. I didn't know how to tell you. I didn't know how to stay without ruining it."

I stayed quiet. Not because I didn't have words. God, I had too many, but because this was honesty. And honesty deserved space.

"Do you ever feel like you're pretending to be okay because no one wants the truth?" I asked softly.

He looked up. "All the time."

We didn't look away.

And then, quietly, like it cost him something, he said, "I should've told you about Sarah. It wasn't fair."

"I know."

"I need you to hear that. Not because it changes anything. Just because it's true."

I swallowed hard. "Then I need to say something too. About Michael."

The air between us shifted.

"That kiss," I said, "it wasn't real. Not for me. I did it because I was angry. Because I wanted to hurt you the way you were hurting me. And I'm sorry. I'm sorry that it worked. I didn't think

110

it through, and when you fought that guy, all I could think was…
this is my fault."

My voice trembled. "You didn't deserve that."

He exhaled, long and quiet. "I don't blame you, Victoria. Not
for the fight. Not for being angry. I should've been honest from the
start. That's on me."

We fell silent again, side by side. Two people who had broken
each other without meaning to. Two people trying to remember
how to breathe in the same space.

The sound of the ocean carried in from the distance, waves
folding over each other like time was restarting.

He turned to me then, really turned, eyes glassy under the
bruises. "You know what scares me?"

"What?"

"That I'll always find you, even when I shouldn't."

My chest ached. "Then maybe stop looking."

He smiled, sad and small. "Can't."

Our arms brushed. The smallest touch. The biggest ache.

For a second, the world was still.

Not fixed. Not healed.

Just still.

And for two broken things, maybe that was enough.

CHAPTER FOURTEEN

It was past midnight, and the sky outside was cloudy, heavy with the threat of rain. The kind of sky that warned you something was coming.

Something always was.

I couldn't sleep.

I tried. God knows I tried. But sleep isn't for the buzzing. Not for the people who throw their meds in the sand and pretend their brain will just behave.

I replayed everything in my head.

My room was too quiet, too loud. I could hear the whisper of waves crashing even from up here, like the ocean was breathing through the cracks in my window.

I got out of bed, shoved on a hoodie over my tank top, and walked barefoot down the stairs and out the front door. The sand was cool and damp against my toes. A few drunks laughed in the distance, but mostly, the beach had emptied out.

And then I saw him.

Elijah.

Sitting on the edge of the seawall, one leg up, the other dangling over the side. His hair was messy, his face bruised, his expression unreadable. He didn't look at me when I walked up.

I didn't say anything. I just sat down beside him, legs tucked up against my chest, our shoulders almost touching.

We sat there for a long time. Silence stretched between us like an unspoken truce.

"I can't sleep," I finally whispered.

"Me either."

I looked at him. "Does it still hurt?"

He blinked like he forgot the bruise was there. "It's fine."

And then I leaned my head on his shoulder.

It was so small. So simple.

But that tiny act broke something open. His hand found mine. Not forceful. Not hungry. Just warm.

Steady. Real.

We sat there until the air grew colder and the silence turned soft.

He stood up and held out his hand.

I didn't ask where we were going.

I just took it.

He led me back up the beach, through the patio doors, into his condo. It was dark except for the blue glow of the TV screensaver bouncing across the walls.

He walked over and sat on the couch. I stood for a second, unsure.

"You can sit," he said. "I don't bite."

I raised an eyebrow. "Not what I heard."

He smirked. "Lies and slander."

I sat beside him, close but not touching. The silence came back, heavier this time. He leaned forward, elbows on his knees, rubbing the back of his neck before bringing his hands down to his legs.

I reached out and touched his hand. His fingers twitched under mine, like the contact startled him.

"You always like this?" I whispered.

He looked at me. Really looked at me. "Like what?"

"Carrying the world but pretending it's not heavy."

He let out a breath, slow and sharp, like it scraped its way out of his chest.

"It's easier that way," he muttered. "No one asks questions if you don't look like you're drowning."

I didn't say anything. Just waited. Quiet worked better on him than pressure ever would.

He rubbed his thumb over my knuckles like he didn't even know he was doing it.

"When I was little, I used to sleep in the bathtub with a towel over me. I told myself it was a spaceship. It wasn't. It was the only place I couldn't hear him screaming."

My heart dropped.

"Your dad?"

He nodded once. "Some days he acts like my best friend, and then other days he's so drunk, he's unpredictable. You know what sucks? You can get used to anything. Even that."

He turned his face slightly, the blue light catching on the bruise under his eye.

My fingers tightened around his.

"Why don't you leave?" I whispered.

"And go where?" he asked, voice flat. "It's not like I've got people lining up to take me in. I've got two more semesters. Then I'm gone."

"You don't have to wait until then," I said. "You could—"

"What?" he cut in gently. "Run away? Crash on someone's couch? Get a minimum wage job and pray it pays for a roof and food?" He shook his head. "I already do that. Why do you think I'm gone so much?"

I swallowed the lump forming in my throat. "You don't deserve that."

He looked at me again. Eyes tired. But warm. "Neither do you."

I didn't realize I was crying until he reached up and wiped a tear from my cheek with his thumb.

"You're not broken," he said. "You've just been fighting for too long."

I leaned into his touch, something inside of me splintering.

"Me too," he added, barely above a whisper.

Our eyes locked.

That's when I moved. Not in a dramatic, passionate way, but like my body was pulled by gravity and I couldn't ignore it.

I slid closer. He didn't stop me.

He didn't say a word. Just stood, still holding my hand, and gently pulled me off the couch.

The moment felt suspended, like the universe was holding its breath. My heartbeat was loud in my ears, louder than the waves outside, louder than anything.

He walked me toward his bedroom, our fingers still laced. I didn't look at the living room as we passed. I couldn't. I wasn't ready to break whatever this was.

His room was quiet, lit only by the soft glow of a streetlight bleeding through the blinds. The bed was unmade, a little messy, like him. A blue comforter and two pillows, one looked like it hadn't been touched in weeks. The air smelled like fabric softener and boy, clean, warm, familiar. And something else. Him.

He let go of my hand and turned to face me but didn't move any closer.

I stepped in first. Because if I waited, I might overthink it. Might talk myself out of feeling everything I'd buried.

"Elijah..." I whispered. I didn't even know what I meant to say after that. But he heard something in it.

116

Something real.

He reached out and gently touched my cheek, like he was afraid I might flinch.

The air between us shifted, thick with something unnamed. My skin buzzed where his fingers lingered.

"I don't know how to do this," I said.

He gave a soft smile, eyes flicking down to our joined hands.

"You're not like anyone I've ever been with."

It shouldn't have mattered, but God, it did. I wanted to be the one he couldn't forget.

And then he kissed me.

God. It wasn't like before. It wasn't heat and desperation. It was slow. Careful. Like he knew I needed to be handled delicately but didn't want me to feel fragile.

My hoodie came off first, then my tank top. He didn't pull or rush. His fingers moved like he was trying to memorize every inch of me.

And I let him. Because I wanted him to know me, all the hidden bruises, all the broken places.

When his shirt came off, I swear I forgot how to breathe. His body wasn't just beautiful; it was carved in pain and survival. Faint scars, bruises still fading, and those deep lines of tension across his chest and stomach.

Every piece of clothing felt like a layer of armor slipping away, and I didn't know if I was more terrified of him seeing me or me finally seeing myself.

I'd never seen anything like it. I wanted to touch all of it.

So, I did.

My fingers trailed across his collarbone, over his ribs, down the trail of hair leading below his waistband. I didn't know what I was doing. My hands shook. But he just stood there and let me explore.

When he leaned in again, his mouth found my neck, then my shoulder, and I melted. Completely. My legs felt like air.

"You're shaking," he whispered.

"I'm scared," I admitted.

He nodded, forehead resting against mine. "We can stop. We don't have to—"

"I want to," I said. "I just... I want it to be you."

Something in his eyes changed. Like the weight of that hit him square in the chest.

He kissed me again. More urgent this time. My bra came off, and my jeans next. He moved like I was a secret he didn't want anyone else to find.

He was slow. So slow.

Time lost its edges.

We made it to the bed, and he pulled the covers back, helping me lie down before stripping off the rest of his clothes. I watched him in the dim light, and I didn't feel embarrassed. I felt seen. Really seen.

For a heartbeat, I felt naked in more ways than one. Like he was looking through every mask I had ever worn, every lie I had told about being fine, and he still didn't flinch. That terrified me. And it saved me all at once.

When he stood above me, completely bare, I stared. Not because I was trying to compare him to anything, how could I? There was nothing to compare him to. But because it was the most human thing I had ever witnessed. A boy stripped of armor, broken in places I recognized in myself.

He came down to the bed slowly, resting beside me.

I didn't flinch when he touched me again. His hand slid down my side, curved over my hip, and then paused.

He looked at me. One last time.

And I nodded.

The moment stretched forever, then it broke.

He kissed me deeply as his hand slipped lower, gentle, easing the tension from my thighs. His fingers found me, and I arched into his touch, the warmth of him grounding me.

"Is this okay?" he whispered against my skin.

I nodded again. "Don't stop."

He kissed my shoulder, my collarbone, and every place in between. And then, when I thought I might fall apart from the sheer pressure of want, he reached into the nightstand, pulled out a condom, and rolled it on.

And then he was inside me.

It didn't feel like losing something. It felt like reclaiming something I didn't know I'd buried.

I gasped, not from pain, but from the overwhelming wave of sensation. It wasn't just physical. It was emotional. Like something inside of me was unlocking. Breaking open.

I wasn't just giving him my body. I was giving him all the pieces of me that I'd been keeping locked up since forever.

His movements were slow at first. Rhythmic. His hand found mine, fingers laced. Our breathing synced like waves crashing in rhythm. My eyes never left his.

His voice was a low groan in my ear. "You feel like fire."

I held onto him tighter. "Don't stop."

When it built, the pressure, the burn, the ache, it wasn't about the orgasm. It was about being full of him.

Of something I'd never had before.

When it hit me, I shook. Moaned. Cried, maybe.

He followed right after, loud, rough, and real, collapsing on top of me in a mess of limbs and skin and sweat.

We lay there afterward, tangled in sheets, both trying to catch our breath. Neither saying anything.

Because the silence said enough.

This wasn't just sex. It was survival.

It was the kind of connection that didn't have a name but left marks anyway.

Neither of us would ever be the same and maybe that was the tragedy of it.

CHAPTER FIFTEEN

The next morning felt like I'd borrowed someone else's life. Not because I didn't recognize it, but because I didn't know how to live in it anymore.

Elijah hadn't said much after. Not even a whispered goodbye. He walked me to the door, kissed the top of my head like that meant something, and then disappeared into the shadows of his condo like a ghost too familiar with vanishing.

Now I was standing in front of the school like everything wasn't upside down.

My insides were sore. My chest was sore. My thighs were sore. My heart? Shredded.

I blinked up at the building like maybe it would let me skip today, but Julie's voice cut through my pity party.

"There you are," she said, linking her arm through mine. "You okay?"

I nodded too quickly. "Just tired."

"Same. My mom was on one last night. Swear to God, if she tries to ground me one more time for breathing."

Her voice faded into white noise as we walked through the doors. Every step I took felt like I was floating six inches above my body.

I didn't see Elijah all morning.

Which only made it worse.

Because I was looking for him.

Every class. Every hallway. Every reflection in glass windows made my heart do backflips for no reason.

By lunch, I gave up pretending. I grabbed an apple from the lunch line and walked to the quad just to get air.

And there he was.

Backpack slung over one shoulder, sitting with Logan, laughing like he hadn't gutted me open less than twelve hours ago.

He didn't look my way. Didn't even glance.

I didn't know what hurt worse, his silence or how easily he wore it.

Julie sat beside me. "You sure you're okay?"

"I said I'm fine."

"You're lying."

I said nothing. Because she wasn't wrong.

He passed me in the hallway right before the bell. Not a word. Not a flicker of recognition. Just a gust of air as he moved past, like I was a ghost he'd already buried.

I thought giving someone all the pieces of you meant they'd hold them carefully.

But apparently, Elijah just liked to watch things shatter.

The fifth period dragged. Sixth was a blur. By the seventh, I was wound so tight I thought I might unravel if anyone looked at me too long.

Julie was chattering about something, and I nodded along like my insides weren't unraveling thread by thread. I kept hearing her voice in pieces, like I was underwater. Like I couldn't quite surface.

He hadn't texted. Hadn't looked for me. Hadn't looked at me.

I shoved my books into my bag and slipped out the side hallway that led to the vending machines, where barely anyone ever went. I needed air. I needed space. I needed to scream into a void or maybe cry until I stopped shaking.

I saw him before he saw me.

Elijah stood by the vending machines, same hoodie from last night, hunched like he was trying to make himself smaller. His hands were jammed into his pockets, eyes fixed on the snack options like they held the meaning of life. He didn't look tense. He looked avoidant. Like he wasn't expecting anyone, especially not me.

I walked straight up to him, heart a goddamn earthquake.

He glanced up, eyes meeting mine. Something flickered. Guilt? Regret? Panic?

"Hey," I said, voice sharp, slicing through the hum of the vending machine.

He startled, like seeing me was the last thing he wanted, and quickly looked away. "Victoria."

"Seriously?" I snapped, arms crossing over my chest. "You disappear on me, and all I get is my name like I'm some random classmate you barely recognize?"

He exhaled like this was a conversation he'd rehearsed and still didn't want to have. "Can we not do this here?"

"Oh, you mean in the middle of school, where you pretend I don't exist? Where you laugh with your friends like you didn't just crawl under my skin and vanish?"

He rubbed the back of his neck, avoiding my eyes. "I didn't mean to."

"You didn't mean to what? Screw me and forget it? Or make me feel like I mattered just long enough to regret it?"

He looked pained but kept glancing around, shifting on his feet like the hallway walls were closing in.

"Can you not do this here?" he said under his breath, glancing around like he was expecting someone to jump out and record us. "People are watching."

"I don't care," I bit back, stepping closer. "Maybe you should've thought about that before screwing with my head."

He shifted uncomfortably, his eyes darting down the hall, voice low. "You're blowing this out of proportion. We never talk at school. Why would that change now?"

"Because everything's different now," I hissed.

His brow furrowed like I was speaking another language. "I don't get why you're so pissed. What did I do?"

I laughed, sharp and humorless. "You really don't know?"

He dragged a hand down his face, muttering, "Victoria, I didn't mean."

"To make me feel disposable?" I snapped, my voice rising despite myself. "Too late for that, Elijah."

He took a step back, glancing in both directions down the hall like he was worried someone might overhear.

"Lower your voice."

"Oh, now you care what people hear?" I laughed bitterly.

His jaw flexed. "We've never talked in school. What did you think was gonna happen today? That I'd bring you flowers and hold your hand in the courtyard?"

My eyes burned. "No, I thought maybe you'd look at me. Like I wasn't just something that happened to you."

He looked genuinely thrown. "I didn't think it'd matter this much to you. We didn't define anything."

"Wow," I said, my voice dropping. "You really don't get it, do you? You act like it was some random hookup, like I should be grateful you even remembered my name."

He flinched like I'd slapped him. Then something snapped in his expression.

"You know what's crazy?" he said, voice low but cutting. "You lasted a whole twenty-four hours before going full meltdown. Didn't even get a full day of peace before you lost your mind over some dick."

126

My jaw locked. "Screw you."

"No, you already did," he shot back, eyes dark. "And now you want fireworks and fairy tales because what, we had sex? You think that makes me yours?"

I stared at him, stunned. "I didn't expect you to be mine, Elijah. I expected you not to treat me like I was nothing."

He scoffed, clearly on edge now. "I'm not trying to be a dick, but what do you want from me, Victoria? Huh? Should I be writing you poetry in homeroom? Parade you through the halls with a crown on your head because we fucked one time?"

I opened my mouth to snap back, but the words stuck in my throat.

He looked at me with something sharp and defensive in his eyes. "Are you done? Or do you want to keep putting on a show?"

I stepped forward, my voice trembling but laced with fire. "No, Elijah. I'm not done. You don't get to act like it meant nothing. Not when you kissed me like I was yours. Not when you held me like you meant it."

He looked like he wanted to argue, but for once, he didn't have anything to say.

My breath caught.

I stared at him one last time, but there was nothing left to say. No apology. No fight worth having. Just ache.

So, I turned and walked away.

Behind me, a loud metallic bang cracked through the silence. I didn't turn around, but I knew exactly what it was.

Elijah had punched the vending machine.

Somewhere deep down, I wished it had been me instead.

Julie's car smelled like peach gum and cheap cologne. Daniel must've left his hoodie in here again.

"So," she said, pulling out of the parking lot. "You've been weird."

I blinked at her. "Weird how?"

She glanced at me from the corner of her eye. "Like smiley but also dead inside. It's giving 'I'm fine' in the worst way."

I let out a hollow laugh and leaned my head against the passenger window. The glass was cool. Grounding. "Maybe I'm just tired."

"Victoria," she warned. "Don't start pulling that 'I'm tired' shit on me. I know what tiredness looks like. You look like someone walked through your brain in muddy boots."

She wasn't wrong. But she didn't know. She couldn't. No one could.

I'd spent the last twelve hours replaying everything over and over again. Elijah's hands on my skin, his breath in my ear, the way his lips whispered things I don't think he's ever said to anyone else. I should be floating. I should feel like I was glowing from the inside out.

But instead, I felt untethered. Like my soul got left behind and my body was just pretending.

And now, all I could think about was how stupid I was for letting my emotions get the best of me. I should've waited. Talked to him at home. Said what I needed to say without turning it into a public meltdown. But I didn't. I lashed out. Loud and messy and raw.

And now? He probably hated me for it. Probably thought I was crazy. And the worst part? I didn't even blame him.

Julie reached for the radio and turned it down. "You've barely spoken all day. This morning, I asked if you wanted coffee, and you just said, 'Sure.' That's not you. You're a two-Splenda, extra-drama, foam-needs-to-be-fluffy-or-I'll-fight-someone kind of girl."

"I just didn't sleep well."

She raised a brow. "Is this about your parents?"

That was the easiest answer. "Yeah. Things were tense last night."

Julie sighed, squeezing the steering wheel. "You want to hang out later? We could go to the pier, eat nachos, scream into the ocean. Whatever helps."

The offer was sweet, but I shook my head. "No. I need to pretend that today is normal. My parents are already breathing down my neck about everything. If I don't show up, I'll be grounded for a month."

We pulled into the parking lot of the condos, and my stomach did a slow, traitorous flip. His car was parked where it always was, like it hadn't moved, like nothing's changed. But everything had.

I saw his windows lit up faintly from the inside. I felt his presence before I even opened the car door.

Thick. Electric. Heavy.

I wasn't ready to face him again, but fate never asked what I was ready for.

And it was fine. I told myself it was fine. Repeatedly.

It wasn't. It never was.

The air by the pool smelled like sunscreen and chlorine.

I stood in the shadow of the stairwell, pretending to scroll my phone while Elijah and Logan leaned against the fence a few yards away.

Logan laughed first. A laugh too loud, too casual.

"So what's the deal with the girl?"

Elijah didn't answer right away. He kicked at a loose tile and stared at the water.

"She's … a mistake I don't want to repeat."

The words hit harder than they should have.

He didn't say my name. He didn't have to.

Logan whistled low. "Damn, that serious?"

Elijah shrugged. "It just … got messy. I don't do messy."

I backed up a step, heart in my throat. The metal gate creaked, and both of them turned.

"Vic—" Elijah started.

I was already walking.

"Hey!" he called. "Wait!"

He caught my arm near the vending machines. His fingers burned through my sleeve.

"Listen, you weren't supposed to hear that."

"Then maybe don't say things like that," I snapped.

His jaw clenched. "You're twisting it."

"I'm quoting it."

He looked like he wanted to deny it, to fix it, but nothing came out. His silence was worse than the words.

"You said it was different," I whispered. "You said I was different."

He swallowed hard. "You are. That's the problem."

I took a shaky breath. "So what? You screw me, then pretend I don't exist?"

"Don't do that," he said, voice low. "It's not like that."

"Then what is it like?"

He stepped closer, and for a second, I thought he might tell me. But his hands dropped back to his sides.

"I don't know," he said finally. "I'm trying not to make things worse."

"Too late."

I pulled away before he could stop me. The gate banged shut behind me, echoing through the humid air.

By the time I reached the street, my chest felt hollow, like he'd ripped something out of me and left the rest behind.

CHAPTER SIXTEEN

The beach is louder than usual. Windy, crowded, the sun reflecting off the water like it's trying to blind us. But none of it matters.

He's here.

And like always, the world shifts to orbit him.

Not with me, of course. That would be too simple. Too honest.

Elijah is out near the shoreline, running across the sand with Logan, Jesse, and Michael, who somehow makes Crocs look like a personality trait. They're kite surfing, laughing, throwing their bodies into the wind like they're invincible.

I'm watching from my towel, pretending I'm not.

Julie is lying next to me in her black bikini top and cutoffs, her eyes hidden behind heart-shaped sunglasses that make her look sweeter than she is. She's passing a vape back and forth with Hannah, talking about a philosophy exam like it's the end of the world.

Me? I'm trying to disappear into the sand.

"You've been watching them for twenty minutes like you're studying wind patterns," Julie says, flicking sand at my leg. "Which one are you crushing on? Please say it's Michael so I can mock you for kissing him and still not dating him."

I fake a laugh and look down at my hands.

If she only knew.

Across the beach, Elijah lifts his kite into the wind and runs, barefoot and golden and so stupidly alive it makes my chest hurt. He hasn't looked this carefree since the night he kissed me.

"I'm fine," I lie again.

Julie doesn't press. She just passes me the vape. I don't take it.

Sarah shows up twenty minutes later like she's stepping out of a music video. Long legs. Tan skin. Glitter on her collarbones. Like she actually planned to look like a distraction.

She walks straight to Elijah's group. He doesn't see her right away.

But I do.

I see everything.

They don't kiss. Not yet.

She just touches his shoulder and smiles. He turns. Smiles back. And I swear my stomach caves in.

"I think I'm gonna go for a walk," I say, already getting up.

Julie looks up. "Want company?"

I shake my head.

I walk down the shoreline, the wind pulling at my hoodie, the waves biting at my feet. It's like the whole world is having fun, and I'm just background static.

I don't cry. I just stared at the water and wondered when it stopped feeling like home.

Sometimes, I wish I were back in Washington. Not because it was better, it wasn't, but because the cold there made sense. The silence made sense. People ignored you and meant it. Here, it's all warmth and sunshine and fake smiles. I gave up everything familiar, and for what? To lie on a beach and pretend I didn't just lose my virginity to someone who won't even look at me?

I feel like I'm going to explode. Like I swallowed something too big and now I'm splitting open from the inside. I don't have anyone to talk to about it, not really. Not about what it means. Not about how my body feels like it doesn't belong to me anymore, and my heart feels even less mine.

There's no language for shame that feels this heavy.

I can't talk to my parents. God, no. My mom would just panic and cart me off to a hundred different doctors, each one poking and prodding and diagnosing until I didn't even recognize myself in their checklists. My dad would probably ground me until I'm thirty. I can't tell them I slept with a boy I've known for five minutes who already looks at me like a regret. I can't even tell Julie. Not the full truth.

A smart, normal girl would have picked Michael. Michael, who kissed me and would do it again in front of the whole school without flinching. Who would hold my hand, call me his girl, make it known. But not me. I never do things the easy way. I chose the boy with walls taller than me, the one who disappears when things get real. Because apparently, I like to suffer.

My brain's a mess. Always has been. And when I try to open up, I just get angrier. I lash out. Break things. Break people. That's why I stopped trying. Because every time I let someone in, I end up regretting it.

It's almost midnight when Julie texts:

You up? I have gummy worms and trauma.

I don't answer. I'm already outside, sitting on a half-buried towel in the sand a few yards from the dunes, hoodie wrapped around my knees, watching the tide roll in like it's trying to swallow the whole coastline.

Another buzz:

I'm walking over. Please don't make me sit out here and cry alone like a sad girl in a Taylor Swift bridge.

I glanced up and spotted her silhouette coming down the path, oversized hoodie flapping behind her like a cape, candy bag in one hand, flip-flops smacking with each step.

She doesn't say hi. Just drops onto the towel beside me, sits cross-legged, and starts untangling the gummy worms like it's the most natural thing in the world.

"You look like hell," she says.

"Cool. That's the goal."

She tosses a worm on my lap. "Eat this. It's red. That means I love you."

We sat there for a few minutes without talking. The only sound is the wind pushing at the water and someone's drunk laughter echoing from way down the beach.

Then Julie sighs, flopping back into the sand. "Okay. What's going on? Because if you don't spill, I swear I'm gonna start trauma-dumping just to fill the silence."

136

I raise a brow. "Like what?"

She lets out a bitter laugh. "Like my mom being pregnant. Again. With a baby we can't afford and a stepdad who's been spiraling since the test turned pink."

My head snapped toward her. "Wait, what?"

Julie shrugs, but it's the kind that looks like it hurts. "Yeah. Alicia and I are gonna get jobs. I already applied to Scoops. She's looking at the boardwalk surf shop. But I'm so tired, V. I'm tired of being the adult. Tired of not getting to be a normal teenager."

The words hit like a mirror. Julie's version of drowning looked different, but I knew the feeling all too well.

She sighs again, softer this time. "Anyway. I shared. Your turn."

I pick at the strings on my hoodie. "Nothing."

"Bullshit."

"I just..." I pause, then shake my head. "It's stupid."

Julie props herself up on her elbows, gummy worm hanging from her mouth. "Was it that girl? Glitter bikini girl? The one who was surgically glued to Elijah's side like a human barnacle?"

I stiffen.

"Yeah," she says, chewing. "Thought so. You looked like someone kicked your soul in the uterus when she showed up."

"I didn't."

"You did. I know your face, V."

I don't say anything. I just stare at the waves like they might pull me in and not spit me back out.

Julie leans over, gently bumps her shoulder against mine. "You like him? And why didn't you tell me? And while we're at it, why kiss Michael if Elijah's the one you want?"

I want to lie. I really do.

But the silence says enough.

Julie just nods slowly, dragging a line in the sand with her finger. "Cool. Okay. Just needed to know whose tires I'm slashing if shit hits the fan."

My laugh comes out more like a sigh. "It's already too late."

She doesn't say "I'm sorry." She doesn't say "Screw him." She just sighs and mutters, "First day, I told you he was the wrong one from the Treasure Island trio. He wasn't the one getting the Tesla."

She just opens the bag again, pulls out another gummy worm, and drops it into my palm like a peace treaty.

After a moment, I say it. Quiet. Scared of the words even as they leave my mouth.

"It wasn't just a crush."

Julie looks over at me but doesn't interrupt.

"He saw me. And for a second, I thought that meant something." She stays still beside me, the candy bag rustling softly in her lap.

"No one's ever really seen me before. Not even back in Washington."

"Because they didn't want to?" she asks, voice low.

I shake my head. "Because I didn't let them."

Julie nods slowly, like she understands more than I expected. "But you let him."

I swallow. "Yeah. And now I wish I hadn't."

She doesn't reach for me. Doesn't say it's gonna be okay.

She just sits there.

Her friendship isn't loud, it's a hand steadying me before I fall.

"Then we sit here," she says, "and mourn the romantic corpse of your dignity and my will to survive another sibling. I brought a playlist called Healing but Still Petty. We're gonna cry, snack, maybe hex someone. Equal opportunity emotional destruction. I'm open."

For the first time all day, the ache in my chest loosens.

Not a lot.

But enough.

And for the first time in weeks, I don't feel invisible.

CHAPTER SEVENTEEN

I woke up already exhausted. Not tired. Just done. Like whatever was holding me together finally gave up sometime around three a.m.

I moved on autopilot. Shower. Clothes. Bag. No makeup. No breakfast. No reason. I don't look in the mirror.

School is noise and color and people laughing too loudly in hallways I used to feel safe in.

Julie talks at lunch. I nodded. Smile. Sip from a water bottle I don't remember grabbing. Pretending like the way I'm drifting isn't obvious.

She watches me like she knows something's wrong. But she doesn't ask. And I don't offer.

Elijah walks past me in the breezeway. Not close enough to touch. Just close enough to ruin my day.

He looks at me. For half a second.

I look away first.

He doesn't follow me. Doesn't say my name. Doesn't flinch.

And somehow, that's worse than anything he could have done.

Because hate would mean he still felt something.

I walk home slower than usual, headphones in, hood up. The wind's stronger today. It bites at my sleeves, kicks sand into my shoes, stings my face like it's trying to wake me up.

It doesn't work.

That night, I sit on the floor of my bedroom while my sister watches TV a few feet away. I told her I have a headache. I told her I need quiet. I told her nothing that matters.

I scroll through maps on my phone. Towns I've never been to. Names I can't pronounce. Places with beaches or deserts or snow or nothing.

It doesn't matter where I go. Only that it's not here.

I don't cry. Crying would mean I still care.

This? This is colder. Cleaner.

This is the part where the girl fades out of her own story.

I crawl into bed without brushing my hair. Pull the blanket over my head like it's armor. And I think: if I left, no one would chase me. And that's how I know I should.

I don't know what pulled me out of bed. Maybe it's the sound of the ocean. Maybe it's the silence in my chest. Maybe it's just habit, sneaking out at night like I'm still the girl who believes he might be waiting.

I threw on a hoodie. Walk barefoot through the sand.

The moon is pale and disinterested tonight, hanging over the waves like it's tired of watching me fall apart.

Even the universe looks bored of my heartbreak.

I tell myself I'm just going for a walk.

I don't believe it.

I found him on the seawall, exactly where I didn't expect him to be. Sitting. Hoodie up. Shoulders hunched.

Legs dangling over the edge like he's one wave away from letting it take him.

His head turns when he hears me. No words. No surprise. Like he knew I'd come.

Of course I did.

I sit beside him. Close, but not touching.

"Didn't expect to see you here," I say, my voice barely carrying over the sound of the waves.

Elijah glances at me, the surprise quick and muted, then turns back to the ocean. "Didn't expect to see anyone."

"Me neither."

I hug my arms around my stomach. "Just needed air."

He nods slowly. "Couldn't sleep."

The silence stretches awkward and wide, but I let it sit.

Finally, he says, "We really are shit at staying away."

I glance sideways at him. "Like ghosts haunting the same wreckage."

The problem with ghosts is they never really leave.

He huffs a quiet breath. "Guess it makes sense. We wrecked the same thing."

There's no apology. No explanation. Just us. Sitting on the edge of something we already know won't hold.

"I should hate you," I whisper, voice shaking. "But I don't. And that's the worst part."

His jaw clenches. He stares straight ahead.

"I never wanted to hurt you," he says.

"But you did."

"I know."

The ocean crashes beneath us.

I don't know who moves first. Maybe it's Elijah. Maybe it's me. But suddenly we're not sitting anymore. We're standing.

Our eyes catch in the dark. That moment stretches, heavy with warning, heavy with want.

I know I shouldn't follow him. I know this will hurt later.

I do it anyway.

His condo is quiet. Dark. The kind of silence that feels intentional, like even the furniture is trying not to make noise.

I step inside and close the door behind me gently, as if I'm too loud, I'll wake whatever this is, and it'll vanish.

The air smells like him. Salt, detergent, and something darker. The windows are cracked. The breeze moves through space like a ghost.

He doesn't turn on the light. Neither do I.

I follow him down the hall. Each step feels heavier than the last. Not rushed. Not clumsy. Just inevitable.

He pushes open the door to his bedroom, and I pause in the doorway.

The sheets are half-twisted like he's been tossing for hours. There's a hoodie crumpled on the floor. A cup of water on the nightstand, barely touched. A photo on the dresser that I can't quite make out in the dark.

I hesitate.

He turns around. Looks at me. Says nothing.

I walk in.

He meets me in the middle of the room, and for a second, all we do is breathe. Close enough to feel it but not touching yet.

And then, finally, his hand finds my jaw. It's soft. Hesitant. Like he's not sure if he's allowed. Like he's touching something he already knows he doesn't deserve.

His thumb brushes my cheek, just once. I think it's meant to be a question.

I answer by kissing him.

It starts slowly. Mouths barely moving. Breath-catching. Fingers grazing over fabric like they're memorizing every layer before it's gone.

His hand moves to the back of my neck. My arms wrap around his waist. His shirt is soft against my palms.

Too soft for the way his heart is beating underneath.

I tug it up. He lets me.

I kiss the hollow of his throat, and his breath stutters against my skin.

My hoodie drops to the floor.

His hands trail down my spine, not hurried, just deliberate. Like he wants to feel every inch. Like he's afraid it's the last time.

Because it is.

We don't say it. But it's there. Humming between our ribs. A quiet knowing.

When we fall onto the bed, it isn't frantic.

It's worship.

It's grief.

It's please let this mean something.

His lips find my shoulder, then my collarbone. His hands slide beneath the waistband of my shorts slowly, his fingers shaking, like touching me is an apology he can't say out loud.

I feel tears build behind my eyes and blink them away.

This isn't about fixing anything. This is about feeling it while we still can.

He looks at me. Really looks. And for a second, neither of us moves.

Then he whispers, "Come here," like he's calling me to safety. Like maybe he's calling me home.

I go to him without thinking.

His hands slid beneath the hem of my shirt slowly, palms warm against my skin. My breath hitches when his fingertips graze the sides of my ribs, featherlight. Like he's memorizing the outline of me. Like he's touching someone breakable.

His shirt brushes my stomach as he pulls it over my head, careful, gentle. It drops to the floor, and he stares for a second too long.

Not with lust, but with something heavier. Reverent.

His hand hovers near my waist like he's asking for permission, even though I'm already standing here, already his.

I pressed into his palm.

That's all the answer he needs.

He kisses me again, this time deeper. Slower. One hand gripping the back of my neck, the other pressed flat to my lower back, anchoring me to him.

I feel his mouth part against mine, and the sound I make isn't soft. It's desperate.

My fingers drag down his chest, over muscle and skin and scar, until I reach the waistband of his sweats. I push them down, and he kicks them off without looking.

His breath catches when I step forward, bare skin brushing bare skin. Every nerve in me sparks. My pulse is everywhere.

He lays me down like I'm something to be handled, not taken.

The weight of him between my legs doesn't feel heavy. It feels grounding.

His hand cups the back of my thigh, pulling it around his waist, and his hips settle against mine in a way that feels so familiar it knocks the air out of me.

But it's not like last time.

This time, he's looking me in the eye.

His hand slides down my stomach, slow and intentionally, until he reaches where I need him most.

I tense, but not from fear. From everything else. From how good he is at this. From how well he knows me.

He touches me like he's learning me again. Like he forgot the map and is redrawing it one soft circle at a time.

I can't help it. I whispered his name.

He leans down, mouth brushing my jaw. "Tell me what you need."

I bit my lip. "You."

His forehead presses to mine, and he breathes me in like he's starving.

When he slides into me, I feel every inch.

It's not fast. It's not hard. It's deep.

My fingers claw at his shoulders. My legs tighten around his waist. His lips move along my neck, down to the edge of my collarbone.

Every slow thrust is purposeful, like he's trying to build something between us with just this moment.

His breath is ragged in my ear. I swear I hear him whisper my name again.

Or maybe I just want to believe he does.

I close my eyes. I feel the way he rocks into me, steady, sure, relentless in a way that's not about claiming me but understanding me. Knowing where to touch. How to move. When to slow down and when to stop altogether and just breathe with me.

The tension builds slowly. Not frantic. Not explosive. Just inevitable.

My body arches into him, and his hand cradles the back of my head like he's afraid I'll slip through his fingers.

"Don't stop," I whisper. It comes out more like a plea.

"I won't," he says.

But something in his voice says he already is.

I break first. Quietly.

My back lifts off the bed, lips parting, breath catching in my throat. It rolls through me like heat. Like grief. Like a goodbye I don't know I'm saying.

He follows, his hand pressed to my hip, his mouth on my shoulder, his body shaking with it.

We stay like that for a while.

Breathless. Quiet. Still.

Eventually, he rolls onto his back. I curled into his side.

He doesn't speak. Neither do I.

And maybe that's what makes it perfect.

Or maybe that's what makes it hurt.

Some love stories don't end, they just stop showing up.

But for once, I don't ask questions.

I just lay there in the dark, pretending we're okay.

Pretending this isn't the last good memory I'll have of him for years.

CHAPTER EIGHTEEN

The hotel pool at the Thunderbird is already buzzing when Julie and I arrive. Sunlight skips across the water, sharp and blinding, and someone's Bluetooth speaker blasts early-2000s throwbacks like a Hot Topic cashier made the playlist on three energy drinks.

Julie's mom is behind the front desk, waving through the glass doors like we're celebrities instead of two girls with beach hair and drugstore flip-flops. She gave us the all-clear this morning, said as long as we don't break anything or call the cops, we can do whatever. I guess that's the teenage version of freedom.

We drop our towels on two lounge chairs near the deep end. The usual crowd is here: Brian and his girlfriend are already glued together like they get paid by the kiss. Nate's bellyflopping off the diving board like he's auditioning for Jackass. Jesse and Logan throw a football back and forth like it's the Super Bowl. Michael's holding court at a table covered in empty soda cans. And Lea's sunbathing with three other girls like this is Ibiza, not St. Pete.

And then there's Elijah.

Sitting at the edge of the pool in dark swimming trunks, wet hair falling into his face, sunglasses hiding his eyes. He looks like a secret and a dare rolled into one. Alone.

Sarahs across the pool in a lime-green bikini, laughing too loud at something a football player says.

Julie flops onto her chair. "Can you believe this weather? It's like the sun finally remembered Florida exists."

"Yeah. Wild."

The truth? I don't even see the sun. I see him. Last night was still burned into my skin, replaying in flashes I can't get rid of—his hand on my spine, the way I curled into him like it was safe. I wonder if he remembers. If it mattered.

He glances up once. Not just noticing me. Seeing me.

One look from him and every version of me I was trying to bury clawed its way back up.

And then he looks away.

I cannonball into the deep end before anyone notices my face.

Sarah's been orbiting the pool for a while.

She laughs too loud at things no one else finds funny. Flicks her hair, checks her reflection in her phone, laughs again. It's desperate in a way that almost hurts to watch.

Every time Elijah moves, her eyes follow. Every time he doesn't look back, her smile falters.

Julie leans over and whispers, "She's one more fake laugh away from a breakdown."

I don't answer. Because I can see it, the way Sarah's pretending she still has a grip on something that's already gone. The way she keeps trying to fix the picture from the outside, not realizing it's already cracked underneath. Because I can see it, the desperation under the eyeliner, the heartbreak behind the tan.

She's spinning her own fairytale out of scraps, pretending the ending hasn't already been written.

When she finally stands, I know it's coming before it happens.

She straightens her shoulders, tosses her hair, and walks toward Elijah like she's marching into battle.

And I hate myself for watching.

For wanting to see what happens when she finally breaks.

I watch Sarah cross the deck, head high, heart breaking loud enough for everyone to hear.

And I hate that part of me that understands her.

The wanting. The trying. The pretending.

An hour later, everyone's sun-drunk and waterlogged. The boys are trying to drown each other on floaties, Julie's trading gossip with Bree, and I'm halfway through a soggy sandwich when Sarah decides to make her move.

She slinks over to Elijah like she's stalking prey. Perches beside him, too close. "You're just gonna ignore me all day?"

"I asked you to leave me alone," he says, flat.

"Oh my God, Elijah. I talked to someone. That's not a crime."

His jaw ticks.

She leans in, voice low but sharp enough for everyone to hear. "At least I'm not sneaking around at night."

My stomach twists.

Elijah finally looks at her. His voice cuts through the noise. "You've been obsessed with me since day one. I didn't ask for this. I didn't ask for you to turn us into something we weren't."

Sarah's face twists. "Then why stay with me? Why pretend?"

"Because every time I tried to end it, you cried or made a scene. I stayed because it was easier than watching you burn it all down."

Her voice cracks. "You're just mad I stopped letting you use me."

His laugh is bitter. "You were never supposed to be serious, Sarah. You forced it. I went along because I didn't know how to walk away. That's it."

"You know what? Screw you, Elijah."

"You already did that yourself."

Cruel words sound prettier when they come from someone you still want to kiss.

Gasps ripple across the pool deck. Someone mutters, "Yikes."

Her lips tremble, but she says nothing. She storms off, slamming a door behind her.

The music cranks louder. People pretend they weren't watching.

And Elijah? He walks straight to me.

"Hey," he says, low. Casual. Like he didn't just light a match in front of everyone.

"Hey." My voice is steadier than my heartbeat.

"You okay?" His knee bumps mine, deliberate.

"Shouldn't I be asking you that?"

He shrugs. "It was just a thing. Doesn't mean it mattered."

"So, it didn't mean anything to you? Then why keep it going?"

He looks at me. Really looks. "It's complicated."

I swallow. "What about last night? Are we pretending that didn't happen too?"

His gaze flickers. "That's complicated."

Before I can push, he changes the subject. "You still write in that notebook?"

"What notebook?"

"The blue one. You had it at the laundromat."

I blink. "You remembered that?"

"Of course I did."

My cheeks heat. Someone calls his name, but he doesn't turn. He leans in, close enough to feel. "You looked happier that day. Like you had a plan."

I laugh softly. "Plans change."

His hand reaches for my necklace, but his fingers brush my neck instead. Slow. Careful.

"Maybe they don't have to," he murmurs.

I freeze. Not because I want him to stop. Because I don't.

It's cruel how the world keeps spinning like nothing sacred just happened.

Julie drops into the chair beside me, obliviously. Elijah pulls back, smiling. "See you in the water?"

I nodded. Too fast.

Later, we're floating in the shallow end, talking about nothing. Elijah drifts closer. Knees brush. Heat radiates off him. His hand slides under the water, grazing the inside of my thigh. To anyone watching, we're just drifting. But his touch is deliberate. Electric.

He guides my hand to his stomach, just above his waistband. His eyes hold mine like a dare. I don't move. Then Julie cannonballs beside us, soaking everyone. "Sorry, not sorry!"

Elijah laughs, pulling back, but not before squeezing my waist under the water. Then he swam off, effortlessly, like I didn't just forget how to breathe.

By the time the crowd thins, he's gone. Vanished.

Julie reappears with a towel around her waist and pizza in her hand. "You good?"

"I don't know."

We sit at the edge of the pool in silence, the night creeping in around us.

"I saw him swim off," she says gently. "Figured you'd need space."

"A minute might not be enough."

155

"Want to talk?"

"No," I murmur. "But I kind of need to."

Julie waits.

"He's different with me. Not just in the obvious way. It's like he's trying not to feel anything, but when he does, it feels real. And I wish we had more time to figure out what that even means."

"Sounds exhausting."

"It is."

She watches me, then grins softly. "Let's stay late. My mom won't care. I'll say we're helping. Besides, this feels like the calm before the storm."

She has no idea how right she is.

We fold towels, change into dry clothes, and sneak sodas from the lobby. The pool is quiet now, almost eerie.

"I don't want to go home yet," I admit.

"Want to walk the beach?"

"Barefoot. Just the waves and stars. A reset."

"Always down for a reset."

The sand is still warm when we step onto it, the night air thick with salt and something fading. We walk until the hotel is just a glow in the distance, until the waves sound like a lullaby.

If I'd known peace was just the pause before heartbreak, I would've never stopped running.

And maybe this is peace. Or maybe it's just the last quiet before everything burns.

CHAPTER NINETEEN

I hear the yelling before I see anything.

It comes from Elijah's building. Violent yelling. Slurred. Muffled crashes. Something heavy thuds against a wall. Then more shouting.

Julie and I froze mid-step, halfway back from the beach. We still have sand on our ankles and damp towels in our hands.

"Was that—?" she starts.

But I'm already gone.

I take off, sprinting barefoot across the parking lot, heart slamming against my ribs. Julie's calling my name behind me, but I can't stop.

I know that voice.

I know his voice.

And it's unraveling.

There's a sound people make when their world caves in. I think that's what I'm hearing.

The door to his condo is wide open, like even the building has had enough.

Inside is chaos.

Elijah's dad is shirtless, red-faced, and drunk out of his skull. A chair is knocked over. Beer cans everywhere. His words slur, spit flying as he shouts something incoherent.

Elijah stands across from him, chest bare, fists clenched, breathing like he's about to explode. His jaw is tight, his hair disheveled, his eyes lit up like a fuse is already burning.

He doesn't see me.

Doesn't see anything but the man in front of him.

"Elijah!" I shout, stepping inside.

His head snaps toward me. His chest rises and falls like he just ran a mile barefoot through glass. There's something feral in his eyes, like he's not even here anymore.

"What the hell is going on?" Julie asks behind me, voice small.

"He tried to swing on me," Elijah growls, voice shaking. "Said I'm just another fucking burden he never asked for. Like I begged to live here."

"You do nothing," his dad slurs, stumbling closer. "You act like I owe you something."

"You do!" Elijah explodes, shoving a hand through his hair. "You owe me a roof. Food. You owe me not being blackout drunk all day, yelling about a woman who left a decade ago."

Julie grabs my arm just as Elijah charges.

He slams his dad into the wall with a sickening thud. A dent blooms behind the man's shoulder. His dad swings, sloppy. He misses and crumples down the wall.

"Elijah!" Julie shouts, stepping between them. "Stop!"

159

I rush forward and reach for him, placing both hands on his chest, feeling the frantic thrum of his heartbeat beneath my palms.

"Please," I whisper, locking eyes with him. I slid one palm up to the side of his face, just barely brushing his jaw with my fingertips. My voice barely makes it out. "Eli, please... just come with me. Let's get out of here. We can go back to the beach. Just you and me. Where things make sense. Where it's always good."

His eyes meet mine, really meet them, and something in him flickers. Like he's about to say something. Like he almost lets the wall fall.

His hand lifts, brushing my wrist, and for a split second, I think he might pull me in.

But then he blinks hard. The flicker dies. The wall goes back up.

He steps back, trembling, gripping the counter like it's the only thing keeping him from combusting.

I can almost hear it—the click of the door locking behind his eyes again.

The universe doesn't knock before it ruins you.

And then she walks in.

Sarah.

Her hair is perfect. Lip gloss gleaming. Tank top like she's here to audition for The Bachelor. She steps inside like nothing happened a few hours ago. She didn't just get humiliated by the poolside and storm off in front of everyone.

"Oh my God. What happened in here?" she says, eyes wide, freezing like she didn't expect an audience.

"Elijah?" she says carefully. "Are you okay? What is this?"

"I'm fine," he mutters, eyes still locked on the floor.

She crosses the room slowly, like she's approaching a wild animal.

"You're not fine," she coos. "You're shaking. Just... come with me, okay? Let's go cool off." Her hands glide up his arms, slow and soft, like she belongs there. Like he's hers.

Something inside me just... breaks.

My jaw locks.

My fists curl.

My vision goes white.

And then I lunged.

I grabbed the front of her shirt and yanked her down. We hit the floor hard. My fists find her face, repeatedly.

"VICTORIA?!" Julie shrieks.

Sarah screams, clawing at me, but I don't feel it. Don't hear her. I'm too far gone.

She touched him.

She touched my him.

"Elijah, DO SOMETHING!" Julie yells again, trying to pull me off.

Elijah stands frozen, eyes wide like he's watching a slow-motion wreck.

"Elijah, DO SOMETHING!"

He snaps out of it.

Grabs me by the waist, dragging me back. I'm still kicking, my foot slamming into Sarah's ribs.

She yelps and curls up, coughing.

"What the fuck is wrong with you?!" Sarah shouts, scrambling to her feet.

Julie steps between us, arms out. "Victoria, STOP!"

Sarah glares at her. "She doesn't even know what's happening! Is she on something?!"

I twisted Elijah's grip, eyes locked on Sarah. "Keep your fucking hands off him."

Sarah blinks. "What?"

Julie gasps. "Oh my God…"

She gets it.

Sarah doesn't.

"Elijah?" Sarah turns to him. "What is she talking about?"

He doesn't answer. Jaw locked. Shoulders shaking.

"She's crazy," Sarah says, voice sharp. "What the hell is she talking about?"

Elijah finally releases me. His hands trail down my arms like he's grounding me before letting go completely.

I turned to him.

My heart sinks.

"Elijah," I whisper, stepping closer. "Come with me. Please." My fingers brush his, like I'm reaching for what's still mine.

Sarah scoffs from behind me. "Are you serious right now? What the hell is this, Elijah?"

Nothing.

Somewhere in the living room, his dad groans from the floor, half-conscious and useless.

Elijah clenches his jaw. His hand hovers over the counter like he's debating something, then pulls back. He rubs the back of his neck, eyes flicking toward me for the briefest second. Then he turns, grabs a backpack from the counter.

He doesn't look back. Doesn't say a word.

Sarah scoffs. "Wait for me."

The door slams behind them so hard it makes the floor tremble.

Julie shifts beside me like she wants to say something but doesn't know how. I don't look at her. I can't.

163

My throat is tight. My heart feels like it's been ripped out and handed to me in pieces.

The silence says enough.

Julie's voice is a whisper. "Victoria… come on." She takes my hand and gently pulls me outside.

We don't need to.

Once we hit the concrete, my knees give out. I collapse onto the ground.

Julie sits next to me, stunned.

And just like that… Elijah is gone.

And maybe that's the worst part—not that he left, but that I would've followed him anywhere.

And he took all of the pieces of me with him.

CHAPTER TWENTY

The next morning is too bright.

Everything feels loud. The birds. The waves. Even the palm trees brushing against the windows sound like they're mocking me. The world dares to keep spinning after last night.

It's cruel how the sun rises even when you don't want it to.

My body aches in places I didn't know could hurt. My hands are raw. My heart is worse.

I don't get out of bed. Not because I'm tired. Not because I'm sick. Because moving feels like pretending he didn't leave.

Pretending is for people who still believe it matters.

He's gone. Not gone in the way people ghost you for a day or two. Gone like the oxygen's been sucked out of the air. Gone like the vacuum left behind when a door slams shut in the middle of a sentence.

I lie in this twin bed surrounded by stuffed animals and glitter pillows, staring at the ceiling and trying not to exist.

Because even in this nightmare of a room, he saw me. All the versions of me. And now he's just gone.

Not leaving. Not fading. Just gone.

Julie texts. I don't answer.

The next day, I try to fake it. I shower. Put on mascara. Staple a smile to my face like it's part of the outfit.

I walk the boardwalk with my chin high, like I have purpose.

Julie meets me near the snow cone stand. She bites her lip like she's holding in questions. "You, okay?"

We walk along the shoreline, waves licking at our ankles. The sky turns a bruised shade of blue.

"I don't even know who I am anymore," I finally whisper.

Julie glances at me. "You're the girl who loves a boy who doesn't know how to let you."

I blink. That's all I do. Because if I open my mouth, everything inside me will spill out.

She links her arm through mine. We walk in silence.

A week passes. Then two.

No one whispers. No one stares. Because no one knew. Elijah was mine in secret, and now he's gone in silence. No questions. No condolences. Just a void only I can feel.

Except Julie. She always sees through me.

"You should write about it," she says one night. "You always used to write when things got bad."

"I don't have the words for this," I whisper.

She hugs me. I don't hug her back, but I don't pull away either.

It gets worse before it doesn't.

I stop sleeping. Start pacing the condo at two in the morning like a restless ghost. I sit on the beach until sunrise, the salt air cracking my lips, my skin sticky with humidity I don't bother to wipe away.

I try to convince myself that this ache in my chest is temporary. That I'll move on. That it's just a phase. But I know better.

Because I didn't just fall for him. He carved himself into me like initials into wet cement. Permanent. Unerasable.

There are nights I swear I hear rocks tapping against my window. I always check. Every time. And every time, there's nothing.

I find his shirt at the bottom of my laundry basket, the one I wore home from the pool. It still smells like chlorine and boy and something I can't name.

I press it to my face and crumble to the floor.

That's when the spiral really begins.

You don't notice yourself breaking until you start sweeping up the pieces.

I count the pills in my anxiety bottle. Twice. Then a third time. I refill the prescription early and tell the pharmacy I'm leaving town. Lie through my teeth because I can't be without it.

But even then, it barely helps.

I lie awake for hours, staring at the ceiling fan blades spinning in endless circles. Sometimes I wonder if I disappeared, would anyone even notice?

Probably not. Because no one ever really has. Not until him. And then finally, I thought someone did. But he left like I was disposable. No warning. No goodbye. Just… gone.

I walk the same stretch of beach we walked, step for step, like retracing it will bring him back.

I sit on the seawall and let the wind slap my face like it's trying to wake me up. I scream into the ocean until my throat is raw. The waves keep rolling in. Indifferent. Unchanged.

A few nights later, I dream of him. His arms are around me. We're tangled in his sheets. His mouth is on my neck. His fingers are brushing mine. That low sound in his chest when I laugh.

For a moment, I forget.

And then I wake up.

The bed is cold. The room is empty.

And all I can do is lie there, eyes wide open, remembering exactly how it felt to be seen by someone who didn't know how to stay.

Elijah is gone.

I keep trying to put myself back together, but he's in every crack.

And now I am just pieces. Raw, scattered, jagged. And every single one still belongs to him.

CHAPTER TWENTY-ONE

Graduation is loud and sticky and suffocating, like being wrapped in plastic wrap under a spotlight, forced to smile while your skin itches and your lungs forget how to breathe.

The caps are too big. The gowns are too hot. The gymnasium echoes with every name shouted, every air horn blasted, every foot tapping restlessly against the floor.

Somehow, even in the chaos, it's the happiest I've felt in weeks. Like a single inhale of fresh air after drowning just long enough to forget what breathing felt like.

It's not peace. Not joy. But it's a flicker of something that isn't pain, and that's enough for now.

Not because I'm free. Not because I'm healed.

But because when they called my name, when the sound echoed across the gym and people clapped like they meant it, I exhaled for the first time in months.

Like the weight of all the rumors and glances and silences finally cracked off my chest.

Like I wasn't suffocating under the memory of him, even if only for that one second.

Because it's over.

And I survived it.

Survival isn't victory. It's just proof that I'm still here.

All the forced smiles. The whispered rumors. The painful walks past his locker like it wasn't the place where we first collided. All of it behind me.

I spot my parents in the crowd. My dad's wearing sunglasses and trying not to cry. My mom's clutching a tissue like it owes her rent. My older sister is waving a handmade sign that says, "YOU DID IT, V!" with way too many exclamation marks.

My younger sister waves like she's the only one who sees me.

And maybe she is.

After the ceremony, we meet in the front hallway near the main office, where families are squeezing in last-minute photos and awkward hugs. Julie's parents are snapping a hundred pictures of her, telling her to smile, turn, smile again.

My dad pulls out a set of keys and dangles them like bait.

"What's this?" I ask.

He points to the parking lot, where a silver Honda Civic gleams under the streetlight like a perfectly wrapped gift.

"You earned it," he says. "You've always worked hard. Even when things were hard."

I blink fast, pretending it's just the gym lights making my eyes water. "Thanks, Dad."

My mom wraps me in a hug that smells like vanilla lotion and home.

"We're proud of you, baby."

I don't say anything. Just nod and lean into it for a second longer than usual.

My mom's not a hugger. I'm not either. We don't do warmth. We do logistics and tension and eye rolls over dinner.

But today, just for a second, we let it be different.

Not fixed. Not healed. Just human.

Later that afternoon, Julie and I head to a local vintage shop called Retro Revival. Not exactly high-end, but better than digging through bins at Goodwill.

We're supposed to be finding dresses for the grad party, but I wander off while she tries on something sparkly.

In the back, there's a shelf of random collectibles. Old record players, dusty books, tarnished belt buckles.

My fingers graze over a worn WWII Iron Cross medal nestled inside a cracked glass case.

It stops me cold.

Because I remember the way Elijah's eyes lit up when he showed me his collection. How he talked about finding each piece.

He said every item had a story.

He wanted to travel the world.

And how he never told me the whole of his.

I open the case and take the medal in my hand. It's heavy. Cold. Important.

I carry it to the front and pay for it without a word.

Julie raises an eyebrow but doesn't ask.

That night, I sit on the floor of my room.

The house is quiet. Everyone's asleep. My new car key rests on the dresser. The medal sits beside my bed.

I dig under my little sister's bed and pull out her old school map. It's faded and creased, like it's been folded and unfolded a hundred times.

I spread it across the floor.

Close my eyes.

Spin my finger in the air.

And when I land, it hits Texas.

Not fate. Not destiny. Just a decision.

Because staying here feels like dying a little every day.

And anywhere else feels better than this.

Maybe it's a place where I won't see ghosts on the seawall. Where my chest doesn't cave in when I hear a car door slam.

Maybe it's a place where no one knows my name. Where I can start over. Where I can be no one.

Not just Florida. But Washington, too.

All the old versions of me.

The girl who broke down behind locked doors. The one who kept her fists clenched and her heart barricaded. The past kept replaying no matter how far I ran.

The girl who got rocks thrown at her head for just walking home. The girl who was called a slut before she ever kissed a boy. The girl who was mocked for her curves before anyone else had them and mocked again for daring to carry herself like she wasn't ashamed.

The girl who didn't want to be a cheerleader, or a stoner, or a band kid, or a debate nerd. The girl who just wanted to read her books in peace.

But they wouldn't let her.

So, when she finally snapped, when she threw the rock, when she screamed, when she stabbed someone, when she lashed out, it wasn't because she was dangerous.

It was because they made her.

This isn't about him. It never was.

This is about her.

The girl who kept breathing.

The girl who survived.

The girl who refuses to stay buried.

I trace the outline of Texas with my pinky.

It feels like touching a future I haven't earned yet.

This isn't just about leaving. It's about letting go.

Of the ghosts. Of the names they called me. Of the parts of me they tried to kill.

I want to be somewhere I can finally get out of my own way.

I stare at the map, still spread across the floor beside me, the corners curling slightly like it's trying to fold in on itself.

My fingers are numb, still tracing the edges of a place I've never been but suddenly need.

But I don't move. I don't pack. I just let the weight of it settle into my chest.

Because even though I spun the map like it could give me direction, like pointing blindly could somehow count as courage, and even though I chose something,

I'm still here.

Still haunted.

Still waiting for the ache to stop.

PART II

—✦—

THE SHATTER LEFT BEHIND

CHAPTER TWENTY-TWO

The first hour feels like freedom.

The rest feels like a mistake.

Freedom isn't supposed to feel like this—quiet and heavy, like grief dressed up as possibility.

I leave Treasure Island with a full tank and a half-broken heart, gripping the wheel of a silver Civic that still smells like new car scent clinging to the upholstery.

Clean. Crisp. Unfamiliar.

A fresh start gift-wrapped in silver.

My duffel bag was tossed into the trunk last night, hidden under a blanket of nerves and determination.

Clothes. Chaos.

My phone is on airplane mode. My playlist is loud.

The sun will not stop being so goddamn bright.

I thought I would cry when I hit the highway.

I thought I would second-guess everything.

Instead, I just drive.

Like I'm afraid to stop.

Like if I pull over, I'll realize I'm not brave—just broken.

San Marcos is still hours away.

I have no place to live, no job lined up, no safety net.

Just a loose plan, a destination, and a head full of ghosts.

By the time I hit Tallahassee, the silence in the car is too heavy.

I scream. Just once. Loud.

It doesn't fix anything, but for three seconds, I sound louder than the pain.

It bounces off the windows and back into my bones.

And then I laugh.

Because maybe this is what it feels like finally being free.

But freedom is lonely.

It's terrifying.

And it doesn't come with instructions.

I pull into a motel on the outskirts of a small town outside Baton Rouge, Louisiana, sometime after dark.

One of those sketchy extended stays with buzzing lights and water-stained ceilings.

The guy at the front desk doesn't ask questions.

I pay cash for the night and haul my bag up the stairs.

The room smells like bleach and burnt coffee.

The kind of place where no one knows your name—and that's the whole appeal.

I dump my stuff on the bed and sit on the edge, knees pulled to my chest.

My chest is tight.

My throat hurts from not crying.

I pull out my laptop and open twenty tabs.

Community colleges. Job listings. Room shares. Part-time work.

Anything to prove I can survive this.

This isn't a vacation.

It's a rebirth.

But no one tells you that being reborn feels a lot like dying first.

I think about the map I spun back in my bedroom.

The tip of my finger landing on Texas like fate was giving me a nudge.

And here I am. Nudged.

I close my eyes.

The room hums around me.

Tomorrow, I'll cross the state line.

I'll find a place to sleep for more than one night.

I'll figure out college applications and job apps and how to survive without losing myself again.

But tonight?

Tonight, I just breathe.

Not because I'm okay.

Because I'm still piecing myself back together in a motel room that smells like bleach and bad decisions.

Because I'm still aching. Still hollow.

Still trying to believe I can make it out of this version of myself alive.

But I'm here.

I'm breathing.

I'm not turning back.

Maybe bravery isn't leaving. Maybe it's gone.

And maybe, for tonight, that's enough to count as brave.

CHAPTER TWENTY-THREE

The walls in this place are paper.

I hear everything.

The coughs, the creaks, the moans, the two-a.m. rerun of Judge Judy playing three rooms down.

Someone is crying. Someone else is laughing.

I can't tell if it's the same person.

The A/C only works if I hit it. The shower won't shut off all the way.

There's a stain on the carpet shaped like Texas, which feels like a sick joke.

The bed is lumpy and squeaks if I breathe too hard.

But it's mine.

Okay, not mine.

A weekly rental, paid in crumpled cash and lies.

But I'm the only one with the key.

No one knows my name here.

No one is asking questions.

And that counts for something. I think.

That first night, I sit on the edge of the bed for hours.

Just sitting.

My backpack is by the door. Shoes still on. Arms around my knees.

Waiting for something. Maybe a sign. Maybe a breakdown.

I've never been alone before. Alone-alone.

There was always someone.

My mom down the hall. My sisters fighting over a charger.

Elijah breathing beside me, anchoring me with the sound of his heartbeat and the heat of his skin.

Even when I was angry, even when I felt invisible, I was still surrounded.

Now I'm eighteen years old in a motel with flickering lights and a lock that doesn't latch all the way, trying to act like I know what I'm doing.

Like I won't fall apart the second I blink.

Spoiler: I blink.

I wedge a chair under the door handle and sit back down.

I don't cry. Not at first.

Because crying means admitting I lost something, and I don't even know what I lost yet.

I shake. Quietly. Like my body is trying to evacuate emotion through tremors.

I try to watch TV, but everything feels too loud. Too fake.

I try to eat chips from the vending machine, but they taste like cardboard, and I panic.

I turn on the bathroom light and leave the door cracked.

I don't know why, but the dark feels too heavy.

At 3:12 a.m., I hear footsteps outside my room.

Slow. Crunching gravel. Then a pause.

My heart drops.

I sit up, frozen. Keys jingle.

Wrong door.

And just like that, his face hits me.

Elijah.

The way he'd lean against his condo door, arms crossed, like the world couldn't touch him.

The way he'd smirk when it already had.

My chest seizes with the memory.

I let out a breath I didn't know I was holding and then burst into tears so suddenly it chokes me.

No buildup. No warning.

Just crack—and I'm sobbing into the motel comforter like I'm seven years old again, begging someone to come get me.

But there's no one to call.

By sunrise, I've barely slept.

I wander to the laundromat with my laptop and a dollar-fifty coffee that tastes like chemicals.

I pretend to job hunt. Apply to anything I can spell.

Smile at strangers so they won't see I'm breaking.

I Google:

How to get a job without experience.

How to open a bank account without an address.

Can fear make your stomach feel like it's rotting?

I haven't written in my journal yet. Not until later, when I'm back at the motel and the silence is thick again.

I buy a spiral notebook at the gas station. Bright blue.

I scrawl across the front in Sharpie:

THE REINVENTION PROJECT.

It feels stupid. Hopeful. Delusional.

But I do it anyway.

Page One: Find a job.

Page Two: Do not die here.

Page Three: Survive the week.

There's a girl at the laundromat who tells me I have nice hair.

I blink at her. "Thanks," I say, but it comes out hoarse.

Like the words are scraping against something broken inside me.

I write it down later anyway.

The girl said I have nice hair.

Proof I existed today. That someone saw me.

Sometimes surviving looks like writing proof that you did.

That night, I scream into a pillow.

Not for drama. Not to be heard.

Just because my bones feel like they're vibrating and there's nowhere else to put the fear.

And then, quietly after, I hear it.

In my head.

Elijah's laugh.

Not the real one, the broken, jagged one he gave me when I told him I was scared of drowning.

It twists in my chest until I'm shaking harder.

I stare at the motel ceiling for hours, wide-eyed and trembling, and realize I'm not afraid of someone breaking in.

I'm afraid no one would stop them.

I'm afraid no one would notice if I disappeared.

Before I fall asleep, I flip open the notebook again and write:

Page Four: Be braver than yesterday.

And under it:

Even if I'm still shaking.

Because I am.

But I'm still here.

And for tonight, that's enough.

The next morning, I walk to the nearest grocery store with fifteen dollars and a tote bag.

The store is too bright. Too quiet.

I wander the aisles like I don't belong, grabbing bread, peanut butter, a pack of apples, and a box of generic mac and cheese like I know what I'm doing.

When I hand the cashier my crumpled bills, my hands shake so hard I almost drop the change.

It feels weird, buying food just for me.

Like survival has suddenly become this tangible, awkward act.

Like freedom means picking out the cheapest cereal and trying not to cry in front of the freezer section.

Back at the motel, I catch my reflection in the cracked bathroom mirror and stare for a long time.

I grab my brush. Then scissors. Then the bleach from the convenience store down the road.

I hold them in my hands, the weight of reinvention heavy and real.

Maybe I could be someone new.

A blonde named something simple. Bree, maybe. Or Amanda.

Someone who doesn't cry into motel pillows or scream into the dark.

Someone who doesn't feel hollow and unlovable.

But when I really look in the mirror, I don't see a stranger.

I see myself.

Wrecked. Raw. Real.

And for the first time in a long time, I don't want to erase her.

I set the scissors down.

Put the bleach away.

Brush my hair smoothly and pull it into a messy bun.

Page Five: Keep showing up.

Even if I still don't know who I am.

Even if I never become someone new.

Even if I stay by myself.

Because maybe she deserves a chance too.

And maybe that's what healing really is—not becoming someone new but finally choosing yourself.

CHAPTER TWENTY-FOUR

The bell above the diner door jingles with a sound too cheerful for how I feel.

Jo's Café sits at the edge of a strip mall off Aquarena Springs Drive. There's a vape shop two doors down and a used bookstore across the street that I already know I'm going to fall in love with.

San Marcos smells different than Florida. Warmer. Drier. A little like cedar and sunburn and whatever cheap cologne the guy behind the counter at the gas station was wearing.

Inside, the walls are yellow and lined with Polaroids of regulars. Vinyl booths, cracked in places and taped back together with black duct tape, run along the windows.

A sleepy hush hangs in the air, just loud enough to remind me I don't belong yet.

"You the new girl?" a voice calls from behind the counter.

Darlene. Late fifties, short red curls, and a smile that doesn't soften her eyes. She's got a pen stuck behind her ear and leopard-print reading glasses like they're a weapon.

"I'm Victoria," I say.

"Doesn't matter what your name is, as long as you show up on time and don't break the coffee pot."

She tosses me a spare apron. "Tie it tight. This place will eat you alive if you look scared."

Too late.

The first hour is a disaster.

I don't know the table numbers. I forget to offer cream with the coffee. I drop a fork and nearly cry when a kid throws his pancake on the floor and starts screaming like I murdered it.

Darlene watches me from the counter like a hawk. She doesn't say much, but every time I mess up, she makes this low grunt in her throat like she's collecting ammo.

"You're not fast," she finally says. "But you're polite. That's something."

I nod, swallowing hard. "Thanks."

"Don't thank me. Just don't quit before lunch."

Midway through the rush, I meet him.

Table seven. Corner booth. Baseball cap. Clean-shaven. Probably twenty.

A worn-out Bobcats hoodie and that effortless college-kid ease I used to roll my eyes at, back when I still had things like routine and certainty and someone who held my hand in the dark.

He smiles when I approach.

"Hey," he says. "You new?"

The word hits different coming from someone who clearly belongs. Like he's welcoming me into something I didn't know I needed.

"Yeah," I reply, tugging at the bottom of my apron. "First shift."

"Well, for what it's worth, you don't look terrified."

"That's because I already cried in the bathroom before clocking in."

He laughs, soft and low. "Good strategy. Get it out early."

I hand him a menu, but he waves it off.

"Just coffee. I'm trying to stay awake through Econ."

"You go to Texas State?"

"Unfortunately. I'd rather be asleep, but here we are."

He watches me write down his order, even though it's just one word.

I can feel his eyes on me. Not in a creepy way. In a human way.

Like he's trying to figure me out.

"You got a name?" he asks.

"Victoria."

"Nice to meet you, Victoria." He pauses. "I'm Jake."

I nod. "Thanks, Jake."

By the time I bring him the coffee, he's halfway through a textbook and hasn't touched his phone.

When I set the cup down, he glances up again.

"I meant what I said," he murmurs. "You don't look terrified. You look like you're fighting something no one else can see."

I freeze.

He shrugs. "Maybe that's none of my business."

"It's not," I say softly. "But… thanks."

For a split second, Elijah's face flashes in my head. The way he once looked at me like he could see everything I tried to hide.

I shove the memory down before it swallows me whole.

But ghosts don't care about boundaries.

By two o'clock, I'm running on adrenaline and two slices of cold toast.

My feet hurt. My back aches. My throat is dry from talking.

But I didn't quit. I didn't collapse.

There's power in that kind of quiet survival. The kind no one claps for.

And no one screamed at me, except the pancake kid.

But he doesn't count.

In the back hallway, I lean against the wall for five minutes and check my phone.

One new message.

Julie: U alive? Text me so I don't call the police.

I stare at the screen. My thumb hovers over the keyboard.

I miss her. God, I miss her so much.

But I can't talk to her. Not yet.

Not when I still feel like I'm going to crumble if someone says my name too kindly.

I lock the screen and slip the phone back into my pocket.

Darlene is wiping down the counter when I finish my last table.

"You didn't run," she says. "I'll be honest, I thought you might."

I smile, even if it's small. "I thought I might, too."

She hands me my tips in a plastic cup. "You'll be sore tomorrow. Don't say I didn't warn you."

I walk back to the rental with the sun dipping low behind me, casting long orange shadows across the sidewalks.

A kid rides past on a skateboard. Laughter spills out from a dorm nearby.

The whole town feels like it's living a life I haven't earned yet.

But maybe someday.

Maybe sooner than I think.

When I get back to the motel, I force myself to text my mom, just a quick: Made it through day one. All good.

It's not because I want to talk. It's because I promised I would check in.

Because the gas card refill and emergency money depend on it.

She doesn't text back right away, which is somehow worse than if she had responded with a guilt trip or unsolicited advice.

Still, I did my part. That has to be enough for now.

I flop onto the bed and pull out my notebook.

THE REINVENTION PROJECT

Page Five: Worked my first shift.

Page Six: A guy smiled at me like I wasn't broken.

Page Seven: Julie texted. I didn't answer. I'm not ready.

Page Eight: I'm still here. That counts.

Then I add one more line, right at the bottom, in tiny letters:

Page Nine: Maybe tomorrow I'll text her back.

And maybe that's what healing looks like. Half promises and small maybes.

CHAPTER TWENTY-FIVE

The sun in San Marcos doesn't whisper you awake.

It punches through the blinds like a reminder: you're not in Florida anymore, and nobody's going to carry you through this.

I roll onto my side and groan. Every muscle in my legs feels twisted. My feet pulse from the memory of yesterday's shift, and I don't even want to think about standing for another six hours.

But I do. Because I have to.

The bathroom mirror shows a girl with pillow-creased cheeks and mascara smudges from two days ago. Her eyes are a little puffy, but not from crying, just from being alive.

I tie my hair up, splash cold water on my face, and brace for day two.

Jo's Café smells like burnt toast and hope.

Darlene is already behind the counter when I arrive. She's in the same cherry-red apron, gum snapping between her teeth.

"Look who came back," she mutters with a half-smile.

"Don't sound so shocked."

She tosses me a fresh apron. "Tie it tight, sugar. This place doesn't get easier."

I grin, just a little. That's as close to a compliment as Darlene gets.

The lunch crowd hasn't hit yet. There's a hum in the air, low and gentle. Plates clinking. Quiet conversation. The hiss of the coffee machine.

Then I see him. Jake.

Same booth. Same hoodie. He's got a book open this time and a coffee half-drunk.

When he sees me, he lifts two fingers in a little wave. It's small. Easy. But it makes something shift inside me.

Maybe hope doesn't arrive with fireworks. Maybe it just sits quietly in a diner booth and waves.

I walk over slowly, bracing myself.

"Round two?" I ask.

"Had to come back," he says, grinning. "You guys undercharged me for the sarcasm yesterday."

I roll my eyes. "You must be disappointed. I'm low on sass today."

"I'll survive." He leans back a little, just enough to make space for conversation. "How was the rest of your shift?"

"I lived. Barely."

His eyes flicker to my hands, nails bitten, knuckles red from wiping down too many tables.

"I meant it yesterday," he says. "You don't look scared. You look... determined."

"Maybe those are the same thing sometimes."

"Maybe," he echoes, voice softer now. "Have you started school yet?"

"Not yet. I will start next week. Just trying to get my bearings and not totally fall apart before then."

He nods like he understands. "What are you taking?" he asks after a pause.

"Just core classes to start. English comp, intro psych, stuff that won't kill my brain first semester."

"Smart move. Avoid econ if you can, it's a soul sucker," he says, and I laugh, surprised by how easily it slips out.

"Noted. I'm just hoping I don't get lost on my first day."

"You won't," he says, sincerely now. "It's a mess, but everyone's just pretending they know where they're going. You'll blend in fine. If you want, I could show you around campus sometime. Help you find your classes, give you the lowdown on which buildings have working A/C and which ones smell like moldy socks."

I nod, and he doesn't press any further. Like he knows that's all I can give right now.

"You like books?"

"I do," I say. "They don't talk back."

Jake laughs. "There's a bookstore not far from here. Reed's. You'd like it. The guy who runs it is cranky, and his parrot curses at everyone."

196

"You trying to get me kicked out of somewhere new?"

"No," he says, serious all of a sudden. "I think you'd feel safe there."

After work, I find Reed's.

It's nestled between a Thai restaurant and a tattoo parlor. The door creaks when I push it open, and the air inside smells like old paper and lemon oil.

Comfort.

Stacks of used books climb toward the ceiling. The lighting is soft. Golden. Like a place that protects you from the outside world.

And yes, there's a parrot.

"Don't screw it up," it squawks as I step inside.

I smirk. "Hi to you too."

The man behind the counter, bearded and balding, doesn't even look up. "Don't mind Elvis," he mutters. "He's an asshole."

I wander. My fingers trail the spines of books older than me. Romance. Sci-fi. Memoir.

I pause in the classics section and pick up a weathered copy of Frankenstein. There's a note scrawled inside the cover: Property of someone who tried.

I hold it close.

The bookstore is quiet. I can hear my own breath. It's the first place since I arrived in Texas that doesn't feel temporary.

It feels like the air itself is holding me together.

I bought the book.

"First time in?" the owner asks.

"Yeah."

"You'll be back," he says. "People like you always come back."

Back at the motel, I collapse onto the bed and open the notebook.

Page ten: Bought a book. Did not cry in public.

Page eleven: Jake is kind. I do not know what I am supposed to do with that.

Page twelve: The bookstore felt like a secret. I want to go back.

My phone buzzes again.

Julie: I will literally call 911 if you keep ignoring me.

I bite my lip. Stare at the screen.

And then I type.

Me: Still breathing. Sort of.

It sends. She replies within seconds.

Julie: Holy hell, V, you scared the shit out of me. Where are you? What are you doing? Are you safe? Do you need me to go there? You'd better not be dead before I can yell at you.

I stare at the messages. My chest tightens, but not in a bad way. I smile.

And for the first time in a long time, I don't feel completely alone.

I call her. She picks up on the second ring.

"Jesus Christ, Victoria."

"Hi," I say, my voice small but steady.

There's a beat of silence, like she's trying to gauge if it's really me.

"You're alive."

"Barely. But yeah."

She exhales hard. "Where are you?"

"San Marcos. Working at a diner. School starts next week."

"Holy shit, you're really doing it."

"Trying. It's not exactly glamorous. I screamed into a pillow last night and bought a cursed parrot book today."

Julie laughs. "That sounds about right. I failed my driver's test again, by the way."

"No!"

"Parallel parking is a lie made up by sadists."

We talk for twenty minutes.

She fills me in on school gossip, her latest thrift store finds, and how my mom keeps pretending she's not checking my location on Life360.

I tell her about Darlene, Jake, Reed, and how Elvis the bookstore parrot called me a bitch.

We're still us. Even with a thousand miles between us, we're still us.

And this time, when we hang up, I don't feel like I've left everything behind.

Maybe beginnings don't always look like fresh starts. Maybe they look like finally breathing without breaking.

I feel like I've started something new.

CHAPTER TWENTY-SIX

School starts on Monday.

I wake up before the alarm. Not because I'm ready, but because my brain doesn't trust me not to oversleep.

There's a nervous sweat under my arms before I even sit up. I pick at my nails, brush my teeth twice, and change outfits four times before settling on jeans and a black tee.

Clean. Plain. Safe.

The kind of outfit that says nothing and everything at once.

I walk to campus with my bag slung over one shoulder and my heart lodged somewhere between my ribs and throat.

The air is thick with heat and nerves, and the sidewalks buzz with students who know exactly where they're going.

I do not.

But then I see him.

Jake's leaning against the edge of a brick planter like he's been waiting all morning. He grins when he spots me, and suddenly, the panic eases just a notch.

"You ready to get lost in a sea of freshmen and overpriced textbooks?" he says.

I shrug. "Define ready."

"Come on. I'll walk with you."

He gives me the unofficial tour—points out the buildings with broken elevators, the coffee cart that serves burnt espresso, and the one hallway that smells like wet socks year-round. His commentary is casual but helpful. Distracting.

"Your first class is where?"

"Old Main. English Comp."

"Classic. You'll love it. Smells like chalk and regret."

We reach the building. Jake gestures toward the doors. "Go be brilliant, new girl. Text me when you escape."

He pulls a pen from his bag, scribbles his number on the corner of a flyer, and hands it to me.

"So, you actually can."

I nod, heart thudding. "Thanks for walking me."

"Anytime."

Inside, the classroom is small. Windowless. The kind of space that makes you feel like you're underground.

I pick a seat in the back corner and try to look like I belong.

The professor walks in. Everyone quiets down.

And just like that, I'm a college student.

The class is fine. Nothing special. We go over the syllabus and icebreaker questions. I mumble something about liking books and writing.

Someone next to me mentions a popular romance author, and I offer a polite smile but say I'm more into writers like Joan Didion or Sylvia Plath—women with bite.

The kind who bleed onto the page and don't apologize for the mess.

It gets quiet after that.

When it's over, I text Jake:

Me: Survived. No casualties.

He replies: Proud of you. Meet for lunch?

I smile.

Maybe I might just be okay here.

After two more classes and one awkward interaction with a vending machine that ate my dollar, I find Jake outside the library.

We sit under a tree with burritos and talk about nothing. Bad professors, weird dorm stories, the existential dread of picking a major.

I tell him I'm thinking about English.

"Figures," he says. "You've got main-character energy."

I laugh. "Is that a compliment?"

"Absolutely."

He takes a sip of his drink, then glances at me. "So, what made you pick Texas? You from around here?"

I shake my head. "Florida. St. Pete area. Moved here a couple of weeks ago. Just needed to get out, start over."

He raises an eyebrow. "Damn. That's a long haul. What made you choose San Marcos?"

I shrug. "Kind of just spun a globe. I landed in Texas. Figured fate deserved a shot."

Jake grins. "That's wild. I'm from here. Born and raised. San Marcos lifer. Thought I'd be out by now, but... here I am."

"You like it?"

"Sometimes," he says. "Depends on the day. And the traffic."

I laugh. "So, you know all the secrets, huh?"

"Some. I could show you around, if you want. Make sure you don't get lost or eaten by the squirrels."

"That'd be nice," I say, surprised. I mean it.

He leans back on his elbows, glancing at me sideways. "So, what really brought you all the way from Florida to this college town in the middle of Texas?"

I shrug, but it's a heavy one. "I needed a reset. Things back home were complicated. I wanted to disappear and start over somewhere that didn't know my name."

"And you actually spun a globe?" he asks, brow lifted.

"Basically. Texas won."

"Lucky us," he says with a small grin. "That's bold. You'll like it here."

"Do you like it?"

"I mean, I haven't run screaming yet. So that's something. San Marcos isn't too bad, once you stop melting in the summer."

I laugh. "Noted."

He nudges a small rock near his shoe. "I can show you around sometime, like properly. Not just coffee carts and wet-sock hallways. The good stuff."

"That'd be nice," I say again, honestly.

"Cool. When you're free again, just say the word. I'm your unofficial tour guide."

"Deal," I say, feeling something warm in my chest that wasn't there a few weeks ago.

He shifts his weight and flashes a grin. "You know," he says, voice low and playful, "I think I've got a weakness."

I raise an eyebrow. "Oh yeah? For what?"

"Sarcasm," he replies, letting the word linger. "And girls who look like they're carrying entire novels inside their heads."

My breath hitches. I look away, but his gaze doesn't budge.

"Or maybe I'm just weak to shy girls with mystery energy."

His tone is teasing, but his eyes don't waver from mine.

I shift in place, my laugh coming out nervous. "Mystery energy? That sounds fake."

"Nope," he says, grinning. "You're like the plot twist in a quiet indie movie. Unexpected, but the whole point."

I roll my eyes, but my stomach flips anyway. "You really lay it on thick."

"Only when it's true."

Maybe he means it. Maybe he just knows how to look at a girl like she's the chapter he wants to keep reading.

Before I can respond, a guy and a girl approach us from the path leading out of the student center.

The guy's tall with a wild mop of curls and a skateboard tucked under his arm. The girl is petite, with a high ponytail, hoop earrings, and an effortless confidence I instantly envy.

"Yo, Jake," the guy calls. "You ditching us for burritos and romance?"

Jake laughs. "Victoria, meet Zane and Naomi. Naomi just transferred here this semester. She's a good person."

Naomi flashes a smile and sticks out her hand. "Nice to meet you, Victoria. Are you surviving your first day, or just faking it really well?"

"Bit of both," I admit, shaking her hand.

"Good answer," she says. "We're heading to the quad if you want to come. It's loud and pointless, but sometimes that's the vibe."

Jake glances at me. "You up for it?"

I pause, just for a second. Then I nod. "Yeah. Why not?"

Jake helps me up, and we follow them, and for the first time in a long time, I don't feel like an outsider tagging along.

I feel like I might actually be part of something.

Even if it's just a walk to the quad with strangers who already feel a little like friends.

By the time I get back to the motel, my shoulders ache from carrying books, and my brain is fried, but there's a strange calm in my chest.

I write in my notebook:

THE REINVENTION PROJECT

Page Thirteen: First day of school. No meltdowns. Minor identity crisis. Success.

Page Fourteen: Jake waited for me. I think that means something.

Page Fifteen: I belong here. Even if I'm still pretending a little.

I fall asleep with my clothes still on and the notebook still open beside me.

And for once, I don't dream about leaving.

I dream about staying.

Maybe staying isn't a weakness. Maybe it's proof I finally stopped running.

CHAPTER TWENTY-SEVEN

Naomi talks with her hands like every word might shatter if it doesn't have the right flair.

Loud. Fast. Animated.

The kind of girl who doesn't just enter a room; she commandeers the oxygen.

She's chaos bottled in glitter and crop tops, and somehow, against every odd in the universe, I like her.

We met three days ago during lunch outside. I barely knew Jake at the time, but he introduced us like we were old friends. Before I could come up with an excuse to escape, Naomi had already launched into a story about getting her tongue stuck in a popsicle mold. I didn't laugh then. I do now.

Today she's dragging me to the mall like it's some sacred bonding ritual.

I almost bailed. Twice.

But she showed up outside my room in a beat-up old convertible with pink fuzzy dice and a playlist loud enough to rattle the sidewalk, so here we are.

"You ever been to this place before?" she asks, merging aggressively while chewing on a straw.

"Nope. I've avoided malls like the plague."

"Girl, what? That's a felony. Malls are where all the tragic character development happens. It's like folklore."

She takes a hard left into a parking spot, bumping the curb without flinching. I grab the door handle like we're about to be ejected into orbit.

Inside, the mall is exactly what I expected: air conditioning set to meat locker, too-bright lights, and a perfume haze from the candle kiosk that slaps you like a toxic ex.

Naomi immediately heads toward Sephora, humming along to whatever pop remix is blasting overhead.

"We need to fix your face."

I blink. "I'm sorry?"

"Not like fix. Just highlight your rage-baby cheekbones. Give you a little Texas shimmer."

I trail behind her, scanning highlighters like they might personally offend me. Naomi swatches three shades on her hand and smears one onto my cheek before I can dodge.

"There. Glow. Mysterious. Like you have secrets and a skincare routine."

"I do have secrets. No routine, though."

She smirks and tosses lip gloss into her basket. "Don't worry. I'll build you one. It'll be tragic, cute, and totally fake. Like all the best ones."

We bounced through half a dozen stores. She tries on oversized sunglasses with rhinestone flames across the top.

I buy socks I don't need.

She convinces me to sample a body mist called Vanilla Lightning, which is somehow both cloying and flammable.

In Hot Topic, she holds up a graphic tee with a vampire biting into a lollipop.

"Tell me this isn't your vibe."

"I plead the fifth."

"That's a yes."

We get side-eyed by a security guard at Spencer's when Naomi dares me to try on a mesh crop top over my tank. She calls it a fashion emergency. I call it emotional terrorism.

She laughs until she wheezes and says I owe her a public meltdown when we reach the food court.

We eat greasy fries at the food court.

She double-dips her ketchup and launches into a story about her old school, where she got kicked out for throwing a cupcake at a boy who called her fat.

"Deadass aimed for his head like a missile. Hit his ear. Not ideal but still satisfying."

"Did you get suspended?"

"Nah. Expelled. Private school with a stick up its butt. Whatever. Their loss."

She says it like it doesn't matter. Like the past can't cut her if she doesn't flinch.

I try to mimic that.

"You ever get kicked out of anywhere?" she asks, biting into a fry like it's just casual conversation.

I pause. Swallow too hard.

"Not officially. Just had to start over."

"Same thing. Clean slates are sexy."

I don't correct her. She doesn't ask again.

But a few minutes later, between fries and stolen sips of my soda, she leans back in her chair and goes,

"So, do you like guys, girls, or are you just vibing in the void right now?"

I nearly choke. "What?"

Naomi grins like she just won a game I didn't know we were playing. "I mean, have you ever dated anyone? Been in love? Crushing hard on some barista with neck tattoos? What's your flavor, Tori?"

My default answer is silence, but she's not pressuring me. Just waiting. Genuinely curious. Like she wants to know me, not dig up dirt.

And I can't help but notice the nickname.

"I guess I've talked to people before. Nothing serious."

"Never even had a weird high school almost-boyfriend or dramatic breakup in a Walgreens parking lot?"

"No dramatic Walgreens moments, sorry."

"Damn. You're overdue. We need to schedule you some emotional damage."

I laugh under my breath. "You first. What about you?"

Naomi leans in like she's about to tell me state secrets. "I dated a girl named Jess sophomore year. She smelled like dryer sheets and played drums in church. And then a guy named Bryan, who told me his love language was vulnerability and then ghosted me for his ex. So, you know. I'm equal-opportunity heartbroken."

"Sounds fun?"

"It was something. But now I'm just out here collecting red flags and turning them into accessories."

I shake my head. She clinks her soda cup against mine.

"To future chaos."

"To chaos."

In the middle of Claire's, she makes me pierce my second lobe.

I flinch, she laughs, and the salesgirl looks one sneeze away from quitting.

We leave with matching cubic zirconia studs and two scrunchies we'll never wear.

We linger in the bookstore longer than I meant to. I drift toward the dark fantasy aisle like muscle memory.

She ends up in romance, of course.

"You read these?" She holds up a pastel-colored cover with an illustrated couple tangled in flowers.

"Not usually."

"That's because you're a Scorpio rising. You want love that threatens to burn the world down."

I laugh, a real one. "You just make this stuff up as you go, don't you?"

"Obviously. But it works, doesn't it?"

She tosses a book into my hands. Pride and Prejudice. I roll my eyes. She shrugs.

"It's nerdy. You'll relate."

Before we leave, she grabs a pack of Tarot cards at the checkout and flips over the top one while we wait in line.

"Opp—The Tower. Total chaos and rebirth. Perfect for your vibe."

"I thought you said I was a Scorpio rising."

"Exactly. Tower energy. Emotional demolition chic."

We leave with two iced coffees and a tote bag full of paperbacks, and we split like divorced parents.

The sun is starting to set by the time we make it back to her convertible.

She drops her sunglasses onto her nose and turns to me.

"Today was fun. You're fun. Even if you pretend not to be."

I smirk. "Don't tell anyone. I have a reputation."

"Of what? Sad mystery bitch?"

"Exactly."

She holds out her pinky. I stared at it.

"For what?"

"Pinky promise you'll come out with me next time. It could be karaoke. It could be breaking and entering. It'll be iconic."

I hook mine around hers. Tight.

"Deal."

And just like that, some of the weight I've been dragging for years shifts.

Not gone. But shifted.

Texas still doesn't feel like home.

But maybe it doesn't have to feel like exile anymore either.

Maybe it just has to feel like living again.

CHAPTER TWENTY-EIGHT

Naomi is bouncing beside me like she just mainlined a Red Bull, her curls pulled back in space buns and her phone lighting up every few seconds with new texts.

"You're coming tonight," she says, not even looking up. "Don't argue. I already told Zane you'd be there."

I gave her a side-eye so sharp it could file glass. "What did I say about ambushing me with plans?"

"That you secretly love it and would rather die than admit it?"

Fair. Dammit.

The party is at someone's off-campus house. The kind with peeling paint, a sagging porch, and Christmas lights still hanging in July. Music pulses through the walls like a heartbeat. Bass, beer, and too much cologne.

There are people everywhere. Some dancing. Some shouting. Some are making out in shadowy corners like extras from a college-themed soap opera.

I hesitated in the doorway, instantly overwhelmed. Naomi grabs my hand and yanks me in before I can bail.

"You're gonna have fun. I promise."

I don't say anything, but I nod. Barely.

Jake spots us before I do. He's leaning against the kitchen counter with a red Solo cup in one hand and a cocky grin like he paid extra for it. He makes his way over with zero urgency, all lazy swagger and dimpled charm.

"Didn't think I'd see you here," he says, eyeing me like I'm a surprise quiz he's about to ace.

"Naomi made me."

"She has good taste. In friends. In music. Probably in chaos too."

Someone passes me a drink. I hesitate for a second. I'm not even old enough to be holding this legally, let alone drinking it, but no one seems to care. My heart stutters. I sniff it like I'm testing for poison, then take a cautious sip. Beer. Warm. Disgusting.

Jake laughs. "You really are new to this, huh?"

"I went to a different kind of school."

"Let me guess. One where fun goes to die?"

"Exactly."

We find a corner of the living room where the music is slightly less deafening. Jake leans in close to hear me. Or maybe he's just using the volume as an excuse. I don't know. But his cologne hits me, peppery and warm. I hate how much I like it.

Naomi is across the room, dancing like the main character of a romcom set in 2003. She catches my eye, winks dramatically, and twirls herself straight into Zane's arms.

Jake nudges me. "You dance?"

"No. I loiter."

217

"Cool. I like loitering. Let's loiter together."

He smiles when he says it. Really smiles. And I feel something uncoil a little in my chest. We stand there for a while, just vibing in the middle of other people's noise. No pressure. No performance.

"You're kind of hard to read, you know that?"

"I get that a lot."

He laughs, but it's quieter now. "I like a challenge."

His hand grazes mine.

I let it.

He leans his shoulder against the wall, a little closer. "So, where are you from anyway? Born and raised in Florida?"

I glance down at our shoes. "Everywhere. Nowhere. I moved a lot. Illinois. Then Washington. Then Florida. And now here."

"Military?"

I shake my head. "Just chaos. My dad chases job opportunities like they're lottery tickets. We were always packing or unpacking. Starting over before I could even get attached to anything."

Jake nods, his smile fading into something softer. "That's gotta mess with your sense of home."

"What home?"

He watches me for a second, not like he's judging me, but like he gets it.

"I've lived in the same town my whole life," he says. "Same bedroom. Same friends. Same corner gas station where the cashier knows my name and my favorite gum. And I used to hate that. Thought it made me boring. But hearing you say that, I don't know."

"Grass is always greener."

"Exactly."

There's a lull. Not awkward. Just reflective. Like we're both standing on opposite ends of something we can't see clearly yet.

He bumps his shoulder against mine, light. "So, what were you running from? Because Texas doesn't exactly scream fresh start."

I almost lied. But something about the question, or maybe the way he asks it, makes me want to tell the truth.

"A mess. Myself. People I shouldn't have trusted. I don't know. Pick one."

"That bad, huh?"

I look away. "That's a story for another beer."

He nods, like he's not gonna push. "Deal. But only if I get to tell you embarrassing stories about my band days."

"You were in a band?"

He grins. "Yep. High school garage band. We were called Emotional Baggage. Terrible name. Worse sound."

"That's honestly iconic."

219

"Don't hype me. I still have the eyeliner somewhere."

I laugh. A real one this time. Not forced. Not filtered.

Jake watches me, a little quieter now. "You know, you're really beautiful."

It hits me harder than it should. I blink, unsure what to do with the compliment.

He rubs the back of his neck, suddenly sheepish. "The day I saw you at the diner, I knew I'd never seen you before. And trust me, in a city like this, you remember new faces. But yours, you kind of stopped time."

My breath catches.

I've been called beautiful before. Once. Maybe twice. Mostly, I've been called intense. Difficult. Crazy. A project. A warning sign. Never something delicate or worth pausing for.

When Jake says it, it hits deeper than I expect. It doesn't settle. It rattles. Like it's trying to change something in me. I don't quite believe it yet.

And under it all, another thought cuts in sharp and cruel: Elijah never said it like that.

It doesn't compute. It presses against the version of myself I've been carrying for years and tries to rewrite her. And I don't know how to let it in without breaking something.

And for a second, just a second, I think he might kiss me.

And I think I might let him.

But someone bumps into us, spilling beer all over Jake's shoes, and the moment pops like a balloon.

He steps back, shakes it off, and makes a joke about cursed footwear.

And I laugh, but it doesn't reach my eyes.

Because part of me is still standing in that almost.

Still wondering if I would've kissed him back.

Still haunted by the truth that even if I had, it wouldn't have been him.

CHAPTER TWENTY-NINE

I don't remember falling asleep.

Just the weight of the night pressing into my chest, beer still bitter on my breath, the echo of Jake's voice circling in my head like a song I didn't ask for.

You're really beautiful.

It should have been sweet.

It should have made me feel good.

Instead, I woke up gasping.

My sheets are soaked in sweat. My shirt's twisted around me like a straitjacket. My throat is dry, and my chest is on fire.

I had the dream again.

The one where I'm back in Florida, on the seawall behind the condo.

The air smells like rain and salt, thick like something about to break.

Elijah is standing in front of me, arms crossed, face blank.

But this time, it shifts.

I see the bruise on his cheek. The way his lip is split. His knuckles scraped raw. He won't meet my eyes.

I reach for him, but he flinches, like even my touch might hurt.

Behind us, I hear yelling.

Slurred rage from his father's voice, echoing like a ghost through the humid night.

"You think you're better than me? You little piece of shit."

Elijah turns away, shoulders tense, and I realize this isn't just a dream.

It's a memory.

A piece of him I wasn't supposed to see.

I call his name.

I beg him to talk to me, to let me help.

He won't.

He just stares out at the black water like it holds the answers he never got.

His mouth moves, barely a whisper.

"I can't be saved."

And then, just like always, he walks away.

Every single time.

I shove the covers off and sit up.

My hands are shaking.

I tell myself I'm fine.

Those dreams aren't real.

I left all that behind when I crossed the Florida state line.

But some things come with you.

Washington followed me to Florida, and now Florida has followed me to Texas.

It doesn't matter how far I drive.

They always find a way to follow.

I drag my notebook from the floor and flip it open, the spiral creaking like bones.

A photo slips out and flutters to the ground.

I freeze.

It's the one from the boardwalk—me and Elijah, grinning like idiots under a cotton candy sunset, arms tangled around each other like we belonged there.

I don't remember tucking it in here.

I don't remember wanting to see it again.

But it's here, like everything else I tried to leave behind.

I stare at the picture for a long time before I move.

I trace my face with my fingertip, then his.

We looked so happy.

So unaware.

Like nothing bad had ever touched us and never would.

I feel the lump in my throat swell, but I don't cry.

I tuck the photo back into the notebook, this time more carefully, like it deserves to be held.

I find the next blank page and start writing before I can talk myself out of it.

I don't know why I can't let it go.

It's been months.

I left.

I chose this.

Texas was supposed to be the fresh start.

But then he shows up in my dreams, and my ribs feel like they're breaking from the inside.

I miss him.

I hate myself for it.

Not just because I still feel something, but because I don't understand why it had to happen at all.

Why was he even put in my life if all he was going to do was tear through it and leave me bleeding?

What kind of twisted joke is it for God, or the universe, to give me something so rare, only to snatch it away without warning?

I keep losing the good ones.

The real ones.

The ones who made me feel like maybe I wasn't cursed.

And it's starting to feel like maybe I'm not meant to keep anything that matters.

I don't go to class.

I don't answer Naomi's texts.

I ignore Julie's too, even though hers come with worried emojis and long messages that ask if I'm okay, if I need to talk, if I'm alive.

I can't bring myself to read them.

Not because I don't care, but because I do. Too much.

And caring right now feels dangerous.

I just curl up on the lumpy twin bed in my cheap motel room with the blinds drawn and headphones blasting static, trying to drown out everything that keeps crawling up from under my skin.

The moment at the party plays on a loop.

Jake.

The almost-kiss.

The compliment.

The way my body reacted like I was in danger instead of being seen.

And somewhere in between it all, a memory pushes through.

The last night in Florida.

My family knew I was leaving. They helped me load the car.

My mom hugged me like she might not get the chance again.

My dad cried but pretended not to.

Even Vanessa and Camila showed up in their pajamas to say goodbye.

Julie begged me not to go alone.

But I still left.

Elijah was already gone.

Long gone.

No goodbye. No closure. Just silence where something used to be.

I still hit the road because goodbyes, no matter how honest, never make leaving any easier.

And I didn't want to be stopped. Didn't want anyone to try. Because I knew if they had, I might not have gone through with it.

The highway was empty. Just headlights and grief.

But before that, before Florida, there was Washington.

A different kind of nightmare.

I remember the girl.

Her name was Brandy.

The kind of pretty that makes teachers go soft and boys go stupid.

Her smile could ruin your life.

And she used it on me every single day.

She shoved me into lockers and once keyed the word "psycho" across my locker.

She whispered. She turned my name into a punchline.

Turned my silence into something suspicious.

Spread lies, laughed when they stuck.

Her favorite game was pretending to be nice while cutting me open.

That day, I don't even remember what started it.

I just knew I was running. Behind the gym. Down the back trail.

My knees were already bleeding from where she shoved me down the embankment.

I could still hear her laughing.

"You're crazy, you know that? You don't belong here. You never did."

And maybe she was right.

The next day in class, I don't remember grabbing the scissors.

I just remember the sound they made when they hit the floor.

And the way everyone looked at me like I'd turned into something else.

Something dangerous.

I wasn't trying to hurt her. Not really. I just wanted her to stop. To shut up. To let me breathe for five goddamn minutes.

No one ever asked why.

They just labeled me.

And that label followed me to Florida.

And now it's here too.

It doesn't matter where I go.

The ghosts always know the way.

I look at the photo again, trace his face one last time, and whisper into the silence, "You always do."

CHAPTER THIRTY

Mornings start before the sun does.

My alarm blares at 5:45, and I roll out of bed in the same clothes I passed out in. Jo's Café opens at six-thirty sharp, and if I'm not there ten minutes early, Darlene glares at me like I just spat in her biscuit dough.

"Cutting it close, huh?" she says, not looking up from the register.

"I'm here," I mumble, tying my apron with fingers that still ache from yesterday.

By seven, the place is buzzing. Coffee brewing. Orders stacking. I'm on autopilot, slinging muffins and halfhearted smiles.

A girl in Lululemon leggings and a Texas State hoodie stomps up to the counter with a latte in hand.

"Um, this has almond milk. I said oat. Are you deaf or just bad at your job?"

My stomach knots. "I can remake it."

She scoffs. Loudly. "Wow. Amazing service. What a concept. What, did they just let anyone in off the street to work here now?"

I feel it like a punch. Not just the words, but the tone. The way she looks at me is like I'm worthless. Like I don't belong here.

Something about her voice splinters something deep.

I see a flash of Brandy's face.

You don't belong here. You never did.

"You, okay?" Darlene asks from the other side of the counter.

"Yeah." I lie. My hands are shaking.

I turn and remake the drink, focusing on the hiss of the steamer instead of the flashback clawing at the edge of my brain.

When I hand it back, the girl doesn't even look at me. Just grabs it and walks away.

I breathe in. Out. Try to swallow the lump in my throat.

But the voice in my head whispers anyway: You're not enough. You never were.

The door chimes.

"Yo, that's her, right?" a guy says.

I glanced up just in time to see Jake walk in with two other guys. Jake gives me a look, casual but not careless.

"Be nice, man," one of them says, nudging him. "You've been acting whipped since you saw her in the library."

Jake rolls his eyes. "Shut up."

"Seriously," the guy keeps going, now talking to me like I'm not standing right there. "You're the café girl, right? The one he stares at like she's a damn poem?"

I feel my face go red.

Jake finally cuts in. "Knock it off. She's got better things to do than talk to you idiots."

"Ohhhhh," the other sings. "So, she's special. Got it."

Jake turns to me, awkward now. "Hey. Didn't mean for them to say all that. They're just being dumb."

I blink at him. Still too raw from the latte girl, still hearing Brandy in the back of my head. My voice comes out flatter than I mean it to.

"I've had worse."

Jake looks like he wants to say something else, but he doesn't.

They leave with their drinks. One of them whistles.

I stared down at the counter, my fists clenched tight around the towel.

Too much attention.

Too fast.

Too soon.

Class.

Community college feels like a weird in-between world. No one knows each other. Everyone's just trying to pass the time or pass the test.

I sit in the back. I don't raise my hand. I take notes even when I don't understand them.

Today, I get back my English paper.

C.

There's a note scribbled at the top in red ink: Too emotional. Unfocused. Lacking structure.

I stare at it like it personally attacked me. Maybe it did.

I shove it into my backpack and walk out of class early. Don't even care when the professor says my name.

Back in the parking lot, I sit in my car with the windows up and scream into my hands.

My chest feels too tight, like I can't get enough air.

I spent three hours writing that paper. I didn't have three hours.

And it wasn't enough.

I'm never enough.

My phone buzzes.

Missed call from Julie. Another text from Naomi. A text from my mom:

Mom: Are you remembering to take your meds? You need protein in the morning, Victoria. Coffee is NOT a meal. And don't forget to email your professor about your assignment—you don't want to fall behind again.

I stare at the screen like it might catch fire.

My jaw tightens.

My fingers curl around the phone so tight I feel the plastic flex.

For a second, I want to throw it across the car, watch it shatter into a hundred tiny pieces just so something, anything, matches how I feel.

But I don't. I just sit there, gripping it like it's the thing holding me together instead of tearing me apart.

I ignore all the messages.

I work another shift.

Burn my hand on the espresso machine.

Forget a guy's order and get called a bitch under someone's breath.

By the time I clock out, my brain is soup.

I sit on the curb behind the café with my head between my knees, willing myself not to cry in the alley like some tragic movie girl.

My phone buzzes again.

Julie: I'm proud of you, even when you're drowning. Call me. Please.

That one breaks me.

I call her.

She answers on the first ring. "V?"

I can't speak for a second. My voice cracks when I do. "Hey."

She exhales, relief and love bleeding through the phone.

Then she's off, asking everything. Am I okay? Am I safe? Am I eating?

I tell her bits and pieces. Enough to make her stop holding her breath. Not enough to scare her.

"You don't have to be perfect to be loved."

I hate how much I needed to hear that.

Julie pauses. Then she says, "You know... I'm not exactly thriving either. I'm taking eighteen credits and working two jobs. I've had ramen three nights in a row, and I cried in the Walgreens parking lot last week because I couldn't afford tampons."

I blink. That sounds familiar.

"Everyone thinks I've got it together," she continues. "But I'm barely keeping my head above water, V. Just like you. If you're drowning, then I guess we both are. And maybe that's okay. Maybe we just tread water together."

My throat tightens again.

But this time, it's not panic. It's something closer to relief.

Later that night, I end up at Naomi's dorm.

She opens the door in sweatpants and glittery eye masks like she's been expecting me.

"Rough day?"

"Something like that."

She lets me in without a word. Hands me a bag of mini-Oreos and a fuzzy blanket.

We don't talk right away.

We just lay there on her tiny bed, watching bad reality TV with the volume too low to matter.

Eventually, she says, "You don't have to do everything alone, you know. You're allowed to fall apart."

I nod, staring at the ceiling.

Naomi is quiet for a beat, then adds, "When I got kicked out of my last school, my parents were so pissed they cut me off. No money. No place to go. I lived in my car for a week behind a laundromat before a professor found out and helped me get into this dorm."

I turn my head to look at her.

She shrugs, but it's the kind of shrug that says it still hurts. "I tried to play it cool at first. Like, oh, I'm just taking a break from toxic energy. But I was scared out of my damn mind."

I blink, speechless.

I always saw Naomi as untouchable. Loud. Fearless. Glittery chaos in human form.

But here she is. Bruised. Real.

"So yeah," she says, squeezing my hand again. "If you're burning down, I'll bring the marshmallows. We don't have to do this perfectly. We just have to keep showing up."

"I don't know how to fall apart without burning everything down."

Naomi squeezes tighter. "Then we'll light the match together."

And for the first time in a long time, I don't feel alone.

I used to think I was the only one carrying this much weight.

Like everyone else was just better at surviving.

But now I see it—Julie with her ramen nights and cracked voice, Naomi with her car-turned-bedroom and broken parental silence.

Everyone has something.

Everyone is crawling through something.

And maybe if I let myself open up more, like really open up, then I wouldn't have to keep pretending I'm made of stone.

Maybe this is how it starts.

Not with healing, but with seeing.

Not being perfect.

Maybe just being okay.

For the first time, I don't want to disappear.

I want to stay.

I don't know what tomorrow looks like, but tonight, I'm still here. And maybe that's enough.

CHAPTER THIRTY-ONE

The next morning, I barely make it through my shift.

The café is louder than usual. The espresso machine sounds like it's screaming bloody murder, and every time the bell over the door rings, I flinch like I'm being shot at. My arms ache from carrying trays, and my knees pop every time I bend. My brain is stuck in glue.

I spill two drinks, forget how to spell the name "Kaitlyn" twice, and drop a ceramic mug that shatters like a bad omen.

Darlene glares at me from the back like she's calculating how many napkin dispensers she'd have to sell to replace me.

"You good?" she finally snaps when I knock over the container of stirrers.

"I said I'm fine."

"You don't look fine."

"Well, maybe that's just my face."

Her eyes narrow. "Watch the tone."

I bite my tongue so hard I taste blood.

The lunch rush hits like a wave I can't get out from under. Orders pile up. A kid throws up near the napkin station. I'm trying to clean it, bag a pastry, run someone's card, and not cry all at once.

My head pounds. My hands won't stop shaking.

Then he shows up.

A regular. Mid-forties. Thinks he's God's gift to women and caffeine. I forgot his muffin. He slams his cup on the counter.

"You're not very bright, are you?"

And I laugh.

Like, actually laugh.

The kind that makes people turn and look.

A sharp, bitter sound that slips out before I can catch it.

"Sorry," I say, my voice tight. "My bad. I'm just trying to keep up while having a complete mental breakdown. Cream or sugar?"

His face flushes. "What, did they just let anyone in off the street to work here now?"

The words hit like a dart right in the chest.

Darlene yells my name from the back, but I don't hear her. Not really. Everything around me warps, like the walls are breathing.

My heart pounds in my ears.

I'm fourteen again, back in Washington.

Brandy's laugh echoes behind me.

You don't belong here. You never did.

My vision blurs. My breath catches.

"You know what?" I snap, voice louder than I mean it to be. "I'm not paid enough to be insulted before lunch. I'm not some disposable cog in your caffeine-fueled machine. I'm a person. I'm trying. I'm barely—"

My voice breaks. Tears sting my eyes, but I blink them back like they owe me money.

"Victoria!" Darlene barks again. "Get it together or get out."

So, I do.

Get out.

I toss my apron on the counter, shove the register drawer shut with a slam that rattles the tip jar, and walk straight out the front door.

I don't quit. I just leave.

Because if I stay another second, I'm going to scream or cry or both.

Maybe I'm already doing both.

I wasn't quitting. I was surviving.

Sometimes leaving is the bravest thing you can do.

By the time I make it back to the motel, I feel like I'm walking underwater.

I don't take off my shoes. I don't throw my bag down. I just sit on the edge of the bed and stare at my hands like I don't recognize them.

My phone buzzes.

A text.

Naomi: Wanna come over and eat snacks until we feel alive again?

A missed call from Julie.

A voicemail from my mom.

I don't open any of them.

I grip my phone until I swear it might crack.

For one awful second, I want it to.

Just to watch something break that isn't me.

I drop it on the nightstand instead.

I fall asleep in my clothes.

I Wake up three hours later to a knock that sounds like pounding on the motel door.

Naomi.

"Jesus, I thought you were dead," she says, barging in. "You look like actual garbage."

"Thanks."

She flops next to me, rips open a bag of mini-Oreos, and hands them over. "Eat before I cry and force-feed you while singing early 2000s emo lyrics."

I take one. Then three. My stomach growls like it forgot what food was.

"I walked out of my job today," I say finally.

"Cool. I got kicked out of yoga for threatening someone. We're thriving."

I snort. "No, like, I actually walked out. Mid-shift. I left the guy's muffin on the counter."

Naomi raises an eyebrow. "Iconic."

"It didn't feel iconic. It felt like I was losing my mind."

She quiets. Then says, "Maybe you are. And maybe that's okay. You're allowed."

I blink hard. Swallow down everything that's rising in my throat.

"I don't know how to keep doing this. The school stuff. Work. Pretending."

"Then don't pretend. Let it suck. Eat cookies. Stay over. We'll braid each other's trauma into friendship bracelets."

I glance at her.

"You ever think we're just... broken?"

"All the time," she says. "But then I remember, even broken girls look hot in eyeliner."

We sit in silence for a long time.

She leans her head against mine.

"You're not alone."

And for the first time in a while, I almost believe it.

After a beat, Naomi shifts and nudges me with her elbow.

"Hey, tomorrow, you and me? We're going out."

I blink. "Out where?"

"The Sports Bra Vault," she grins. "Some of the girls from campus go there on Thursdays. Cheap drinks, loud music, and questionable decisions. It'll be great."

I groan. "Sounds like a hangover waiting to happen."

"Exactly. It's called healing, babe. Come on, just a few hours. You need a reason to wear that one dress you pretend you don't like."

I roll my eyes but don't say no.

Maybe I'm not ready to celebrate.

But maybe I'm ready to stop feeling like the world's on fire for one night.

And maybe that's the closest thing to peace I've had in a long time.

CHAPTER THIRTY-TWO

We came to The Vault Bar to celebrate passing our finals. Naomi and I slipped in two hours ago and made a beeline for the bar. Three shots of vodka later, we were dancing like we owned the place. Naomi, with her arms thrown around my neck, both of us shrieking the lyrics to a song we barely knew. Her hair stuck to her forehead from the heat, and my cheeks ached from laughing. We spun and stumbled like we had no past, no scars, no names to live up to. She grabbed my hand and twirled me again, and I let her because, for once, it felt good to forget.

Naomi shouted something about finding the hottest guy in the room and making him regret his whole life, and I just laughed, the vodka making me bold enough to consider it. That was the thing about Naomi: she made me feel like the world could be fun again, like I wasn't just a ghost haunting the edges of my own story.

And for a minute, the world cooperated. The music, the flashing lights, the press of sweaty bodies—all of it swirled together into a dizzy blur of freedom. I wasn't the girl with a broken past. I was just a college girl in a tight black dress, dancing with her best friend, high on vodka and temporary amnesia, like the heartbreak and bullshit of life didn't cling to our heels like gum.

The lights flash pink, then green, then a strobe so violent I lose track of which direction is up. I don't care. I throw my head back, arms in the air, heart thudding like it's trying to escape my chest. Naomi yells something in my ear. I think it's about shots, and then she disappears into the crowd.

I'm alone on the dance floor for half a breath. And in that breath, the dizziness shifts. Freedom curdles. I catch my reflection in a cracked mirror behind the bar. My eyes are too wide. My smile is too sharp. There's a haunted edge to it, like I'm not dancing to feel alive, but to outrun the ghosts nipping at my heels.

And then I see him.

Elijah.

Time stutters. My skin breaks into goosebumps despite the heat. The music. The lights. Naomi's voice. It all slips underwater. He's standing by the wall, under a neon beer sign, scruff on his jaw and eyes darker than I remember. Enough of the same to wreck me. Different enough to make it hurt.

He sees me. Of course he does. And in one second, just one, my whole body forgets every reason I ever had to hate him.

I shot back a fourth shot. For courage. For spite. For the ghost standing in front of me.

And then I'm moving toward him, my fingers tapping his shoulder like we're strangers.

He smirks.

That fucking smirk.

"Why are you here?" I blurt.

He lifts his beer. "Are you drunk, Ariel?"

So, he does remember me.

Elijah motions to the door and says something about it being too loud in here. I nod and follow right behind him, like I haven't spent all this time trying to forget his very existence.

Outside, the air is cooler, cutting through the heat of vodka and sweat. He leans against a streetlamp, studying me like I'm still a puzzle.

"What are you doing in Texas?" I ask.

He shrugs. "Work. I do ironwork now."

"And this week it brought you here? To San Marcos?"

"Guess so. We travel all over the place. You live here now?"

"College. And waitressing."

"Never pegged you for a people person."

"I'm not. I desperately want to toss coffee at the customers at least five times a day."

He laughs, rougher than I remember. "Still dramatic."

We trade questions. What happened after he left? What happened to me. His dad is still a drunk. My motel room has bleach-stained walls. Logan sometimes. Jesse never. Julie is in pieces but still tethered to me by texts.

Then, after a quiet beat, he shifts his weight. "You eaten tonight?"

I shake my head. "Vodka counts, right?"

He smirks. "Not unless you're planning to die young. There's a diner up the road—or, uh, my hotel's got room service. Decent burgers. We could... talk."

It's not an invitation that feels dangerous. It's one that feels inevitable.

I hesitate for half a second, then nod. "Okay."

He leads the way down the street, the two of us walking in silence except for the buzz of neon and the faint hum of traffic. My heels click against the pavement, echoing in time with my pulse.

At the hotel, the food sits mostly untouched, curly fries growing cold. He leans back against the headboard, watching me.

"So... why Texas?"

"Needed a clean break. Somewhere no one knew my name. I got a job at this shitty diner, and I live in a motel that smells like bleach and broken dreams. My mom probably hates this version of me, but I'm free. College makes me feel like maybe I'll survive this version of me."

His voice softens. "Are you happy here?"

"Sometimes," I admit. "It doesn't hurt the same way. And that's something, right?"

"Yeah," he murmurs. "That's something."

And when his hand brushes mine on the bedspread, the spark is so familiar it hurts.

I meet his eyes. "Did you miss me?" My voice is unsteady.

His breath stutters. His hand tightens on the sheets. "Always."

The air shifts. My heart is a war drum. We stare at each other, a silent tug of war happening right here in this hotel room.

I breathe out his name softly.

That's all it takes. The gravity between us snaps, and he is up from the bed and coming at me in one swift movement.

Mouths crash. Teeth. Tongue. Hands in my hair. Lips on my throat. He lifts me like I weigh nothing, slamming my back against the door as his mouth devours mine.

I claw at his shirt, dragging it up over his head. He shucks it off and goes back for my neck, sucking hard enough to leave a mark. I gasp as his teeth scrape my collarbone.

"Fuck, I missed this," he growls. "I missed you."

"Then show me."

He peels off my dress with a growl, unclipping my bra in one practiced motion. My breasts spill out, and he doesn't hesitate. His mouth is on me, hot and greedy, like he's starving. He bites, just enough to sting, and I arch into him with a cry.

He lays me down on the bed and rips off my panties in one swift motion. I'm bare. Spread. Vulnerable. And he just stares.

"You're going to be the death of me," he groans.

"Then die slow," I whisper.

His mouth is on me before I can blink, tongue flicking, teasing, worshipping. He eats me like he's punishing me for ever leaving. My thighs tremble as I come undone, legs shaking around his shoulders. But he doesn't stop. One orgasm isn't enough. He wants me ruined.

"Elijah. Fuck. Please."

He comes up for air, lips glistening, eyes dark. "You still want this? After everything?"

I meet his eyes. "I need to feel something that doesn't hurt."

I scoot down the bed, never breaking eye contact, and reach for the waistband of his jeans. He steps closer to the edge, and I ease them down along with his boxers. His cock springs free, and I suck in a breath. He's hard, thick, and already leaking, the sight of him undoing me all over again.

He hesitates. Swallows. "You don't get it. I never stopped wanting you. But I don't get to have you. Not really. Not the way you deserve."

I rub my thumb along the underside of his cock and drop to my knees. I guide him into my mouth slowly. His hands fist my hair. A broken groan falls from his lips.

"Jesus fucking Christ."

I take him deeper, tongue swirling, cheeks hollowed, dragging moans from him that sound like they've been buried for years. He grips my hair harder, trying not to fall apart.

"I'm not going to last," he growls.

I pull off with a pop. "Then fuck me. Now." It's drunk courage. Sharp and shameless, teetering on the edge of recklessness. But it's the truest thing I've said all night.

He yanks me up and flips me onto the bed. He doesn't ask. Doesn't pause. He just plunges into me in one hard, perfect thrust. I scream.

It's brutal. Deep. Unrelenting.

He fucks me like he's trying to erase the years. Every stroke is a memory. Every thrust is a scream. We're both crying, gasping, holding onto each other like lifelines.

I hear my own voice, small, cracked, aching. "You left."

"I went back. You weren't there."

He flips me over, dragging me onto all fours. His hand slides up my spine, then grips the back of my neck as he drives into me again.

He leans in, breath ragged. "I tried to stop running, Victoria. I swear I did."

I claw at his back, nails digging deep as he drives into me repeatedly, every inch of him pushing past my sanity. He grabs my jaw and forces my eyes to meet his own—raw, glassy, desperate.

I grab his face between both hands, breath trembling. "Please... tell me I'm yours. Even if it's a lie."

He leans his forehead against mine, breath shaking. "It doesn't matter what I want. It never has."

He rubs rough circles over my clit, and my whole body seizes as I come again, harder this time. It's violent and ragged. He follows with a strangled cry, burying himself so deeply I swear I can feel him in my soul.

He collapses on top of me, breath hot on my neck, both of us trembling like we've just survived the end of the world.

Later, tangled in sweat and sheets, bruises blooming across my skin, I stare at the ceiling with my heart wrecked and my body still trembling.

And I know.

This is the night everything changes.

Because I am his.

And now, there's a piece of him inside me that will never leave.

The TV flickers against the wall, blue light spilling across tangled sheets and half-eaten fries. His hand twitches in his sleep, fingers brushing mine like muscle memory.

Outside, a siren wails.

Inside, everything is quiet. Too quiet.

The kind of quiet that comes right before a storm.

His heartbeat slows against my skin, steady and real.

I close my eyes and pretend it means forever.

But deep down, I know how this story goes.

Morning always ruins the miracle.

CHAPTER THIRTY-THREE

I wake up to cold sheets and the echo of a slammed door.

The room is dim, washed in the gray-blue light of early morning. The air is stale with what we did. Sex and sweat and heartbreak cling to the walls like smoke. My body aches. My heart aches worse. I reach across the mattress, half-asleep, still hoping to find him.

But he's gone.

The other side of the bed is empty.

Not just empty. Erased.

The burger wrappers? Gone. The Jack in the Box bag? Gone. His wallet, the rest of his clothes, his scent. Gone. Like he was never here at all.

But I'm still wearing his shirt.

It hangs off my shoulders like a lie. The collar is stretched from his hands. The hem curled from where I clutched it in the dark, like it meant something. Like he meant something.

I curl my knees to my chest and press my face into the sleeve. It still smells like him. Faintly. Like laundry soap and salt air and a cologne I don't recognize. Something new. Something I won't get to know.

No goodbye. Just a crumpled Jack in the Box receipt on the nightstand.

I almost don't see it at first. It's the only thing he didn't erase. No wrappers, no clothes, just this receipt. Like he wanted to be sure I'd find it. I reach for it, afraid it might disappear if I blink.

His handwriting is messy, rushed.

I'm sorry. You were never a mistake.

—Eli

I sit in the silence, not sure what to do now.

Then I see my phone, tossed on the dresser last night. On the screen, a notification glows.

Voice Memo: 2:17 a.m.

I don't remember recording anything. My fingers shake as I unlock the screen. I press play.

There's a pause. A rustle. And then his voice.

"You're asleep. Thank God you're asleep. I wouldn't be able to say this otherwise. I don't know how to do any of this. Not right. Not with you. You were always the thing I got too close to, like fire. Like something sacred. I never knew how to hold it without burning myself. But you should know…"

A breath.

"I never stopped. Even when I left. Even when I made you hate me. I never stopped. Even when I tried to."

The audio cuts off there. No explanation. No follow-up. Just those last five words, carved into silence.

I blink at the phone like I can force more words out of it. My mouth moves before my brain catches up.

"Never stopped what?" My voice cracks. "Say it. What did you never stop?"

I press the screen again. Rewind. Play. Rewind. Play. I hold the phone to my ear like it can answer me if I just get closer.

"Say it," I whisper to no one. "Say it. Say it."

Nothing. Just the breath, the confession, the cliff.

I sink to the floor like my knees just gave out, the phone clutched to my chest like it's a lifeline or a loaded gun. My heart is beating so loud it drowns out the silence.

He was here.

He was here.

Now he's gone.

And I break.

It doesn't come soft. It comes like a body being torn in two. Ugly sobs crack my ribs open and leave me heaving on the carpet of a hotel room I never wanted to remember. My nails dig into the shirt I'm still wearing, as if I can claw his name out of the threads.

I scream into the pillow until my throat is raw. Until the world tilts. Until my soul goes quiet.

This is what love looks like when it's left behind.

This is what it means to be the girl someone almost stayed for.

And this time, there's no one left to come back.

He left me with five words and a silence that still won't shut up.

SOMEWHERE AFTER HIM

The air still smelled like him. Smoke and salt and rain.

I kept telling myself it would fade, that if I opened the windows and scrubbed the sheets, the scent would stop clinging to my skin.

It didn't.

I spent the next few days moving through the world like a ghost. Work. Shower. Sleep. Repeat.

I didn't eat much. Didn't talk much. Just kept pretending that silence was the same thing as peace.

People at the café asked if I was okay. I smiled and said I was just tired. Everyone's tired. It was an easy lie to believe.

I tried to write, but every word looked like his name.

I tried to sleep, but my body didn't trust the quiet anymore.

It kept waiting for his voice, for the knock, for something that wasn't coming.

The world kept moving like nothing had happened.

Cars honked. The neighbor's dog barked. My phone lit up with reminders to pay bills and buy groceries, like grief could be scheduled between errands.

I started counting things. Steps to the door, tiles on the kitchen floor. Only because numbers didn't hurt the way memories did.

There wasn't a way to reach him, and maybe that was the point.

The world had folded in on itself and left him on the other side.

Even if I screamed loud enough for the sky to crack, he wouldn't hear me.

He was gone, and I was the echo.

There wasn't a clean break between before and after.

It was just one long ache that stretched across everything.

I learned how to exist with it. To keep my face steady when people talked.

To nod when someone said "you're strong" like it was a compliment instead of a curse.

The night it finally rained again, I stood outside until I was soaked through.

The water wasn't cold enough to shock me, not warm enough to comfort me.

It just was.

Like me.

Somewhere after him, the world kept spinning. Bills still came in the mail. My alarm still went off at six. The coffee still burned my tongue.

Somewhere after him, I learned that you could keep breathing even when you don't want to.

You just forget how to live while you do it.

And then one morning, the ache stopped being special. It just became the day

CHAPTER THIRTY-FOUR

The world doesn't end in a bang. It ends in the monotony of routine. That's what I tell myself, over and over, as I rinse out coffee pots at Jo's Café, coming back to a dead-end job that I walked out on and trying to cram flashcards into my skull during breaks that don't feel like breaks at all.

I wake up. I work. I study. I sleep. Repeat.

And when I say sleep, I mean black out from exhaustion and wake up in the middle of the night drenched in sweat, Elijah's name on my tongue and my heart trying to claw its way out of my chest.

There are no good days anymore. Just the less-bad ones.

Naomi notices.

"You look like a ghost that forgot how to haunt," she says one morning as I slam the fridge door harder than necessary.

I grunt. "I'm fine."

"You've said that every day for the past two weeks. You're like one 'Can I speak to your manager' away from snapping."

She's not wrong.

My body is out of sync. My emotions are either numb or unhinged, no in-between. I've snapped at three customers this week, and I nearly cried when I dropped a tray of food in the kitchen. Over onion rings. Fucking onion rings.

Julie texts me, and I ignore it.

My mom calls. I silence her.

Then she calls again. And again. On the fourth call, I answer.

"Hello?"

"Finally! I've been calling you for days. Are you eating right? Have you been taking your medication? Your skin looked terrible in that photo you posted. Are you sleeping enough? You sound awful."

"I'm fine," I grit out, already seeing red.

"You don't sound fine. You need to stop staying out so late. And you better not skip class again. I didn't raise you to be some college dropout working in a greasy diner."

"I said I'm fine!" I snap, voice cracking.

There's a pause. "Don't take that tone with me, young lady."

I slam my hand on the counter. "I am not a kid anymore, Mom! I'm an adult. You don't get to micromanage every second of my life just because I don't answer your calls fast enough. Maybe I'm busy trying not to fall apart!"

Another pause. "You need to calm down."

I hang up.

My psych professor gives me a "C" on a paper again that I barely remember writing, and I storm out of class before the bell even rings. The hallway spins, and I lean against the wall, breathing hard like the air's been sucked from the building.

"Hey."

I don't even hear Naomi come up beside me. She slides a cold Sprite into my hand without asking.

"You gonna pass out, or should I call an exorcist?"

"I don't know what's wrong with me," I whisper.

She studies me. "Well, if it's not demonic possession, maybe it's just grief. You ever let yourself feel it?"

I laugh, but it sounds hollow. "Feelings are dangerous. Look where they got me."

She nudges me. "Okay, broody. You gonna keep living in that depressing motel forever?"

"It's cheap."

"So is a cardboard box, but I'm not recommending it."

I exhale sharply through my nose. Naomi doesn't push, but she doesn't let go either.

That night, she makes me promise to at least consider looking at apartment listings. "Crash with me until you figure it out. I'm a disaster, but my floor doesn't creak like a horror movie."

I tell her I'll think about it. And I mean it. Maybe.

The next morning, Jo's Café is slammed, and I'm two seconds from throwing a plate of waffles at someone. The bell above the door chimes again, and I plaster on my dead-inside smile.

A girl with a too-tight ponytail and a sorority sweatshirt snaps her fingers at me like I'm a dog. "Um, hi? We've been waiting for, like, ever."

"We're short-staffed," I say through gritted teeth. "I'll be with you in just a minute."

She scoffs. "That's not good enough. What do they even pay you for?"

I grip my notepad so hard the spiral digs into my palm. "Look, I said I'll be with you in a minute."

"Is that the best you can do?" she sneers. "Honestly, you look like someone who peaked in high school and never recovered."

Something inside me snaps.

"You know what? You're right. I did peak. Right around the time I didn't have to serve spoiled brats who think the world revolves around their iced coffee. You want service? Try basic human decency first."

Her mouth drops open. "I want to speak to your manager."

"Great," I spit. "She's in the back crying over the soul she lost training people like me to put up with people like you."

Naomi shows up out of nowhere like a guardian angel with rage-management issues and pulls me toward the kitchen. "And we're walking, and we're breathing," she mutters.

In the back, she stares at me. "Okay. So. Uh. Wanna talk about it?"

I lean against the wall, chest heaving. "Nope."

"Cool. Let's not do that again unless we want to get sued."

"Copy that."

She hands me a half-eaten muffin. "Break-room therapy snack. On the house."

I sink to the floor, muffin in hand, heart barely hanging on.

This is not healing. This is surviving. And even surviving feels like a full-time job.

Jake texts me later that night. Something casual. Something safe.

Jake: Dinner? No pressure. Just food and maybe a mediocre milkshake.

I stare at it for twenty minutes before replying.

Me: Sure.

He picks me up in a beat-up truck that smells like cinnamon gum and gasoline. I climb in, and he glances at me sideways. "You okay? You look like you haven't slept since the Cold War."

"Close," I say, forcing a smile.

Dinner is at a diner that isn't Jo's. Somewhere, I don't have to wear a name tag. The silence isn't romantic, but it's comfortable.

Jake dips his fry in ketchup and leans back. "My roommates are idiots. Like, one of them thought you could microwave tinfoil. Spoiler, you cannot."

I laugh, a little too loudly. "Seriously?"

"Swear on my dog's life. Speaking of, he once ate an entire pair of flip-flops and didn't even look guilty."

I shake my head, smiling. "Dogs are chaotic like that."

He tilts his head, eyes warm. "What about you? What's your chaos?"

I stir my straw in the milkshake. "I'm a psychology major. I work at Jo's Café. And I live in a motel where the faucet leaks and the walls are so thin I can hear my neighbor snore."

"Sounds… cozy."

"Sounds like survival," I say, half-joking, half-not. "But I'm trying. I like figuring people out. Psychology makes me feel like there's a reason for the way people break."

He nods seriously for once. "That makes sense. You're the kind of person who wants to understand before you judge. I respect that."

"What about you?"

Jake grins. "When I'm not pretending to be an Econ major, I'm actually in the mechanic program. I know, doesn't make any sense, right? I just like engines more than essays. Always loved taking things apart and putting them back together. Especially cars. Greasy, loud, obnoxious things. They make sense to me."

"Wish I could say the same for people."

He shrugs. "People are like cars. They break down, yeah. But if you know what you're doing, you can fix them. At least a little."

264

I glance at him, eyes soft. "That's dangerously close to poetic."

He laughs. "Don't tell my shop teacher."

I laugh too. Real, actual laughter.

And then he asks, carefully, gently, "So... are you seeing anyone?"

I stab a fry. "No. Not really."

He nods like he already knew the answer. "You deserve something good, you know? Not just something that makes sense on paper."

"Like fries for dinner?"

He grins. "Exactly like fries for dinner."

He drives me home. Doesn't ask to come in. Just leans across the console and tucks a piece of hair behind my ear.

Then he hesitates. His eyes flick to my mouth, and before I can react, he leans in.

His lips press to mine. Warm. Gentle. Not wrong, but not right either.

His lips aren't as full as Elijah's. His tongue doesn't move with the same urgency, the same hunger. His breath tastes like cinnamon gum, not salt air. His kiss is soft, careful. Almost sweet.

But it isn't fire. It isn't danger. It isn't him.

It's the smallest kindness, but it feels like a life raft. And maybe that's worse. Because I don't want to be saved by someone who isn't Elijah.

Jake pulls back, a little flushed, smiling like it meant something.

"Goodnight, Victoria."

I force a smile. "Goodnight."

And when I step out of the truck, the weight of it hits me. No matter who touches me. No matter who tries.

I'll always taste Elijah in the absence.

And maybe that's what loving him really means—he's everywhere, even when he's gone.

CHAPTER THIRTY-FIVE

ONE MONTH LATER.

The nightmares haven't stopped. If anything, they've mutated.

It's not just Elijah in the dark now. It's blood and shadows and slammed doors. It's the feeling of being left behind over and over until I wake up drenched in sweat, convinced I'm drowning in a bed that isn't even mine.

I throw myself into the grind. School, work, repeat. I'm sprinting through days like if I move fast enough, the pain won't catch me. But grief has endurance. It lingers in the still moments, when I stop to breathe and my chest caves in.

Naomi watches me like I'm a houseplant that she forgot to water. "You need a night out," she says one afternoon while we're cramming for psych. "Come out with me tomorrow. Sports Bar Vault. Trivia night. Drunk karaoke. Whatever it takes."

I nod, but it's a lie. I don't want fun. I want numb.

The next few days blur. I'm nauseous all the time. Smells make me gag. Coffee, perfume, the inside of the break-room fridge. I'm constantly exhausted no matter how much I sleep. My boobs feel sore and heavy. I chalk it up to stress. Or karma.

Jake texts me again. "Another date? I promise this one won't involve flip-flop-eating dogs or econ jokes."

I agree. I need a distraction.

The night comes. I'm in the bathroom, mascara wand in one hand, when my stomach flips so violently I barely make it to the toilet.

Date canceled.

The next few days pass in a blur of saltines and Sprite. Everything makes me gag—the smell of bacon, car exhaust, even my own shampoo. I throw up at work, at school, on the sidewalk. I try to power through, but my body has turned against me.

I skip meals, then feel dizzy and shaky. I sleep for twelve hours and wake up tired. Naomi side-eyes me every time I run to the bathroom. "If you puke in my car one more time, I swear I'm buying you a bucket necklace," she mutters.

"It's just a bug," I lie.

But the ache in my chest won't let up. And the queasy pit in my stomach feels less like the flu and more like dread wrapped in biology.

The next morning, I drag myself to Walgreens, convinced this stomach bug is the flu on steroids. I wait in line at the pharmacy counter, rubbing my temples, trying not to throw up under the buzzing fluorescent lights.

"Hi, I think I need something for a really bad stomach virus," I tell the pharmacist. "I've been nauseous for days. Dizzy. Exhausted. Everything makes me gag."

She gives me a once-over, then nods slowly. "We've got a few over-the-counter remedies for nausea and fatigue."

As she turns to grab the items, I catch her sliding something else across the counter with a practiced motion.

A pregnancy test.

No words. No judgment. Just a quiet suggestion.

I stare at it, my stomach dropping even further. My hand trembles as I pick it up and add it to the pile.

Twenty minutes later, I'm in the flickering fluorescent haze of my motel bathroom, crouched on the cold tile floor beside the tub. My palms are sweaty against the porcelain. The test lies face down on the counter, mocking me with its silence.

My heart is a jackhammer in my chest. I close my eyes and count backward from ten, trying to slow my breathing, but it only makes the dizziness worse. My stomach churns with something deeper than nausea. It's dread, thick and paralyzing.

The silence feels too loud. I wipe my palms on my jeans, stand up on trembling legs, and flip the test over.

Two lines.

Two. Fucking. Lines.

The world doesn't explode. It just folds in on itself, quiet and cruel.

My vision blurs as the air disappears from the room. The tiles tilt beneath my feet. I stumble backward and collapse onto the edge of the tub with a hollow thud, gasping like I've been sucker-punched. My chest heaves. My fingers clutch the sides of the tub.

I try to make sense of what I just saw, but my brain short-circuits, caught in an endless loop of disbelief.

I scramble forward and grab the box. Rip it open. Shake out the instructions with trembling hands. I scan the paper again and again, desperate for a loophole, a mistake, anything. But there it is, in black and white: two lines mean you're pregnant.

I lower the instructions slowly, staring at the test like maybe it will change if I just keep looking.

But it doesn't.

"No," I whisper. "No, no, no."

The tears start slowly, then fast. I slide down until I'm curled on the floor, my body folding in on itself. I rock back and forth, fists clenched, biting down hard on my knuckle to muffle the sobs.

This can't happen.

This isn't my life. I'm nineteen. I live in a weekly-rate motel. I work double shifts to pay for textbooks. I'm not even old enough to drink legally. I had to get vodka from someone else. I've never dated a boy, not with the title. I haven't been to Paris. I haven't earned my degree. My parents will kill me. I can't afford this. I can't be this.

I press my face into the edge of the tub, trembling. The test lies inches from my nose, taunting me.

Two lines.

Two lines.

Two.

Lines.

I slide to the floor, shaking. I laugh. I cry. I dry-heave. I hug my knees and press my face into them.

Then I pick up my phone.

Julie answers on the second ring. "V? Oh my god, are you okay?"

I don't speak. I just sob.

"Hey. Hey. Talk to me. What happened?"

"I messed up, Jules." My voice cracks like glass. "I messed up so bad."

"What are you talking about? What happened?"

"It was one night," I whisper. "One night."

Julie's voice cuts in, sharp and confused. "What do you mean one night? What are you talking about?"

Silence. Then a sharp inhale.

"Julie." My voice is high and tight and barely mine. "It was just one night."

"Victoria, if you do not tell me what you are talking about, I cannot help you."

"Elijah. I saw him." I finally exhale.

She doesn't respond right away. I imagine her jaw dropping, her eyes going wide like she used to when I'd spill a secret too big for our tiny lives.

"Elijah, Treasure Island Elijah?"

I nod like she can see me. "Yes. Him. And now this. And I don't even know if he knows I'm alive anymore. Or if he ever cared. I don't know anything. Except that I'm fucked. I know that."

"Okay. Okay. Deep breath. You're not alone. I'm here. Tell me everything."

And I do.

I tell her about the bar. The shots. The hotel. The way he kissed me like the world was ending and held me like I was the only thing worth surviving.

I tell her how he left.

How I woke up in his shirt with nothing but a receipt and silence.

How I've been pretending I'm okay when I'm splintering apart.

How the test had two lines.

"Victoria…" Julie whispers. "I wish I could hug you right now."

"I don't even know what I'm going to do. I live in a fucking motel. I make minimum wage serving waffles. I can't do this."

"Yes, you can," she says firmly. "You're the strongest person I know. And this? This doesn't define you. It's a moment. Not the whole story."

I let out a shaky breath.

"I don't even know how to tell him because I don't even know where he is."

"You don't have to decide that today. Right now, just breathe. I'll come to visit you, or you could come visit me if you want a change of scenery. We'll figure this out. Together."

My throat tightens. "Promise?"

"On my life."

I close my eyes and let her words wrap around me like a blanket.

Because for the first time since that night, I don't feel entirely alone.

CHAPTER THIRTY-SIX

I didn't collapse. I didn't scream or shatter. Not out loud, anyway. The pain folded in on itself, curling deep in my chest like a fist I couldn't unclench.

I waited until I was alone.

Then I packed.

No makeup. No hairbrush. Just clothes, my charger, and the test shoved in a grocery bag like it was nuclear waste. I booked a last-minute one-way flight to North Carolina with shaking fingers, scrolling until I found the cheapest seat I could afford. No checked luggage. No plans. Just escape.

The airport in San Antonio was a hive of noise and movement. Security lines snaked through barriers. Kids screamed. Someone dragged a suitcase with a busted wheel that clicked against the tile like a ticking bomb.

I checked in at a kiosk, my fingers trembling so badly I kept misspelling my own name.

When the TSA agent asked me to remove my hoodie, I did it silently, robotically. My socks were mismatched. My eyes were hollow. I made it through security without speaking a single word.

In the terminal, I sank into a plastic chair near Gate C7 and stared out the window. Rain smeared the sky gray. The tarmac was slick. Planes taxied and took off like they knew where they were going—like the whole world had direction but me.

When my boarding group was called, I walked to the gate like I was in a dream. Found my seat by the window and sat. A mom with a crying toddler took the aisle. A man in a neck pillow was already snoring in the middle.

I pressed my forehead to the cool glass and watched San Antonio disappear.

In the air, I gripped the test in my pocket like a secret grenade.

Charlotte Douglas Airport was loud in a different way. Polished. Gleaming. All glass and steel and strangers.

I moved through it on autopilot. Followed the signs to baggage claim even though I had no bags. Found a bench near Arrivals and texted Julie:

Just landed. I'm outside.

Julie didn't answer right away. I wrapped my arms around my knees and stared at the palm of my hand like it might hold a map.

Minutes stretched like years.

And then Julie's car pulled up.

She jumped out before it even stopped moving. Barefoot in Adidas slides and a hoodie that said Don't Talk to Me Before Coffee. Her hair was a frizzy topknot. She looked half-asleep and fully panicked.

"Holy shit," she breathed, wrapping me in a hug before I could blink. "What happened? Are you okay? What—?"

I didn't answer. I just held on.

We didn't talk about it that first night. Julie reheated leftover Chinese takeout, and we watched some mindless baking show until

I fell asleep with rice stuck to my hoodie and a half-eaten egg roll on the coffee table.

The next morning, it all came out. Over coffee. Bitter. Black. No creamer.

I didn't cry. I just talked.

About the motel. The test. The fact that my life was now officially off the rails. That I didn't have a job or a degree or a goddamn clue. That I couldn't even find Elijah.

Julie listened like it was her full-time job. Occasionally nodding, sipping from a mug that said Chaos Coordinator in gold foil.

Then, gently: "Okay. What do you want to do?"

I stared at the table.

"Do you want to keep it?" she asked, her voice even.

I swallowed. My hands shook. "I don't know. I can't even wrap my brain around what that looks like."

Julie didn't flinch. "Then let's figure it out. We can look at clinics. We can talk about adoption. We can talk about what it'd be like if you kept it. Whatever you need."

I blinked fast. "You're not mad?"

"I'm your best friend, Vic. I'm mad at the world. Not you."

I let out a breath I didn't realize I was holding. For a second, the chaos inside my chest softened.

We spent the rest of the afternoon curled up on her couch. Chick flicks. Chocolate ice cream. Crumbs on our leggings. For a minute, things felt survivable.

Until she said it.

"I saw something."

I glanced over. "What?"

Julie bit her lip and exhaled like she was holding a live wire behind her teeth. "There's something I need to tell you," she said slowly, her voice low. "I didn't want to text it. I didn't want to say it over the phone. Hell, I didn't want to say it at all."

My stomach dropped. "Say what?"

Julie swallowed. "Elijah's married."

The words dropped like a detonated secret, echoing through the room before I could even process them.

Married. Elijah. Married.

My world didn't just tilt, it split like glass hit with a hammer.

Something in me split clean down the middle, like lightning through glass.

I blinked. "No. That's—" My voice cracked.

Julie didn't argue.

She unlocked her phone with a shaky thumb and pulled up a screenshot. "I was trying to find him the night you called," she said quietly, not meeting my eyes. "Searching everything. Facebook, Instagram, Google… and I found this."

She held the phone out.

I leaned in.

It was a photo—blurry, like it was taken quickly and uploaded without a second thought. Elijah dressed nicely. Standing in front of a dull government building. A courthouse. His arm around a girl in a plain white dress who was grinning like an idiot. No guests. No flowers. Not even a smile on his face. Just a quick, clinical moment captured in pixels.

I squinted at the screen. My heart stuttered. "Wait…" I whispered. "That looks like Sarah."

Julie exhaled. "It is. That's whose Facebook I found it on."

I jerked back. "What? No. What the fuck? Are you serious?"

Julie nodded slowly. "They got married, Vic. Last year. It was posted around graduation."

I recoiled like the words hit me physically. My voice spiked, brittle and defiant. "No. That's not—no. He would've told me."

Julie watched me carefully. "I didn't want to believe it either. But it's real."

"No, it's not. That picture, maybe it was fake. Maybe it was staged. Maybe it was some bullshit photo-op. He would've told me, Julie. He wouldn't have slept with me and then just… lied like that."

Julie sighed. "Vic, I know you're hurting, but it's her Facebook. The post is still up. She changed her last name. This isn't fake."

I stood up, pacing. My fists were clenched. "No. No, he wouldn't do that. That night, he was real with me. He looked me in the eye. I know him. He would've told me."

"Would he?" Julie asked gently. "Because he didn't. And now you're here."

I opened my mouth to argue again, but the words collapsed on my tongue.

My eyes darted to my phone on the couch.

I snatched it up with trembling fingers. Opened my voice memos. Scrolled. Tapped.

Play.

Elijah's voice crackled to life.

"You're asleep. Thank God you're asleep. I wouldn't be able to say this otherwise. I... I don't know how to do any of this. Not right. Not with you. You're always the thing I got too close to. Like fire. Like something sacred. I never knew how to hold it without burning myself. But you should know..."

His breath hitched.

"I never stopped. Even when I left. Even when I made you hate me. I never stopped. Even when I tried to."

The audio cut off.

I'd forgotten the sound of his voice until it became the only thing that kept me breathing.

I clutched the phone like it might turn into an answer. Like there might be more. But there wasn't.

And now the silence felt louder than the message ever did.

Julie broke it gently. "That... didn't sound like someone who didn't care, Vic."

My head snapped up. My expression felt wild, unsteady. "Then why didn't he say something? Why didn't he tell me about her? About any of it?"

Julie hesitated. "I don't know. But I don't think he meant to hurt you. People get scared. They make stupid, cowardly choices when they don't know how to deal. That message sounded like he was falling apart."

I shook my head, eyes filling. "Then he should've stayed."

"Yeah," Julie said softly. "He should've. But maybe he didn't know how. It doesn't mean you weren't real to him. It doesn't mean he didn't love you."

She paused, then added, "Maybe he loves her too. Or maybe it was impulsive. Maybe he regretted it the second it happened, and that's why he didn't tell you. People do stupid shit when they're scared. When they think they've messed everything up. That voice memo? It didn't sound like someone happy."

Julie met my eyes. "Maybe he didn't tell you... because he didn't know how to fix what he broke."

I pressed the phone against my chest like it could plug the hole. But nothing stopped the bleeding.

I stopped pacing, my chest rising and falling fast. My mouth opened, then closed. My entire body stiffened like I was trying to hold in a scream.

"He would've told me," I whispered one last time, like saying it enough could make it true.

"How do we find him?" I asked, my voice cracking. "Where would he even be? Do you think he stayed in Florida? Or did he go somewhere else with her?"

Julie exhaled. "I don't know. But if we start looking, we can find something. His last name, her Facebook, any mutuals... There has to be a trail."

"It's not like he left a forwarding address," I said bitterly. "It's like he vanished. Like he planned this."

"Maybe he didn't plan it," Julie said gently. "Maybe he panicked. Maybe he thought you'd never forgive him."

My lip trembled. "He didn't even give me the chance."

Then I stood up. Walked to the bathroom. Closed the door quietly.

And finally broke.

Not loud. Not violent. Just a slow, quiet unspooling. My body sank to the floor as my heart caved in.

Because this wasn't just abandonment.

It was confirmation.

I was not worth his goodbye.

I was not worth remembering.

I was a mistake.

And now… I was carrying a piece of him.

Alone.

CHAPTER THIRTY-SEVEN

The motel light buzzes like it's just as tired of being here as I am.

I stare at the peeling ceiling above the bed I haven't slept in for two days, my body stiff and hollow from the flight. My bag's still in the corner where I tossed it. An empty chip bag and a half-drunk water bottle sit on the floor near the bathroom.

I should probably care. But I don't.

I got back to Texas an hour ago, and the silence is already deafening. No calls. No texts. Nothing.

Not that I expected one.

After Julie showed me the photo—Elijah standing in a courthouse, ring on his finger, her on his arm—I broke in ways I didn't think were still possible. I shattered.

And then I booked a last-minute flight back to Texas without thinking twice. I needed distance. I needed numbness. The plane touched down, and I still didn't know what I was doing, only that I couldn't stay there.

Now I'm here. And I still don't know what the hell to do.

I pull my phone from the charger and open my messages for the hundredth time, even though I know what I'll see. Nothing from him.

Just the voice memo.

I can't bring myself to delete it. But I also can't press play again. Not yet.

I close my eyes and press the phone to my chest.

Later that night, I sit cross-legged on the bathroom floor, my knees pulled to my chest, the motel's scratchy towel beneath me. The light flickers like a bad horror movie, and honestly, I wouldn't mind if a demon just showed up and ended it all. Saves me the decision fatigue.

I hold the pregnancy test box in my lap like it's going to speak first. Three more tests line the counter. All positive. No variation. No confusion. Just pink lines and a brand-new universe I didn't sign up for.

I reread the instructions, like maybe I misunderstood. I didn't.

This is real.

He married someone else.

And I'm pregnant.

A whole world collapsed inside a single heartbeat.

The bathroom door creaks open, and Naomi's voice cuts through the silence.

"Okay, I let you have your dramatic motel meltdown. Now what the hell is going on in here?"

She steps in, sees the tests, and goes still.

"Shit. Are those yours?"

I nod slowly, not looking at her.

She exhales like she's trying to reset the entire atmosphere. "Holy shit, Victoria. That explains the stomach bug. And the weird crying. And you were eating syrup straight out of the bottle last week."

She sinks to the floor, staring at the pink lines like they're spelling out doom. "Are we in a Lifetime movie right now? Should I call craft services?"

I laugh, but it dies fast.

Naomi glances at me. "Wait, do you even know who the—? Never mind, that can wait. Are you okay? On a scale of one to completely losing your mind?"

I swallow. "Somewhere between imploding and floating off into the void."

She squeezes my hand. "Okay. Cool. We're spiraling, but we're doing it together."

She tilts her head. "Are you gonna tell me who the mystery guy is, or are we playing Guess That Daddy?"

"It's... someone from that night at Vault. When I disappeared."

Naomi raises an eyebrow. "The hot, haunted-looking one who hadn't slept since 2012?"

I huff a tired laugh. "Yeah. That one."

Her eyes widen. "Okay, I thought this was just a hot one-nighter. Vault hookup, maybe a few tears, dramatic lighting, end scene. But this?" She gestures toward the counter. "This is season-cliffhanger chaos."

"It wasn't just a hookup."

She studies me, softer now. "Is he... in the picture?"

I shake my head. "No. It's complicated. We have history. He showed up out of nowhere, and it completely knocked the air out of me."

Naomi frowns. "So why are we not calling him and telling him he seriously messed up?"

"It's not that simple."

"You're growing a whole human, and he just peaced out? You don't get to ghost someone after something like that."

I swallow. "He didn't ghost me. He didn't know. I didn't even know. And now it's too much."

She leans her head back against the door. "Well, what now? You keeping it?"

I don't answer.

Naomi throws her hands up. "Seriously, why are we not calling him? Why are we not telling this man he's about to have a legacy walking around?"

I let out a bitter laugh. "Because I didn't even ask for his number. I thought I could handle seeing him again. I couldn't."

She starts tapping on her phone. "Then we cyberstalk. Vault boy has to exist somewhere online. He didn't crawl out of a swamp in cowboy boots."

I laugh once, sharp and quiet. She has no idea how dead-on that is.

"Don't bother. Just leave it. He's gone. I need to figure out what I'm doing, not what he's doing."

Naomi smirks. "This doesn't mean you're weak. This means you're rewriting the rulebook. I expect killer eyebrows and a vengeance playlist."

"I don't know," I whisper. "I feel like I can't breathe most of the time. Like everything's cracked wide open."

Naomi nudges my shoulder. "Hey. Whatever you decide, you're not doing this alone."

For the first time all night, I believe her.

And for the first time in forever, that tiny sliver of belief feels like oxygen.

I stand slowly, legs weak but steady enough. I walk to the sink, splash cold water on my face, and stare at my reflection.

My eyes are red, swollen, tired, but they're still mine.

The flickering light buzzes overhead, sputtering out for half a second before coming back on.

I don't look away.

Because maybe surviving isn't a choice.

Maybe it's a rebellion.

CHAPTER THIRTY-EIGHT

The next day, I call my mom because I don't know what else to do.

The phone rings three times before she answers.

"I think you should come home," she says. Her voice is quieter than I remember. No judgment. Just tired.

"Why? So, you can tell me how stupid I was?"

"No," she says gently. "I should have made it easier for you to come home instead of making you feel like you had to run."

I pace the cracked sidewalk outside the laundromat, the smell of detergent and damp air clinging to me. The phone shakes in my hand. "You have no idea what I've been dealing with."

"Then come tell me. Or don't. Just come home. You don't owe me your pain, Victoria. You never did. I just want you safe."

"You always wanted me quiet. Obedient. Not falling apart."

"I wanted you okay," she says softly. "I just didn't know how to handle it when you weren't."

Silence stretches. It is thick. Unspoken. The kind that hurts more than yelling ever could.

"I can't tell you everything," I whisper. "Not right now."

"Then don't. Just come home. We'll figure it out together."

I bite my lip, close my eyes. "I don't know who I am anymore."

"You're my daughter. That's enough for now."

My throat burns. My voice splinters. "Okay," I whisper. "I'll come back."

When the call ends, I just stand there, the phone still pressed to my ear like I'm waiting for someone to tell me what happens next. The world hums around me. Traffic. The low thrum of a dryer spinning behind the laundromat window. A bird pecking at crumbs near my feet.

It's all so painfully normal.

And I am anything but.

I sink onto the curb, the sun beating down on my shoulders. My reflection stares back at me in the laundromat glass. Hollow-eyed. Pale. Lost. A girl who ran until there was nowhere left to go.

I pull my knees to my chest, resting my chin on top.

Home. The word feels foreign. Like a place I used to belong to but forgot how to find.

I picture my mom standing in the kitchen, hands wrapped around a coffee mug, pretending not to cry. I picture the smell of her laundry detergent, the way she hums off-key when she's nervous, the sound of her footsteps in the hall.

And for the first time in months, I want to go back. Not because I'm ready. Because I'm tired.

So tired of being the girl who breaks things and calls it surviving.

I stare up at the sky, gray clouds gathering like bruises.

Maybe this is what surrender looks like. Not weakness but finally admitting you can't keep running forever.

I pull out my phone again and type a message to Naomi.

Me: I'm going home for a while.

Naomi: Good. Maybe let someone else hold you up for once.

I smile, small and shaky. She's right.

That night, I pack the same duffel I brought to Texas. Clothes, charger, nothing else. The motel hums behind me as I zip it closed.

When I step outside, the air smells like rain.

I tilt my head back and let the first drops hit my face. They are cold. Cleansing. Almost cruel.

"I'm going home," I whisper to no one.

And for the first time, it doesn't sound like defeat.

It sounds like the beginning of something I might finally survive.

CHAPTER THIRTY-NINE

TWO DAYS LATER, ON THE ROAD.

I didn't say goodbye. Not to Texas. Not to school. Not to the diner. Not to the motel that smelled like bleach and heartbreak.

Naomi already knew. She didn't try to stop me this time. She just texted:

Find peace. I'll be here when you do.

For a second, I almost texted Jake too. I thought about saying thank you or I'm sorry or in another life, maybe.

But this isn't another life.

This isn't a perfect story.

It's the one where I leave before the ending can hurt any worse.

The first hour was silent. Just the hum of tires and the steady ache in my chest.

Then Louisiana hit me like a wall.

Somewhere near Lafayette, I had to pull over. The sun was too bright, the sky too open, the thoughts too loud. I sat in a Waffle House parking lot with my forehead pressed to the steering wheel and cried until my ribs hurt. I screamed into my hoodie. I pounded the steering wheel like it owed me answers.

But he didn't show up.

Mississippi smelled like wet earth and regret. Every tree reminded me of him. Of that night. Of his voice in the dark.

Every gas station bathroom felt like a checkpoint in purgatory.

And then came Georgia. The sky turned gold, the sun low and soft against the trees. The kind of light that makes even broken things look holy.

That's when I see it.

A billboard off the side of the highway. Faded, crooked, forgotten by time. Four words clinging to the rusted frame:

What You Carry Matters.

I ease onto the shoulder and kill the engine.

The cicadas are screaming from the trees. Heat shimmers above the asphalt. Cars blur by in streaks of white and red, everyone else barreling toward a life that makes sense.

The words hover over me like a verdict.

My hand hovers over my stomach. I am afraid to touch it, like naming it will make it real in a way I can't undo. But I press my palm there anyway. Warm. Human. Mine.

The voice in my head tries to be practical. You don't have a plan. You don't have money. You don't have him.

Another voice answers from somewhere deeper. You have you.

For a second, I swear I hear his voicemail inside the rush of the highway.

I never stopped.

The words echo. A promise. A curse. A ghost.

I close my eyes and breathe through it. The air burns my lungs. The world hums on without me.

I picture the motel sink. The pregnancy tests lined up like soldiers. Naomi's hand in mine. Julie's voice on the phone, promising that I am not alone. I picture the girl I used to be, the one who thought running could outrun the ache, and realize she isn't here anymore.

I roll the window down. Warm air floods in, thick and alive.

For a moment, I let the silence settle. I let myself feel the weight of it all. The loss. The fear. The small, flickering hope that maybe, somehow, this isn't the end.

I reach for the duffel bag in the passenger seat. Inside, folded neatly on top, is his shirt—the same one I woke up wearing the morning he left. I press it to my face, breathing him in one last time.

Then I fold it again, slower this time, and place it beside me. Not in the backseat. Not packed away. Just there. Like a reminder. Like closure.

I rest my forehead on the heel of my hand and let the truth land.

I am carrying more than a mistake.

I am carrying a future.

I am carrying a piece of myself.

The wind catches my hair as I start the car. I pull back onto the highway.

The billboard shrinks in the rearview mirror, but the words do not.

Because I do carry something.

And it matters.

The highway stretches ahead like a promise I'm finally brave enough to keep.

And for the first time, I stop looking back.

PART III

THE RECKONING

CHAPTER FORTY

THREE YEARS LATER.

The air smells different here.

It isn't the salt or the humidity, or the faint sweetness of sunscreen baked into pavement. It's something else. Something quieter. Heavier.

Maybe it's because I'm not seventeen anymore.

Maybe it's because I'm not just me anymore.

The baby's asleep in the back seat. Technically, she's not a baby anymore. She turned two in March and already thinks she runs the entire eastern seaboard.

Her name is Isla—like an island. Because that's what she was. A place apart. A piece of peace in the middle of everything that drowned me. She is the only reason I've made it this far without completely crumbling.

I pull into the driveway of the one-story condo we'll be renting—the one my mom helped me find after I finally saved enough to move out on my own. It's not much, but it's safe. It's in Madeira Beach, close to work and daycare. Close to whatever version of home I can still make for her.

The neighborhood is quiet. Run-down but not unsafe. Mostly older, retired people who keep to themselves. I don't really fit in, but it's what I could get. I can live with that.

I turn the car off and just sit there for a second, listening to the engine tick and the silence settle in.

Three years.

Three years since I left Florida.

Three years since the night that rewrote my life.

Three years since Elijah.

He doesn't know. About the baby. About me. About any of it.

I never told him.

And now we're back in the same state, the same city, the same stretch of broken pavement that tried to destroy me the first time.

But I'm not that girl anymore.

I check the rearview mirror. Isla's head is tilted to the side, her thumb in her mouth, curls stuck to her forehead with sleep sweat. She looks like peace. Like the one good thing that survived the wreck.

My pregnancy wasn't something I ever expected, and definitely not something I was ready for. I spent most of it working and studying, trying to finish my associate's degree while holding myself together with duct tape and denial. I kept it quiet. Didn't post about it, didn't announce it, didn't make it into a celebration. Just survived through it. Quietly. Furiously. Like maybe if I protected her hard enough, she'd never feel the ache I did.

After she was born, I squeezed into my parents' condo with a baby like we weren't already squished before. I took night shifts and bounced between temporary places until I landed the assistant position at Logan's family's firm. They gave me a shot when no one else would. Logan's dad, especially. He said he remembered me from back in the day and that I seemed like I could handle myself. I could. And I did.

Now I answer phones, meet with clients, draft documents, schedule court dates, and file motions in neat little stacks. Like organizing other people's chaos might give me some kind of control over my own. It's not glamorous, but it pays the bills. And most days, it's quiet enough that I can breathe.

I don't really talk to anyone. Not beyond polite coworker smiles or short texts from Julie, who checks in when she can. It's mostly just Isla and me, clocking in and out of life like it's a shift we can't afford to miss.

Sometimes I wonder what Jake and Naomi are doing right about now. If they're still close. If they ever think about that messy semester we all survived. I wonder what it's like to be twenty-one with no baby on your hip and no secrets eating you alive. Just school, friends, maybe a few hookups, and late-night pizza runs. Normal things. Not this tightrope walk I do every day, hoping I don't screw up the only thing I've done right.

I made her, and sometimes it feels like she's the only thing I've ever done right. But when she laughs too loud or furrows her brow in that stubborn way that mirrors his, it sucker-punches me. Like a ghost with green eyes lives inside her, and I don't know if I want to hold on or run.

I take a breath, open the car door, and step into the heat.

Time to start over. Again.

Inside, the condo smells like dust and Pine-Sol. The air conditioner wheezes like it's not sure it wants to live another summer, but it kicks on anyway. I carry Isla in, still asleep on my shoulder, and drop my keys onto the chipped countertop.

There are boxes everywhere. Clothes. Dishes. A few framed photos I haven't decided if I can look at yet.

Isla stirs when I lay her down on the tiny toddler bed in her room. I smooth her hair back, kiss her forehead, and whisper, We're here, baby. We made it.

She doesn't wake up.

I walk into the kitchen, open the fridge, and find it empty except for a bottle of water and one leftover juice box. It'll have to wait until tomorrow.

My phone buzzes on the counter with an incoming text.

Julie: Are you alive?? or did the heat stroke win

I pick up the phone and text back:

Me: We're alive. The house is a mess. Isla's out cold.

A second later:

Julie: I'll try to get time off to fly down and spend time with you guys soon.

I smile. A real one. First in a while.

I grab the water bottle and my old spiral notebook, the same kind I used to write in back in Texas and walk out onto the tiny front porch. I sit on the step and let the sticky heat settle into my skin. The cover's new, but the need is the same. I flip it open to a blank page, click the pen, and stare at the paper like it might know what to say before I do.

Then I just start writing. Scribbled truths I can't say out loud.

I don't know who I am without the ache.

I still check doors and windows twice, like danger might still be out there—or maybe it's still inside me.

She looks like him, and it terrifies me.

I'm scared she'll grow up to be broken just like her mother.

Some days, I hate him. Most days, I miss him.

I want to forgive myself, but I don't know what for.

I don't want to be the angry, crazy girl inside anymore.

I stare at the page until the words blur, like maybe if I look long enough, they'll stop being true. But they don't.

I close the notebook and press it to my chest like a secret.

This isn't the life I planned.

I wonder how long until I feel like the wound's finally starting to heal. Like maybe life won't always feel like it's built on bruises and breath-holding.

The sky outside deepens to violet. A storm brews somewhere offshore. I listen to the faint thunder roll through the air and think, maybe this time, I won't run from it.

And so, I stay there, in the heat and the hush, listening to the world go quiet again.

At least until everything catches fire again.

CHAPTER FORTY-ONE

It's been a few weeks since the move, and everything still feels like it's held together with string and stubbornness.

My days are a rinse-and-repeat cycle of daycare drop-offs, case-file chaos, and carefully constructed normalcy. I keep my head down, show up early, and work hard enough to keep the whispers at bay. I don't do happy hours or linger in the break room. I clock in, grind through, and leave just early enough to grab Isla before the daycare's late fee kicks in.

But there's comfort in the quiet. The hum of the copier. The soft shuffle of papers. Logan's dad called me into his office to fix a typo that wasn't even mine. It's not glamorous, but it's mine. It's something.

Sometimes at lunch, I sit in my car with the windows cracked just enough to hear the gulls from the bay. The air smells faintly of salt and exhaust, and for a few minutes, I let myself pretend I'm somewhere else. Someone else. Not the paralegal with a secret, not the single mom counting minutes before daycare closes. Just a girl breathing again.

Julie kept her promise and came down for a long weekend. She took me and Isla to the boardwalk for ice cream, dragging us from one salty snack stand to another like it was a mission.

"Your kid's a menace," she said, laughing as Isla tried to grab her entire cone.

"She gets it from her godmother," I said, deadpan.

"Rude," Julie replied, licking the melting swirl from her wrist. "Also, not wrong."

We found a shaded bench and sat, legs stretched out, soaking in the humid breeze. Isla babbled in between bites, fingers sticky and wild.

"You okay?" Julie asked after a beat, softer.

"I'm fine."

She raised a brow. "Victoria."

I sighed. "As fine as I'm gonna be."

Julie didn't push. She just leaned her shoulder into mine and said, "Then I'll be fine with you." And for a second, I was.

We stayed there longer than we meant to, talking about nothing and everything. The kind of easy conversation that used to fill whole nights. Julie told me about her new boyfriend, about the apartment she's thinking of buying. I listened, smiling, pretending my chest didn't ache at the reminder of all the versions of life that kept moving without me.

We ended the day walking the pier. The sun dipped low, turning the water peach and gold. Julie bought Isla a pinwheel and a chocolate-dipped pretzel, and Isla promptly dropped both. I laughed harder than I had in months.

"You need more of this," Julie said as we packed the stroller into the trunk. "More moments that don't feel like survival."

"I'm trying," I whispered. "It just doesn't come easy."

Julie wrapped her arms around me, holding tight. "You don't have to make it easy. You just have to keep showing up. And I'll keep showing up too."

She left the next morning, hugging me like she knew the weight I was carrying and pretending not to notice how long I held on.

After she left, the apartment felt emptier. I washed Isla's bottles, folded laundry, filled the silence with cartoons that played too loud just so it wouldn't echo. When I looked around at the boxes still half-unpacked, it hit me how temporarily everything still felt. Like I'd built a life out of placeholders.

*****

Later that afternoon, it was a Sunday. Hot. Muggy. I was at the flea market just outside Clearwater, dragging Isla along in a stroller with a wobbly wheel, scanning the tables for cheap used books.

I was bent over a box of paperbacks when Isla started fussing.

"Hold on, baby, almost done," I muttered, fishing out a copy of something beachy and predictable.

The air was thick with sunscreen and frying oil. People moved slowly, sweating through tank tops and bad tempers. Isla's curls stuck to her forehead, and I dabbed them with a napkin, promising we'd go home soon.

That's when I heard it. Sharp. Angry.

A man's voice. Followed by a woman.

"You're fucking impossible, Sarah." Elijah's voice.

My chest locked. I froze behind a rack of tank tops, heart slamming against my ribs.

"I told you not to come," he said, quieter this time, clipped and exhausted.

"And I told you I'm not going anywhere until you listen to me!" she snapped.

It was them. Sarah. Elijah. Standing on the other side of a booth selling knockoff sunglasses, having a fight like they didn't care who heard.

I edged closer, tucked behind a wall of beach towels.

Elijah looked wrecked. Still beautiful, still Elijah, but worn. He rubbed a hand over his face like he hadn't slept in days. Sarah looked manic. Her hair was piled in a messy bun, eyeliner smudged like she'd cried or was on something or just didn't care.

"You don't get to show up and cause a scene every time you get caught," he said. "Not here. Not again."

"Oh, don't act like you're some innocent now," she spat. "You still come home when you want. Still take what you need."

"That's not true."

She laughed, loud and sharp enough to turn heads. "You think just because you've got some job with a hard hat and a union card that you're better than me?"

He didn't respond. His jaw clenched.

"You think you can do better than me? You think some other girl's gonna deal with you? No one else wants the broken, bitter version of you, Elijah."

He stepped back. "I never asked you to deal with anything."

Sarah's voice cracked. "But you let me. You let me ruin myself loving you."

Elijah's face twisted. It was part disbelief, part disgust. "No, Sarah. You ruined yourself by clinging to something I never asked for. You throw love around like it's currency and expect me to cash it in. I can't even stand being around you anymore."

People were staring now. A vendor stopped stacking bracelets. Someone pulled out their phone. Sarah noticed and snapped, "What are you looking at?" before kicking at a crate of hats. The display toppled, scattering across the walkway.

"You're making a scene," Elijah said, low but dangerous.

"You made me this," she said, tears and rage tangled in her voice. "You don't get to stand there like some saint while I drown in what you started."

He didn't flinch, but something in him went cold. "You were the simple choice. The safe one. I kept trying to convince myself that meant something, but it never did."

The words hit like a slap. Sarah's breath hitched, wild and shaking. "You're mad, that's all. The other guy didn't mean anything," she said quickly, desperate. "You know that. He was just—he wasn't you. He was never you."

He caught her wrist as she lunged forward. "Enough. You're not doing this here."

"Let go of me," she hissed, wrenching her arm free. "You don't get to silence me. You don't get to walk away."

"You've got nothing left to say that I need to hear."

She stormed off, nearly knocking over another table on her way. A few people clapped awkwardly, the way crowds do when they're relieved the tension's over.

And then, as if the universe couldn't be more twisted, Elijah turned. Looked up.

And he saw me.

The world narrowed. The noise of the market fell away. No chatter, no music, just the thud of my heartbeat in my ears. His eyes locked on mine, confusion flickering into recognition, then disbelief, then something darker.

My knees nearly buckled. I gripped the stroller handle like it was the only thing tethering me to the ground.

He took a step forward. Just one. Then stopped himself.

I don't know if it was guilt or shock or the ghost of every word we never said, but for a second, he looked like he might cross that space between us.

And I looked like I might let him.

Then Isla whimpered, small and innocent, and the sound snapped me out of whatever spell had pulled me under.

I turned fast, shoved Isla's stroller into motion, and practically ran for the car.

My pulse roared in my ears. The air thickened around me, sound collapsing into white noise. Every step felt like the summer I spent running from him and never really getting far enough.

Did he recognize me?

Of course he did.

But did he see her? Did he see Isla? Her wild curls, her tiny fists clutching the stroller bar, those bright green eyes just like his?

I didn't stop until I was back in the driver's seat with the AC on full blast, Isla whining softly as I clutched the wheel.

He's here.

And he's still a storm.

And I'm still the girl who never learned how to survive him.

And three days later, like fate wasn't finished gutting me, he walked into the law firm.

But that's its own kind of story.

CHAPTER FORTY-TWO

I'm already late. Like, borderline losing-my-job late.

Isla screamed through the entire morning. Wouldn't eat. Wouldn't wear pants. She cried so hard she hiccupped her way through daycare drop-off, clutching my neck like I was leaving her at a prison camp.

Then, just as I wrestled her into the car seat, she blew out her diaper like a confetti cannon of regret.

We were both crying by the time I dropped her off. And I hadn't even had coffee.

I parked crooked in the office lot and jogged inside, hair barely brushed, blouse clinging to sweat and formula.

The receptionist didn't even look up.

"Victoria, Landon's in Conference Room B. Friend of Logan's. New client. He needs you in there to take notes."

"Seriously?" I panted, clutching my oversized bag like a weapon.

She shrugged. "He said ASAP."

Of course he did.

I flew down the hall, heels clacking like gunshots. My bag slipped off my shoulder, and I reached to adjust it. That's when it happened. The heel of my left shoe caught on the warped tile just outside the conference room.

I went flying.

Straight through the half-open door.

My tote exploded. Pens, files, a crushed fruit pouch, and Isla's spare sock scattered across the carpet like confetti.

Landon looked up from his seat, eyes wide before cracking up. "Fashionably chaotic as always, Victoria."

"Kill me," I muttered, scrambling to gather my dignity and the sock.

I looked up.

And there he was.

Elijah.

Sitting at the end of the conference table in a fitted T-shirt, dark jeans, and well-worn Nikes that looked like they'd walked through hell and back. His arms were crossed, but his entire body went still the second I hit the floor.

His eyes locked on mine. And stayed there.

Everything around me went silent.

Landon kept talking. Something about legal intake, a misunderstanding, restraining order drama, but I heard none of it. My blood turned to static. My skin to fire.

Elijah blinked, slow and heavy. His mouth didn't move. His expression didn't change. But his gaze... his gaze tore through me.

311

I sat down in the chair next to Landon and tried not to tremble as I flipped open my legal pad. My pen tapped against the page, betraying me with shaky fingers.

"Victoria, this is Elijah," Landon said, oblivious to the inferno. "Friend of Logan's from way back. He's here about a personal legal matter. Thought it might help having a familiar face in the room."

Ha. Familiar wasn't the word I would've chosen.

Elijah finally looked away.

I exhaled. Barely.

I took notes. I think. Something about a false report, a domestic call that got messy, a restraining order filed in anger and later recanted. Elijah's jaw clenched the whole time. I watched him from the corner of my eye, hyper-aware of every breath he took.

He hadn't said a word to me.

But I could feel him.

And then, just before Landon stood to leave, Elijah's gaze slid back to mine.

One second. Two. Three.

Did he know? Did he recognize her? The toddler at the flea market? The green eyes? The curls?

He nodded, almost imperceptibly.

Then Landon clapped him on the back and opened the door. "Victoria will get those notes typed up and sent to Logan by tomorrow. Good seeing you, man."

Elijah stood, tall and slow, but said nothing.

As he passed behind me, I caught a whisper of his cologne. Clean. Familiar. The kind of scent that rewires your nervous system.

He didn't look back.

And that was almost worse than if he had.

I stared down at my notes, at the empty page I hadn't written a single word on, and realized my hands were still shaking.

Three years apart, and my body still remembered him like a language I'd spent my whole life trying to forget.

CHAPTER FORTY-THREE

The office was too quiet after he left.

The air felt heavier, like his presence had rearranged it. The scent of his cologne still lingered, faint and familiar, impossible to ignore. I sat there long after Landon was gone, pretending to organize my notes, pretending my hands weren't shaking.

The clock on the wall ticked too loud. My pulse kept trying to match it.

When I finally packed up my things, the hallway felt longer than usual. My reflection in the elevator doors looked unfamiliar—tired, pale, eyes too bright. I pressed the button, exhaled, and whispered to no one, "What the hell are you doing here, Elijah?"

The elevator dinged, but I didn't move right away. For a second, I half expected him to step inside, say something, anything. He didn't.

The drive to daycare was a blur of headlights and humidity. Every red light felt like a countdown I didn't want to reach. I rolled the window down, hoping the air would quiet the noise inside my chest. It didn't.

By the time I pulled into the daycare lot, the parking spaces were nearly empty. Through the window, I spotted Isla sitting near the cubbies, her bear in her lap, eyelids heavy with sleep.

"Rough day?" her teacher asked, handing me the clipboard to sign.

"You could say that," I murmured.

Isla looked up when she heard my voice. Her face lit up like I was the only thing in the world that made sense. She reached for me, her little arms wrapping tight around my neck.

"Hey, baby," I whispered, kissing the top of her head. "Let's go home."

By the time we made it back, the sky had bruised purple and gold. The condo was dim and still when I unlocked the door, one arm cradling her against me. I set her on the couch, slipped off her shoes, and covered her with the soft throw blanket. She was asleep before I could even straighten up.

For a long moment, I just stood there, watching her chest rise and fall. The tiny curls on her forehead stuck with sweat. Her thumb rested against her mouth. She looked like peace itself.

I brushed her hair back and whispered, "You're safe," though I wasn't sure I believed it.

In the kitchen, I poured a glass of water and stared at the window over the sink. My reflection stared back, faint and ghostlike, eyes rimmed red.

Elijah.

I could still feel the way the room went still when he looked at me. The air between us had changed, thick and electric, like gravity remembered our names.

I should have been furious. I should have walked out. Told Landon I wasn't the right person for that case. But I didn't. I sat there and let it happen.

315

My phone buzzed.

A text from Naomi.

Naomi: You alive? Or did daycare mom life finally win?

I smiled weakly and typed back.

Me: Barely. Long day at work.

Naomi: You sound weird. Everything okay?

Me: Just tired. Really tired.

I didn't tell her who I saw. I couldn't. Not yet.

The condo was quiet again. Too quiet. I turned off the kitchen light and walked to the window. Outside, the streetlight flickered, casting everything in pale gold. A shadow moved across the sidewalk, slow and deliberate.

Probably a neighbor. Probably nothing.

Still, my pulse jumped.

I checked the lock on the door. Then I checked it again. Old habits die hard.

When I sank onto the couch, the silence felt alive, stretching thin around me. I pulled the blanket over my lap and stared at the ceiling.

I thought about his face in that conference room. The way his jaw tightened. The way his eyes softened for just a second before he shut it all off again.

I told myself this meant nothing. That tomorrow would come, and he'd disappear like he always did.

But deep down, I knew better.

He never just disappeared.

He always came back like a storm you swore had passed.

And somewhere out there, I could feel it again. The quiet pull, the gravity between us waking up after three long years.

The kind that doesn't ask.

The kind that takes.

CHAPTER FORTY-FOUR

There's a knock at the door. Sharp, impatient, and completely unexpected.

I freeze mid-step, a cereal bowl in one hand and a trash bag half-tied in the other. A cartoon hums softly in the background, little giggles echoing off the walls. Isla's shoes are by the door. Her tiny jacket is slung over the couch like a warning. There's a crayon under my foot.

The knock comes again, louder.

Panic punches me in the chest.

I lunge for my phone. One unread text from Logan.

Logan: Elijah's swinging by to drop off the discovery forms. I gave him your address since you were out sick. Hope that's okay.

No, Logan. It is not okay.

My stomach flips. I glance down at myself—bare feet, oversized band tee with a grape-juice stain near the hem, hair in a chaotic mess of knots and a claw clip that gave up hours ago. It looks like I haven't slept because I haven't. My bra is missing. My dignity went with it.

Another knock. Three fast raps this time. It sounds like him. It feels like him.

I open the door just a crack. And of course, there he is.

Elijah. Six feet of unresolved history in a hoodie and jeans, holding a manila envelope and a face I used to memorize in the dark.

"Elijah." His name hits my lips like a sin I swore I'd never say again. I grip the doorframe, not for balance, just to keep from reaching for him. "Seriously? What are you doing here?"

His expression doesn't shift, but the energy does. "Logan said you needed the forms. I'm just the delivery guy now, I guess."

I glance over my shoulder at the chaos behind me. Sippy cup on the counter. Stuffed octopus on the floor. A kid-sized hoodie peeking out from under a blanket on the couch. Everything in this condo screams I'm a mom now, and all I can do is stand there like a deer in headlights.

He holds up the envelope but doesn't say anything at first. Just watches me, like he's still waiting for something. Permission, maybe. Or just proof that I'm still me.

After a beat, he says, "Here."

I reach for it, but he doesn't let go. His fingers graze mine. Slowly. Deliberately. A pulse of heat shoots up my arm. I don't move. Neither does he. It's a stare-down wrapped in static and muscle memory. The air between us crackles.

He glances past me again, eyes narrowing.

"Can I come in? Just to drop these off," he says. His tone is careful, cautious, like he's testing the limits of how close he's allowed to get.

I hesitate. Every instinct screams no, but my body betrays me. I step back just enough for him to take a single stride inside.

He doesn't move far. Just over the threshold. Close enough that I can feel the heat coming off him, smell the soap and cologne and something that's just him.

He looks around once, slow.

Then his gaze catches on the couch.

"You got a kid here or something?" he asks.

I freeze. "Seriously?"

He nods toward the couch. "All this kind of speaks for itself."

I don't answer. Just shift my weight and glare like that's a response.

He doesn't drop it. "You gonna tell me what's going on, or should I just keep guessing?"

"Like you're owed an explanation?" I snap. "That's rich coming from the guy who disappeared into a courthouse wedding with the psycho ex."

He cocks his head slightly, like he's weighing whether to call bullshit. There's a pause, long enough to set my whole body on edge.

"Didn't figure you for the juice-box-and-crayon type."

I smirk, but it's tight. "Guess I'm full of surprises."

His eyes drag over me like a match waiting to strike. The oversized tee I slept in. My bare legs. My flushed cheeks. He lingers on my mouth too long, and something dark shifts in his expression, like he remembers exactly what I taste like.

He doesn't speak. Doesn't have to. I feel his judgment like static clinging to my skin.

"I won't stay," he mutters. "Just figured it'd be easier than going through the office."

"Right." I take the envelope, grip it too tight. "Thanks."

Still, he doesn't move.

"You okay?" The question is simple. Loaded. It sits between us like a live wire.

"Yeah," I lie. "Just tired."

He nods, slow. His knuckles flex against the envelope like he's holding back more than words. Then his eyes flick toward the fridge.

And I forgot about the drawing.

Crayon. Purple stick figures. One labeled Me. One labeled Mommy. A big red heart between them.

His face shifts, just barely. A flicker of something sharp. A puzzle piece turning the wrong way.

"You serious about this new life?" he asks.

"What?"

"This." He gestures vaguely, eyes narrowing. "Cozy little domestic vibe you've got going on."

I fold my arms over my chest. "What's that supposed to mean?"

"Nothing." He shrugs, but it's tight, controlled. "Just didn't picture you like this."

"Like what?" Say it. Say it out loud so I can break something over your head and get this over with.

He doesn't. Just shakes his head and lets out a dry laugh that makes me feel fifteen again and already ruined.

"You dating someone?"

The words are low. Too low. Like a dare whispered across a bar. Like he's already picturing someone else's hands on me and wants to burn the image out of his head.

I blink. "Excuse me?"

"You heard me."

I tilt my chin up, spine straightening like it will shield me. "Are you seriously asking me that right now?"

He leans against the counter, arms crossed, and I swear he's smirking.

"I'm curious."

"Well, don't be."

"That's a no, then?"

I scoff. "Why do you even care?"

His jaw flexes like he's biting something back. "I don't." But his eyes say otherwise.

I go to close the door, but he doesn't move.

"I just figured," he says, voice low now, "maybe you found someone normal. Someone who doesn't drag you into messes."

I freeze. "Is that what you think this is? That I'm living some picture-perfect life now?"

He looks me dead in the eye. "I don't know what the hell you're doing, Victoria. But you sure didn't wait around to ask why I left."

Something inside me snaps.

"You don't get to act wounded," I say, stepping into his space. "You were the one with the secrets. You were the one with Sarah and the courthouse wedding and the disappearing act."

His expression hardens. "Don't turn this around on me."

I laugh. It's hollow. Mean. "You showed up married, Elijah. I don't owe you anything."

He pushes off the counter with a bitter laugh. "Of course. This is exactly how it always goes, isn't it? Whatever. You got the papers. We'll keep it professional from now on."

He turns, hand on the door. The words slip out before I can stop them.

"She's yours."

It's barely a whisper. Raw. Shaken. The kind of secret that rips skin when it slips free.

But he doesn't hear it. Or maybe he does and chooses not to turn back.

The door creaks shut. His footsteps fade.

The envelope slips from my hands, papers scattering across the floor like pieces of a life I can't keep together.

I sink down next to them, knees pulled to my chest.

He was here. He saw everything.

He left again.

But this time, he didn't even know he was leaving himself behind.

CHAPTER FORTY-FIVE

I haven't heard from him for two days.

Not a call. Not a text. Nothing dropped off at the office. Nothing from Logan. Nothing at all.

Which is worse than yelling. Worse than if he'd called and said every awful thing I already whisper to myself in the mirror.

Because silence? That's his specialty. His disappearing act? Legendary.

But that look on his face when he saw the drawing on the fridge, that haunted, calculating flicker behind his eyes. I can't stop seeing it.

He knows something's off.

I feel it every time my phone lights up and it's not him. Every time I walk through the kitchen and glance at the fridge, considering just tearing the whole damn thing down. Like maybe erasing it will rewind time. Maybe it will put the truth back in the box I kept it in for three years.

Julie says I'm spiraling.

She's not wrong.

She called this morning, voice tight with concern but trying to play it cool. Julie never pushes unless she has to. But she knows me too well.

"You okay?" she asked.

"I'm fine."

"Victoria."

"I'm. Fine."

The kind of fine that's unraveling at the seams.

I made it through half a cup of coffee and four back-to-back client calls before I had to run to the bathroom and lock the door just to catch my breath.

Because he knows.

And any minute now, he's going to do something about it.

I try to distract myself with work. It's laughable.

Sarah's case file sits on the edge of my desk like it's mocking me. Open. Incomplete. Messy. Just like her.

A handful of citations. A DUI. Two counts of resisting arrest. A "misunderstanding" at a Waffle House that ended in broken glass and someone needing stitches. And that's just what's on paper.

What doesn't make it into the file is how she weaponizes her tears. How she twists reality until she's the victim in every room. How she once accused Elijah Garrison of hitting her in a Walgreens parking lot because he wouldn't let her drive drunk.

Logan says we're just helping Elijah file a response and coordinate deposition prep. Nothing major.

But nothing about Sarah is ever just anything. She's the kind of girl who turns breakfast into bloodshed. Who cries in court and claws your eyes out in the parking lot. Who dials 911 with crocodile tears and then winks at the officer when no one's looking.

And what kills me most is that he stayed.

For years. Through all the chaos. The fights. The false reports. The arrests. The threats.

I used to ask myself what kind of spell she had over him. Was it guilt? Obligation? Or did he just want to be punished that badly? Because Sarah didn't love him. She owned him. Like a possession she could ruin, repeatedly, just to prove she still had the power.

And maybe that's what scares me. He let her.

And now she's tangled up in Elijah again. Somehow.

And I'm tangled with him. Again.

I sit at my desk and stare at the legal pad in front of me for twenty minutes without writing a single word. Just pressing the tip of the pen into the paper until it almost breaks through.

My brain drifts backward. The way it always does when I feel trapped.

"You made me do this, Elijah," she screamed once outside a party senior year. "You don't love me! You never did!"

Only it wasn't Sarah screaming in that memory. Not at first.

It was Brandy.

Brandy with her pink claws and fake tan. Brandy, who cornered me in the girls' locker room in ninth grade and told me

I'd better stay away from Justin, or she'd find out where I lived. The same Justin I was only tutoring because he was failing Algebra, and I had no idea who he was outside of that class. Brandy, who cried to the principal about being bullied after she shoved me into a locker.

It's all the same girl.

Different names. Same poison.

And the worst part is that no one ever saw through it. No one stopped them.

Not even Elijah.

He used to come back to the condo with this look in his eyes. Cold. Detached. Like something inside him had been scooped out and buried. And still, he stayed. Still, he said she didn't mean it. She was just confused. Maybe she was only doing it to make him jealous.

But it wasn't the drinking or the drama or the chaos.

It was all the guys.

She'd sleep with them. Post about it. Let him find out secondhand. She'd twist the knife slowly and deliberately, then cry about how it was all his fault for not loving her right.

And the worst part? He believed it. Or pretended to. He tried to make it make sense. Like it was what he deserved.

I remember the first time I saw Sarah slap him across the face. It was at the Bilmar, right by the pool. I watched it happen from behind the bar rail while pretending not to.

She laughed like it was a joke.

He didn't even flinch.

He just picked up her towel and handed it back to her like he owed her something.

I couldn't breathe.

Because I knew that look. I'd seen it before, in the mirror. After Brandy. After being told I was too much. Too angry. Too violent. That it was my fault when people cracked.

And now Elijah wears it too.

Like an invisible brand.

That's the part that keeps me up at night. Not that Sarah hurt him.

But that he let her. That some broken, bleeding part of him wanted to be hurt.

Maybe he never really left the chaos. He just stopped calling it by name.

The thing about ghosts is they never stay dead. They wait until you're standing on solid ground again, and then they haunt you all over.

And Elijah Garrison? He was never just a ghost. He was the wildfire I thought I survived.

Turns out, I'm still burning.

And now the fire is standing at my door.

CHAPTER FORTY-SIX

There is a knock at the door.

Not a gentle tap. Not a drop-off knock. No pretending this is casual.

Three sharp raps. Intentional. Loaded. Like the sound of judgment arriving in person.

I already know who it is. My stomach tells me before my ears finish processing.

It is late. Isla is not here. She is spending the night with my parents. First time in weeks. I planned to do laundry and maybe breathe for once.

Instead, I open the door and find a storm.

"Elijah."

He does not answer. He does not smirk. He does not lean like he used to. He walks right past me like I am nothing more than a threshold.

"Come on in," I mutter under my breath. "Make yourself at home."

He stops in the middle of the living room. Same black hoodie. Hands in his pockets, as if he lets them out, they will do something he cannot take back.

He does not turn around.

"You could have told me."

My spine tightens. "Told you what?"

He spins to face me. "Do not."

There is venom in that single word. A threat buried in restraint.

"I talked to Logan," he says. "He said you have a daughter. He thought it was weird that I did not know. Figured you were keeping it private. Until I started thinking about the timing."

"Elijah—"

"No. You do not get to 'Elijah' your way out of this."

He is pacing now. Like he has been coiled for days, waiting for the chance to come unglued.

"I saw you in Texas three years ago. You moved back three years ago. Took a job with my friend, Logan. You had a baby the same year. I kept trying to remember if I wore a condom, if you told me you were on birth control or not. Would I even know if you were with anyone else? It is all too much to remember, but the math adds up. I am supposed to believe that is just a coincidence?"

I take a shaky breath and backpedal, crossing my arms like a barrier. "You are reading into things. This is crazy. You have no idea what you are talking about."

"Really?" he bites. "Because I think I do. And I think you are just pissed I figured it out before you had to come clean."

I cross my arms, but it is not armor. It is instinct. "You were not around."

"Because you left!" he snaps.

I snap back before I can stop myself. "You left me. You walked out of that hotel room like I was nothing. Not even a goodbye, Elijah. Just gone. You disappeared first. Do not rewrite history like I vanished on you."

His brow furrows, voice suddenly tight. "I left you a note. A voicemail. I thought…"

"A note?" I shout, my voice rising fast. "You think that counts as a goodbye? You think a voicemail is enough?"

His jaw tenses. "I did not know what else to do."

"In what world do you walk out of someone's life without leaving a number? Without any way to find you? You left me in that bed like I was just some mistake you regretted the second the sun came up."

He drags a hand through his hair, exasperated. "I had to leave for work, Victoria. I did not know what to do. I thought giving you space was the right thing."

"Bullshit." My throat burns. "You thought vanishing was better than being honest? You really thought leaving a note and then ghosting me was the grown-up choice?"

"You should have found a way to tell me."

"You were with Sarah."

"Do not talk to me about Sarah."

"No?" I laugh, bitter. "Why? Because you married her?"

He grabs the edge of the kitchen table like he is trying to steady himself. "That was not… Jesus, Victoria. That was not real. That was a mistake. A punishment."

"A mistake for what? You treated her like she won a prize and treated me like I was the mistake. How does that make any sense in your head?"

His silence answers better than words ever could.

I swallow, throat dry. "You stayed with her. You let her lie. Hurt you. Sleep around. Humiliate you."

"And you," he growls, stepping closer, "hid my child from me."

There it is. The bomb. Silence rings in its place.

"I did not know how," I whisper.

"No. You did not want to."

"You do not get to walk back into my life and pretend I owe you an apology for trying to survive you." I push past him, breath ragged, fury shaking loose.

"I flew to another state to see Julie. She helped me try to find you. I was so wrecked I did not even know how to begin. And you know what we found, Elijah? We did not find a sad, broken boy. We did not find the Elijah I loved."

My voice breaks, then spikes again, louder. "We found a married Elijah. You tied yourself to her. You did not leave a number. You did not leave a way for me to reach you. I had no way of contacting you unless I wanted to go through your wife."

He slams his hand against the wall hard enough to make the frame rattle.

"Do you know what it did to me," he screams, voice cracking now, "to come home and feel like a fool? You think I am stupid? You think I would not figure it out?"

"I was going to tell you," I shout back, stepping toward him, eyes burning.

"When?" he roars. "After her high school graduation? Or after I missed every moment that mattered?"

"You think it was easy for me?" I scream. "You disappeared."

He is pacing, wild, furious. "You had my kid and you did not think I deserved to know?"

"You chose her," I throw back. "You made that decision. You picked your poison. You were gone, Elijah. What was I supposed to do? Show up at your door and hand you a baby and hope to God your wife did not break me in half?"

"Do not twist this on me."

"I had no way to contact you," I scream. "You left. You always left."

He walks toward me. Close enough that I have to tilt my chin up to meet his eyes. His jaw is tight. His eyes are wild.

"You knew I did not have parents there for me. You knew what I went through with that man. You knew I would never want that for my kid."

I flinch.

His voice is guttural, barely human. "You knew."

Then, like a fuse snaps inside him, he lunges, not at me, but toward the counter.

His arm sweeps, and the vase of flowers crashes to the floor. Water splashes across the tile. Glass explodes in every direction.

We both stand there, panting, unblinking.

I step toward him, chest heaving, throat raw. "What is wrong with you?"

He steps into me. Inches. "You. You are what is wrong with me."

"Then say it," I scream. "Say you regret all of it."

"I regret nothing," he spits. "That is the problem."

"You should have stayed," I throw back.

"Then why did you not tell me?"

"I was scared."

"Of what? Of me?"

"Of losing everything all over again."

My voice cracks, and for a moment we just breathe each other's air. Both of us are trembling. Both of us are on the verge.

Then I say it. The one thing I never wanted to admit. "I did not think you were strong enough to stay."

Something in his face breaks. Not soft. Not tender. Just a fracture.

My heart is pounding so hard I think I might drop too.

"I want to know my kid," he whispers.

Tears spill down my cheeks.

"I still want to."

He takes one step back. Then another. Toward the door.

"Do not leave," I say, voice cracking.

He does not answer. He opens the door, and the night presses in. Broken glass glitters behind him. He does not step out.

He shuts the door. The sound is a gunshot.

His footsteps charge back toward me like a storm surge.

"Say it," he growls, barely audible.

"What?" My voice is shredded.

"Say you did not want me. Say you moved on. Say it."

I laugh. Short, sharp, bitter. "You left me in a hotel bed and vanished. What was I supposed to do?"

He grabs my wrist. Not hard. Not soft. Just enough to make my breath hitch. His eyes search mine.

"Tell me you still feel it," he growls. "After everything. After all this time."

"Feel it?" My laugh shakes. "It never stopped. You never stopped." I grab his hoodie, drag him closer. "And I am so tired of pretending it did."

Our mouths crash together. Angry. Desperate. It is not a kiss. It is war. His hands tear into my hair. Mine yank his hoodie over his head. Buttons fly off my blouse as he rips it open.

"I hate you," I whisper against his mouth.

"Good," he growls, lifting me onto the counter. "Then hate me right."

His mouth trails down my neck, rough and shaking, like he is tasting every word he never said. My back hits the cool counter, and for a second, it is not anger. It is ache. He looks up, breathless, eyes wild and wrecked.

"I do not have a condom," he pants.

"I am on birth control," I say, breathless.

"I trust you," he says. "Do you trust me?"

I hesitate, heart pounding, then nodding. "I do. Yes."

We do not make it to the bedroom. We do not make it past reason or pride. We crash into the wreckage.

His mouth finds my collarbone, my neck, the underside of my jaw. It is messy and raw and the most alive I have felt in years.

He lowers me to the floor. Our knees scuff tile, hands skimming glass. Shards of the vase surround us, the one he shattered minutes ago.

"You are bleeding," I pant, staring at a nick on his hand.

"I do not care," he growls, hitching my leg around his waist.

He tears at the rest of my clothes, every motion frantic. Like he is trying to strip off the last three years along with the fabric.

My nails drag down his back. He shudders.

"Did anyone else touch you?" he demands, forehead pressed to mine.

"No," I gasp. "Only you. There has only ever been you."

His breath catches. For a second, his eyes soften, just barely. Then he kisses me again, and we fall apart.

Right there on the cold floor. In the ruins. In the pieces of our chaos.

I do not care about the cuts. Or the bruises. Or what it means tomorrow.

Because right now, in this disaster we built together, we have finally found a way to feel whole.

But even as I lie there, tangled in him, skin stinging and heart thudding, I know.

This does not fix anything.

This is just the eye of the storm.

CHAPTER FORTY-SEVEN

My eyes peel open to the burn of daylight slicing through the blinds.

My throat feels like sandpaper. My skin stings.

I am on the kitchen floor.

My blouse is somewhere across the room. There is a gash on my thigh that I do not remember getting. The tile beneath me is tacky from sweat and blood and something I do not want to name. My hair is knotted. My chest aches. My legs feel like lead.

And he is still here.

Elijah lies on his back beside me, one arm flung over his face like he could not bear to see the sunrise. There is dried blood on his forearm. A shard of glass near his elbow. One of the buttons from my blouse is stuck to his chest.

He breathes like he ran ten miles and finally collapsed.

For a second, I just stare. This is the first time I have ever woken up next to him. The first morning after that was not a dream or a memory I tried to rewrite. In the chaos and the blood and the bruises, we are still here.

He shifts. Blinks slowly. Winces.

"Shit," he mutters.

"Yeah," I whisper.

We do not say anything else.

Because what do you say when the explosion has already happened, and you are both still standing in the rubble?

He sits up. The movement is slow, deliberate. Like everything hurts. Like he is afraid he will step wrong and shatter again.

"You are bleeding," I murmur.

He looks down at his palm. The cut is deep, dark now. "So are you."

I look at the gash on my thigh. Dried blood crusts the edge. There is a smear on my stomach. A bruise is blooming on my hip.

"We need to clean up," I say, voice like broken glass.

He nods. Stands. Offers me his hand.

I hesitate. I take it.

He helps me up. Neither of us flinches. It feels like we should.

I limp to the bathroom. He grabs the broom.

When I come back, he is sweeping the glass. Shirtless. Quiet. Focused. Like if he stops concentrating, he will fall apart again. He nudges a little circle of glittering shards, then pauses and lifts something small from the floor. He turns the loose button in his fingers once and sets it on the console like an apology he does not know how to say.

I pass him the first aid kit. "We probably need stitches."

He shrugs. "We probably need therapy."

It almost makes me laugh. Almost.

We patch ourselves in silence. Gauze. Tape. Disinfectant that burns. Bandages over bullet holes.

He finally breaks it. "Did she know?"

I pause, pressing gauze to my hip. "Who?"

"Julie."

"Yes."

He nods like he already knew the answer. Like it still hurts. "Why did she not tell me?"

"Because I begged her not to. Because she is loyal to me. Because I was a mess. Because I could not handle the thought of you showing up and seeing it on your face. That moment when it hit you that you missed everything."

He nods again. Stares at the floor.

"You never asked me," I whisper.

"What?"

"If she were yours. You never even asked."

He looks at me then. Straight through me. "Because I already knew."

Silence falls again. Not heavy now. Just tired.

He picks up a photo from the console table. Isla on the beach, hair windblown and sun-kissed, sand stuck to her cheeks as she laughs at something out of frame. He stares for a long moment, something unreadable passing through his expression. He sets the photo down, takes a blanket from the couch, and wraps it around my shoulders.

I sit. He sits beside me.

We stare at the cleaned floor where the vase used to be.

His voice is rough. "What is her favorite color?"

"Purple. Only if there is glitter involved."

He huffs a worn-out chuckle. "What else?"

"She loves everything ocean. Dolphins, sea turtles, jellyfish. She can name them all. She thinks she is a mermaid and talks to seagulls like they are her army. She sings in the bath like she is on Broadway."

"What is her favorite food?"

"SpaghettiOs. She throws them everywhere and still somehow wins the argument."

He swallows. "Does she have your temper?"

"Worse. She launched a full bowl across the room because her show ended."

He closes his eyes for a second. "She sounds amazing."

A beat.

"Does she know about me?"

I hesitate, then shake my head. "She knows she has a daddy who lives far away. That is all I could give her."

He nods. Takes a breath like it hurts. "What else is she like?"

"She scrunches her brows the way you did when you were pissed off but trying to hide it. And when she smirks, it is you. Same eyes too. She is smart. Stubborn. I think she is trying to take me out before kindergarten."

He rubs his palms down his thighs, a nervous tick that undercuts his steady tone. "Can I ask something weird?"

I nod.

"Tell me about when she was born. Who was with you? What it was like."

The questions tumble out like they were dammed for years.

"She was early," I say, steadying my hands in my lap. "I went into labor two weeks before my due date. It got complicated. Her heart rate dropped, and they rushed me for an emergency C-section."

He goes still.

I add softly, "My mom was there. That was it."

I rise, step toward him. Gently, I take his hand and guide it under the hem of my shirt to the scar just below my navel. His fingers brush the raised skin. Rough calluses against a place that still aches sometimes. His eyes flick up to mine. I do not look away.

The birthing room was too bright. I did not hear my name, only her first cry, thin and furious, and I knew I would never be alone again.

343

"That is what brought her into the world," I whisper. "That scar."

He does not speak, but his thumb moves, a soft stroke across the line. Reverent. Memorizing.

"What is her name?" he asks, low, like the question is heavy.

"Isla."

He repeats it quietly, like a prayer. "Isla."

"It means island," I say. "A place apart. Like the island where we first collided. Where the chaos finally felt like peace."

He closes his eyes for a beat and opens them more softly. "Isla," he says again. He says her name like a promise he was late to.

There is a beat of quiet.

"Do you have a picture I can keep?" he asks, voice careful.

I pull a doubled print from the back of a frame on the shelf. The same beach day. I press it into his hand. He tucks it into his pocket like it belongs there.

"I want to meet her," he says.

"Okay."

"I want to meet her," he repeats, quieter. "Really meet her."

"You will."

"When?"

My voice is soft. "Tomorrow, if you can be here."

He nods, like gravity just changed.

I draw a breath. "Tomorrow we are parents first."

He nods again, slower this time, like he understands the cost of that sentence. "Nine a.m. I will be here."

I glance toward the hallway, toward the room that holds every piece of the life I built without him. "I need to get ready. She is with my parents. I will text my mom and bring her home."

Hope creeps in around the edges of his expression. He looks at the console, at the small button he placed there, then back to me.

We sit quietly. Still bleeding. Still bruised. But for the first time in forever, there is forward motion.

Still wounded. No longer alone.

Tomorrow, he meets her. But tonight, he remembers what he lost.

CHAPTER FORTY-EIGHT

He showed up at 9:00 a.m. sharp.

I know because I had been pacing since 8:00, checking the time. Rearranging the throw pillows. Trying not to hyperventilate into the curtains.

When the knock finally came, it was gentler this time. Hesitant. Not like last night's storm. This one was careful. Hopeful.

I opened the door and saw him standing there in jean shorts, a white T-shirt, a huge bag from Target in one hand and a bouquet of flowers in the other. There was a stuffed alligator wedged under his arm, a kite rolled up and tied with a blue ribbon, and a nervous wreck of a man trying not to shake out of his own skin.

"Hi," he said, like it was the first word he had ever spoken.

I swallowed. "Hi."

We stood there for a beat. Then I stepped aside.

He walked in, careful like he might break something. Like he already had and did not want to make it worse. He set the bag down gently, as if it contained explosives instead of toddler clothes and a plastic sea turtle.

"She is still asleep," I said.

He nodded. Then exhaled. "Okay. That is good. Gives me a minute to freak out in peace."

I glanced at the bag. "You brought gifts?"

"Yeah," he said sheepishly. "Clothes. A stuffed animal. Plastic toys. The lady at the store helped me figure out the sizes. I had no idea what I was doing. Then I just grabbed anything with ocean animals on it. Dolphins, jellyfish, sea turtles. And of course, the alligator and the kite, because those were our things. They still feel like ours."

I smiled, but it trembled at the edges.

We sat. Same couch. The same two people who were bleeding on the tile twelve hours ago. Only now we were dressed, stitched, and raw in a different way.

"Tell me more about her," he said.

I nodded. "She hates naps. Talks to shells on the beach like they are secret agents. Her favorite word is no. She uses it like a punctuation mark. And she has this way of asking the same question seven different ways just to see if I will break."

He grinned, wide and crooked. "Definitely my kid."

"She knows all the ocean animals by heart. Her room is full of fish and mermaids. She calls manatees sea potatoes."

He chuckled, low and worn. "That is valid."

"She has this ritual where she lines up all her bath toys in a very specific order, and God help you if you move one."

"Chaos toddler."

"Exactly."

He rubbed his hands along his thighs. Still nervous. Still trembling beneath the surface.

347

"What else?" he whispered. "What is her laugh like?"

"Like bubbles and trouble," I said.

He smiled like he had just heard his favorite song in a stranger's car.

"And does she know who I am?"

I took a second. Then nodded. "Yes."

Without thinking, I turned and disappeared into my bedroom. A moment later, I returned with a photo clutched in my hand—the one from the boardwalk that summer. I handed it to him, silent.

He took it carefully, eyes scanning the image, locking onto the younger versions of us, sun-drenched and smiling like the world had not fallen apart yet.

He nodded. Jaw tight. Eyes glassy.

Then came a soft shuffle from down the hallway. Tiny feet. A door creaking open.

I froze.

He turned toward the sound like it was a miracle.

And then she appeared. Bedhead tangled, holding a blue whale in one hand, rubbing her eye with the other.

Elijah knelt like someone dropped the gravity in the room, and he was obeying it.

She saw him. Blinked. Looked at me.

She tugged on my shirt and pointed, her brow furrowed in that curious toddler way.

"Who dat?"

I swallowed a lump the size of Florida. I crouched to her level. "That is your daddy, baby."

She looked back at him. Then stepped closer. Head tilted. Studying him like a sea creature she had not seen before.

He knelt lower. "Hi, Isla," he said. "I brought you a gator."

She stared at him. Then at the stuffed alligator.

"Who dat?" she asked, pointing at the gator.

He stammered. "Uh, I did not name him."

She hugged the stuffed gator tightly, rocking on her heels as she stared at it with delight. "Pickle," she announced with toddler certainty.

Elijah chuckled, voice catching. "Pickle it is." Verdict rendered. No appeal.

She looked up at him, eyes wide with curiosity. She scrunched her eyebrows at him. He scrunched back without thinking. Same face. My chest hurt.

He showed her the rolled-up kite. "I brought this too. It is a kite. You know what that is?"

She stared at him, wide-eyed, not quite understanding.

He crouched lower. "It goes up in the sky. Like this." He lifted the rolled-up kite and mimicked it flying with a whooshing sound, his hand sailing through the air.

She watched him, silent for a beat, then looked down at Pickle and hugged him tighter, clearly more interested in her new friend than in his animated explanation.

Elijah smiled under his breath. "Okay," he murmured. "Maybe later." He exhaled like he had been holding his breath for years.

Then she wandered toward the kitchen like she had known him forever.

Elijah was still on his knees, staring like he had just met his whole world.

I sat beside him. He did not look away from her, his eyes tracing every movement like he was trying to memorize her.

"I missed everything," he whispered, the words cracking as they left his mouth.

I exhaled, shaky. "You get this now. She is still little. There is time."

He nodded slowly, like it hurt. Like agreeing meant admitting all the years he lost.

"I was not there when she cried for the first time," he murmured. "Or when she took her first steps. Or said her first word. I missed her birthday. Her first laugh. I missed her whole beginning."

I rested my hand lightly over his. "She is not going to remember what you missed. She is going to remember when you were here."

He did not answer right away. Just stared at our hands like he was afraid they might vanish. His breath hitched. He rubbed his palms on his jeans, like he was trying to scrub off guilt that would not lift.

"I do not know how to be this," he finally said, voice raw. "What if I mess her up? What if I do not know what the hell I am doing? What if I turn into him?"

My throat tightened. I knew who he meant.

"You will not," I said, firm but quiet. "You are already nothing like him."

He clenched his jaw. Shook his head. "You did not see what I saw growing up. You did not hear the things he said, the way he slammed every door. I have spent my whole life running from becoming him, and now I am standing here, terrified I might not be any better."

"You showed up," I said. "You are here. And she does not need perfect. She needs you."

He looked at me, really looked at me, and something crumbled. He pressed his hand over mine again, tight, like he was anchoring himself.

"I want to be good," he whispered. "For her."

"You will be." I held his gaze. "But I need one thing."

351

His eyes lifted. "Name it."

"I do not need perfect," I told him. "I need consistent. Show up when you say you will. That is the rule."

He nodded once, like it landed where it should. Not a favor. A vow.

Across the room, Isla climbed onto a dining chair and kicked her heels against the rung. Elijah stood and drifted toward the Target bag, pulling out a tiny T-shirt covered in jellyfish. He fumbled with the crinkly tag, thumbs clumsy. It made my throat ache.

"What is her size again?" he asked, squinting at the label.

"Three T," I said, and he grinned at himself like he had just passed a test.

He dug deeper and pulled out the kite again. The plastic clip at the tail snagged the ribbon, and he fought it for a moment, swearing under his breath. I took it from him and unhooked the line. His smile was sheepish and grateful.

A small voice broke the quiet. "Juice."

I moved to the kitchen, grabbed her cup, then paused. Elijah was already there beside me, hand out.

"Can I?" he asked.

I passed him the sippy. He rinsed it, filled it carefully, twisted the lid, tested the seal, then set it on the counter. No big speech. No performance. Just a task, done right.

Isla toddled over, grabbed the cup, and plunked Pickle next to it like they both deserved refreshments. Elijah crouched and lined up her bath toys on the low shelf by the sink in the exact order she preferred—duck, turtle, boat, mermaid. He looked to me for confirmation. I nodded. He smiled, small and real.

Some men bring excuses. He brought a Target bag and sat on the floor.

He glanced up at me, worry and wonder tangled in the same expression. "When can I see her again?"

"Tomorrow," I said. "And the day after. Show up when you say you will."

"I will."

We sat there, knees almost touching, while across the room, Isla hummed to herself and made Pickle dance. The house felt different. Lighter. Not fixed. Not healed. But tilted a few degrees back toward possible.

He missed her beginning.

He does not plan to miss her life.

He does not say goodbye when he leaves. He just looks back once, and it feels like the start of something new.

CHAPTER FORTY-NINE

The house was quiet in a different way now. Not tense. Not loaded. Just still.

He left around noon to shower and came back at six with takeout and nerves. After dinner, he asked if he could put her to bed. I said yes.

Isla curled into Elijah's side as he read her Goodnight Moon like it was something he had done a hundred times. She did not ask where he would be in the morning. She did not cry or cling. She just said, "Night, Daddy," like it was the most normal thing in the world.

He answered, "Night, bug," like he had been practicing it for years and just needed the room to be dark to try it out.

And maybe that hurt the most.

I stood in the hallway, arms crossed tight over my chest, watching from the shadows like I was not sure I belonged in this scene.

When he kissed the top of her head and whispered something too low to hear, something only meant for her, I had to look away.

Because how was I supposed to protect her from him when that did not sound like a lie?

He stepped into the hallway and eased her door shut. For a second, we just stood there. The space between us was filled with all the words we had not said yet.

"I did not know if I should leave," he said, rubbing the back of his neck. "Or if that would make this weirder."

"It is already weird."

"Fair."

"You can stay," I said. "If you want."

His eyes met mine. "Do you want me to?"

Loaded question.

"I do not know," I said honestly. "But you are here. I guess that counts for something."

He nodded slowly, careful not to push. "I will take the couch."

I did not argue.

I went to my room and sat on the edge of the bed until the silence felt itchy under my skin.

The front door creaked, and my whole body locked. What if he left? What if this was it again? The door, the silence, and then nothing.

The door closed. Footsteps. The soft pad of bare feet on tile.

Relief hit so hard it made me dizzy.

I picked up an extra blanket and stepped into the hallway.

The bathroom light was on.

The door was cracked.

I should have turned around. I did not.

Through the steam, I saw his silhouette. Water running over his back. One hand pressed to the tile like he was holding himself up. His head bowed. His shoulders slumped. The mirror was fogged, a single clean handprint sliding down.

He looked broken.

That hurt worse than anger ever did.

I was back on my bed before he got out of the shower, pretending to read my phone, pretending I had not seen him that raw.

He knocked once and peeked in. Hair damp. Black T-shirt. Joggers. Face flushed from the heat.

"I keep a bag in the truck," he said when he caught me looking. "Work makes me live out of it more often than not."

I nodded too quickly. "Makes sense."

"Can I sit?"

I motioned to the edge of the bed. "Sure."

He sat. We did not speak.

A minute. Two. Five.

"I did not stay away because I did not care," he said at last. "I need you to know that."

I looked over. "Then why did you?"

He exhaled through his nose. "Because I did not think I was allowed to come back."

"You left without a word, Elijah."

"I know."

"You left me bleeding in more ways than one."

His shoulders dropped. "I know."

"And I looked for you. Not because I needed saving. Because I needed closure."

"I was scared," he said. "Of what I would say. What I would do. Of ruining whatever was left of you."

"You do not get to decide what ruins me."

That hung there like a slap.

He did not flinch. "I have thought about you a lot."

My throat burned.

"I did not know about her," he added. "If I had—"

"I know."

"I would have come back. For you. For her. Even if you hated me."

I looked down at my hands. "She was born in March. The air smelled like rain. I wanted you there so badly I almost called the hospital operator just to scream your name into the wind."

He looked punched.

"I deserved that," he said.

"Maybe."

Silence again.

"I do not know how to be a dad," he admitted.

"You show up," I said.

He nodded, slow. "I will try. Every day. If you let me."

Something cracked inside me. Not forgiveness. Not peace. A step. A small bridge in the rubble.

"Are you still with her?" I asked.

His jaw clenched. "No. I was. Not like that. Not after the other day. I have not called her back. I will not."

"I am not asking because I care who you date or marry," I said. "I am saying it because Isla is my priority. I do not want Sarah around her. Not ever."

His head snapped toward me. "She will not be. I swear. I am done. No more taking her back. No more excuses."

"She will not go quietly."

"She can scream all she wants," he muttered. "I am not listening."

Silence again, but it did not suffocate. It just hung there, open.

"We are not going to be together," I said. My voice shook from exhaustion, not uncertainty. "Whatever this is, it is for Isla. That is all."

He nodded, and I kept going.

"There were nights I did not want to wake up. At night, I held her and cried until I could not breathe, and all I wanted was for you to walk through the door and hold me too. You did not. You were with her."

His face went pale.

"I will never forget the way you walked out of that condo when I was seventeen," I said. "You left me on the floor and walked out with Sarah. I do not know if I will ever get those pieces back. Not from then. Not from the hotel."

He stared at his hands. "I did not know what I was doing. Girls wanted me. I was used to that. Sometimes I told myself you were just another one who would get over it. Then there were nights with you when everything felt different. Like we could be something real."

He rubbed his palms together. "I did not know what to do with that. I did not know how to be someone who stayed. I was so messed up, I did not know what love was, so how could I know what you felt? Or what I was allowed to feel back. When it felt real, I panicked. I ran. I picked the chaos I understood over the calm I did not know how to live in."

"You mattered more than anything," I said. "You still do. That is the problem."

The silence turned jagged.

"We are broken," I whispered.

"Yeah," he said, voice cracked. "But maybe we can be better for her. Even if we never fix ourselves."

"Are you leaving in the morning?"

He turned his head, and his profile cut in the dark. "I do not know yet. Do you want me to?"

"That is not what I asked."

He sighed. "Then no. Not unless you tell me to. I am not running this time."

"So what does this look like now?"

"I do not know," he said after a beat. "Day by day. Even if it is awkward. Even if it is hard. Even if it is just for Isla."

"I am scared," I said.

"Me too."

"I took some time off," he added. "A few days. Then I have to go to work. Out of town. Weeks at a time sometimes. I will come back as soon as I can."

"So this will be off and on."

"Maybe. Not emotionally. I will be here for her, even if I am not sleeping under this roof."

I did not feel angry. Just tired.

"I am here now," he said. "That is what I can give you tonight."

"I am tired," I said, standing.

He looked unsure.

"You can stay in here," I added, motioning to the bed. "If you want."

"I can take the couch."

"I know. You do not have to."

He paused, then nodded. "I will stay on my side."

I slid under the blanket and kept my back to him as he settled on the other side. We did not speak.

We lay there, breathing. Quiet. Rigid.

The mattress felt too small for the space between us. Every shift and exhale echoed.

I felt his presence like static.

We were both afraid to be the first one to fall asleep.

We lay in the dark like two ghosts learning to haunt each other gently.

For the first time in years, I did not feel alone.

Just scared.

His hand brushed mine under the blanket. Not grabbing. Not pulling. Just there.

I did not move.

Seconds passed.

I turned my hand over and laced my fingers through his.

He squeezed once.

Neither of us spoke. He did not let go.

His thumb drew a slow line across the back of my hand. A steady rhythm. Comfort. Reassurance. Maybe even an apology.

Tomorrow, the real world will crash in again.

Tonight, we just breathed.

And neither of us ran.

CHAPTER FIFTY

The sound that woke me was not loud.

It was soft. Familiar. The rhythmic thud of tiny feet on tile, then the creak of a door pushing open.

I blinked against the thin morning light cutting through the blinds.

Isla stood in the doorway, curls a full riot, clinging to the fuzzy stuffed alligator she refused to sleep without. Her thumb was halfway to her mouth when she noticed Elijah lying behind me.

She did not say anything. Her eyes just widened.

"Hey, baby," I whispered, brushing hair from my face.

She padded over, climbed up with zero hesitation, and wriggled between us like she had done it a thousand times.

Elijah stirred when her hand touched his arm. Confusion flashed. Then he saw her.

Something unspoken shifted.

He did not speak. He just looked at her like she was a fragile miracle he had no right to witness. She rested her palm on his chest and hummed, curling in like it was the most natural thing in the world.

He looked at me.

I could not breathe.

"Is this okay?" he whispered.

I nodded, throat burning.

For the first time, I saw it. Not just the guilt or the regret, but the want. He wanted to know her. Be with her. Protect her. I was terrified it was too late.

We lay there in silence, all three of us, the weight of reality heavier than Isla's arm on my ribs.

His phone buzzed.

Once.

Twice.

A third time.

He did not move at first. His jaw tightened.

I looked over. The screen lit on the nightstand.

Sarah.

I said nothing.

It flashed again.

SARAH: 8 MISSED CALLS.

Then a voicemail notification.

He reached for the phone, stared at it like it might explode, and set it face down.

I slipped out of bed.

"Victoria," he said, sitting up fast.

"Do not. Just do not."

He followed me into the hallway, phone still in his hand.

"She will not stop," he said, frustrated. "She is calling because I did not answer yesterday. I told her it was over. I told her to leave me alone."

"And she just happened to call the morning after you slept in my bed?"

He flinched. "No. It is not like that. I have not spoken to her since I left."

"Do you get that it does not matter? Seeing her name light up your phone like an alarm ruins this."

He did not respond.

"You can block her," I said.

"I will."

I stared at him. "You will. God, Elijah. You married her. You do not get to shrug this off like she is some random girl from your past. She is your wife."

His face paled. "It is not like that. We have been—"

"Do not." My voice cracked. "Do not stand in my hallway, in my house, after sleeping next to our daughter, and pretend this is not complicated. You married her. You picked her. You stayed with her while I raised our daughter alone."

He lifted his head, something sharper behind his eyes. "You raised her alone because you chose to. Do not put that all on me.

365

You could have found me if you really wanted to. You knew who I was. You knew where I came from."

I froze.

"You think I did not want to?" I hissed. "You think I did not wake up every day praying you would come back first, so I did not have to chase someone who already left me bleeding?"

He did not flinch.

"No," he said, cold. "I think you liked playing the victim. You made me the villain so you would not have to admit you never even tried. You let me become the ghost, Victoria. Now you are mad I haunt you."

That broke something. Because it was not entirely wrong, and he knew it.

"You are unbelievable," I snapped. "You act like I owed it to you to chase you down after you left me on the floor and walked out with her. Or the time you left me in bed with a note on the nightstand. You think I was supposed to track you down and beg? While I was eighteen, alone, pregnant, and trying not to fall apart every time someone said your name?"

"I think you wanted to be the only one hurting," he shot back. "You wrapped your pain around yourself like armor and decided no one else was allowed to be wrecked too. You think it did not kill me to walk away? To wonder if I made the biggest mistake of my life every single day?"

"You did make the biggest mistake of your life. Now you want a gold star for regretting it?"

"I want a chance to fix it. You will not let me try."

"Because I do not know who the hell you are anymore," I yelled. "You are not the boy I loved. You are not the one I gave my heart to. That version of you died the day you chose her."

His jaw clenched. "Maybe you are not the girl I fell for either. Maybe we are strangers now. We still made a kid together. We still owe her something."

"I owe her everything," I said. "Which is why I cannot let you walk in and pretend time did not pass without you."

"I am not pretending," he said, voice hardening. "I am trying to catch up before it is too late. I will not be like my parents. You do not get to decide that."

"No? And you do not get to rewrite history because you feel bad now," I snapped. "You do not get to play house like the last two years did not happen."

"I am not playing anything," he growled. "I am showing up now. You are punishing me for every minute I did not."

"Because those minutes broke me," I shouted. "While you were out there building some fake life with her, I was here. Carrying it. Alone. Every diaper, every fever, every tear. Mine. You do not get to breeze back in and call that catching up."

"And what, you want me to grovel forever? Crawl across glass for a sliver of trust?"

"Maybe I do," I said. "You made your choice. I had to live with it. Maybe you get to live with what it costs."

He looked at me like he did not recognize me.

"I am trying," he said again, quieter but still edged. "God, I am trying. You do not want that. You want me punished. Maybe I deserve it. But do not lie and say this is only about Isla. You are angry because it still matters. Because I still matter."

Fury collided with heartbreak in my chest.

"Do not flatter yourself," I said, but my voice shook.

He raked a hand through his hair. "I will get breakfast. For Isla. Give you a minute."

He grabbed his keys, opened the door, and left like he could not stand the air around me.

I stood there, listening to the door slam. Listening to nothing at all.

I did not chase him.

Not this time.

I slid down the wall to the floor and pressed my palms to my eyes.

Maybe he was right.

Maybe I was not just angry.

Maybe I was scared.

Scared that if I let him back in, I would not survive it if he left again.

As the quiet stretched around me like a wound, I realized something worse.

I wanted him to come back.

I did not know if I would let him in even if he did.

CHAPTER FIFTY-ONE

The minutes ticked by like hours.

The house felt colder without him in it. Isla's quiet breathing from the other room was the only proof that the world had not ended.

But I did not know if I would let him in even if he did try to come back.

I wandered the kitchen like a ghost. Opened the fridge. Closed it. Poured coffee. I did not drink it. Every sound felt too loud. Every shadow reminded me of him.

His toothbrush still sat on the counter. His duffel bag was by the door. I should have thrown it outside. I almost did.

I picked up my phone more times than I could count. Just to check. Just to see.

Nothing.

No call. No text. No I'm sorry.

And that silence gutted me worse than the yelling.

Because deep down, some part of me believed that if he left again, he would stay gone.

And this time, I did not know if I would survive it.

The day dragged.

Isla was restless, maybe because I was. She toddled around the living room, clutching her gator and pointing to the door every few minutes like she expected it to open. Like she expected him.

She pulled at his bag once. Tried to unzip it. Sat beside it like it was a toy. I could not take it. I moved it to the closet and shut the door.

She did not cry, but she kept checking. Kept glancing toward the hallway like she knew something was missing. Like she could feel the fracture in the air.

By night, I was raw. Strung out on hope and spite.

I told myself I did not care. I did not need him.

I still had not eaten. Still had not changed out of the shirt I slept in. Still had not erased the way his voice sounded when he said he was trying.

He said he would come back with food.

He did not come back at all.

I put Isla down early. She did not protest. She just clung to me a little longer than usual before rolling over, thumb in her mouth.

When the house went quiet again, I stood in the middle of the living room and realized I was waiting.

Waiting for headlights.

For the knock at the door.

For something that never came.

By midnight, I finally turned off the lights. Not because I was tired, but because the shadows looked less empty than the room with them on.

I crawled into bed with a weight in my chest so thick it hurt to breathe.

The pillow still smelled like him. Like citrus and storm.

I flipped it over.

Then back again.

I hated him.

I missed him.

I wanted to scream, but I did not want to wake Isla.

Instead, I stared at the ceiling until my eyes burned.

When sleep came, it was not rest.

It was a surrender.

Temporary.

Fragile.

CHAPTER FIFTY-TWO

When I woke up, the silence had not changed.

Elijah still wasn't back.

I moved on autopilot the next morning. Dressed Isla in an outfit from the dryer. Brushed her curls into something less chaotic. Poured dry cereal into a cup and handed her a juice box.

She kept looking at the door.

So did I.

The daycare drop-off blurred. The woman at the desk smiled like everything was normal. Like I wasn't unraveling from the inside out.

At work, I filed reports. Answered emails. Stared at the same spreadsheet for fifteen minutes without typing anything.

People talked to me. I smiled back. Said things like yeah and totally, and I'll get that to you by the end of the day.

I didn't remember any of it.

By the time I got back to the house, the sun was already low.

I stopped for takeout on the way. Something quick. Easy. I wasn't hungry, but Isla had to eat. She babbled from the back seat the whole ride home, kicking her feet and singing to herself like nothing in the world was broken.

I wished I could join her in that kind of peace.

At home, I unlocked the door with a sigh that shook something loose in my chest. The lights were off. Everything still in its place, including the Elijah-shaped absence.

I carried the food to the kitchen, got Isla into her highchair, and turned on a cartoon she liked just to fill the space with sound.

I set her tray in front of her. She squealed and dug in with her hands, totally content.

I sat at the table with my takeout and stared at it.

Tried a bite. Didn't taste it.

And then.

A knock at the door.

I froze. My heart slammed against my ribs like it wanted out.

I stood slowly, my chair scraping the tile, and crossed the living room with shaking hands.

When I opened the door, Elijah was standing there. Hair a mess, keys in hand, like he didn't know if he was supposed to knock or run.

The quiet exploded inside me all over again.

He opened his mouth, but nothing came out. Just a shaky exhale.

"I didn't know if you would answer," he said finally.

"Then why knock?"

"Because I didn't want to walk away again."

My hand tightened on the knob. "You kind of already did that."

He flinched. Barely. I saw it.

"I shouldn't have left like that," he said. "I needed time."

"Time?" I barked a humorless laugh. "You said you were going to get breakfast, Elijah. Not disappear for two days."

"I know. I panicked."

"Panicked," I echoed, blinking hard. "Must be nice. Just leaving when things get hard."

He looked down. "That's not what I meant."

"No, I think it is."

Behind me, Isla's show filtered through the house. Soft voices. Cheerful music. The clatter of her tray.

"You left," I said, quieter now. "Again. And I spent the last forty-eight hours convincing myself it was better this way."

He looked up at me. "Was it?"

I hated him for asking that.

I hated myself for not having an answer.

I stepped back and motioned him in. "She's eating. Don't keep her waiting."

He stepped in cautiously, like the floor might give out. He set his keys on the counter like they weighed a hundred pounds.

Isla spotted him first. She lit up instantly, legs kicking, a little squeal escaping her lips.

Elijah paused like the sound physically hit him. Then he crossed to her and knelt beside the highchair, brushing his hand gently over her curls.

"Hey, baby girl," he whispered. "You miss me?"

She grinned around a mouthful of chicken nugget and reached out with sticky hands.

My throat burned.

I turned away. Cleaned an already clean counter. Anything to keep from watching him be the father he could have been all along.

"Victoria."

I didn't turn.

"I'm not good at this," he said. "Any of this. I never learned how to stay when it mattered. I'm trying to figure it out, but I mess it up. Every time."

I turned slowly. "And what do you want me to do with that, Elijah? Pat you on the back? Tell you it's okay that you vanished for two days without a word?"

"No." His voice was thick now. Raw. "I want you to see that I came back."

I stared at him. At the circles under his eyes. The wrinkled shirt. The way his fingers trembled as he held Isla's hand.

"Coming back isn't enough."

"I know."

"I needed you," I said. "I needed you when I was throwing up every morning alone. When I was figuring out how to work and take care of a newborn. When I was so sleep-deprived I forgot what my own name sounded like."

He stood still, absorbing every word like a punch.

"I needed you when I stopped recognizing myself in the mirror," I whispered. "And I hated you for every second you weren't here."

His mouth opened, but he didn't speak.

Isla dropped her juice box. The sound snapped us both out of it.

"I'll get it," he said softly, crouching to grab it.

I stepped aside. Gave him space. The ache didn't.

"I don't trust you," I said quietly, arms crossing.

"I know," he said. "But I want to earn that back. Even if it takes years."

"You can start by giving her a bath. It's almost bedtime."

He blinked. "A bath?"

"You know, water, bubbles, little plastic duck. Very advanced parenting."

"Victoria." He rubbed the back of his neck, unraveling. "I don't. I've never bathed a toddler before. What if I do it wrong? What if I hurt her or—"

"You can wrestle gators and jump into swamps," I cut in, a laugh that wasn't funny. "But bathing a two-year-old is where you draw the line?"

His face twisted, half-ashamed, half-amused. "Point taken."

"She likes the yellow cup. Use that to rinse her hair. Not the purple one. She throws that one."

He nodded like I'd handed him nuclear codes.

We moved through the rest of the evening like we were learning to breathe underwater. He followed me to the bathroom while I ran the tub. I handed him the baby shampoo, the washcloth, and the towel with little bear ears. He knelt beside the tub like it was sacred.

When I handed Isla over, she giggled and kicked, splashing both of us.

"She isn't glass," I muttered.

"I feel like she is," he whispered.

He washed her hair carefully, let her play with the bubbles, and held her like she might vanish if he blinked. When she splashed his shirt, he smiled like it was the first real thing he'd felt all day.

We dried her off together. Pajamas. The pink ones with little alligators. She tugged at her bedtime book. Elijah sat on the edge of the bed while I read, his eyes on Isla the whole time, like he was memorizing her.

When her thumb found her mouth and her breathing slowed, he stood frozen, watching like he couldn't move.

"She's okay," I said quietly.

He nodded once. "Because of you."

I didn't answer. I turned off the light and walked out.

He followed.

For the first time in two years, it felt like maybe we were doing something right.

We didn't talk down the hall.

My room was darker than I remembered, shadows curling in the corners. I flipped the switch. Warm yellow light flooded the space.

Elijah stood just inside the doorway like he wasn't sure he was allowed in.

"You can use the shower," I said quietly. "If you want."

He let out a breath, low and hoarse. "Yeah. I probably should."

"Towels are under the sink. Your bag is still in the closet by the door."

He didn't move.

"Elijah," I said, finally meeting his eyes.

He looked like he'd been holding his breath for two years.

"Can I stay?"

The question cracked through me, jagged and dangerous.

"Yes."

Just that. Yes.

He disappeared down the hall, and I sat on the edge of the bed trying to remember how to breathe. I didn't know what tonight was supposed to be. I just knew something was about to change.

The water ran for a while.

When he came back, his hair was damp, curls falling over his forehead. Black basketball shorts hanging low on his hips. Eyes like they hadn't closed in weeks.

He stood there, bare feet on my floor, like a ghost that had finally come home.

"I didn't know what to do," he said.

"With Isla?" I asked.

"With you."

That shut me up.

"I tried to hate you," he whispered. "Tried like hell. It never stuck."

My voice barely existed. "Then why didn't you come back?"

He looked down at his hands. "Because I was living in a cage and convincing myself it was a home."

My breath caught.

"She made sure I couldn't leave," he said, voice shaking. "Every time I tried, she broke something. A plate. A lie. Me."

"Elijah," I whispered.

"She went through my phone. Faked panic attacks if I didn't answer right away. Said she was pregnant, then said she lost it, then said she lied about losing it, then said it was never mine. I still don't know which version is real."

I covered my mouth.

"She told everyone I was abusive. Screamed so loud once the cops showed up. I hadn't even touched her."

His jaw clenched. "And I stayed. Because I was scared I'd never get out clean. Because she said if I left, she'd ruin me."

He paced, memories spilling. "I never understood her hold on me. She was always with someone else. Every time I left. Someone would tell me she was off with a new guy. A coworker. A neighbor. A guy at the bar."

He laughed without humor. "My dad went to a strip club once and saw her there. Said she was dancing under a fake name like nothing had happened. Like she hadn't spent the week screaming at me and threatening to kill herself if I left."

He shook his head. "She got that job for attention. Or revenge. I didn't even know."

I didn't realize I was crying until he stepped forward and brushed a tear from my cheek.

"She was never just crazy," he whispered. "She was calculated. And I was too tired to fight."

My voice cracked. "So how do you leave her now? How are you around Isla and keep her safe?"

I swallowed, chest tight. "I'm not just scared you'll leave again. I'm scared you'll bring all that chaos with you. That it will find my daughter. And she'll be the one who ends up hurt."

"I saw Isla's face," he said, his hand warm on my cheek. "And I knew I couldn't survive another night pretending I didn't have something worth saving."

"Does she know you're here?" I asked, voice shaking. "Are you in town?"

He hesitated. "She knows I left. She doesn't know where I went."

"How do you know she won't find out? Elijah, how are you keeping her away?"

My voice broke. "She sounds unhinged. What if she follows you? What if she shows up here?"

He sighed, rubbing his neck. "I won't answer her. I told the landlord I'm breaking the lease. I left no clues. She doesn't know where I'm staying or who I'm with. She'd never go to my dad for answers. She knows he hates her."

My stomach twisted. "That isn't a long-term plan. She won't just let you go."

"I know," he said, shame and exhaustion flooding his face. "But I had to start somewhere. I had to choose something that wasn't her. Even if I don't have it figured out yet."

"You'd better figure it out fast," I said. "Because I'm not putting Isla in danger. I need to know she's safe. I don't want any drama around my child."

He nodded, jaw tight. "Our child. You know she belongs to me, too, right?"

I crossed my arms, heart racing. "She might share your blood, but you haven't been here, Elijah. For two years, it's been me."

His jaw clenched. "Don't act like she's only yours."

"I'm not acting like anything. I'm protecting her."

He stepped forward, eyes dark. "You wouldn't even have a child to protect if I hadn't given her to you."

The words hit like a slap. He looked as shocked as I was, but he didn't take them back.

"Wow," I whispered. "You really want to go there?"

"Yeah, I do," he snapped. "Because I'm sick of standing here like I'm some stranger who knocked you up and disappeared."

Tears burned hot now. Not sadness. Rage. "You did disappear. You left me to raise her alone while you played house with a psychopath."

"I didn't play house," he bit out. "I survived in it. There's a difference."

"You think I didn't survive, too? You think carrying your baby while the whole town whispered wasn't survival? You think sitting alone in a hospital room, pushing out your child while you were God knows where, wasn't survival?"

His face twisted. "Don't you dare make this like I chose to be gone. I didn't get to be there. I was buried under a woman who blackmailed me, gaslit me, isolated me, and made me question my sanity."

"But you stayed," I shouted, stepping into him now. "You stayed. While I was bleeding and scared and trying to figure out how to raise a child who looks just like you, you let her crawl inside your head and shut every door."

His jaw flexed.

"You didn't come for me," I said, lower now. Broken. "You didn't come for her."

He dragged both hands through his hair like he could tear the guilt out by the roots. "I know. I know I messed up. But don't erase me. Don't act like I don't matter. She's mine too."

"Then act like it," I snapped. "Fight for her. Not with me. Not when it's convenient. Show up. Stay. Prove me wrong."

His chest rose and fell like he'd taken a blow. For a second, I thought he might yell. Or leave. Or explode.

Instead, he whispered, "I don't know how to be what she needs."

"Then learn," I whispered back. "Because she isn't waiting. And I'm not doing this halfway."

The tension in his shoulders eased. Something softer slipped through.

"Let me stay with her tomorrow," he said suddenly. "While you're at work. Just for the day. Let me try. Let me see what it feels like to be around her. To be responsible for her."

My instinct was immediate. I shook my head. "No. That's too soon. You don't know her schedule, her food, her moods."

"Then teach me," he cut in, firm but not angry. "I'm not asking to be her full-time dad tomorrow. I'm asking for a chance. Just a few hours."

I hesitated, arms locked across my chest.

"I get it," he said, quieter. "You're scared. I'd be scared too. But she's my kid. I won't let anything happen to her. Not on my watch."

I searched his face for cracks. "If she gets even a bruise."

"I'll call you before she hits the floor," he said. "I swear it."

"She's picky about food. She doesn't like loud noises. If she doesn't nap, she turns into a demon."

He smiled, barely. "So, she's already like you. Noted."

I rolled my eyes but didn't argue. "Fine. One trial run. Tomorrow. If she looks overwhelmed, it's over."

"Deal." He held my gaze. "You won't regret it."

The silence that followed felt different. Like we were no longer on opposite sides. Like maybe, for the first time, we were starting to parent from the same page.

The tension still pulsed under the surface.

"Are we stopping here tonight?" he asked, voice low. "Just talking about Isla?"

"I don't know," I said. "Should we?"

His eyes dropped to my mouth. "Depends. If I kiss you, will you let me? Or will you hate me for it?"

I didn't answer. I didn't know.

He took one step closer. Just one.

I didn't move.

"I don't want to do something stupid," he said, quiet but raw. "But I can't walk out of this room pretending I don't still feel you everywhere."

"Then don't walk out," I said.

He crossed the space in two strides.

His hands didn't grab. They hovered until I tilted my face up and nodded once.

Then he kissed me.

Soft. Slow. Barely there at first, like he was afraid I might vanish if he moved too fast. His lips brushed mine like a memory, like a question.

I kissed him back just as slowly.

No urgency. No fire. Just heat. A low burn that simmered in the silence while his hand cupped my face and his thumb swept under my jaw, anchoring me.

He walked me backward, steady, until the backs of my knees hit the bed. He didn't ask again. He didn't need to.

I was already peeling my shirt off when he dropped to his knees.

His hands slid up my thighs, thumbs dragging under the waistband of my shorts. "Can I taste you?" he asked, voice rough, almost reverent.

"Yes," I whispered.

He didn't wait. He pulled them down, slowly and deliberate, watching my face the entire time. When he leaned in, his mouth was hot and unrelenting, tongue flicking and sucking like he knew exactly how to break me apart.

My fingers threaded through his hair. I anchored myself to the only thing that felt real.

"Fuck," I gasped, hips arching.

He groaned against me like the sound of me falling apart was something he needed. "I almost forgot how good you tasted," he whispered, thick with hunger and awe.

When I came, loud and shaking, thighs trembling around his head, he didn't stop. He kissed up my stomach, dragging his mouth along every inch of skin until he hovered above me.

I tugged at his shorts. "I want to feel you," I breathed.

He yanked them down. God, I forgot how much I missed this, missed him. Thick and heavy and already leaking for me.

He lined himself up, eyes locked on mine. "Say it."

"I want you inside me," I said, raw and needy. "Now."

He gripped himself and ran the head of his cock slowly through my slick, dragging up and down like he was studying every part of me with the tip. He watched it glide through the wetness, paused to press against my entrance just enough to make me gasp, then pulled away again.

"Look how ready you are for me," he murmured. "I almost don't want to ruin it."

I writhed, hips arching. "Elijah."

He didn't let up. He rubbed along me again, slow and deliberate, teasing my clit before circling my opening once more.

"You feel that?" he whispered. "That's mine. Every inch of you."

Finally, with one slow, aching thrust, he slid inside.

We both groaned like it was the first breath after drowning.

He moved slowly at first, grinding deep, each thrust dragging moans out of me like confessions. Then faster. Harder.

"I'm going to come," I warned, nails digging into his shoulders.

"Then come," he whispered. "Let me feel you lose it on me."

I shattered.

Body clenching. Heart cracking. Lungs begging for air.

His rhythm stuttered. His breath broke. "I'm close," he managed.

"Elijah," I gasped, pulling him deeper. "I'm on birth control."

His eyes searched mine even as he moved. "Tell me what you want."

"Stay," I said. "I want you to stay."

He hovered, breath caught. "Mean it, Vic."

"I do."

He groaned, a sound that cracked something open in my chest, and came inside me, deep and hot and relentless, holding me so tight it felt like he was trying to fuse our bodies together.

For a moment, neither of us moved. We just breathed.

Then he kissed my collarbone. My shoulder. My cheek.

He stayed inside me, forehead pressed to mine, like he didn't want to let go.

And neither did I.

The house was quiet. No cartoons, no clatter, no empty rooms swallowing sound.

There wasn't an Elijah-shaped absence anymore.

There was an Elijah-shaped weight on the bed beside me, warm and real.

And I didn't want it to move.

CHAPTER FIFTY-THREE

Morning came soft and golden.

The kind of light that didn't belong to people like us.

For a second, I didn't remember. The sheets tangled around my legs. The faint smell of him on my skin. The warmth pressed against my back. It all felt like a dream that hadn't decided if it wanted to be good or cruel.

Elijah's arm was draped over my waist, heavy and protective, like muscle memory had taken over before guilt could. His breathing was slow. Deep. Safe.

I stared at the ceiling, half expecting the universe to come crashing through it just to remind me this wasn't real.

Because it couldn't be.

Not after everything.

My body ached in ways that weren't just physical. My heart thudded like it was confused whether to race or rest. I should have felt shame. Or regret. Something sharp. Instead, I felt still.

Dangerously still.

Isla stirred in the monitor on the nightstand, a soft whimper pulling me back to reality.

I slipped out from under his arm carefully, like one wrong move might break whatever fragile peace we'd built last night.

In the kitchen, the air smelled like salt and leftover coffee. I poured myself a cup and stared at the sunrise bleeding through the blinds. Elijah's hoodie hung on the chair. A ghost of normalcy.

He came out a few minutes later, hair damp, shirtless, eyes soft. He made pancakes. Burned the first batch. I laughed quietly before I could stop myself.

For one terrifying moment, it felt like a family.

By the time I had Isla in my arms, rocking her in the early light, the quiet was already shifting.

Last night wasn't forgiveness.

It was a pause between storms.

And I knew when he woke up, we'd have to figure out what came next.

Not just for us.

But for her.

Morning

I paced the condo staring at the ceiling, trying to talk myself out of letting him stay with her. My mind ran every worst-case scenario on a loop like some anxiety-fueled doomsday prepper. What if he didn't feed her enough? What if he lost his temper? What if he got distracted and she wandered outside? What if Sarah showed up?

I hovered like an over-caffeinated helicopter, listing every single thing Elijah already knew because I needed to say it out loud just to feel like I was doing something.

"Her nap is usually around noon, but don't force it. Watch her cues. Her sippy cup is in the cabinet. Don't let her eat the cheese puffs unless you want orange handprints on every wall. And she gets weird about loud noises during cartoons. Don't ask, just keep the volume on eight."

Elijah just stood there calmly, like I wasn't unraveling in front of him. He kept nodding, like he actually gave a damn about cheese puffs and sippy cups.

"You don't have to do this," I muttered again, my hand gripping the doorframe like it could keep me from leaving.

"Yes, I do," he said again.

My chest clenched. I looked at Isla, still in her footie pajamas, tugging on her stuffed bunny like it was any other day. She didn't know her whole world was about to be flipped. Again.

When I finally left, I sat in the car with the engine running for a full ten minutes before pulling out of the driveway.

Mid-Morning

I called. Twice.

Once when I parked at work and again during my first break. Both times, he answered on the first ring.

"She's fine," he said, amused. "We're building a fort. She kept grunting and throwing pillows when I stacked them wrong."

My throat tightened. "She did?"

"Yeah. Dragged one over and shoved it where she wanted it. I think she was showing me how you usually do it."

A dry laugh slipped out. I tried to mask how much it got to me.

"Call me if anything— I mean anything—happens."

"I will."

Afternoon

The third time I called, he didn't answer.

Neither the fourth nor the fifth.

Panic bloomed like a sickness in my chest. My hands shook as I texted:

Me: Everything okay?

Me: Elijah?

Me: Where are you?

No answer came, so I called again.

When the sixth call finally connected, all I heard was him shouting—female voices in the background, shrill and muffled.

"I told you to fucking stop calling me. Are you this fucking delusional? I don't want you. I will never come back. You are done. We are done."

My heart plummeted.

"Elijah?" I said, quietly.

Silence. Then a broken sounding, "Victoria?"

I hung up.

Then I opened his contact, hit Delete, and stared at the confirmation like it might save me.

Five seconds later, hands shaking, I restored it. I couldn't make myself choose.

Evening — Beach Walk

I didn't even want to go. But Isla grabbed her sandals and pointed to the door like it was a command from God. So I packed her up, and Elijah came along because I let him. Barely.

The walk was quiet. Just waves, wind, and the sound of my blood boiling.

"You said you weren't talking to her," I said finally. Not a question. A reminder.

"I wasn't," he said quickly. "I haven't. She's relentless. Calling from new numbers. Texting repeatedly. I lost it. I thought it was her again."

I stopped walking. "You really screamed at me like I was her."

His face fell. "I didn't know it was you. I swear."

"But you still said it. You let her drag you down, and I got to be her punching bag because you didn't check the caller ID."

He tried to reach for me, but I stepped back.

"I threw the phone across the kitchen after I realized. I blocked everything. I swear to God, Victoria, I'm not letting her near either of you again."

Isla shifted in my arms. I kissed the top of her head, trying to stay calm.

"She scares me," I said, quieter. "Not for me. For her. If that woman ever got near my baby, Elijah, I—"

"She won't," he cut in. "I won't let her."

I didn't speak for a long moment. Then, "Are you going to divorce her?"

He flinched.

"Are you going to file? Or are you just going to keep pretending this isn't the mess that it is?"

His jaw tensed. "It's complicated."

I narrowed my eyes. "You think I don't know that? I live complicated. I'm asking if you're going to do better. For you. Not even for me."

He looked away, the ocean wind pulling at his shirt like it was trying to drag him off somewhere else. "I haven't figured that out yet."

Something inside me snapped. "That's your answer? After everything? You still won't cut her off completely?"

He turned back to me, but I was already fuming.

"You came into my house. You held our daughter. You looked me in the eye and said you wanted to be better. But you don't even know if you're going to sign a piece of paper that tells her it's over?"

396

His mouth opened, then shut.

"You want to be a father?" I hissed. "Then act like a man. Because this limbo isn't good for anyone. Especially her."

And then Isla started squirming. She twisted in my arms, reaching toward him, fingers stretched and wiggling. "Dada."

I froze.

It wasn't the first time she had said it. But it was the first time she said it here. The first time around him.

Elijah's whole body stilled. "Can I?"

I hesitated. Then passed her over.

The blue ribbon from the rolled-up kite brushed his wrist as he reached for her, a thin strip of sky between us. She melted into him like she belonged there. Like she knew.

Tears burned the corners of my eyes.

"She doesn't do that with anyone," I whispered.

He looked at me over her head. "She knows."

Maybe she did.

And maybe it scared the hell out of me.

Later That Night

We didn't talk much after the beach.

Isla went down fast, heavy with sleep and sun. I didn't offer Elijah the couch. He didn't ask. He followed me down the hall like he had always belonged there, and when I climbed into bed, he lay down beside me.

Neither of us touched.

The air felt thick. It had things to say but didn't know how.

After a while, I whispered, "So what happens when you go back to work?"

He was quiet for a beat. Then, "I have another job lined up. Out of town again. A couple of weeks at a time. On and off."

My stomach turned. I stared at the ceiling. "And Isla?"

"I want to see her. As much as I can. However I can. I'll FaceTime every day I'm gone. I'll give you my schedule, every hour if you want it, so you know exactly when I can see her when I'm back."

I turned to look at him.

He continued, "You don't have to worry about anything. I'll help with whatever she needs. If you need daycare covered, I'll pay for it. If she needs clothes, toys, or medicine, I'll get them. Or if you want money every week to help out, say the word. I'm not walking away from her, Victoria."

I swallowed hard. "You're going to have to show up, Elijah. Really show up."

"I know."

Another pause.

"Did you tell anyone I'm back?" he asked.

"No."

He looked at me. "No one?"

"Julie. That's it. She's the only one who knows you're the father."

His jaw tightened. "You didn't tell your mom?"

I shook my head. "I didn't tell anyone. I didn't want to answer the questions."

He rolled onto his back, staring at the ceiling like it personally offended him.

"Are you embarrassed by me?" he asked suddenly, voice tight.

"What?"

"Your parents. Your friends. Would they not approve? Is it because I don't come from money? Because I don't have some big shiny life with a family that sends Christmas cards and takes beach vacations together?"

"No," I said quickly, sitting up. "It's not like that. I just kept it to myself."

He turned his head, eyes sharp. "Your mom knows you had a one-night stand, but not that it was me?"

"She knows I got pregnant. That's all. I didn't tell her anything more than that."

"Why?"

I exhaled slowly. "Because I wasn't ready to accept it myself. You were gone. I had no clue if you'd ever show back up, and I didn't want the world to know something I barely had a grip on. Julie knew because I needed one person. Everyone else felt too raw. Too fragile."

He didn't speak. He stared up at the ceiling like he was trying to memorize the cracks.

"Elijah," I said, reaching for his hand.

He didn't pull away, but he didn't squeeze back either.

And just like that, the wall started to go up again.

I hated how familiar it felt.

Later That Night — Continued

The silence between us stretched like barbed wire. Every second that ticked by made it harder to breathe, harder to pretend things weren't unraveling inside me.

He hadn't looked at me since I told him. Since I admitted I kept him a secret.

I hated the way it felt, like he was already gone again.

So I did the only thing I knew how to do. The only thing that ever cut through the noise between us.

I rolled toward him. Let my hand slide across the sheets until it found the warmth of his bare stomach. He didn't move. He didn't even flinch.

"Elijah," I whispered.

Nothing.

I dragged my fingertips lower until I found the waistband of his shorts. Still, he didn't react.

But he wasn't stopping me either.

My hand slipped beneath the fabric. He was already hard.

"You're mad at me," I said softly, wrapping my fingers around him.

He inhaled sharply through his nose.

"I know. But I need you to trust me tonight. Let me take care of it."

He still hadn't looked at me.

So I shifted, pulled the covers back, and slid my hand deeper. I wrapped my fingers around him, hard and waiting, before gently pulling him free. Then I lowered my head.

I kissed the skin just above his waistband. Then lower.

His breath hitched when I took him into my mouth.

Slow. Deep. Intentional.

He still didn't speak, but his hand found my hair. Not guiding, just holding.

I worked him slowly and wet and unhurried, until his breathing changed, until I felt his stomach tense beneath my palm.

Then I pulled away, dragging my tongue up his shaft, watching the way he pulsed against my lips.

"Is it crazy that I never slept with anyone else?" I whispered, dragging my tongue over him. "I never wanted to erase you from my body."

He finally looked at me.

His eyes were wild. Ravenous. Still unsure.

I pulled my shirt over my head and tossed it aside, baring myself to him. Then I swung a leg over and positioned myself above him, lowering until I was straddling him.

I pulled my panties to the side, grinding against him with nothing but soaked friction between us.

He hissed, hands flying to my hips.

"I want you to let go," I whispered. "Let me have you tonight."

His jaw clenched. He didn't stop me.

I dragged the head of his cock up and down my slit, teasing us both, watching his eyes lock on the place our bodies touched.

When I sank down on him, he gasped like he'd been holding his breath since the moment I touched him.

I moved slowly. Torturously. I had never done this before. Never been the one in control like this. I hoped I was moving the way I was supposed to. I hoped he couldn't feel the nerves rattling inside me. Every shift of my hips was careful and shaky with doubt I refused to show. Part of me wanted to ask if it felt good, if I was doing it right. I didn't. I kept going, trying not to think about how experienced he was. I didn't want to compare. I wanted to be enough, right now, like this.

His hands gripped me tighter, but he let me lead for once.

Then one of his hands moved slowly and deliberately. He slid it up between us, over my ribs, then my collarbone, until it reached my mouth. Without a word, he slipped a finger between my lips. I sucked it in slowly, curling my tongue around the pad of his finger, our eyes locked in a silent rhythm. It wasn't just sex. It never was. This was how we spoke when words failed. A language carved in the dark.

He stared at me like I was a religion he was ready to burn for.

I hate that it still feels like home.

"Tell me when," I whispered, low and shaking with control. "When you want me to get off you. When you need me to stop, say it."

Every inch of him inside me lit a fuse under my skin, and I couldn't stop the way my body reacted. The tightening. The ache. Drowning in the fullness of him. I dug my nails into his chest and leaned closer, breath catching.

"I love you," I whispered, the words slipping out like a gasp. Raw. Unfiltered.

I didn't care if it ruined everything. It was the truth, and it had waited long enough.

When I felt him start to lose control, when I felt the way he twitched and throbbed inside me, I knew.

He didn't pull out.

I collapsed forward, bracing my hands on his chest, panting against his neck.

"I told you," I said, breathless and wrecked.

"I know."

His arms wrapped around me like he was afraid I would disappear.

I let him.

Because sometimes loving someone means holding still while the wreckage settles—

just long enough to see what's left standing.

CHAPTER FIFTY-FOUR

It started with a phone call.

Elijah's phone buzzed on the counter. When he answered, I watched from the hallway, arms crossed, already knowing. The way his expression shifted told me everything. His job had finally come through. South Carolina. He would be gone in two days. Three weeks, maybe more.

He didn't say anything right away. He just slid his phone into his back pocket like he didn't know he had just broken the quiet we were pretending wasn't fragile.

"That was work?" I asked.

He nodded, eyes unreadable. "Yeah. I leave Thursday."

"Oh."

Silence stretched between us like old wallpaper peeling at the corners. I waited for him to say more, to explain, to soften the blow. He just stood there.

I sat on the edge of the bed, legs pulled to my chest, while he folded the same shirts and jeans he had worn days ago, clean now, fresh from the dryer. The air between us felt jagged. We had been playing house, pretending the world wasn't waiting to tear it down.

"You weren't planning to stay, were you?" I whispered.

He froze mid-fold, the hoodie heavy in his hands. "What?"

"This was just a break. A pit stop. You were never going to stay."

"I never said that."

"You didn't have to."

He stood up and ran his hand through his hair, frustration flashing behind his eyes. "What do you want me to say, Victoria? You want me to quit? Stay here with nothing figured out and crash on your couch while I sort my life out?"

"No," I said, my voice tighter than I wanted it to be. "I want to know what I am to you. I want to know what we are before I keep letting you sleep in my bed. Before I let you keep holding my daughter."

"Our daughter," he snapped, louder. "She's not just yours."

I flinched, but he wasn't done. He stepped forward, hands clenched at his sides. "Do you even hear yourself? You say your bed. Your daughter. Like I'm some visitor who got a free pass. I'm her dad, Victoria. You have to stop acting like I'm not."

My breath caught. I wanted to bite back and say I was the one here every day, every night. The words jammed in my throat.

"She wouldn't even exist if it weren't for me," he said, voice cracking. "So stop pretending I'm a stranger who doesn't have the right to be in her life."

I swallowed hard, the sting leaving a mark, and forced myself to sit up straighter. "I know," I said, quiet at first. "I know. I'm sorry. I just…"

I looked down at my hands, twisting my fingers until the knuckles went white. "I don't like not knowing what we are. Or how long you'll stay. I don't like feeling out of control. Every time

I think I've figured out how to keep Isla safe, how to keep myself safe, it changes. You show up and it changes again."

He didn't speak. He watched me. I met his eyes, and my voice dropped to something raw. "It's not that I don't want you here. I'm scared to want you too much. And then lose you all over again."

He dragged a hand through his hair and let out a long breath. "Vic, last month, I didn't even know I was a dad. Now I have a daughter, and a ghost from my past has reappeared. I'm still married to a woman I can't stand, and I have legal shit hanging over my head."

His voice cracked. His shoulders sagged. "I'm trying to figure it out. But I need a second to breathe. Just one second to breathe."

The way he said it—like breathing was a luxury—made me realize how much I'd been holding mine too. Maybe we were both drowning, just in different oceans.

I didn't know what to say. I wanted to crawl into his chest and make it all go quiet. All I could do was nod, slow and small.

The room felt too full. Or maybe too empty.

He showed up the next evening, after I got off work, with three garbage bags and a beat-up cardboard box.

"This is it," he muttered, setting them by the door. "Everything I own."

I stood a few feet away, arms crossed. "What are you planning to do with all of it?"

"I'm not staying anywhere long-term," he said. "I was thinking, if it's okay, I could leave my stuff here. Just until I find my own place."

I blinked, caught off guard. "Yeah. I guess that's fine."

He ran a hand over his jaw. "I left all the furniture. Let her do whatever she wants with it. I grabbed the stuff that mattered. Clothes, a couple of things from my mom, and my tools. I wanted to get in and out before she got home. She doesn't even know I was there."

I exhaled slowly. "At least if your stuff is here, I'll know you're coming back."

He looked at me, eyes serious. "I'd come back for my kid either way."

My chest squeezed. I didn't want to be just the place that held his things. I wanted to be the reason he came back. I didn't say it. Not then.

He hesitated at the door, untying the blue ribbon from Isla's kite. He looped it around the inside handle and pulled a small knot. "So you know I'm coming back," he said, barely above a whisper.

I stared at the ribbon fluttering against the wood. I didn't trust my mouth to say anything that wouldn't betray me.

That stupid ribbon broke me more than his goodbye ever could. Hope, tied into a knot I didn't remember agreeing to.

That night, after dinner, he asked if he could help put Isla to bed. I watched from the doorway as she curled against his chest, her tiny fingers tangled in the collar of his shirt. He sang something low and off-key. She didn't care. She was asleep within minutes. He didn't move. He just held her.

When I came back to check, they were both passed out. Her cheek on his shoulder. His head tilted back. Mouth slightly open, like he hadn't slept in weeks. I stood there for a long time, the lump in my throat burning. I didn't wake him. I turned off the lights and left them there.

The second he left, the walls cracked.

I became obsessive. Checking my phone every ten minutes. Refreshing messages that weren't coming. I wasn't okay, and the worst part was pretending I was.

Three nights later, I sat with Logan in his office while Isla napped in the corner playpen.

"She's not going to drop this," I said, watching Logan flip through Sarah's old court records.

"She already has," he said. "She didn't even show. Judge tossed the whole thing."

"She's planning something," I muttered.

"She's unraveling. That's good for us."

Good for us didn't mean safe. People like her didn't fade; they waited.

I wasn't so sure.

When Elijah called that night, I picked up from the kitchen, my voice barely a whisper. "It's over. Logan had it dropped."

"She didn't show?"

"No. Not a word. Nothing."

He exhaled, the sound jagged. "She thinks playing nice will fix it. That if the charges disappear, I'll come running."

"Will you?" I asked too fast.

He paused. "No. But that doesn't mean she won't try harder now."

And she did.

Three more days. That's all it took.

Elijah's messages went from full paragraphs to fragments. Then to one-word replies. Calls stopped coming altogether.

I sat outside the daycare after drop-off, staring at nothing. My chest ached in places I didn't know existed. That night, after putting Isla down, I finally lost it.

I sent him a text:

You're not doing this again. I won't be your in-between. You either come back or don't bother calling again.

No response.

Not until 2 a.m.

I'm trying, Vic. I swear I am. I don't want her. But I feel like I'm buried under everything, and I don't know how to dig out without destroying the pieces I still have left. I don't know who I am right now, and I'm scared I'll mess up everything if I move too fast.

My fingers hovered over the keyboard before I typed back:

Just figure it out.

I rolled over in bed, staring into the dark.

The baby monitor crackled softly.

His bags were still by the door.

The blue ribbon was still on the knob.

And my heart was still with him.

CHAPTER FIFTY-FIVE

The next morning came quietly, but nothing about me felt still.

I moved through the kitchen like a ghost, making Isla's breakfast on autopilot. Toast, blueberries, the exact cup she liked, with the pink straw that couldn't bend. She didn't ask for him. She never did. But her little eyes glanced at the doorway like maybe he would appear there again, like magic. Like last time.

He didn't.

By the time I dropped her at daycare and pulled back into the driveway, I sat in the car for ten minutes just staring at the front door. His bags were still inside. Still untouched. Still daring me to believe.

I didn't.

I walked past them like they weren't there. Like I wasn't dying a little more each time I looked at them. The silence in the house wrapped around me like a warning.

The bathroom light flickered against the mirror; even my reflection looked like it didn't want to be here.

I didn't cry. Not until I was in the shower, head against the tile, mouth open in a silent sob that no one could hear. I didn't cry until the water ran cold. Even then, it didn't feel like enough.

Later that night, Logan texted me.

Logan: You okay?

Me: I don't know how to answer that anymore.

Logan: Want to come by tomorrow? I have a client cancellation at noon.

Me: Maybe.

Logan: Bring Isla if you want. Or don't. Just come.

I stared at the screen for a long time. Then I put my phone down and lay in bed, back to the door, trying to convince myself I didn't care if he walked through it or not.

I was lying.

The next day, I went.

Isla was with my mom, and the office was quiet. Logan handed me coffee without asking how I took it. He knew. He always knew.

"You look like hell," he said lightly.

"Thanks. So do you."

He smiled, then sobered. "You have that look again. The one where you want to burn everything down."

"Maybe I do."

"Vic, have you thought about talking to someone? Really working through your past, not just burying it? I'm not judging. I think it might be time to find a way that actually helps you heal. You've been carrying this for so long. You act like it doesn't touch you, but I see it. It does. Every day."

My mouth opened, then closed. The truth sat heavy in my chest, sharp-edged and splintered.

"I've thought about it," I whispered, voice cracking. "I don't even know where I'd start. How do you talk about things you spent your whole life pretending didn't break you? I also tried the whole talk-and-medication theory when I was younger. It didn't work."

I looked down at my hands, fingers clenched tight around the cup. "I feel like if I let it out now, it'll swallow me whole. And if it doesn't, then what? Then I have to admit I've been carrying it this long for nothing?"

My throat burned. "I don't know how to do this the healthy way, Logan. I never have."

Logan leaned back in his chair, studying me. "I never really understood the thing you two had growing up. It was over as quickly as it started, and yet somehow it never really ended. You held on to something you never even had. Both of you. Like the idea of each other meant more than anything that happened. Maybe it still does."

My throat tightened.

"I think he's scared to come back because part of him thinks he'll mess it up again. If he does, he won't survive it. Not this time."

Logan exhaled slowly and rested his arms on his knees. "I've known Elijah a long time. I knew what his dad was like. How he got when he drank. How Elijah used to show up at my place with bruises he never explained. He never let anyone in, not really. He learned to keep the peace and survive. That kind of pain rewires you. It makes you believe love only exists if you earn it."

He paused, eyes on mine. "Sarah wasn't love. She was something he didn't know how to push away, because part of him thought that was what he deserved. It's not. Deep down, he knows that."

I blinked fast and refused to let the tears fall. "I don't know who I am without him."

Logan sighed, rubbing his hand through his hair. "You love him. I get it. But you can't sit in limbo forever. At some point, you have to decide if you're going to keep hurting yourself with hope or start stitching up the wound."

He paused again. "You know I'm Elijah's friend. I always will be. I'll look out for him where I can. But I care about you, too, Victoria. I want you to be okay. Even if that means walking away. Even if that means choosing yourself."

He reached across the desk, gently squeezing my hand once before letting go. The warmth lingered longer than it should have.

For the first time in days, I let someone's words sink in.

I wasn't ready to let go.

But maybe neither of us had to keep bleeding just to prove we were worthy.

Maybe Elijah didn't have to carry the weight of everyone else's damage to make up for his own.

Maybe I didn't have to keep setting myself on fire and hope someone noticed the smoke.

In the parking lot, the air felt heavy and bright at the same time. I sat in the driver's seat, stared at my cracked screen, and pulled up a list I had saved months ago. Local counseling offices.

I tapped the first number. It rang twice.

"Clearwater Counseling, this is Ana. How can I help you?"

I swallowed, steadied my voice, and said, "Hi. My name is Victoria Drayton. I'd like to set up an appointment."

CHAPTER FIFTY-SIX

The parking lot smells like hot asphalt and old sunscreen. Moms wave. Kids wobble under backpacks. I'm almost at the daycare door when I see her.

Sarah. Leaning against a silver Nissan with a cracked taillight and a smile that doesn't reach her eyes.

My stomach drops. The old heat crawls up my neck. I don't move closer. I don't move back either.

She pushes off the bumper and starts toward me like we're old friends.

"Victoria," she says sweetly. "What a surprise."

"It's pickup time," I say. "Not visiting hours."

Her mouth curves. "You look tired."

"I'm raising a two-year-old."

Her gaze flicks past me to the door. "So, I heard."

I step sideways and block her line of sight. "You're not welcome here."

Her voice lowers. "He's my husband."

I hold her stare. "I'm the mother of his child."

For a second, something mean lights her face. The performative part drops. She steps closer, too close.

"You think a baby makes you special," she whispers. "It makes you easy."

I smile without warmth. "Try another line."

The door clicks behind me. I don't turn. If she thinks Isla is within reach, she'll sink her teeth in.

I text one word to Elijah.

Me: Here.

He replies instantly.

Elijah: Two minutes.

I keep my body between Sarah and the glass.

She circles like a shark that smells blood. "You stole him."

"I didn't steal your husband," I say calmly. "He walked out of your house by himself."

She laughs, bright and fake. "He always comes back."

"Not to you."

Her jaw twitches. "You don't know him like I do."

I tilt my head. "Then why are you out here begging in a daycare parking lot instead of inside a home where he wants to be?"

She flinches, then smiles again. "You can't keep me from him."

"I can keep you from us."

Her eyes sharpen. "Us." She rolls the word like it tastes bad.

She takes another step. I don't give ground. My heart thunders so hard it hurts.

"Back away from the entrance," I say. "Now."

"Or what?" she whispers.

"Or I call the police, and the director walks out with a trespass notice and a witness list."

Her eyes flick left and right. She's measuring the audience, the lobby camera, the teacher holding the door cracked with a phone in her hand, the dad by the minivan pretending not to watch.

The growl of a truck cuts through the heat.

Elijah turns into the lot like he hasn't slept. He kills the engine and crosses the pavement in long strides. Jaw tight. Eyes locked first on Sarah, then on me.

He stops at my shoulder.

His voice is quiet. "You need to leave."

Sarah lets out a shaky laugh. "There he is. My husband finally decided to show his face."

He doesn't look at her ring. He doesn't look at her mouth. He keeps his eyes level. "Not yours. Not anymore."

"You think this is a game," she spits. "You think you can throw away vows because you got bored and knocked up a girl who never stopped fantasizing about you?"

Elijah doesn't move. "I didn't throw anything away. You did."

She sneers. "You're a liar. You always were."

I take my phone out, unlock it, and hit record. The red dot glows.

Sarah notices. "What are you doing?"

"Protecting myself," I say. "And my daughter."

Her voice spikes. "You can't record me."

"We're in a public place," I say softly. "You came to me. Keep your volume down if you don't want an audience."

She takes a breath like she's about to scream. Elijah steps half a pace in front of me. He doesn't touch her. He doesn't touch me. He just plants himself like a wall.

For the first time, I realize he's not fighting me anymore.

"Here's how this goes," he says. "You will not contact Victoria. You will not step on this property again. You will not show up at her home. If you need to speak to me, use counsel."

"Counsel," she mocks. "You found a lawyer who'll hold your hand through a tantrum."

She looks past him at me. "You're proud of this."

"No," I say. "I'm tired."

She snorts. "You think he'll stay. You think you're different."

"I don't think anything," I say.

420

She laughs, high and ragged. "You can't stand there and pretend you're better than me."

"I'm not better," I say. "I'm done."

She goes still. For a beat, I see the moment she decides to try claws instead of words.

Her hand flashes. Elijah catches her wrist midair.

"Don't," he says. Calm. Firm. Final.

She yanks free, the movement jerky, ugly. She looks around again, realizes the lobby door is still cracked and there are eyes on her from every angle.

Her voice drops. "I'll ruin you."

"You already did," I say. "Ruin yourself."

Color floods her cheeks.

Elijah's phone buzzes in his pocket. He ignores it.

Sarah steps in close enough that I can see the smear of mascara at the corner of her eye. Her whisper is acid. "You think he's safe with you. You think he won't crawl back the first time you make him feel small."

I lean in the tiniest bit. "I don't make him feel small. I make him show up."

For a breath, no one speaks. The cicadas scream. A car door thunks. Heat shimmers over the asphalt.

The daycare director pushes the door wider. Her voice is steady. "Ma'am, you need to leave the property. We've already called authorities."

Sarah turns her head. Reads the woman's face. Reads the room. Picks the only door left.

She smiles a knife-edge smile. "He'll call me. He always does."

"No," Elijah says. "He won't."

She stares at him like she can will it true. When it doesn't work, she swallows the fury and pastes on a new face.

"You two deserve each other," she says lightly. "Enjoy your little family, for now."

She pivots on her heel and walks back to the Nissan like she's on a stage. The engine coughs. The car peels out too fast. Gravel spits.

The lot exhales.

I don't. Not yet. My hands are shaking so hard my phone clicks against my palm.

Elijah looks at me. "Are you okay?"

"No," I say honestly. "But I'm upright."

We stand there in the heat. Neither of us moves for the door. Neither of us looks away.

Inside, I hear Isla laugh.

I hit stop on the recording. I save it. I forward it to Logan with two words: For the file.

We sit on the curb like teenagers after detention. I press my palms to my knees and count my breaths.

He rubs his thumb over the scar on his knuckle. "I shouldn't have let that get this far."

"You didn't swing," I say. "You didn't shout. You set a line. That's farther than before."

He watches the glass door like the ocean's behind it.

"I won't let her near you."

"You won't let her near Isla," I say.

His mouth hitches. "Both."

I look down at my shoes. The laces don't match because I tied them in the dark this morning. "She wanted a scene," I say. "We didn't give her a good one."

He huffs a breath. It almost sounds like a laugh.

The director opens the door a few inches. "All clear."

"Thank you," I say.

She nods. "We'll document it." She glances at Elijah. "Nice to see you stand where you should."

He swallows. "I'm trying."

She closes the door again.

Elijah turns to me. "You want me to go in with you?"

"Yes," I say. "But stay behind me."

He nods. "Always."

We walk inside together. The cool air hits my skin. My heartbeat finally starts to settle.

Isla sees us and lights up like sunrise. She shouts "Dada," then "Mama," and the sound knocks something loose in my chest.

He stops a step behind me, like I asked. He waits. He doesn't reach for her until I pick her up and tilt her toward him.

His palms rise. Gentle. Open.

She tips forward into his hands like she's been doing this her whole life.

I feel my throat burn. I swallow it down.

He presses his mouth to her hair. Closes his eyes for a second that's longer than a blink.

When he looks at me, there are a thousand things in his face. All of them are messy. None of them is fake.

"What now?" he asks quietly.

"Now," I say, "we go home."

He nods. No argument. No promises. Just that.

We walk past the lobby camera and out into the heat. The sky is white with sun. The parking lot is empty again.

I buckle Isla in. I stand there for a beat with my hand on the car-seat clip like it's a talisman.

Elijah rounds to the driver's door of his truck. He stops. Looks at me across the roof.

"It's over with her," he says. "I promise."

"Good," is all I manage.

He nods.

I close Isla's door. He gets in his truck. I get in my car.

Before I start the engine, I pull out my phone and open a new note.

I type three sentences.

He stood in front of me. He didn't yell. He said he's done with her.

I read them twice like they're a spell.

Then I drive.

CHAPTER FIFTY-SEVEN

The smell of sleep and something burnt clung to the air. Morning light filtered through the blinds, soft and indifferent, like it hadn't watched my whole world collapse twelve hours ago. The house looked the same, but everything inside it had shifted.

I sat on the edge of my bed, elbows on my knees, staring at the bruises on my knuckles. One of them had split just slightly. Nothing serious. Nothing worth explaining.

A soft whimper floated from the hallway.

"I'm here, baby," I called, voice steady because it had to be.

I met Isla in the hallway and scooped her up, pressing my cheek to her curls. Warm. Solid. Real. She tucked her thumb into her mouth and melted into me, heavy with sleep.

We padded toward the kitchen. I glanced into the living room and saw him. Elijah. Still in jeans. Shirt wrinkled. Curled awkwardly on the couch like he hadn't moved all night. It was cruel how peaceful he looked. I stood there too long, just watching his chest rise and fall. Some part of me wanted him to wake and say something that would make the night disappear.

He didn't.

I set Isla in her booster and handed her a sippy cup while the waffle iron heated. She drummed her palms on the tray and giggled to herself, blissfully unaware that her mother had turned into a monster last night.

I felt like I was watching myself from the ceiling. Crack the eggs. Measure the mix. Pretend my hands aren't shaking.

I didn't hear him entering the kitchen. I felt it. The air changed the way it always does around him, like my body senses him before my eyes do.

He leaned against the doorway, sleep still clinging to his eyes and shame painted across his face. "Morning," he rasped.

I kept whisking like he wasn't standing five feet away.

Isla perked up at the sound of his voice and let out a high babble. He crossed to her and crouched beside the booster.

"Hey, baby girl," he whispered, kissing her cheek. "You sleep good?"

She squealed and slapped her hands on the tray. He stayed there, soft and steady, pointing at her cup, naming colors, asking about her stuffed animals.

I didn't look at him. I flipped the waffle. The sizzle was louder than it needed to be.

"I'm sorry," he said at last.

I didn't answer. The apology hung there, useless and heavy, like the smell of burnt mix. For bringing her here. For letting me spiral. For not stopping it. For not loving me enough. Which part was he sorry for?

"What was she doing here, Elijah?" I asked, voice flat.

He rubbed the back of his neck. "I didn't know she would find me here."

"You didn't even try to stop it," I said. "You just watched it happen like it wasn't your mess to clean up."

427

"I didn't know what to do." His voice dropped, cautious, like the moment might crack if he breathed wrong. "I froze."

"You always freeze," I muttered. "Until it's too late."

His jaw tightened. "I'm not doing this right now."

"Of course you aren't." I slid the waffle onto Isla's plate and cut it into tiny squares. Syrup. Berries. Ritual over ruin. "You never want to talk when it's real."

"You think I don't care?" he asked, quieter. "You think any of this has been easy for me?"

"No," I said, finally meeting his eyes. "I think it's been easy for you to leave."

His lips parted. Nothing came out.

"Eat," I said to Isla.

He sat across from her and picked at a corner of an empty plate. Then he cleared his throat. "I need to head out for a bit. Just to clear my head."

His pupils went small. He kept rubbing the same spot on his wrist. He looked past me like he was checking exits.

I rinsed the mixing bowl and set it in the rack. I didn't look up.

"I won't be long," he added.

Silence.

He stood, wiped his palms on his jeans, and turned toward the door.

He put his hand on the frame and opened his mouth twice before nothing came out. He nodded at the floor. I recognized the nod. It was the one he uses when his words fail.

The latch clicked. The door closed.

The quiet that followed was worse than any screaming.

I sat with my daughter and watched her eat waffles, syrup shining on her cheeks like war paint. She kicked her heels and hummed at a cartoon I forgot to turn on.

Maybe she had it right. Maybe pretending was the only way to survive it.

CHAPTER FIFTY-EIGHT

The afternoon light cut sharp through the blinds, striping the floor like bars. I stood at the sink with my hands in the dishwasher, watching the suds cloud around my knuckles. Bruised. Swollen. They looked like they belonged to someone else. It was strange, feeling this calm after all that fury. Like the storm had moved through and left me hollow instead of clean.

The door opened. Elijah came in quiet, like he was trying not to exist too loudly. Shoulders slumped. Face drawn. He leaned against the frame and stared at the floor like it was easier than looking at me.

"How is he?" I asked. My voice came out flatter than I meant it to.

He dragged a hand down his face. "Bad. Worse than last time. He didn't even recognize me at first. Thought I was his brother. Bottles everywhere. He's just gone."

I dropped the towel on the counter. "So you sit there and watch him kill himself, then come back here and make us live with it too?"

His head snapped up, eyes flashing. "What do you want me to do, Vic? Walk out on him?"

"I want you to stop dragging his poison into this house. I want Isla to be safe. I want you here, not halfway gone every time you walk through the door."

He swallowed and looked away.

"You went to him again," I said, sharper now.

His shoulders lifted in a weak shrug. "What else am I supposed to do?"

"Not make his wreckage our life," I snapped. "Don't show up half-present at my table and leave me to sweep up what's left of you. Don't let our daughter grow up thinking this is normal."

He winced. "You're angry all the time."

"I'm angry because I keep bleeding to keep this family alive. I'm angry because you keep choosing everyone else's ghosts over us. You sit in silence and freeze until I'm the one throwing punches at the air."

His jaw tightened. He still didn't fight me. That almost made it worse.

The silence between us was thick enough to choke on. I stared at the sink until my reflection blurred in the steel. The words were already forming before I even decided to speak them.

"Maybe we shouldn't live together right now," I said. My voice was quiet, steady. "Maybe you should stay with your dad until you figure yourself out. I can handle Isla on my own. I can't handle this with you sitting on the couch like a shadow."

His face twisted. "You want me gone."

"I want safety," I said. "If you can't give that, then yes. I want you gone."

He pressed his palm to the windowpane, his reflection warping in the glass. "He doesn't have much time. I can't just leave him."

"If you're haunted by him, you can't be haunted here too," I said. "Not with my daughter under this roof."

His shoulders sagged. "I don't want to lose you again."

"You've been losing me," I said. "Piece by piece."

The silence stretched so long it thinned the air. A knock rattled the door.

I opened it. Carter stood there with a folder and a stack of mail. He had that easy smile, soft around the edges.

"Hey," he said. "Clinic paperwork. Thought I'd drop it off before the end of the day."

"Thanks," I answered. My voice was steadier than I felt. He handed me the folder, and our fingers brushed. Polite. Nothing intentional. It still jolted something in me. He carried that safe kind of energy, the kind that didn't set off alarms.

Behind me, I felt Elijah's stare like heat on my neck. The air shifted again, tighter this time.

"If you need anything, call," Carter said. His eyes lingered on me for a beat, then flicked to Elijah. He nodded like he didn't see the storm in the room, then stepped back. "Take care."

The door closed. Elijah let out a laugh that was short and brittle.

I sat with the folder in my lap. My pulse wouldn't slow. There was something greedy in me that liked the way Carter had looked at me. Like I wasn't broken. Like I wasn't haunted. For a moment, I felt dangerous.

For a moment, I felt seen.

Elijah didn't sit. He paced, dragging a hand through his hair.

"Does he even know who you really are?"

"At least he saw me," I said.

His mouth opened like he had an answer. Nothing came. He looked wrecked.

"I don't want to lose you," he said again, softer now. Almost pleading.

"You already are," I whispered.

He started pacing faster, like a man trying to outrun himself. "I can't keep losing everything. My dad is dying, and she's still calling. I go there and he looks at me like a stranger, and she calls, and I get stupid, and I can't—"

"You can't stop her," I finished for him. It was what he believed. It was the loop that let him slide back into silence.

"Maybe I'm not enough," he said. The confession landed like an accusation against both of us.

"You're not enough if you sit and watch," I said. "You can be enough if you do something that matters. Not promises. Not words. Actions."

He laughed then, small and broken. "You make it sound so simple."

"You made it sound simple once," I shot back. "You used to be my anchor."

He closed his eyes and leaned into the cushion like the seawall boy had shrunk into a corner. "I don't know how to be him again."

"Then learn," I said. I was tired of holding a life together with duct tape and threats. If I didn't push him, he'd stay in the web of the past and drag us both down.

He left eventually. Not loud. Not dramatic. Keys on the table. A soft click of the front door. The house felt too big after that. Isla slept in the next room while I slid into a chair, put my head in my hands, and let the rage break into something less raw.

I got up. Went to the door. Locked the deadbolt. Set his key on the counter and stared at it until my eyes burned.

This didn't fix anything. It didn't solve the divorce or the dad, or Sarah's ugly orbit. It did something else. It shifted a fault line. It made a choice loud enough that the ground under all of us would move.

When the house settled, I went to Isla's room and watched her breathe. Even little waves. I wanted to keep that. I wanted to be the thing that made her not afraid. I promised myself then, in a vow colder than love, that I would stop pretending safety was something anyone else could hand her.

Outside, thunder rolled somewhere far off, low and distant. The kind that always comes before the real storm.

I'm done setting myself on fire so someone else can keep warm.

CHAPTER FIFTY-NINE

Dinner was lasagna because I didn't care enough to try. Isla smeared sauce across her tray with her fist, dragging her stuffed bunny into it until its ear was red. I didn't stop her. Let it stain. Let something else in this house look ruined besides me.

The silence was wrong. Too wide. Too sharp. I kept waiting for the click of the door, the shift in the air when Elijah walked in. Nothing came. Just the sound of Isla chewing, the scrape of my fork against the pot.

I slammed the pot into the sink harder than I meant to. Water splashed up my arms. Isla startled, her wide eyes locked on me with sauce across her cheek. My chest tightened.

"Eat," I said. My voice was gravel.

She shoved another noodle in her mouth. Her quick obedience cut me deeper than if she had cried.

The hours between blurred. I cleaned until my hands ached, just to have something to do that didn't require thinking.

Bath was lavender bubbles and plastic whales lined up in the tub. Isla splashed, laughing so hard she hiccupped. It should have healed something in me. Instead, it scraped everything raw. I wrapped her in a towel and held her too tight.

She fell asleep fast, thumb in her mouth, bunny tucked to her chin. I stayed by the bed, staring at her breath until I was dizzy. I promised her the same lie I always do. Safe. Always safe. Even if I had to rip the world apart to make it so.

The house turned into a coffin once she was out. Too clean. Too still.

I poured wine into a glass, stared at it, and threw it into the sink. Shards exploded. I laughed, harsh and broken, then choked on it. The sound startled me. For a second, I thought it came from someone else.

Isla cried.

I sprinted to her room and scooped her up. Her fists clutched my shirt, hot tears soaking me. "It's okay. You're okay. Mama's here." I kissed her hair until the crying softened. She forgot fast. I didn't.

Back in the kitchen, I swept glass into the trash. A shard cut my thumb, blood welling bright. I sucked it until the taste turned metallic. Shame burned hotter than pain. I wrapped it in a paper towel, then ripped the towel down the middle just to hear something tear.

On the table sat the folder Carter left. Paperwork for normal people. I slammed my palm against it until the edge cut into my skin. I wanted to shred it. I wanted to fill it out and pretend I was someone else. I did nothing but press harder, like force could make me belong.

My phone lit up. His name. I let it ring out. It lit again. And again. Then silence. Then the voicemail icon.

I pressed play.

His voice cracked before the first word. "Vic. I don't even know where to start. I went to his house tonight, and he didn't know who I was. He looked at me and called me by his brother's

436

name. I cleaned him up off the bathroom floor, and he laughed because he thought it was a joke. I don't know how much longer he has, but it feels like he's already gone. And I don't know how to keep going without drinking myself into the same grave."

He sucked in a breath. I pictured him on the curb outside, head in his hands.

"Sarah keeps calling. She knows I won't pick up, but she won't stop. Every time the phone rings, I feel like I'm going to crawl out of my skin. And you. God, Vic, I know you hate me right now, but please don't shut me out. You're the only person who ever saw me when I wasn't worth seeing. If you close the door on me too, I don't know what I'll do."

Silence stretched on the recording, broken only by his shaky breath. Then his voice dropped, low and ruined.

"I keep thinking about the day you broke my kite strings on the beach. I was furious, but it was the first time in my life someone pulled me out of the sky and made me stay. I should've told you then that you meant everything. I should've told you before I lost the chance."

The message ended.

I pressed the phone to my ear until it hurt. My throat closed, and my chest heaved. Tears came fast, hot, blinding. I hated him for leaving. I hated him for calling. I hated him for making me remember the boy on the seawall who had looked at me like I was the only thing keeping him breathing.

"Fuck you," I whispered, shaking until my teeth ached. "Fuck you for making me care when I swore I wouldn't."

The phone slipped out of my hand, clattering across the floor. I kicked it under the counter like a rat I couldn't look at.

Both palms pressed to the counter, I bent forward and finally let it break loose. A sound ripped out of me that wasn't crying and wasn't screaming, both at once. My body shook with it until my knees gave out and I slid to the floor.

I stayed there, gasping, fist still wrapped in a bloodied paper towel. The house was still. Too still.

I crawled into Isla's room and sat against her bed until her breathing pulled me back from the edge. She curled her hand around the bunny's ear. I saved the voicemail. I hate that I saved it.

The streetlight outside flickered once, then held steady. I took it as a warning. Or a promise.

I swore it again. Nothing touches her. Nothing.

The phone lit once more in the dark. His name burned across the screen. I didn't move. I stared at my daughter instead and whispered the truth.

Safe won't last. Not like this. And if he can't give it to us, I'll build it myself. Even if I have to destroy everything else.

CHAPTER SIXTY

My mom showed up at the door with her usual forced smile and a plastic bag of snacks. "Sleepover night," she announced like it was a gift. Isla squealed, bouncing in place with her bunny.

"You look awful," Mom said before she even crossed the threshold. Her eyes flicked over my face, sharp and searching. "What happened to your lip?"

I touched the faint split without thinking. "Nothing."

She made a low sound in her throat, the one that says she doesn't believe me but isn't going to press. "I hope you've been taking your medicine. You can't afford to be reckless now. Not with her." She nodded toward Isla, already rummaging in the snack bag.

My jaw tightened. "I'm handling it."

"You always say that," she muttered. Then, louder, "You need to remember you're a mother before anything else. Whatever mess you're wrapped up in, Isla comes first. She doesn't need to see you fall apart."

I zipped Isla's bag, crouching low so my daughter wouldn't see the heat in my eyes. "There's something you should know," I said, forcing the words out. "Her dad found us. He wants to be in her life."

Mom froze, eyebrows shooting up. "Her dad? That guy from Texas?" Her voice sharpened. "How did he even find you in Florida?"

"Does it matter? He found me."

She set the snack bag down a little too hard. "Of course it matters. Men like that don't just show up after years and suddenly want to play father. He wasn't around then, and he won't stay now. You're fooling yourself if you think otherwise."

"He's different," I said, and the lie burned my throat.

Her mouth pressed tight, eyes narrowing. "He'll never be different. And if you're foolish enough to let him circle back in, you better not let that child pay the price for your choices. If something happens to her because of you, I'll go to court myself. Don't think I won't."

The threat hit like a slap.

She glanced at Isla and shook her head. "Vanessa never gave me this kind of grief. She grew up, made good choices, and settled down. Why can't you ever just be responsible?"

The words sank like stones. I didn't answer. I couldn't.

I kissed Isla's curls, breathed her in, and told her I'd see her tomorrow. Mom stood in the doorway, waiting, still holding her judgment like a weapon. "Try to pull yourself together while she's gone. Be responsible, Victoria. For once."

The door shut behind them, and for a long time I just stood there, listening to the quiet press against my chest like punishment.

I walked through the house like I didn't live here. Every room echoed. Every surface gleamed too clean. I ended up in the bathroom, the mirror pulling me in like gravity.

The light was cruel. White and sharp. It showed everything—the hollow under my eyes, the faint scar on my lip, the way my hair clung to my cheek. I leaned closer until the glass fogged with my breath.

"This is you," I whispered. My voice sounded foreign.

I thought of Sarah. Sarah with her perfect eyeliner and polished nails. Sarah who never walked into a room and made people stiffen. I pressed my fingers against my cheekbone until it hurt. If I pushed hard enough, maybe I could force the softness out. Maybe I could carve myself sharper.

My reflection blurred. For a moment, I didn't see myself at all. I saw the girl in the hallway at school, gripping a pencil so tightly the wood splintered. I saw her lunge. I heard the scream. The gasp of the crowd. The word freak whispered like a curse.

My grip on the sink tightened until my nails carved crescents into my palms.

I pressed my palms to the sink until my wrists ached. "You were always the problem," I said to the mirror.

Elijah's voicemail slipped through the cracks of my brain. You're the only person who ever saw me when I wasn't worth seeing. My chest seized. I wanted to smash the phone just for daring to remember. Instead, I stared at the mirror and dared it to argue.

My hands shook. I grabbed the edge of the sink and yanked. The toothbrush holder crashed to the floor, spilling bristles and paste. The sound wasn't loud enough. I picked up the hairbrush and hurled it against the wall. A crack bloomed in the drywall.

Breath ripped out of me in short, ragged gasps. I clawed at my hair, pulling until my scalp burned, until strands came free and clung to my fingers. The quiet that followed was almost holy. Then came the truth.

"You were always the problem," I said again, softer this time.

My knees buckled, and I collapsed against the cold tile.

The sobs came guttural. Not tears. Not whimpers. Animal sounds. My body convulsed with it, shaking until I couldn't breathe. I pressed my forehead to the floor and let it all pour out— every memory, every scream, every time I'd been left, every time I'd been too much.

In the mess of it, Sarah's face flashed again. Her smile on my porch. Her hand on Elijah's arm. My stomach flipped. If she were here right now, I would… I would…

I slammed my fist into the tile just to stop the thought. Pain bloomed in my arm. My knuckles split, tiny blooms of blood staining the grout.

I crawled back to the mirror. My face was streaked. My hair was wild. My eyes were swollen red. I looked like something feral. Something already halfway to the monster people always said I was.

I put my hands on the counter and leaned close. "This is who you are," I whispered. My voice cracked. "This is who you've always been."

For a long time, I just stared. Waiting for the reflection to change. Waiting for some sign I wasn't already gone.

It didn't.

I laughed then, sharp and bitter, the sound bouncing off the tile. I pressed both palms flat against the mirror like I could climb through it and find a version of me that didn't ruin everything. The glass stayed cold. My skin stayed hot.

My chest rose and fell too fast. I forced it to slow down. I looked myself dead in the eye. "Fine," I whispered. "If I'm the monster, then I'll decide who burns."

Somewhere outside, thunder rolled, low and distant, like the world was warning me what came next.

I shut off the light and left the wreckage where it fell. The house swallowed me whole.

CHAPTER SIXTY-ONE

ELIJAH

The apartment smelled like bleach and old cigarettes. I used to think bleach meant clean. Here, it meant someone trying to erase a mess that would not leave.

"Dad," I called from the doorway. "I'm here."

He did not answer. The TV hummed with a game show that felt like noise from another planet. I found him in the bathroom on the tile, shirt half-buttoned, belt threaded wrong. He was staring at the ceiling like the lights held a secret.

"Easy," I said, dropping to my knees. "I've got you."

His skin felt thin, papery and hot at the same time. When I got my arms under him, he laughed. It sounded like a cough that forgot how to be a cough.

"Mike," he said. "You took your time."

I am not Mike. I swallowed the name like a pill that stuck. "It's Elijah."

"Right," he murmured, drifting. "Right, right. Come here, boy."

I got him onto the couch. I wiped his face with a damp towel. I cleaned the spot on the floor because stepping over it felt like stepping over a body. The towel went gray even though the tile had looked white.

I'd been cleaning up after him my whole life. It never stayed clean for long.

He dozed with his mouth open. His breath rattled. Every few minutes, he flinched like someone had shouted his name inside a dream. The bottles on the kitchen counter clicked when the air conditioner kicked on. I wanted to sweep them all into a bag and drop them down the trash chute. I did not. I lined them up by size like a child making order out of chaos.

I took out my phone and typed a message to Victoria. I wrote, I'm here with him. I wrote, I should never have left you in Texas. I wrote, I'm sorry. I deleted every word. My fingers hovered, trembling. Not from withdrawal. From wanting to reach for something I kept breaking. The little blinking cursor looked like a heartbeat I could not regulate. My thumb rubbed the same line on my wrist over and over like I could trace the seam that brought Isla into the world.

I drank the last of the coffee I found in the pot. It tasted burned and metal. I drank it anyway. I needed the jolt. I needed something that did not feel like grief.

He woke and stared at the ceiling fan. "You're late," he said, finally finding a word that made sense. "You're always late."

"I'm here now," I told him.

"You're late," he said again, then closed his eyes like the argument took all his energy.

A number I knew by heart lit the phone. I should have turned it off. The screen kept glowing against the laminate like a lure. I let it ring out. It rang again. I answered because I make dumb choices when I'm tired.

"I filed this morning," Sarah said, sweet like a bruise. "I wanted it to be me. I want the record to show I threw you away."

I gripped the counter. "Send them to me."

"Oh, I will," she said. "And I want you to remember it. Every time you play house in that little whore's kitchen, remember why I went first. Because you are the bag on the curb, Elijah. People set you out and feel better. Your father forgets you. Your friends forget you. I will forget you. I'm just making it official."

"Go to hell, Sarah."

She laughed softly. "I only need yours on the line that says respondent. Make sure to sign when the courier comes. Papers won't save you. Married or divorced, you're not done with me."

The line went dead.

I opened her thread and scrolled all the way up. Block. A gray badge appeared. I stared at the word until it meant more than a button.

The silence afterward felt heavier than the call itself, but cleaner somehow.

My father stirred. "Who was that?" he asked without opening his eyes.

"No one," I lied.

"Always no one," he said, and drifted back under.

I cleaned his kitchen. It was something I could do that did not require a miracle. I scrubbed the stovetop, threw away empty cartons, and pulled out the trash. I found a coffee mug with a

446

lipstick print that did not belong to anyone I knew. I rinsed it and tried not to think about what that meant.

I rolled my sleeves to my elbows and took the warm can from the back of the fridge. The tab hissed. I touched the rim to my mouth, just enough to taste metal, throat working once. Then I turned slowly and poured it into the sink. Foam climbed, died.

I want the burn. I choose the ache of staying.

I let cold water run over my forearms until the veins stood. I crushed the empty in one hand and dropped it in the bin.

My dad needed a shower. He would not get one without a fight. I coaxed him up, and we shuffled to the bathroom like a two-headed animal. I kept my voice steady. I told him every step before we did it. Water on. Shirt off. Towel ready. He complained about the pressure. He complained about the heat. He called me by the wrong name again, and I let it pass.

The name landed like it always did — familiar, wrong, and sharp enough to bleed me from the inside.

I held the back of his neck while the water ran over him and tried not to think about a childhood where this had been the other way around.

After, I dressed him slow. Socks. Sweatpants. The one soft T-shirt he still liked. He smelled like drugstore soap and an old man. He looked at me for a long time, and for one breath, I saw recognition come back like a wave that wanted to reach the shore and failed.

"Elijah?" he said.

"Yeah," I said too fast. "Yeah, Dad. I'm here."

He blinked like a light found its way back in. "Your mother used to sing in the kitchen," he whispered. "Off key. Made the coffee too sweet. I miss her. I didn't say it enough."

"I know," I said. My throat tightened.

He looked at me, softer than he ever let himself be. "She was the good one," he said. "Tell her I remember. Tell her I'm sorry."

The light faded from his face. "Where's Mike?"

I miss her too. I should call her. I should tell her he asked.

"I don't know where Mike is," I said. "I'm here."

I got him settled with a glass of water and a show he used to like. He watched it like a man trying to remember a language he once spoke. I sat on the floor by the couch because my legs would not hold me. I put my head against the cushion and closed my eyes. He snored. I matched my breathing to his because I am pathetic like that. It calmed me anyway.

I called my mother and let it ring into the dark. "He asked about you," I said to the tone. "He said he's sorry."

The voicemail I left Victoria circled back like a tide. I heard my own voice, begging a little, apologizing a lot, talking about my father on the bathroom floor and how it felt like losing him while he was still alive. I heard the line about the beach. The kite. How angry I had been when the strings snapped, and how relieved I had been when the wind stopped trying to take us. I had not said it right. I never do. I always arrive late to the words that matter.

I typed a new text and did not delete it. The courier can bring the papers at any time. I will sign. Sent.

I made a list on an envelope because paper sometimes makes things real. Sign divorce papers. Block Sarah for good. Find a clinic for Dad that will take him. Sleep for more than an hour. Eat food that is not from a gas station. Call my mom. Try not to lie to the woman you love. I wrote each item like a command. I added one more. Do not ever drink. I underlined it twice.

The phone buzzed again. Sarah on a new number. A mirror selfie no one sends at noon. I turned the phone over and blocked it. Block. A small gray word that tasted like metal and mercy. My hands shook. I let them.

My dad woke late in the afternoon and asked if his mother had called. She has been dead for fifteen years. I said not yet. He nodded and smiled at something I could not see. He asked if I would make eggs. I made them wrong because his pan was wrong and his stove was wrong, and because I am not my mother. He ate two bites and fell asleep in the chair with the fork still in his hand.

The sun slid down the blinds. The room got longer and more yellow. The air tasted like dust. I stood and stretched, and every muscle protested like I had carried a house on my back.

I could feel the part of me that wants to quit. The part that wants to leave the door unlocked and walk until the road decides where I am allowed to stop. I could see the bar on the corner. I could picture the morning after with my face in my hands and another apology that Victoria did not deserve to hear.

I went to the sink and ran cold water over my wrists until they ached. I counted to thirty. I did it again. I looked at my reflection in the dark kitchen window. I looked like a man who wanted to be better and had not learned how.

"Dad," I said without turning around. "Do you remember the beach?"

He did not answer. His breath rasped from the recliner like a saw through soft wood.

"I met a girl there," I said. "She was trying to hurt herself. Instinctively, I dove in after her. I was so mad when the kite strings broke. I thought I had lost something special. I thought she had ruined it. I was wrong."

My voice shook. I hated it did. I kept talking because if I stopped, I would not start again.

"I should have told her then," I said. "I should have said this is the first time I feel tethered to a person, not a bottle or a street or a story about myself that hurts me. I should have told her I didn't save her. She saved me."

I sat on the floor again. I pressed my shoulder into the couch. The fabric smelled like dust and skin and the last ten years.

He snored. The show asked contestants to name a capital. I could not have named my own if someone paid me.

"I will sign the papers," I said to the room. "I will stop letting Sarah decide what I am. I will not drink tonight. I will try to be a father my daughter can rely on."

The promises tasted like metal. I held them in my mouth anyway.

I taped the envelope list to the refrigerator with blue painter's tape. The hum of the motor felt like a clock. I let it count me through one more minute.

Outside, a siren slid past. A dog barked. A kid rode a skateboard down the cracked sidewalk and laughed like the world might let him keep it.

I closed my eyes and saw the kite again. The string in my hands. The girl on the sand with hair in her eyes, cursing me out like a prayer. I saw the wind snap and the fabric fall and the sky come closer. I felt relief and fury and a new kind of gravity.

"Isla," I whispered to no one. "I'm trying to be the man your mom pulled down to earth."

My father breathed like a tired engine. I matched him. I let the rhythm pull me through another minute. Then another. I did not drink. I did not call. I did not run. I sat with the living and the almost gone and the ghost of a kite that still tugged at my hands. I decided that would be enough for tonight.

CHAPTER SIXTY-TWO

The doorbell rang while my coffee was still deciding if it wanted to help. Isla sat on the rug with her blocks, serious as a surgeon, bunny faceplanted beside her. I wiped my hands on my shirt and opened the door.

A courier held a thick envelope like it was radioactive. "Elijah Garrison?" he asked, pen hovering.

"He doesn't live here," I said. My voice stayed level, but my pulse was a hammer in my throat.

He checked the label. He checked my house number. He made the face people make when they choose paperwork over common sense. "This is the address on file."

"Then the file is wrong," I said, and shut the door.

The mail slot whispered. The envelope slid across the floor and slapped the baseboard.

I stared at it until the print came into focus. In re: Marriage of Sarah Garrison and Elijah Garrison. Petition. Service at my address, the very porch where she had already dared show herself. I picked it up and dropped it on the table like it could bite. Another mess that somehow had my name on it.

Isla toddled over and pressed a blue block to my thigh like a medal. I kissed her curls and swallowed the taste of metal.

Another knock. Not the courier. A woman with a clipboard stood on the step, and a deputy hovered half a step back, hands visible.

"Ms. Drayton," the woman said. "Child and Family Services. This is Deputy Kline. We received a call about yelling and loud noise last night. We need to do a welfare check."

The word call went cold under my skin. "From whom?"

"Anonymous," she said. "May we come in?"

I stepped aside. Refusing only invites a different report. The deputy stayed near the entry, scanning. The woman's eyes moved quickly, competent, not cruel.

"Is your daughter here?" she asked.

"She's right there," I snapped.

The woman crouched to Isla's level, verified breathing, limbs, and eyes. She glanced at the food on the counter, the outlets, and the sink.

"Sleeping space," she said.

I showed her the crib. Fresh sheets. Clean blanket. Sound machine shaped like a cloud.

"Any substances within reach?" she asked.

"No," I said. "The only bottle close enough says dish soap."

"May I see your hands?" she asked.

I opened my palms. Thin slice along my thumb. She nodded and checked a box.

"We are not here to be punitive," she said. "We just verify safety. If someone is harassing you with false reports, document everything. Deputy Kline will note extra patrol."

The deputy tapped a card on the table. "Camera on the porch is good, but you should get one for the back," he said. "Motion lights help."

"Thank you," I said, because I was raised right, even when I wanted to bite.

They left. I locked the door and pressed my forehead against the wood for three breaths. Isla tapped from the other side with her block like she was checking on me. That was my timer. I turned. I picked up the envelope. I slit it open with a knife.

Dissolution. Irreconcilable. Respondent. Words that flatten a life into lines. Her name. His name. My vision pulsed.

I am a paralegal. I know exactly how a line item like welfare check looks inside a packet if someone wants it to hurt. I know exactly what it means that Sarah used my address after showing up here and swinging. It is not an accident. It is a message.

I pictured scissors. I pictured a string. I pictured what I would cut and what I would keep.

Fear burned off quickly. What was left was focus.

I did not think. I called Elijah.

He answered on the second ring. "Victoria."

"A courier just shoved your petition through my mail slot, and ten minutes later, I had a welfare check in my living room."

"I did not give them your address," he said. "Sarah filed. I swear I did not—"

"I am not asking you to explain for her. I am telling you this is my house and my child, and I am not doing another morning like this."

He went quiet for a beat. "Are you both okay?"

"Yes," I said. "And I am furious."

"I hear you," he said, low. "I will change the service address today. I will get a P.O. box. I will keep you both out of this. I am sorry."

"Good," I said. "Please handle it today."

"I will," he said. "I should have done it already."

"Also," I said, and my voice thinned because the truth scraped, "do you understand what it felt like to open the door to a social worker and a deputy with a clipboard while our daughter stacked blocks on the living room rug?"

He breathed in. "I am sorry that happened. I hate that it happened because of me."

Silence stretched. I looked at Isla. She was feeding a block to her alligator and humming to herself like the world still made sense. I wanted to keep it that way.

"I am not your punching bag," I said. "I am not hers either. Keep my name out of it. Keep my address out of it. If you need something from me, ask like a man who knows what it costs."

"I will," he said. "I am calling the service company now. Then the clerk. I will text you when it is done."

"Okay," I said. "Thank you."

I hung up before he could try to make it softer.

The kitchen hummed. I stood there with the envelope and the deputy's card, and the blue block Isla had handed me like a medal. I put the block on top of the papers like a seal.

Isla toddled over and lifted her arms. I picked her up and she tucked her legs around my waist like she was built for that space. My hands were still shaking. She did not mind. She patted my cheek and said a word that meant nothing and everything.

My phone buzzed a few minutes later.

Elijah: New service address set. Box confirmed. Your address has been removed. I am sorry you had to deal with that.

I stared at the message until the letters steadied.

I checked the locks. I checked them again. I made us lunch and watched Isla eat like the world had not tried to crawl inside my house.

I taped the deputy's card inside the cabinet where the coffee lives. Not as fear. As a reminder. I am not helpless.

The house listened. It always did when I meant it.

When the room finally went quiet, I stood in the middle of my kitchen and said it to the air so the walls would remember. "No one touches her."

Then I slid the petition back into its envelope, shut the drawer, and waited for the day to try me again.

CHAPTER SIXTY-THREE

I had just put Isla down for a nap when someone knocked again. The hair on my arms stood. My chest tightened.

I opened the door to see Elijah on the stoop with empty hands and the kind of tired face that makes you want to be cruel and kind at the same time. The air between us hummed with everything we weren't saying yet.

"I came for the papers," he said. "I will sign them and drop them at the attorney's in the morning. I have to leave for work in the morning, so I wanted to see Isla before, if that is okay."

I motioned for him to come in.

The envelope sat on the table like a verdict. He did not flinch. He pulled out the response and the acknowledgment, found a pen in the junk drawer without asking, and set the papers flat. The room went quiet enough that I heard the tiny click of the pen and the soft rasp of paper against wood.

He signed. He paused after the E, like the rest of his name weighed more than ink, then finished it anyway. The pen dragged a small groove in the table. Proof, not a promise. I hated that closure sounded like paper tearing.

He set the pen down. No speech. No performance. Just ink on lines that cut us free. He took out his phone, snapped a photo of the signature page beside the date on the recipe-card magnet, and texted it to me without a caption. Evidence.

He glanced toward the hallway. "Can I see her now?"

"In her room," I said.

He went in and sat on the floor beside the toddler's bed, forearms resting on the rail. He did not reach for her. He waited. When she blinked awake and saw him, her face went from soft sleep to sun. She popped up, grabbed her bunny, and held it out like an offering.

He took the bunny and pressed its ear to his mouth like it was a phone. "Hello, Miss Bunny," he whispered. "Did you sleep well?"

Isla climbed into his lap like she had not been born during a war. He stayed cross-legged on the rug and let her show him every block like it was a treasure. No baby voice. No show for me. He held up a triangle and said, "Yellow," and she stole it and set it on a blue square like she was building the world with shape and stubbornness.

They wandered to the kitchen. He washed his hands before he touched anything, and something in me unclenched. He cut strawberries the size of postage stamps and set them on a plate with a circle of crackers and a small scoop of yogurt. He wiped her face once, then handed me the cloth so I could be the one who finished. It was nothing and it was everything. A faint thumbprint of strawberry juice stayed on the plate. It felt truer than any apology.

When the plate was empty and her eyes got glossy, he took her to the couch and opened the soft book with the animals that roar and quack when the batteries are good. The batteries were dying because life is accurate like that, so he made the sounds himself without being stupid about it. She laughed like she had forgiven the whole day. Then she tucked her head into his throat and fell asleep a second time, heavy as trust.

He stayed still for a long time. He breathed slow so she would match. When he finally shifted, he carried her back to bed and set her down with both hands under her body the way you place something you cannot afford to drop. He checked the corner of the fitted sheet. He checked the cloud machine. He still remembered the small things, the ones that make homes instead of headlines. He closed the door without letting it click.

Back in the living room, he poured two glasses of water and brought one to me before sitting down.

"My mom came for Isla last night," I said. "I told her you found us. She asked how you found me in Florida, like I had invited a stranger in. She told me to take my medicine. She threatened the court. She compared me to Vanessa for sport."

His jaw flexed. "I am sorry."

"You did not do it," I said. "But you are in the middle of why she thinks I cannot be trusted with a life."

He nodded, throat working. "I called my mom," he said, eyes on the table. "Finally. I did it while I was with my dad. It was short. Awkward. She asked if I was eating. I lied. I asked how she was doing. She said, "Better than last winter. We did not talk about the parts that hurt. I want to try again when I can say the rest."

"That is good," I said, and I meant it.

He looked at my hands. "Are you alright after that welfare check mess?"

"No," I said. "But I will be. It is easier when I have a list."

He half-smiled. "What is on it?"

460

"Another camera. Motion light. Remember to breathe." I tapped the papers. "And this. Ending what should have ended a long time ago."

He nodded. "I am afraid I will be just like my dad, and that scares me."

"Then do not be," I said.

He looked up. "I meant what I said in the voicemail. The beach. The kite. All of it."

"I know," I said, and I did. "I felt suffocated in that condo with my parents. I felt suffocated by my mom. I know she loves me, but she makes you want to run. I cannot explain it. Like, I will never be good enough for her, so I want to run. I pulled the map out and pressed my finger on places like spells. Then Isla breathed in my face, and I remembered I do not get to leave. Not anymore."

We sat in the quiet where the past usually shouts. It hummed instead. He reached across the couch and set his fingers over mine. He did not grip. He just covered, like a roof.

"We are broken kids," he said. "I can be gentler with the kid in you. You can be gentler with the kid in me. That is all I know how to promise tonight."

"It is a good start," I said.

His eyes went to the monitor. Isla rolled and threw a leg over the bunny like it was a horse. He smiled without showing teeth. It was the look of a man whose heart belongs to something small. It was not fair that the same heart that broke me was the one teaching her how to love.

461

"Tell me something true," I said.

"My father is falling in pieces," he said. "I hate that I am angry at him, and I hate that I am angry at myself for being angry."

"Tell me another," I said.

He looked at me for a long time. "When I think about you in high school, bloody and furious, I do not see a monster. I see a girl who decided she would not be hunted. I want that girl on my side. I want to be on hers."

"My turn," I said. "When you left me in Texas, I told myself I liked the quiet better than the ache. That was a lie. I liked the ache better because it felt like proof I had loved something real."

He covered his face with his hands and let out a breath that sounded like grief and relief at getting married.

We leaned back on the couch with our feet on the table like teenagers who had stolen a night from the world. He told me about calling the service company from a parking lot and the way the woman on the phone read his confirmation number like she was naming his fate. He touched the corner of my split lip. I touched the scar on his eyebrow and the tendon that jumps in his wrist when he is trying too hard not to feel.

We did not kiss. Not then. We let the quiet work like a balm instead of a weapon.

When he stood to leave, he paused at Isla's door and listened without opening it. The house breathed. The day finally let go.

"I will call her every day," he said. "I will text in every city."

"Okay," I said.

At the door, he stopped and pressed his mouth to my forehead like an apology and a prayer. "Goodnight, Vic."

"Goodnight, Elijah."

After the door clicked, I stood in the kitchen for a moment. I pictured scissors. I pictured a string. I kept what mattered and cut what tried to own me.

The house felt different. Not safe. Not fixed. Just less alone.

I checked Isla one more time and came back to the couch. The blanket still held its shape. I pulled it over my lap and stared at the ceiling until my body believed that morning would come and we could survive it.

Morning would come. I would meet it standing.

CHAPTER SIXTY-FOUR

The morning air smelled like salt and sunscreen before I even opened the sliding door. Isla pressed her nose to the glass, palms spread, fogging it with every impatient breath. She was already in her strawberry swimsuit, one shoulder strap twisted, hair bent into two lopsided pigtails by Vanessa, who had shown up with iced coffees and a towel bag like she had been waiting all week for me to ask.

The gulf stretched out in front of us like it had secrets. Not the blue postcard you send to people in winter, but green-gray, restless. The kind of water that remembers storms even when the sky is clear.

"Careful," I called as Isla shot forward, feet slapping wood, sand sticking. Vanessa laughed behind me, the easy kind that comes when you are not the one raising a toddler. She tossed me a bottle of sunscreen like it was a grenade I better not forget to pull the pin on.

We set up halfway down the beach where the shells were sharp and the tide reached high. Isla darted in and out of the shallows, squealing every time the foam chased her ankles, then running back to throw herself on the towel only to get up again.

Vanessa stretched out beside me, sunglasses swallowing her face. "She's fearless."

"She does not know what to be afraid of yet," I said. My voice sounded heavier than I meant to.

I watched Isla scoop a plastic cup of wet sand, dump it, then clap like she had built something permanent. The sun lit her hair so bright it looked like spun glass. She ran toward the water again, this time straight in until it reached her knees. She lifted her arms to balance, stubborn, daring the tide to knock her over.

And then I was gone.

The beach blurred. The sound of Isla's laugh warped, stretched. My chest pulled tight like it remembered something my head tried to forget.

It was another shoreline, years earlier, same stretch of sand, but a different sky. The moon was thin as a fingernail, the water black enough to swallow us whole.

Elijah had stripped his shirt off and dropped it in the dunes, daring me to follow him down where the waves broke hard. I remember my fists balled tight even then, anger buzzing under my skin like a live wire. He had grabbed my wrist before I could throw it at the world.

"Stop fighting shadows," he said, voice low enough the wind almost carried it off.

"I am not fighting shadows," I spat. "I am fighting everyone who thinks they own me."

He laughed once, not mocking, just raw. Then he tugged me down to sit in the wet sand, water rushing up to our thighs and retreating like it could not make up its mind. My jeans stuck cold and heavy, but he did not flinch. He just stared out at the horizon like it owed him an answer.

"You ever wonder if we are just gonna disappear?" he asked. "Like one night the ocean takes us and nobody notices until morning?"

His profile was all bone and stubbornness, jaw set against everything that had tried to break him. I should have been scared. Instead, I leaned into it.

"I would notice," I said. My voice came out smaller than I wanted, more truth than armor.

He turned his head then, really looked at me, eyes dark enough to drown in. He lifted a handful of wet sand, let it sift through his fingers. "That is all I need to hear tonight."

For a moment, the world felt lighter. Just a girl with a boy in the tide, not broken kids with broken homes.

"Mama!" Isla's voice cut through, sharp as sunlight.

A gull cried overhead. A lifeguard whistle cut somewhere down the beach, thin and far.

My chest lurched. The moon, the tide, Elijah's hand, they all vanished. I blinked back into the present, where my daughter was wobbling knee deep in the gulf, arms flapping as a small wave broke against her. Vanessa was already half up, ready to sprint, but I beat her there.

I scooped Isla into my arms, water streaming down her legs, sand clinging to her skin like proof she had been braver than sense. She squealed against my neck, triumphant.

"See. Mama. Big," she shouted, legs kicking.

Vanessa laughed, softer this time. "She is you, Vic. All over again."

I kissed Isla's wet hair, heart pounding. My throat burned with something I did not say. Because if she were me, if she carried the same wild in her veins, then she would also carry him. Elijah. Always him.

I set her down on the towel, and she plopped cross-legged, digging into her snack bag with wet fists like nothing had happened. The gulf rolled behind her, endlessly. I took a picture for my mom, then almost sent it to him. I did not.

I lay back on the sand, eyes on the sky, pulse still too loud. The past pressed close, as insistent as the tide. No matter how far he had gone, no matter how many ghosts hunted me or how much time we spent apart, Elijah lived in my daughter's laugh, in her stubborn feet chasing water, in the way my heart still jumped at shadows that looked like him.

And I hated it.

And I needed it.

Both at once.

The tide kept coming.

I cannot forgive the ocean.

But I can teach my kid to kick.

CHAPTER SIXTY-FIVE

I had almost convinced myself he would not come back that soon. That I would have weeks to breathe before the air in my house carried his name again. The knock came anyway, low and steady, like he knew I had been listening for it even when I told myself I had not.

When I opened the door, Elijah stood there with his duffel on one shoulder. He looked the same and not the same, sunburn at the edges, face drawn from travel, a weariness that clung like smoke.

"Rotation changed," he said. "I have a few days."

Behind my knees, Isla barreled in with her bunny tucked under one arm. "Dada," she squealed, hitting his shin like she wanted to topple a tree.

His face broke. Not the guarded half smile he rationed out, the real thing, ragged with relief. He dropped the duffel without looking and scooped her up, pressing his mouth to her hair like oxygen.

"I missed you, bug," he murmured.

She patted his cheek with a sticky hand. "Snack?"

He laughed under his breath, cracked and tired. "Of course. Snack first."

I stepped back so he could come in. He carried her to the sink, washed his hands, and started slicing strawberries like he had been born to it. I leaned on the counter, arms crossed, watching him cut the pieces small enough for toddler teeth.

"You did not call," I said.

"I did not know until this morning," he answered, eyes on the knife. "I did not want to promise if I could not make it."

The words sat between us like a pile of unsorted laundry.

Isla shoveled fruit into her mouth with both fists and juice painting her chin. He wiped her once, gentle, then passed me the cloth so I could finish. He always did that, like he wanted me to be the last hand she felt.

When she wandered off to stack blocks, he stayed where he was, palms braced against the counter.

"You look tired," he said.

"You look gone," I said.

He gave the ghost of a smile. "Fair."

My phone buzzed. Unknown number. I almost ignored it, then the preview lit enough letters to slice me open. You think he is yours. He is always mine.

I flipped the phone face down. Elijah saw. His voice turned rough. "Sarah."

I did not confirm. I did not have to.

"She signed the papers," he said, jaw tight. "This should be done."

"Should be," I said. "You know she will not let go."

"I will not let her touch you or Isla."

The way he said it put a hurt in my chest. Not a promise. A vow carved out of bone.

Blocks toppled with a crash. "Uh oh," Isla yelled, rubbing her eyes. The fight with sleep had started. She crawled into his lap like she had always owned that space.

"She is down," I said quietly.

He nodded, stood, and lifted her. Her head fell heavy on his shoulder. I followed down the hall, watching the line of his back, the steadiness of his stride.

He set her in bed with both hands under her body like she was glass. He tucked the bunny into her arm. He checked the corner of the fitted sheet. He pressed his lips to her hair, not loud, just enough for her to sigh and turn her face toward him.

"Night, bug," he whispered.

"Dada night," she mumbled, already gone.

He stayed one breath longer, breathing with her. Then he closed the door without a click.

The quiet pressed close.

I stepped into him. He did not move away.

The kiss came slow, almost careful, like neither of us wanted to snap what little was held. His hand slid into my hair, thumb at the back of my neck, until I shivered. He bent me to the couch, not a throw, a lay-me-down, stay still so he could take his time.

When his mouth left mine, it found my jaw, my throat, the soft line of my collarbone. Each press was unhurried, reverent, like he was mapping old ground to convince himself it still existed. My breath caught every time, not because it surprised me, but because it did not. My body had always known his script of him.

"Elijah." It slipped out broken. My hand clutched his shirt.

"Shh," he said into my skin. "Do not rush me."

He peeled my shirt up sensually enough to hurt. He looked at me like I was not a body, like I was an answer. His palms slid over my ribs, up to the curve of my breast, thumbs circling until sound left me. His mouth followed, teeth grazing, tongue softening. I arched, desperate to close the last inches of space.

"God," I whispered, fingers in his hair, "Do not do this slow with me."

"Yes," he said. "Tonight I can."

Jeans gave under his hands. He dragged them down, knuckles warm against my thighs. He looked up at me from between my legs, eyes darker than I remembered. He kissed the inside of my knee, then higher, then higher, until I trembled.

"Please," I said, shameless.

"Always with the fight," he murmured. "Even when you beg."

Then his mouth was on me. Slow. Devastating. My hand slammed the couch back. My hips bucked until he steadied them with his palm. He took his time, patient and relentless, until I broke with a sob and pulled at his shoulders to bring him back to me.

When he pushed into me, it was slow and deliberate, every inch a choice. I dug my nails into his back. He set his forehead to mine.

Tears burned the corners of my eyes from the weight of it. He kissed them away without a word. He moved deep, unhurried, like he could pour the things he could not say straight into my body.

"You are killing me," I breathed.

He caught my mouth. "Not tonight."

We moved together like we had nowhere else to be. My body remembered him. My soul ached with him. Release came in long waves, a breaking open I did not want to end.

After, he stayed inside me. Our breaths tangled. My hand rested on my stomach. He covered it. He held me there like an anchor. No words came. He never gave me the ones I wanted. He gave me silence heavy enough to count as a confession.

We lay that way for a long time. The quiet hummed, not sharp, just full. His heartbeat thudded steadily against my side. I wanted to ask if he would stay the whole stretch. I wanted to ask if he would keep coming home here and not just to a city. I did not ask. He wanted to say he was sorry. He wanted to say he could fix it. He did not say it.

He shifted at last. His gaze slid to the counter where my phone sat facedown. The weight of it waited. She was still circling. He looked away.

Again tonight, his hand fell to the scar below my navel. He touched it without thinking, thumb brushing the line. He touched the scar like it was the hinge of a door he meant to keep open.

He breathed out deliberately. I felt him look toward the door where his duffel crouched by the frame, proof that pause is not staying.

"I am here," he said at last, almost a whisper.

I nodded against his mouth because I could not ask for more. Not tonight. I wanted him to say Stay. He did not. I wanted to tell him I was terrified. I did not.

We let the quiet ask for us. It was not enough.

CHAPTER SIXTY-SIX

I woke up to the weight of him. Warm, solid, steady where he had never been steady before. Elijah was on his back, arm bent behind his head, breath deep and even. For a second, I did not move, afraid that if I blinked too hard, he would vanish, the night before dissolving into nothing but a fever dream.

Then came the sound of little feet on the floor. Isla's bunny dropped first with a thud, and then she scrambled onto the bed with all the force of a toddler who had not yet learned the word gentle.

"Dada," she squealed, climbing onto his chest like he was a mountain made just for her.

His eyes opened instantly. No hesitation, no groggy confusion. Just a grin that broke across his face like he had been waiting years for that moment. He wrapped her up, kissed the top of her head, and muttered, "Morning, bug."

She giggled, patting his face with sticky fingers, babbling sounds only he seemed to understand.

I turned my face into the pillow so they would not see me break.

For a few minutes, it was only us. Isla bouncing in toddler rhythm, Elijah laughing in a way I had not heard in forever, and me, memorizing the shape of his hand against her back. Too easy to imagine this was permanent. Too easy to believe we could live in that bubble.

But bubbles always pop.

I pushed myself up, brushing hair from my face. "I have to work today."

Isla whined, clutching her bunny tight.

"I can keep her," Elijah said, like it was nothing. Like he had not missed two years of mornings.

I froze at the closet door. "You will keep her?"

He sat up, Isla anchored to his lap. "I can handle snacks and cartoons. You do not have to drag her out."

My mouth went dry. He had not been there for tantrums in the car seat or the little daycare cubby with her name on it. But she leaned into him like he had always been there.

"Yeah," I said finally. "Okay."

At work, I barely touched a file. I checked my phone every ten minutes, waiting for the other shoe to drop. By lunch, my jaw ached from clenching. The silence did not feel like peace. It felt like a storm cloud waiting to split.

When I pulled into the complex that evening, my mom's car was already crooked in the visitor spot. My chest caved in. Her perfume reached me before her words. Powder and worry.

She stood in the doorway with her arms crossed, eyes drilling into Elijah, where he sat on the couch with Isla balanced on his knee, bunny dangling from her hand.

Her voice cut sharp. "So. You are him."

Isla lifted her bunny to my mom like an offering. Mom did not take it.

Elijah looked up, steadily. "Ma'am."

"Do not ma'am me. You are the man from Texas, are you not? The one who showed up looking for her?" Her gaze flicked to Isla, then back to him. "Then maybe you can explain why my granddaughter is sitting here with you, alone, when my daughter is not even home."

The air went brittle. Isla blinked between us, bunny halfway to her mouth. Elijah didn't move. The quiet had a pulse.

The heat rushed into my face. "Mom."

She snapped her head toward me as I stepped inside. "Do not mom me. You told me he found you, Victoria. You never said I would walk in and find him living in your apartment, playing daddy while you are at work."

I swallowed hard, every word slicing deeper. "It is not like that."

"Then what is it like?" she shot back. "Because this morning I got a phone call. Anonymous. Some voice telling me I needed to check on you. That you were not safe. And now I walk in and see this."

The air thickened. My stomach turned. Elijah's jaw flexed once, then locked. "She called you."

Mom frowned. "Who?"

I did not answer. I did not have to.

Mom's eyes narrowed on Elijah. "What is your name?"

"Elijah," he said, voice low but steady.

"Elijah," she repeated, testing it like a sour taste. "I do not know you. And I do not trust a stranger with my granddaughter."

Elijah shifted Isla on his knee, his arm snug around her middle. Calm, measured, but there was iron underneath. "You do not have to trust me yet. But she is my daughter. She is safe. She is happy. That is what matters."

Mom looked at me, fire blazing in her eyes. "I raised you better than this. Better than to keep me in the dark. Better than to drag a man with a past you will not even explain into your child's life."

I bit the inside of my cheek hard enough to taste blood. "It is not your call. This is my life. If you cannot accept that, then that is on you."

Her mouth pressed into a line so thin it could have cut. "One of these days, Victoria, your anger is going to burn everything down."

Maybe it already had.

She swung her bag over her shoulder and left, slamming the door hard enough to rattle the frames.

The silence she left behind was suffocating.

Elijah set Isla down gently. She toddled off toward her blocks, obliviously. He glanced at the door, jaw tight, then stepped closer to me, his hand brushing my arm.

"I will deal with the calls," he said. "I will keep your door clean."

I wanted to believe him. But the phone in my bag was still hot with that anonymous call, and the truth was humming like a live wire.

Sarah was not done.

CHAPTER SIXTY-SEVEN

Elijah was in my bed when the sun came up. Not tucked away on the couch pretending distance. Warm skin against my back, his arm heavy over my waist, his breath stirring the hair at my neck. Isla's bunny was wedged at the foot of the mattress, her gift from the night before, and the sight of it nearly broke me.

When Isla clambered into the room, clutching her bunny by the ear, she squealed the word she had claimed overnight. "Dada."

He shifted, pulled her onto his chest like he had been practicing for years, and pressed his mouth to her crown. "Morning, bug."

Her laugh filled the room. Mine stuck in my throat.

By midmorning, it was almost domestic. The three of us moved through the store, Isla perched in the cart, babbling at the bananas while Elijah pushed. The air smelled like freon and citrus. Back at the condo, he peeled one for her, wiped her hands when she smeared pulp across her cheeks, tightened the loose handle on a cabinet door without being asked.

It was too easy. Too natural. Too dangerous.

Because my head did not stop there. My head leapt ahead, building futures, tearing them down, starting again.

That night, with Isla asleep, it boiled over.

"So, what is this?" The words snapped out of me.

Elijah leaned against the counter, arms folded, solid as stone. "What is what?"

"This." I gestured. "You are here. Sleeping in my bed. Taking her to the store. Fixing cabinets like you live here. Do you live here now? Is this it? Are we together? Or are you going to keep showing up and disappearing until I cannot breathe anymore?"

His jaw shifted. He held his silence like it might protect us.

I kept going, the questions tumbling fast. "Do we start dating other people now that you are divorced? Or are we dating each other? Are we just cohabitating for Isla? Or are we actually together? Because I cannot live in this gray space where you are everything to me in private and nothing to me in public."

His eyes flickered, but he stayed locked down, and it gutted me.

"You claimed Sarah in front of everyone. You married her. You flaunted her when you did not even want her. But me? I have always been the secret. Now my mom walks in and looks at you like you are a one-night stand I dragged home. If you had ever claimed me, if you had said out loud what I was to you, maybe she would not look at me like that."

My voice cracked on the last words.

He pushed off the counter, slow and deliberate, until he stood close enough that I felt the heat of him.

"I do not have answers for everything you asked," he said, voice low and frayed. "I will give you the truth. With Sarah, it was easy. I did not care about her. I did not love her. I did not worry about breaking her. She was nothing. You have never been that. You were the opposite. I did not know how to survive it."

480

He dragged a hand through his hair. "I do not know what I am doing here, except trying to figure out how to be a dad when I got thrown into it overnight. Most days, I do not know what I am doing at all. But do not think for a second I do not care. If I did not, I would not be here. That night in Texas was a coincidence, but I was relieved. I had wondered if you were happy somewhere, not drowning in the same mess I was. I wanted that for you. I did not want to drag you into my life."

The fight should have split us.

Instead, I surged toward him.

I gripped his shirt, yanked him down, and kissed him hard enough to bruise.

His hand locked in my hair, tilting my head back, his mouth crushing mine like a storm. He spun me, lifted me onto the counter, and pulled my thighs open with a hunger that left no space for air.

My sleep shirt was gone in a rough tug. He shoved my panties aside. He unbuttoned his jeans, pushed them low, and freed himself. When he slid into me, it was deep and merciless, like every question I had thrown at him was burning through his body instead of his voice.

I gasped, clutching his shoulders, nails carving into his back as his thrusts rattled the cabinet doors.

"God, Elijah," I choked, my forehead pressed to his. "You wreck me."

His mouth took mine, swallowing the confession. He stayed hard and relentless, each drive demanding more than I had to give.

My cries spilled against his lips, sharp and broken, until the tension snapped and heat tore through me.

He groaned into my mouth, his rhythm faltered, and then he shuddered deep inside me, his arms locking me in like a man refusing to let go.

The room smelled like salt and skin. My pulse had not found its way back yet. His breath brushed my shoulder, steady where mine was not.

Later, we collapsed into the bed, sweat-slick and tangled. His arm stayed around me, heavy, anchored. His hand found the scar below my navel. His thumb brushed the line once, careful. He took a breath and left his palm there, warm and present.

My phone buzzed on the nightstand. Unknown number. The silence before I looked hurt more than the sound.

You can play house all you want. He always comes back to me.

My heart seized.

Elijah shifted, voice rough. "Who is it?" His eyes cut to mine. "Her?"

I nodded, throat tight.

He cursed and dragged a hand over his face. "I should have cut her out years ago. I am doing it now."

His voice sounded like a vow. My chest knew better.

The night held its breath. Morning never stays kind.

CHAPTER SIXTY-EIGHT

Isla was at my mother's.

The apartment was too quiet. Not peaceful. Fake. I wiped the same corner of the counter until my wrist hurt. I tried ten different books. A movie. Nothing could fill the silence of Isla and Elijah not being here. I used to love silence. Now it terrified me.

I told myself I had locked the door. I stared at the deadbolt like I could turn it tighter with my eyes.

The handle turned.

The door clicked and opened an inch. My stomach dropped through the floor. I had not set the latch. Maybe I had and forgot. None of it mattered. The door was open.

I let out a breath. "Elijah? I am glad you are home. I am so on edge, I thought..."

Sarah stepped inside like she paid rent. Sunglasses in her hair. Perfume gone sour. A pale boutique bag hanging from her hand like a dare.

"Oh," she said. "Look at that. Open."

"Get out."

"Relax." She did not stop. She drifted into the living room as if the air belonged to her. Two fingers skimmed the back of my couch, testing. She toed one of Isla's stacked blocks. The tower toppled and scattered under the coffee table.

Cold prickled my scalp. My feet would not move. My brain kept saying this is not happening while my eyes watched her move deeper into my life.

"House looks borrowed," she said. "Fits you."

"What do you want?"

"A present," she said, setting the bag beside the vase of roses Elijah brought home two nights ago. The water was clear. The petals were a deep, sweet red.

"Do not talk about her," I said.

She smiled, pleased. "I did not say anything bad. I said she is yours. And you. You are not his. Not really. You are the side dish he orders when he needs to feel something. He will go home when he is finished pretending."

Brandy in my head, clear as glass. Move, fat girl. Books slapping tiles. Sneakers squeaking. Laughter in a hallway that smelled like bleach.

My mother under that, low and tired. Lock the door. Use your head.

My jaw locked until my molars ached. "Say it and get out. He chose to be here. Not with you."

She tilted her head at the framed photos. She plucked one up between two fingers. Isla at the beach. Crooked grin. Salt-stiff hair.

"Cute," Sarah said. "Where is her father? Try him. Go pretend with a man who actually wants you."

I was already moving. I took the frame from her hand hard enough that the glass clicked. I set it back in its exact spot. My fingers shook.

She nudged Isla's stuffed bunny with her shoe. Not a kick. A flick, curious to see how far it would slide. The bunny spun on its ear.

"Do not touch her things," I said.

"Touchy." She tapped the vase with her knuckle. The roses trembled. "He bought these? Let me guess, grocery store. Last-minute apology."

"What do you want?" I said again.

Light flashed in her eyes. "I knew I recognized you. The neighbor from that summer. The one he snuck to when I was gone."

The floor tilted.

"I was out of town with my parents that whole summer," she went on. "If I had been here, he would not have looked at you. You were the filler. The secret. Not a friend, he would claim. Not a girl he would stand beside in daylight."

Brandy again. Closer. Ugly.

A shove. The soft tear of a folder.

My palms are hot. The weight of the scissors.

"You do not belong here," I said.

"Neither do you," she said, parting the tissue in the bag, neat and nosy. "Yellow. Loud. Cheap. Just your style."

Heat climbed my throat. I yanked the bag away. The handles cut my palm.

"Where is her father?" she asked. "Do you even know? Or was it another woman's husband? Same old game. Crawl into someone else's bed and call it love."

My mother is in my ear. You bring fire into your own kitchen and then cry when it burns.

"Get out," I said.

She took one more step, eyes on the blank square of wall where family photos would go if I believed in those. "He likes his games. He will be finished with this one soon."

The room shifted. I could see her mouth moving, but I did not hear her anymore.

I heard hallways. Rubber bands snapping my wrist. My mother is at the sink. Stop. Think. Stop.

I stepped into her space. Shoulder to shoulder. "Leave."

She smiled like she had found a new animal and wanted to see what it did when it was cornered. "No wonder he hid you. Men do not parade trash."

I moved.

I shoved her off the shelf. Her hip struck the coffee table. The vase rocked. Her hand shot out and knocked it anyway. Water spilled. Roses slid. The glass rolled, slipped off the edge, and

486

shattered. Red petals scattered. Thorns scratched patterns in the puddle. The cover image of my life smashed itself and bled on my floor.

She looked at the mess, then at me, and smiled wider. "There she is. The girl who never learned."

On the console: renewal forms, a dead pen, a marble bookend, square and brutal. Cold and heavy in my palm.

"Put that down," she said. "Do not embarrass yourself."

"I told you to leave." My voice stayed steady. My hands did not.

She stepped closer. A tilt of her head. "You are so dramatic, Victoria." The smile sharpened. "Take your bastard baby and disappear. Leave him alone. I am not leaving until he is back with me."

"Back up," I said.

She did not.

Brandy snapped hard. Trash.

My mother is in the doorway of our old kitchen. Stop.

I moved.

She leaned in, enjoying herself. "You want details? He puts me on the counter and tells me to keep my heels on. He likes my mouth in the shower, his hand on my throat, my back to the tile. He never begged with you. He begs with me. After that summer, I asked him about the neighbor girl. He laughed. Said you were nothing. A distraction. I told him to prove it. We were at the courthouse by noon. You were never important."

Static filled my head. Roses and metal climbed the room. The water crawled around my shoes. She smiled like she had found the lever that opened my chest.

"Do you want more?" she asked, almost kind. "You are the secret he keeps in the dark. The stand-in he uses when his real life is busy. He walks past you in daylight, and you follow like a shadow. You talk and talk, and he goes quietly. You cry. He leaves. He never says your name." She tipped her chin at the roses. "Did you get those because he forgot about you? Ask him about Jessica. I am surprised you do not know about that one yet."

My nails cut my palm. Copper hit my tongue. The edges of the room were pin-holed.

I set my feet. Left forward. Right braced. I drew the bookend back to my ear and let the breath leave my body.

The first swing landed with a sound that did not belong here. Not a crack. A thick, wrong thud. Her head hit the wall. A frame rattled and hung crooked.

She blinked, shock flaring into rage. She came at me. Nails raked my cheek. Her fist caught my ribs, and heat burst under my skin. She gripped a fistful of my hair and yanked me into the counter. The edge bit my hip. The bookend slipped in my wet grip.

I wrenched free and hit her again. Lower. Temple. She screamed and shoved. We lurched in rose water. Our feet slid. We crashed into the table. My knee went sideways. She clawed for my throat, breath sweet and metallic. I drove my shoulder into her and bounced her off the wall.

"Stop," she screamed.

For a blink, it was my mother. Then Brandy. Then no one.

She swung her forearm into my face. Stars burst. She kicked my shin, and we went down. Knees, petals, glass grit. She kept my hair and wrenched. Pain shot hot through my neck. The bookend skittered. I grabbed it back with both palms, marble slick.

She was still spitting my name.

I brought the weight down.

Once. Twice. Again. My shoulder burned. My forearm went numb. Red splashed the baseboard. Lipstick dragged across her cheek like a bright crayon. Petals stuck to the tile. The water ran pink. The room narrowed to the arc of my arm and the wet weight in my hand.

Everything went quiet.

The bookend was slick. I let it go. It hit tile with a blunt thud and slid to the table leg.

Sarah slid down the paint and ended up crooked. Her eyes looked past me. Her mouth was open. Nothing came out.

The room smelled like iron and roses and something animal.

"Get out of my apartment," I said, voice breaking. "Leave me and my daughter alone. Do you hear me? Get out!"

She did not move.

I swung again without thinking, an open-handed slap that smeared red across my fingers. "Get up." Nothing. "Sarah, get up. Now."

A high, thin sound filled my ears. I dropped to my knees. Two fingers to her throat, too hard, then lighter. Nothing. Wrist, slick, slipping. I bent to her mouth and waited for air and got only roses and metal.

"Sarah," I said, shaking her shoulder. Her head lolled. My hands would not obey. Adrenaline burned my chest and left my fingers clumsy. "Please. Get up."

I waited anyway. One breath. Two. A twitch. Anything. I already knew.

"I killed her," I said. Saying it made it real. The words rang through my chest like a bell.

I should call 911. I should call my mother. Julie. Someone.

My brain ran in circles and went nowhere. I found my phone, scrolled until his name steadied.

He answered on the second ring. "Victoria."

Air scraped my throat. "I need you."

"What is wrong?"

"I need you." I pleaded.

"Where are you?"

"Home."

"Give me a few minutes. I will be there." He kept talking. I hit end.

The room rushed in. The phone clattered to the tile. I slid down beside her, shaking so hard my teeth clicked. "Wake up. Please wake up." I shook her once, twice, as if I could rattle time backward. Nothing. The edges of my vision salted black. The AC clicked on, and the cool air hit my ankles. Roses and iron rose in my nose. My stomach heaved.

Brandy in my head. Ugly.

My mother, hoarse. Look at what you have done.

The bookend sat like a blunt animal. Petals clung to red. The bag breathed in the corner of my eye.

The world kept moving like it did not know I had changed its shape.

I stood. I locked the latch. I unlocked it because he would need it open. My palm stayed flat to the wood. I tried to breathe like a person.

I looked at where Sarah ended. I did not touch her. The picture frame hung crooked. I fixed it. It tilted again.

Keys at the door. The knob turned.

"I left it open," I whispered. My chest felt too tight to hold.

"Elijah," I said when he stepped in. His name felt like a plea and a confession.

The hall light framed him for a heartbeat. "What the fuck." His gaze swept the room. Smashed glass. Roses bleeding into water.

Red on tile. The marble bookend. Then he saw her. "What the fuck," louder.

He moved before I could speak. He dropped to his knees beside her. Two fingers under her jaw. Nothing. Wrist. Nothing. He bent, ear near her mouth, hand flat on her chest, waiting for a rise. Nothing. He lifted one lid, checking for light. Still nothing.

He sat back on his heels. "What the fuck," again, softer now.

He crossed to the door and turned the deadbolt with a solid click. Shock burned off his face. His eyes came back to mine. He took one long breath, then another.

"What happened?" he said. "Victoria. What did you do to her?" He took a half step closer. "Tell me what happened."

Heat flashed through me. "Do not talk to me like that. She walked in. She would not leave. She touched Isla's things. She would not stop." My throat burned. "Do not ask me what I did. Ask what she did."

His chest rose hard. He looked at her again, then at me. His voice scraped raw. "Tell me what happened. Oh my God." He stepped closer, and something in me snapped. I came off the floor swinging, open palms and fists. His chest. His shoulders. Anything I could reach.

"You told her I was a mistake. You married her. You loved her. I was just your secret. I hate you. Who is Jessica? I wish I had never met you. I wish my kid had a different dad!"

He caught my wrists. "What are you talking about? I never talked to Sarah about you. Jessica was years ago." He shut his eyes and pulled in air. "Stop. Just stop, Victoria. We have to figure out what to do about the woman not breathing on our floor."

I sagged and shoved him again. He wrapped his arms around me and held on until the fight shook out.

He let go and paced once, twice, rubbing his face, forcing his brain to work.

"I wish I had never slept with you," I said. "I wish Isla had a different dad."

"You do not mean that," he said. "Stop arguing. We have to figure out what to do right now before Isla does not have any parents."

Something broke loose again. I surged, voice rising, hands up. He pushed me back, firm, and steered me onto the couch.

"Calm down," he said, palms on my shoulders, until I stayed.

He stepped back. The panic drained off his face, leaving the hard, quiet version that solves problems.

I cracked. The crying came hot and ugly. I folded in on myself, elbows on my knees, hands in my hair, rocking once, twice, to keep my body from coming apart. "Tell me who Jessica is. Why did Jessica get into a relationship with you? Why did Sarah get married to you? Why am I the one no one claims? Maybe I deserve this. Call the cops. Put me in jail. My mother will be happy. She can raise Isla into a perfect robot. Or you take her, and maybe Jessica can be her mom."

He crouched in front of me, hands on his knees. "Jessica was a girl I dated for a few months. It ended because I did not care

493

enough to try. Sarah was not love. I married her because it was loud and easy, and I thought that was what a man like me gets. I did not tell her about you. I did not laugh at you. I kept you to myself because I was a coward and because I did not want you in my mess." His jaw worked. "You are not the one no one wants. I am the one who ran. That is on me." His fingers touched my wrist, careful. "You are not a bad mother. You are not a mistake. I kept coming back for a reason."

He drew a slow breath. "This is not the time for us to talk about us. She is not waking up. We must fix this."

He stood. "Okay. Listen to me."

The room finally breathed. It did not fill my lungs. It kept me upright.

I nodded. I could do that. I could listen.

The night opened.

We walked in.

CHAPTER SIXTY-NINE

He straightened. "Okay. Listen to me."

I nodded. I could do that. I could listen.

The hum of the fridge filled the silence. A droplet slid from the shattered vase and hit the floor with a tiny, deliberate sound. Then he moved, fast and precise, like muscle memory taking over.

He stepped around the rose water without touching it. His eyes tracked everything. Petals. The smear on the baseboard. Glass grit. The marble bookend. Sarah.

He swallowed once, and the wild shock left his face. What stayed was focus.

"Phones," he said. "Both stay here. Nightstand. Chargers in. Volume up. We do not take them out of the apartment."

I handed him mine. He set it on the table, then pulled his out and set it beside mine. Two black rectangles, still and harmless.

"Shoes," he said. "Do not change yet. Keep them on. We bag them when we are done. For now, cover them."

I moved. I brought an old gym bag and a roll of trash bags. He slipped a bag over each of my shoes and tied the plastic at my ankles, quick and tight. He did the same to his. "No prints," he said. He watched me stand and checked the knots, as if seeing me follow orders kept me upright.

"Gloves. Do you have cleaning gloves?"

My hands trembled. My voice did too. "Why are you so calm? How do you know what to do?"

"If you were raised with my dad, you would understand. I have cleaned up worse than this."

He kept his eyes on the work. "Do what I tell you. Turn it off. She is nobody right now. Think about our daughter. Do what I say."

He crouched beside Sarah and did not touch her yet. He looked at her wrists, her hair, the angle of her neck. He looked at the puddle of roses creeping toward her shoulder.

"We do not drag her through this," he said. "Towel under the head. Then the blanket. Do you have a spare?"

I brought the blue moving blanket from the hall closet. He folded it in half and laid it beside her like a bed. He slid a towel under her hair, then looked at me.

"On three. Arms. Hips. Do not look at her face if you do not want to."

We lifted. It felt like a bag of wet sand with the heartbeat gone. Something in me split then. Quietly. My stomach lurched and then steadied because his voice kept counting. We wrapped. We taped the folds.

"Her keys," he said. "She came in a car."

"I do not know." I scanned the room in jerks: the counter, under the mail, the coffee table, the rug by the couch. I tugged open the pale bag, shook it once, patted my pockets, and came up empty. "I do not see them anywhere. She must have them on her."

496

He squatted at the edge of the blanket and peeled back the tape, quick and careful. The adhesive let go with a gummy rip, lifting a few strands of hair. He folded the blue from her hip and slid two gloved fingers into the pocket of her jeans. He did not look at her face. He looked at his hands. The fob came free with a small click, keys clinking once like coins, a ring with a house key and a cheap charm shaped like a tiny palm tree. He set the palm tree charm aside; cheap gold flaked at its edges. He checked the other pocket and pulled a lipstick the color of bleeding fruit, the cap hairline cracked.

He set the fob on the table and stood. "Got it."

"You want me to drive my car with a dead body in it? What if I get pulled over?"

He looked at my face for the first time and touched my cheek with the back of his knuckles like I was breakable, and he did not want to prove it.

"Blanket," he said. "Tape."

We lifted again on three.

We moved like a team that had practiced.

We did not.

Out the front door. Down the short walkway to the driveway. Past the dead porch light. His hood up. My head down. No neighbors outside. The night smelled like heat and oil and the last of the day.

My car waited under the streetlight, a gray BMW sedan. He opened the trunk. Rubber and dust breathed up from the carpet.

"On three," he said. Knees bent. My hands under the blanket at her shoulders, his at her hips and calves. The weight sagged and shifted; the wrap rasped against our gloves. We tipped her in, careful, feet first, angling so the bumper stayed clean. The bundle landed heavily on the trunk carpet with a dull thump. He tucked the loose edge of blue under, smoothed the fold, then wiped the lip and latch where our wrists had brushed. The metal was cold through the towel. He dropped the lid. The sound felt like a lid on a box.

We walked back to the condo like nothing had happened. We went inside and moved through the rooms in a slow, weird blur, gathering everything that could tie this place to us tonight.

He went straight to the drawer and pulled the hard drive. He wrapped it in a towel and crushed it on a concrete step outside the door with the hammer from the toolbox. Fast. No ceremony. Next, he unscrewed the door cam and smashed that.

He collected towels, the blanket, the mop head, any cloth that had held blood or smell, and shoved them in without looking. We sprayed cleaner on the counters and the table, wiped until our hands burned, swapped bottles without a word, then brought out the bleach. We went down on our knees and chased the pink into the grout until the water ran clear and the smell of iron was gone. He folded the towel and the ripped pieces of fabric and shoved them into a second bag, tied it tight, and set both by the door. I double-checked the doorframes, the light switches, the spot on the wall where she had hit. He emptied the vacuum into a plastic sack and shook out the rug like we were erasing footprints.

By the time we finished, the condo smelled like chemical warfare. After blood and a body, the irony was that it was the bleach that made me think I might die.

He stripped his shirt and dropped it into a bag. He handed me a trash bag for mine. I changed in the hallway and could not remember what I did with my hands while I was doing it.

He dragged his hoodie on and tossed one to me. "Hood up."

I went to the closet and pulled on my rain boots, sliding them over the plastic he had tied at my ankles. He tried for light, out of touch. "You still wear those hideous rain boots."

I did not laugh. He looked past it and kept moving.

By the sink, a pair of sunglasses sat upside down. I did not remember when she had set them there. He looked at them for a beat. Then he picked them up and dropped them into the bag with the rest.

He paused. On the counter, the pale boutique bag still sat with its yellow bow. He took it, tied the handles, and added it to the larger sack like he was packing up a set from a play that had ended.

Elijah had the bags slung over his shoulder as I did a final walk-through to make sure all the evidence was erased.

Outside, he lifted the fob for Sarah's car and clicked unlock. A white coupe blinked two stalls over.

"I will take hers," he said. "You follow me in yours."

My legs worked because his voice gave them a job.

On the road, the world felt too bright. Brake lights. Tail lamps. The neon pharmacy sign pulsing like a heartbeat. I kept my eyes on his taillights and did not look anywhere else.

499

He turned off at the next town. A bar lot with a busted sign and a pool table painted on the window. Two pickups. A handful of cars. He parked the white coupe in the far row like it had been there for hours. He walked to my driver's door and opened it.

"Switch," he said. "Leave it."

I slid across the seat to the passenger side. He got behind the wheel of my BMW. We pulled out quietly. No hurry. No sprint. Just a curve back to the highway and then away.

The car went silent except for the engine. I watched the white line on the shoulder and tasted roses at the back of my throat.

"Where are we going?" I asked finally. My voice sounded wrong.

His hands stayed steady on the wheel. "Do you remember when I took you to Mary Jean's?"

My chest pulled tight. "Yes."

"Do you remember what I told you about the alligators?"

I closed my eyes and saw another night. Teen heat. Black water under stars. His voice in my ear, telling me why a person who did not want to be found would choose water with teeth.

"Yes," I said.

Three hours of highway and hush unspooled under the tires. Miles and mile markers. Tolls and flat dark. He drove. I watched the clock crawl and gripped my knees until my fingers went numb. They trembled anyway. When the lights of everything finally fell away, we turned off onto a narrow road with no name. Then a

500

rutted track. Palm fronds reached into the headlights and drew back. The night was a wall of sound. Frogs. Cicadas. Mosquitoes. Water breathing in the dark. When I pictured opening the door, I did not trust my legs to hold me.

He turned into Mary Jean's drive and killed the headlights. "Wait outside," he said. "Do not move." He jogged up the porch and went inside. When he came back, he was rolling an old hard-sided suitcase. "We are taking the airboat," he said. "This will make it easier to load her. We will go to the bait stretch. There should be gators there."

I waited on the porch, shaking, counting breaths, listening to insects buzz and the car tick as it cooled. When he came back with the suitcase, relief hit so hard my knees went loose. Something to do. A shape to the night again.

He popped the BMW trunk and unzipped the suitcase. He tipped it on its side, mouth open.

"On three." We slid the wrapped weight in. The zipper bowed. The hard shell groaned. He looped a rope around it twice and knotted it, a belt to keep the lid from springing. The handle creaked when he rolled it. Wheels clicked over the porch boards. The night smelled like river and rot.

At the dock, he heaved the suitcase onto the airboat deck and climbed in. He reached for me. I stepped in and kept to the dry spots. He thumbed the ignition. The engine revved up and settled into a heavy roar. The fan pushed the air flat. We skimmed into the dark.

The grass parted in silver sheets. He leaned on the stick and threaded channels he knew by memory. We cut the motor at the bait stretch. Posts leaning. Rope scars whitening on wood. The water moved under us like it was thinking.

He dragged the suitcase to the center of the deck and unknotted the rope belt. He unzipped it and folded the lid back.

"Look away if you need to," he said without looking at me.

He reached in and lifted the bundle, peeling the tape back with slow, precise movements. He folded the blue blanket aside, keeping it in the suitcase like a promise to remember. Her clothes were bunched and twisted, stuck in ways that made it clear she had not gone willingly.

He dug in his pocket and pulled out a small folding knife. The blade flashed once in the moonlight. He did not hesitate. He slid the knife under the hem and cut, careful and efficient, slicing fabric away in long, quiet strips. The sound of cloth parting was loud in the still air. He kept his face turned, never looking at her, never letting himself see more than he had to.

When the last piece fell free, he folded the blanket back over her and tucked the strips of clothing into the corner of the suitcase, like he was closing a book. Then he zipped the lid shut with a soft, final sound.

He set his palms under her ankles and behind her knees, angling her toward the rail. The boat rocked in a slow, stomach-deep way, like even the water was waiting.

He lifted her in small, careful motions, the kind a person makes when they are doing something they cannot take back. The air felt heavy, pressing against us from all sides.

502

For a second, he just held her there, halfway between the deck and the dark. His arms trembled. The muscles in his forearms went tight. I could hear the soft rasp of his breath, steady but forced, the kind of breathing people do when they are pretending not to feel.

The water lapped quietly against the hull, black and endless. The sound made my skin prickle.

He shifted his grip, slid his hands lower, and eased her feet over the side. The water accepted her without a splash, only a dull ripple that spread out and disappeared.

For a heartbeat, she hovered there, suspended by his hands and the pull of the current. Then he let go.

The suitcase creaked beneath my feet as the balance shifted, and I swear I could feel it, the weight leaving the deck, the silence deepening, the world closing in around what we had done.

He did not move for a long time. Just stared at the water, shoulders heaving, like he was waiting for it to reject her.

There is a point in the night when nothing has happened yet, and everything already has.

We waited. Long enough for my heartbeat to count a hundred. Silence but for insects and the motor ticking down. Then the surface broke. The log shape turned and opened. Teeth. It took her calf in a slow clamp and pulled. Another slid in from the left, mouth wide, and they twisted. The water went white and loud. Tearing. Then darker.

"Look away," he said.

I could not. My nails bit into the railing. The air smelled like metal and rot.

I watched until the ripples swallowed the light and the dark closed like a mouth finishing a sentence. The motor idled, soft and uneven, like it was afraid to interrupt. Elijah stared at the horizon, jaw locked, eyes empty. I stared at the water, both of us waiting for something to come back up that never would.

We watched until the ripples lay down. Elijah stuffed the blanket and tape back into the suitcase, zipped it, and tied the rope around it again. He turned the key, and the fan rose. We slid back along the channel the way we had come.

At the dock, he killed the engine. The night swallowed the sound.

He wiped his hands with a bleach-damp rag before he spoke again. The motion was slow, deliberate, like he needed something to scrub the memory off his skin.

We walked to the car, and Elijah popped the tailgate and pulled out the bags. Plastic crackled in the dark.

*****

I followed him to the back of the property, through the knee-high grass and the smell of salt and smoke that always lived out here. The old fire pit waited, half-filled with ash and rainwater.

He dumped the bags in. Paper towels, rags, the hammer, his shirt, my shirt. The suitcase. The rope. He unscrewed the red gas can and poured it carefully. The liquid splashed, darkening everything it touched.

He struck a match and tossed it in.

The fire caught with a hiss, then roared, hot and fast, the heat pushing us back. The smoke curled upward, thick and oily, carrying the smell of bleach and plastic and something that used to matter.

He pulled his shirt over his head and let it fall. "Yours too," he said.

I stared at him. He did not look angry. Just done. I peeled mine off, dropped it into the dirt, then kicked off my pants just like he did. The night air wrapped around us, cool against skin still vibrating from the fire's heat.

We stood there in our underwear, the flames painting his skin gold and mine red.

He doused the rest with gasoline.

The fire burned hotter.

I watched the smoke twist up through the night.

Neither of us spoke. The pit crackled and popped, a thousand tiny endings eating themselves to silence.

When the flames finally started to shrink, he went to the car and came back with a clean shirt and pajama pants. We dressed without looking at each other.

He tied the gas can closed, kicked dirt over what was left, and turned back.

When we got back in the BMW, he looked toward the water one last time, like a man checking a door.

"Are you sure nothing will come up about Sarah? Will Mary Jean ask questions?"

"She is gone," he said. "They will not leave anything behind. Mary Jean does not ask questions."

I looked at him and tried to understand what that meant. What kind of history makes a person say it as fact?

We drove back the way we came. The white line reached and reached. Neither of us spoke. The car smelled like swamp and rope and fear.

The fire did not just eat the evidence.

It consumed the girl I used to be and left behind someone who would never flinch at the dark again.

CHAPTER SEVENTY

We parked and came in through the front door. No one saw us.

Or if they did, they would not remember.

I stood in the living room, waiting for his next instruction. Still in shock. Still unsure what to do.

As if reading my mind, he said, "Shower."

I nodded in response.

"When you wake up, you are going into the city to trade your car. You decided you wanted an SUV. You test drive three. You sign paperwork. You post a picture if you have to. We go about our day like we were here all night asleep."

I nodded again and did what I was told.

I sat on the floor of the shower and let the water run over me. My skin felt too tight. My hands would not stop shaking. The water hit my scalp and turned static. It was not washing anything away. It was just noise filling the space where panic should have been.

Memories lined up and walked past.

Sarah and Elijah as teenagers. The hood of his Chevelle, warm under her back. Her head thrown back, laughing. The sodium lights on the beach parking lot making halos on wet asphalt. Me across the street in a window, watching like a ghost. Want pressed against the glass. He never looked up.

Then a screen lit blue in a dark room years later. A wedding post. A courthouse step. Peonies. Her new last name spelled out in a pretty font. Comments with hearts and forever. My thumb kept scrolling even when my chest forgot how to beat.

Tonight replayed next. The roses she mocked. Sarah's mouth moving. Jessica in her teeth like a dare. My mother's voice telling me to stop. Brandy's laugh from another life. The marble bookend heavy in my hand. The arc. The sound. The world going small and bright.

I tried to make sense of the heat under my ribs. Why was I this angry? What had I done to deserve being the secret, the punchline, the target?

The water kept falling. Pink gathered at the drain and disappeared. It was proof of something, but I did not know if it was guilt or relief.

I counted tiles until the numbers stopped making sense.

When I came out in a clean shirt, the apartment looked like a staged room after a showing. Blank. Fresh. A lie with good lighting.

"I am going to shower," he said. "Try to sleep."

I nodded. The words inside my mouth had no shape yet.

Then he disappeared into the bathroom.

I walked to the front door and locked the deadbolt. I stood in the middle of the room and listened to the building breathe. I walked to the guest bathroom. The pipes knocked. The air still smelled like bleach and endings.

I pressed my palm to my stomach and felt my own pulse there. The nausea rose fast and mean. I crawled to the toilet and vomited until there was nothing left, only bile and shaking.

I rinsed my mouth, pressed my forehead to the cool porcelain, and slid back to the tile. Knees to my chest. Breathing through the sting.

The night kept going. The clock ticked. The pipes groaned. Somewhere down the hall, Elijah turned off the water.

I stayed very still and tried not to come apart.

Sleep found me like shock does. Slow, merciful, and cruel all at once. Eventually, my body did what my mind could not. It shut down.

CHAPTER SEVENTY-ONE

Morning found every surface too bright. The blinds did nothing. The light came in and sat on the floor and made a point of itself. My eyes ached. I scrubbed my nails until the half-moons went pale. The smell of bleach lived in the back of my throat.

The world looked normal again, and that was the cruelest part.

Elijah came back just after seven with coffee and a paper bag. He set both down and stood a few feet away like he was checking for cracks.

"Dealer opens at nine," he said. "Keys, license, insurance. We do paperwork. Then you go to your mother's to get Isla. I will be here when you get back."

I nodded because my head knew how. My stomach did not. I drank coffee that tasted like soap and sugar.

He watched me find my purse and check for what I needed three times. He did not tell me to hurry. He did not touch me.

"Phones go with you now," he said. "Normal."

"Normal," I repeated. The word felt foreign, like a sound I was trying on for size.

Before I left, I stood in the doorway and looked at the clean room. The lie held. The flowers were gone. The glass was gone. The marble bookend was not there to glare at me. The air still smelled like a pool that had been shocked too hard. It was spotless. Sanitized. Like grief with a good scrub.

The city was awake. People had errands and playlists. I had a story to build.

The first dealership said they had two SUVs on the lot that matched what I wanted. I did not know what I wanted. I said space for a car seat and a stroller, and grocery bags that did not explode in the trunk. The salesman smiled like he could sell me a boat too.

We test-drove one with seats that swallowed me and a camera that showed me how close I came to the curb. I kept both hands on the wheel and pretended I cared about stitching. I made a joke about needing more cup holders. He laughed. I laughed because he did.

Every laugh felt like a lie I had to pay for later.

In the finance office, the air smelled like printer ink and lemon cleaner. I signed my name until it stopped looking like mine.

When the last page slid back across the desk, I pictured string and what I would keep.

I traded a gray BMW for a black Lexus SUV and a promise that I would be safer. The salesman took a photo of me next to the hood with keys raised and thumbs up.

I posted it with a caption that said new chapter.

Heart emoji. The screen glowed too bright, like it was mocking me for pretending to be alive.

The little spinning wheel felt like a lie loading.

I watched my old car roll away like a stranger. My knees shook so hard I had to sit in the driver's seat of the SUV before I could make the engine turn. My phone lit up with little hearts and someone I barely knew saying she was proud of me.

Elijah texted: Status.

Me: Signed, I wrote. On my way to Mom's.

Elijah: Good.

My mother's kitchen smelled like coffee and fried bread. Isla sat in her highchair, face milk-sweet and sticky. She lifted both arms when she saw me and made the sound she makes for me that is not a word yet.

Her bunny's ear stuck to her cheek; when I lifted her, it left a damp crescent on my shoulder.

"You traded your car," my mother said, looking out the window at the driveway. "Since when?"

"Since today," I said. "The old car was too small."

She made a sound that could mean anything. She wiped Isla's hands with a warm cloth. "You look tired."

"I am fine."

Fine tasted like ash on my tongue.

She glanced toward the hallway. "Is that man still staying at your place? Are you planning to let us meet him properly?"

"I do not know," I said. "Soon."

"Are you coming for dinner tonight?"

"Maybe. Text me."

When she turned away, I pressed my face into Isla's hair. She smelled like milk and safety. I wondered how long until that smell was gone too.

On the way home, Isla fell asleep in the new car seat without protesting. She looked so small from the driver's seat. I drove like every taillight was a test.

The new seat crackled under its plastic once, like it was learning our names.

Even the silence sounded different now. Trained. Obedient.

*****

Elijah had cleared the counters again when we came in, even though they were already clean. He took Isla from my arms and held her like he always does—whole body, two hands. He looked like he might cry, and then he did not.

"It drives nice," I said, as if we were regular people. "Backup camera that makes me look competent."

He looked out the window at the SUV. "Good."

We moved through the noon hours pretending to be busy. He took out the trash that did not weigh enough to be this heavy. I did laundry that did not need doing. The condo smelled less like bleach and more like soap, but my head still leaned in that direction.

Everything we touched felt staged. Like props from a life we had already burned.

At three, my phone buzzed with a number I did not know. A survey from the dealer. I deleted it. Another buzz. A coupon. Not her. The silence around Sarah was louder than questions.

My fingers went cold anyway. I set the phone face down on the table and walked to the sink. I washed a clean plate. Elijah watched my back.

"What?"

"Nothing," I said. "No one is asking about her."

"They will not yet," he said. "She disappears. People will assume she is out or with someone."

I nodded. The clock kept going.

Time was cruel that way. It refused to stop even when everything else had.

The afternoon stretched. The clock made each minute take a long way around. By five, the condo felt hollow and loud at once.

We fed Isla early. She dropped peas to the floor one by one. Bath. Pajamas. Bunny. Her eyes closed on my shoulder before I could lay her down.

We stood in the doorway and listened to her breathe until my chest came quietly. She slept like the world had not changed, and maybe that was mercy.

Elijah stood with his hands braced on the counter, head down. He looked tired in a way his body would feel tomorrow.

"Are you sure nothing will come up?" I asked. "About her. About last night."

"I am sure she is gone," he said. He did not look at me. "Mary Jean will not ask me a thing."

I wanted to ask what kind of woman never asked Elijah questions, and why I felt a little safer and a little more scared because of it. There was always something dangerous about the people who loved him quietly.

He moved to the stove and set a pot to boil. Olive oil and garlic hissed in a skillet. He sliced zucchini into coins and salted them with his fingers. Pasta went in. Lemon over the pan. A handful of parsley from the jar by the sink. The condo smelled like dinner fighting bleach.

Garlic won by inches. It almost smelled like forgiveness.

He set two plates. Forks. Water with lemon. He ate because he had to. I pushed pasta into patterns and counted out three bites, then a fourth that sat in my throat until water forced it down.

He did not say to eat. He said, "Enough is enough."

He reached and brushed a crumb that was not there off my shoulder. "We clean up," he said. "We try to sleep."

Sleep sounded like a word from another language. I nodded anyway.

Outside, the sky went the color of clean bone. The condo windows held the light for one last moment and then let it go.

Everything let go eventually.

The condo was too quiet. The kind of quiet that made every breath sound like a confession.

We had washed the plates, scrubbed the counters, and folded the towels back on the bar. Normal things. Fake things.

When we finally slipped into bed, Isla's room down the hall hummed with the sound machine. Elijah stretched out on his back, arms behind his head like this was any other night. His chest rose steadily, his eyes fixed on the ceiling. Calm. Always calm.

His thumb tapped twice against his bicep, the only tell.

I lay stiff beside him, sheets tangling at my knees. My body was electric, nerves firing in places words could not reach. I turned my head toward him, searching for his profile in the shadows.

"You are not even shaken," I whispered. "Why? Why would you help me?"

His jaw tightened, a muscle twitching once. He did not look at me. "Because I have cleaned up worse."

That was it. No lecture. No fear. No promise of absolution. Just that.

I stared at him, throat raw, wanting to press for more. Why not turn me in? Why not leave? Why not scream? But his silence swallowed every question.

The ceiling fan turned above us, blades chopping the night into smaller, quieter pieces. I curled into him because I did not know what else to do. His arm lifted, heavy, certain, and settled around me.

Normal is a costume. We wore it anyway.

We did not sleep. But we stayed there, pretending.

The dark did not judge. It just listened.

CHAPTER SEVENTY-TWO

The morning started with Isla's blocks clattering against the rug while I wrestled my hair into something that passed for professional.

Elijah stood in the doorway, barefoot, holding Isla on his hip like he'd been born for it. Her curls tangled against his chest, and her sticky hand clutched the hem of his shirt.

"You're good," he said, watching me button my blouse with shaky fingers. His voice was flat. Not a compliment. Just a fact he was trying to make true.

I didn't feel good. I felt like my body was too tight for my skin.

"You sure you've got her today?" I asked, even though I knew the answer.

He gave me a look that sliced through the space between us.

"She's mine too."

That was the end of that.

By the time I pulled into the office parking lot, my jaw ached from clenching. The radio had been background noise I didn't hear.

I sat there for one extra minute, forehead against the steering wheel, whispering promises to myself that I'd make it through another day.

The office smelled like burnt coffee and toner. Phones rang, keyboards clicked, laughter spilled out of the break room like nothing bad ever happened anywhere.

I slid into my chair, opened my inbox, and felt the walls tilt.

By ten, I was in the restroom, palms flat against porcelain, forehead nearly touching the mirror.

The paper towel dispenser coughed once, the light hummed like it was judging me.

The fluorescent glow carved shadows under my eyes I didn't recognize.

My lips moved, but no sound came out.

Get it together.

I said it again, louder this time, until the words scratched in my throat.

The reflection didn't listen.

Back at my desk, I unlocked my phone.

Me: How's Isla?

I typed with trembling thumbs.

Elijah's reply came fast.

Good.

I wanted a paragraph. I got a period.

I stared at the single word until the letters blurred.

Lunch break.

Me: Did she eat?

Elijah: Yes.

Two o'clock.

Me: Napping?

Elijah: Sleeping.

Answers like lifelines.

Answers like knives.

By midafternoon, my phone buzzed again.

This time it wasn't a word. It was a photo.

A photo-booth strip.

Four tiny frames, glossy with cheap shine.

In the first, Elijah grinned, crooked and unguarded, Isla perched on his lap.

In the second, she had spaghetti on her cheek, and he was trying to look stern.

In the third, she grabbed his beard, both mid-laugh.

In the last, he kissed the top of her head.

The fourth frame hurt the most.

My lungs forgot how to work.

I remembered another strip. Years ago.

Us as teenagers in the same booth, pressed together like we were daring the world to notice.

Salty hair, motel lighting, two kids with fire in their eyes.

Same rectangles. Different lives.

The walls of the office bathroom closed in.

My mind turned on me like an animal.

What are we doing? How did we end up here, from summer fuck buddies to a one-night stand to this? Playing house.

Is this real or just convenient?

Why is he so calm? Isn't he afraid of me? I killed a woman. Doesn't he know I could destroy him too?

Is Isla safer with him? He doesn't need pills to get through a day. He doesn't tremble when the phone rings.

What if she gets my temper instead of his patience? What if she grows up and fears me the way I fear myself?

Why did he come back at all? Because he had nowhere else? Because I was the bottom of the barrel, like everyone always said?

My hands were fists. My jaw was a vice.

I pressed my knuckles against the mirror until my skin ached, until I could almost imagine cracking the glass.

I opened my mouth and let out a sound that wasn't words at all. Just rage. Just grief. Just noise.

When I left the bathroom, my face was wet in the fluorescent mirror, mascara ticking like raindrops down bone.

I walked to my car after work like a woman leaving a funeral.

I gripped the steering wheel so hard the leather bit back.

I drove to an empty strip mall, parked, and screamed until my throat burned.

My throat tasted like rust.

The AC unit dripped onto hot concrete, no one looked up.

Nobody came. Good.

When I pulled back into the driveway, the condo looked the same.

Elijah answered the door with Isla on his hip, calm as ever.

He didn't ask where I'd been. His thumb tapped twice against his bicep, then stilled.

He smelled like baby shampoo and citrus.

He looked at me, then at the tear tracks, and just said,

"Did you eat?"

His voice, as always, was blunt and practical.

I wanted to throw the photo in his face and demand to know if he ever worried this would all implode.

Instead, I marched into the kitchen, made tea I couldn't drink, and slammed the cupboard so hard a plate slid and cracked in the sink.

A hairline lightning bolt across cheap porcelain.

He didn't comment. He bent, picked up the broken pieces, and tossed them in the trash with the same precision he used to lift Isla from the rug.

I wanted to scream that it wasn't just the plate.

I wanted to tell him the booth had shown me a future I couldn't live inside.

I wanted to confess that I didn't feel safe, not from the world and not from myself.

But I only stood there, shaking, while he carried our daughter down the hall to bed.

Later, when the condo was silent, I crawled into bed beside him and whispered apologies.

For the mop. For the bleach. For all of it.

I wanted absolution. I settled for air.

"You don't have to say sorry every five minutes."

His voice was flat, eyes fixed on the ceiling fan spinning shadows across the room.

"I do. Because I can't stop breaking things."

His jaw tightened. He turned his head, eyes catching mine, and for a second, I thought he might agree.

Instead, he reached for my hand, laced his fingers through mine, and held on.

"You're not the broken one, Victoria."

His voice was low and rough.

A promise he wasn't sure he could keep.

But he didn't let go.

And still,

the pieces between us didn't fit right.

Not yet.

CHAPTER SEVENTY-THREE

The news was on in the break room when I went to refill my coffee.

I wasn't listening, not really. My ears were full of fluorescent buzz, the chatter of keyboards, the faint click of high heels down the hall.

Then I heard her name.

Sarah.

I froze.

Her face flashed on the wall-mounted TV, smiling in a photo so staged it made my teeth ache.

The caption in yellow block letters:

MISSING FOR ONE MONTH.

The reporter's voice was bright, practiced, almost cheerful.

"Sarah Price, twenty years old, was last seen outside—"

The mug slipped.

Ceramic hit linoleum, shattered, coffee bleeding across the floor like ink.

"Jesus, Victoria," one of the paralegals gasped, rushing for napkins. She laughed too loudly, like broken dishes could be funny if you framed it right. "You okay? You look like you saw a ghost."

I bared my teeth in something that was supposed to be a smile.

"Just clumsy." My throat was made of glass. "Long night with the kid."

Nobody questioned it. Nobody ever does if you package it neat enough.

I crouched down, scooping jagged pieces into my palm. They cut, not deep, but enough to sting.

The reporter's voice droned on behind me until someone finally muted the TV.

At my desk, my hands shook too much to type.

I unlocked my phone and fired off a text to Elijah.

Me: How's Isla?

The reply came instantly.

Elijah: Good.

I stared at the word until it blurred. My reflection in the monitor looked like it wanted to vomit.

Lunch break came.

Me: Did she eat?

Elijah: Yes.

Two o'clock came.

Me: Napping?

Elijah: Sleeping.

I wanted more than one-word replies.

I wanted him to say something human, something that reminded me we weren't balancing on a knife.

Instead, I stared at three syllables until they became hieroglyphics.

By three, the whispers started.

Two women stood near the copy machine.

"That girl Sarah," one said, lowering her voice like it mattered. "So sad. Pretty, too. My cousin knew her from Clearwater. Said she was always wild. Maybe she ran off."

The other one snorted. "Or worse. Girls like that don't just disappear."

Their laughter was nails in my spine.

I dropped a stack of briefs on my desk so hard the papers fanned out like wings.

No one looked up.

I pressed a paper staple into my palm until it left a crescent.

I ducked into the restroom and locked the stall.

My phone buzzed.

Elijah again. This time, a photo.

The walls closed in.

My mind turned on me like an animal.

The photo hit harder than it should. Elijah's smile, Isla's hand on his cheek.

They looked untouched by anything dark, like the world forgot what we did.

My hands started shaking before I even realized I was holding the phone.

The office hummed around me, printers, voices, the smell of burnt coffee, but all I heard was the news playing behind my thoughts.

Her name again. Her face again.

I couldn't breathe right.

I told myself it was fine, that no one knew, that I was imagining the way people glanced at me, but my body didn't believe it.

Elijah was calm, steady, like this was just life now.

But how could he be so calm?

Didn't he see the blood still clinging to my memory?

Didn't he hear the lies whispering under the static?

I kept thinking someone was going to walk in and tell me they found something. That they knew.

And then I looked at Isla's picture again, at her eyes, and the fear turned inside out.

What if she found out who I really am?

What if she's safer without me?

I used to know what kind of person I was.

Now I can't even trust my reflection.

When I stumbled back into the hall, my mascara had bled into bruises under my eyes.

No one looked twice.

At home that night, Sarah's face was still waiting.

On our TV this time, smiling, teeth perfect, eyes bright, a ghost trapped in pixels.

"I told you not to watch this crap," I snapped.

My voice was too sharp, a knife across the room.

Elijah didn't flinch.

He pressed the power button.

The screen went black.

His thumb tapped twice against his knee, then stilled.

"You don't need to hear it," he said.

"I already did," I shot back. My hands shook as I pulled off my coat. "At work."

He leaned forward, elbows on his knees, looking at me like I was a car about to blow a gasket.

"So don't listen again."

"That's it? Just pretend?"

"Yes."

The word dropped like a stone in water.

Final. Heavy.

After Isla went to bed, I couldn't sit still.

My nails tapped against the kitchen table until the sound drove me mad.

"People are going to keep asking," I whispered. "They're not going to stop until—"

"They'll stop." He twisted a screw into one of Isla's toys like it was life or death. "They always stop when they don't get answers."

"Do you even care?" The words sliced out of me before I could swallow them.

His head lifted. His jaw clenched. "Don't start."

"I'm serious, Elijah. You act like none of this touches you. Like we didn't—"

"Stop." Quiet. Deadly.

I bit down on my lip so hard I tasted blood.

He set the toy down.

Leaned forward until his eyes speared me to the chair.

"It's us, Victoria. No one else. Say it."

My heart rattled like it wanted to escape my ribs.

"I can't—"

"Say it."

The silence stretched so long I thought I'd suffocate.

"It's us," I whispered.

The tension slid from his shoulders, just enough to look like he believed me.

He picked up the toy again. Twisted the screw. Conversation over.

I lay awake that night, staring at the ceiling, his words repeating until they hollowed me out.

It's us. No one else.

But Sarah's face was still there when I closed my eyes.

Smiling. Bright.

A paper tiger the world kept waving in front of me, daring me to admit it wasn't real.

CHAPTER SEVENTY-FOUR

The night hung heavily, tense and waiting, as if the air itself knew what was coming.

A thin fog clung to the parking lot, low and stubborn, the kind that made headlights smear.

Isla was asleep.

Her doll lay face down on the hall rug like it had fainted.

I stood at the sink with my sleeves pushed to my elbows, rinsing a glass I had already washed twice.

The faucet hissed. The fridge hummed. Every sound in the condo was a machine pretending to be a heartbeat.

Elijah checked the time and slid his keys off the hook.

"I'm dropping those groceries," he said. "Then I'll be back."

He said nothing else. He never knew what to say where his father was concerned.

There were words that rotted if you touched them too often. Father was one of them.

Then he bent over and kissed Isla's hair, even though she was asleep and did not know it.

He pressed his mouth to my temple the way you press a thumb to a bruise to make sure it still hurts.

The door clicked shut.

The room exhaled.

I stood there with the dish towel in my fist and listened to the quiet roll back in.

Time passed like thick syrup. Ten minutes. Then fifteen.

I loaded the dishwasher for the pleasure of the clatter.

I put on water for tea I would not drink.

I opened the window because the air felt used.

The night outside smelled like wet concrete and someone else's supper.

Somewhere, a dog barked at nothing.

When the first siren sounded, I thought it was far away.

The second came closer.

The third threaded the street like a blade.

I turned the burner off and went to the window.

Orange.

Far to the west, where the old condos sat shoulder to shoulder, a dull orange pulsed upward and painted the underside of the low clouds.

It looked like a city remembering how to burn.

I did not call him.

I texted.

Me: You good?

No answer.

Me: Answer me.

The tiny bubbles did not come.

The kettle clicked as it cooled. My breath fogged the glass.

Another siren shrieked and cut short like it had run out of room.

I put my shoes on without thinking.

I checked Isla. She slept on her side with one knee tucked up like a comma.

I tucked the blanket around her and stood there listening to the soft whistle of her nose.

She would not wake to thunder. She would not wake to the fire two miles away.

She would wake for me, saying her name.

I did not wake her.

I locked the door and stood with my hand still on the deadbolt.

That was when the phone lit up, screen bright against the dark.

But no message came through. Just his name. Just the silence of an unanswered thread.

I stared at the screen until it went dark, then I called him anyway.

It rang once. Then nothing.

I called again. It did not even ring.

I set the phone on the counter and stared at it as if I could bring him back with my eyes.

Another pulse of orange rolled against the clouds.

The dog stopped barking.

The night took a long breath and held it again.

I do not remember deciding to move.

Only the sound of my own shoes, the keys in my hand, the hall light flicking across the doll's eyes.

I locked the door behind me and ran.

*****

The air tasted like metal the closer I got.

People lined the sidewalk in pajamas and sandals, faces tipped up to the heat as if watching the weather.

Tape unrolled. Voices bounced off stucco and chain link.

The old man who sold lottery tickets stood with his hands on his head and said nothing for once.

I pushed between bodies until I could see the street.

Then I saw him.

He stood behind the line, one hand at his mouth, the other curled in on itself like it had forgotten how to open.

His shirt was streaked gray. Ash clung to his hair and made him look older by ten winters.

He did not see me at first.

He did not see anything but the condo with smoke bleeding from its windows and the balcony railing warped by heat.

His thumb tapped twice against his thigh, then stilled.

"Elijah," I said.

It was not a shout. It was a name carrying itself across the heat.

His eyes found me like a magnet finds nails.

Something broke across his face and was gone before it could call itself a feeling.

He shook his head once.

"Victoria," he said. Just that. As if that were enough for both of us.

The windows belched smoke and glass, fire curling out in uneven breaths.

People around us flinched as another section of the balcony gave way with a cracking sound.

The night carried it like a wound.

"What happened?" I asked.

Not a question that wanted details. A question that needed a place to be set down.

"He was drunk," Elijah said. "He was always drunk. There was the stove. There was a match. There was me at the door, and him with that look."

His mouth pressed thin.

"He told me to get out of his condo. So I did."

He said nothing else about it, only that when he came back the second time to check on his father, the condo was already burning and there was no saving him.

His jaw worked. He did not meet my eyes.

His chest moved, shallow and mean, like breathing was a job he no longer wanted.

"Did you try?" I said.

I heard what it made me sound like and hated the shape of it.

"I did," he said. "They pulled me back."

He lifted his hand. The knuckles were scraped. The skin was bubbled in one place where heat had licked it.

He looked at the red like it belonged to someone else.

"I did," he said again, quieter. "I did."

A firefighter moved past us with a coil of hose like a sleeping snake.

The steam came in sheets.

Someone called out numbers. Someone else answered with numbers that made sense only to the men carrying them.

The upper floors gave in by sections, fire chewing through drywall and wood.

The orange light dimmed as firefighters drowned it, not suddenly but in waves, until only smoke remained.

The crowd shifted.

A woman beside me started to cry and did not seem to know it.

I touched Elijah's sleeve. It was gritty.

He did not pull away, but he did not lean in.

He was a post in a storm. The last straight line in a notebook full of torn pages.

"They will ask you things," I said. "You will say as little as you can. You will say the truth that fits inside a box. You went to bring food. He yelled. You left. That is the shape."

He nodded once, like a man agreeing with a sentence he had already written.

We stood while the condo sagged into itself, walls scorched, windows hollowed, until nothing was left but a dark, wet frame against the streetlights.

The air cooled and tasted of coins.

Somewhere, a radio spat names none of us knew.

The tape lifted and fell in the breeze like a weak wrist.

The first time I saw them bring a sheet out, I thought it might be for show.

That is a small, mean thought, and it fit too well in my head.

Elijah did not look.

He stared at the curb with sudden, brutal interest.

His mouth drew thin.

The muscle in his jaw ticked its little metronome.

"We should go," I said.

He shook his head.

"Not here."

"Home," I said.

"No," he said. "Not here."

As if the ground could hear him if he said it more than once.

A woman in a heavy coat asked him his name and wrote it down on a clipboard.

He answered without looking at her.

When she thanked him, he nodded at her shoes.

When we were finally allowed to leave, the crowd thinned into clusters on the sidewalk.

I led him to the truck.

He climbed in like a man told to perform a task he did not fully understand.

The seat belt clicked.

He turned his head as we pulled away and watched the last of the orange collapsing into a wet, black thought.

We did not speak on the drive.

The light at Forty-Fifth turned red.

We waited there with three other cars while the cross traffic moved through their ordinary night.

A boy in the next lane sang with his window down to a song I could not hear.

A pair of women in scrubs laughed at something on the passenger's phone.

A stray cat threaded the dumpster behind the taco place like a shadow sewing its own seam.

The world did not look different at all.

That felt like violence.

At home, the hallway smelled like someone drying laundry and someone else trying to cover cigarette smoke with lavender spray.

The doll lay where I had left it, facedown.

I wanted to kick it and hated that I wanted to.

Elijah locked the door.

He stood with his back against it like he was the lock.

"Go shower," I said. "You're covered."

He did not move.

I went to him and pulled on his T-shirt because he was looking at nothing, and it scared me.

The fabric was stiff in places where steam had kissed it, and ash had married cotton.

He let me peel it off him, let me take his hand and lead him to the bathroom like he was a patient, and I was a nurse who had already seen too much.

The mirror gave us a version of ourselves I did not recognize.

His hair was gray with ash.

My face was white with the kind of fear you cannot confess without sounding ungrateful for breath.

I turned the water on.

Steam climbed the glass.

He stepped in.

He stood with his hands braced against the tile and let the water carry gray down his back.

It ran in dirty veils and then turned clear and then dirty again as I worked the soap into his hair.

I was gentle where the heat had raised his skin.

I was not gentle where it had not.

He did not flinch.

When he stepped out, the towel I wrapped around his shoulders turned a dull, ugly color.

He sat on the edge of the tub and stared at the grout line like it had a secret.

I took a washcloth and cleaned the ash from his ears and the crease beside his nose.

The sink water grayed and then cleared.

I kept going until the cloth came away clean.

"Say something," I said.

My voice sounded thin to me.

"What," he asked.

It sounded like a man who had been asked to lift a car.

"Anything."

He swallowed. His eyes looked past me.

"He reminded me he hated me. That's the last full sentence he said."

I nodded. I did not say I was sorry.

Sorry is for accidents. This felt like a long plan finding its last step.

He set his elbows on his knees and bent forward.

For a breath, he looked like a boy.

Then he straightened, and the boy slid back under the water.

We dressed him in a clean shirt.

He stood at the mirror.

His hands were steady.

That frightened me more than if they had shaken.

He went to Isla's room and stood in the doorway without stepping over the threshold.

He watched her breathe.

He lifted one hand to the jamb and left it there without touching anything.

In the kitchen, I filled a bowl with water and set it in the sink.

I put the washcloth in it again, though there was nothing left to lift.

The motion gave me a job. I needed a job more than I needed breath.

He came behind me and set his palm on the counter next to mine.

Our hands were a mirror that did not quite match.

He looked at the water circling the drain.

"He's dead," he said. "And I'm not."

There was no victory in it. No relief. Only the simple weight of the sentence.

He let it sit there a long time.

"I left when he told me to. I didn't try to be a hero."

"You tried to get him," I said. "They pulled you back."

He nodded once. "I tried."

The word sounded like a stone skipping once and then sinking.

"And I walked away when they told me to. I walked away because I knew what it would do to her if I didn't."

His eyes cut toward the hallway where Isla slept.

"I picked our life. I chose our life. I chose it to know it was the only way forward."

I pictured string and what I would keep.

I reached for him.

He let me take his wrist.

His pulse thudded against my fingers like a thing trapped and tired.

"It's over," I said.

I did not know if I meant him and his father, or us and the story we had been trying to outrun.

The sentence could hold both.

He nodded again.

He did not cry.

He did not throw anything.

He did not say the things I thought he might, that he had wanted an apology and got a fire, that boys raised in heat learn to shape themselves into the flame that does not ask.

He only stood there and let the smoke out of our kitchen.

He only stood there and let me hold his wrist until my hand went numb.

When the clock clicked past midnight, I made tea I still could not drink.

I set the cup near him for the heat of it and left it there to cool.

He drifted down the hall and back, the way people do when a room will not hold them.

He opened the front door and looked out at the quiet parking lot as if it might give him a different answer now.

He closed it again and locked the bolt.

We did not speak of the word funeral.

It waited in the space between us like a folded suit.

Near two, he sat at the table and looked at the wall and finally said,

"He's gone."

"Yes," I said.

"I'm still here."

"Yes," I said.

"And you."

"I'm here."

He leaned his head back and stared at the ceiling as if it could explain us to ourselves.

I watched his throat move when he swallowed.

I watched the set of his shoulders and how they did not slump.

I waited for the storm I had known would come since the moment I saw him inside that orange light.

It did not come tonight.

When the tea was cold and the air tasted like old coins again, he stood.

He came around the table and put his palm on the back of my neck.

It was not tender. It was not rough. It was a hand with a purpose.

He held there a moment, then let go.

"Sleep," he said.

I shook my head. "You."

He looked at the dark room beyond me.

"I can't. I'll be out here."

I went to Isla's door and looked in, then looked back at him.

Then I went to the bedroom and lay on top of the covers and stared at the ceiling that had nothing.

CHAPTER SEVENTY-SIX

The condo carried the silence of a graveyard. Every cupboard I opened sounded too loud. Every footstep echoed. The fire might have been miles away now, but it followed us home, stitched into the air, hanging off Elijah's shoulders like a second skin. Isla pressed her face into his chest, and he almost smiled. Almost.

The funeral came fast, quiet, and mean. A folded program with the wrong picture on the front, too much gray in the photocopy, a name that meant nothing in church air. Men who had shared beers with his father stood and spoke, voices thick with praise about how he would give the shirt off his back, how he had a laugh that filled a room, how he was the kind of man you could call at midnight, and he would show up. Each word landed like a stone in Elijah's chest. Because the boy who had lived in that man's shadow remembered nights without dinner, mornings with bruises, afternoons spent alone. He remembered the door slamming, the silence that followed, the hunger that never left. The lies stacked up around him until he could barely breathe. He didn't blink. Elijah stood at the back, hands locked behind him, shoulders straight as a guardrail. His thumb tapped twice against his wrist, then went still. He didn't go forward when the preacher called the family. He didn't look at the coffin. He didn't cry. The AC coughed cold over the pews, hymnals rasped like dry leaves.

I watched him the whole time, wondering when he would break. Wondering if he could. Wondering what it meant if he didn't. The only sign he was still alive was the tick in his jaw and the way his fists closed when people touched his arm in passing. When it was over, he walked out before the last prayer was done, his boots loud against tile, his shadow dragging me with it.

That night, when Isla was asleep and the condo was silent, the storm finally came.

"You keep looking at me like I'm stone," he said, voice low, rough. He stood by the window with the blinds half shut, city lights cutting stripes across his face. The vent clicked on, and cold air reached my ankles. "Like nothing got in. Like I'm not already split open."

I froze with the dish towel in my hands. "I never said."

"You don't have to." His eyes were sharp. "You think I don't hear it in your silence? You think I don't feel it every time you watch me breathe?"

"Elijah."

"I pulled at that door until my skin burned off." His hand curled into a fist. "I tried. And I left him. I left him because he told me to get out, and maybe part of me wanted him to burn."

His voice cracked on the last word. He swallowed hard and kept going, like stopping would kill him. "You dragged me into blood and bleach and graves I didn't ask for, and I stayed. I stayed because of you. Don't you dare look at me like I'm the one who can't feel."

The towel slipped from my hands. My chest burned. "I never said you couldn't feel. I just... you never let it out. You never let me in."

He laughed once, sharp and hollow. "Let you in? You want in, Victoria? It is fire. It is fists. It is a kid growing up too fast because nobody looked. It is a mom playing family in another state. It is me staying with a whore, so my life looked normal, wanting her

549

gone and going back anyway because chaos was all I knew. It is walking around town thinking every guy had slept with my girl, and she would still pick me just to twist the knife. I tried to date someone else, and it made my life worse, because broken is the only language I ever learned. Maybe I didn't care she was dead. Maybe that is why I was calm. Maybe I am not the man you keep building in your head. Maybe I am more messed up than you."

I crossed the room before I knew what I was doing. "You stayed this time. Even when I'm the one who ruins everything."

He slammed his hand against the window frame hard enough that the blinds rattled. "Stayed? Do you know what it costs me to stay? I see her face every time I close my eyes. I hear him screaming. And I walk back here, and you look at me like you're waiting for me to shatter. Maybe I already did."

My throat tightened. I wanted to run. I wanted to fold myself into him. "I'm terrified," I admitted. "Of losing you. Of losing Isla. Of myself. What I've done. You think I don't hate myself every day?"

His chest rose and fell like he was holding back a hundred words at once. Finally, he let some out. "You think I don't? You think I don't wake up wishing I'd been the one to burn instead of him?"

The words cut me open. "Don't say that."

"Why not? It's true. He's gone and I'm still here, and maybe the world got it wrong."

I shook my head, tears hot. "No. The world got it right, Elijah. Because you're here. Because Isla needs you. Because I need you. And if you ever think you're replaceable, you're lying to yourself."

550

For a second, his face broke, just long enough for me to see the boy he used to be. Then he pressed his palms to his eyes, dragged them down, and whispered, "God, I'm so tired of fighting ghosts." His hands fell, eyes locking on me. "And you. Why me, Victoria? Why anchor yourself here? You had Texas. You had a chance to be free. You could have walked away and built a life that didn't smell like smoke and rot. But you stayed tethered to me. Why? Because I ruined you? Because I ruin everything? My mother. My father. And now you. Maybe I'm the wreck you keep choosing because you don't know how to stop."

He stepped toward me, voice ragged now, fury and grief tangling. "You want truth? Then answer me this. Why me? Why cling to me like a damn anchor when you had the chance to cut free? In Texas, you could have built another life, pretended I was just some mistake from your past. But you stayed bound to me. Why? Because I wrecked you? Because I ruin women the way I ruined my mother? The way I ruined my father? Maybe you stayed because you knew I would ruin you too." His breath came harsh. "Maybe I'm not the fantasy you dreamed up. Maybe I am every ugly thing you fear in yourself. Maybe you chose me because you're as broken as I am."

I snapped then, words ripping out before I could stop them. "You think you ruined me? You think you're the only one who destroys everything you touch? I stabbed a girl before I even knew your name. I killed someone with my own hands. Don't act like I'm the innocent clinging vine and you're the poison. I am just as wrecked. Maybe worse. Maybe I chose you because you're the only one who looks at me and doesn't flinch." My voice climbed and cracked. "I don't need a new life. I need this. I need you. Even if it kills me."

Loving him felt like choosing the knife and handing it over.

551

He took another step, eyes wet, furious. "Then we're both sick. Both cursed. Both chained to a fire we can't put out." He pressed his palm against his chest. "I walked away from you once because I thought it was the only mercy I could give. I married another woman just to keep myself from crawling back, to prove I could live without you, to keep from ruining you the way I ruined my mother. And then Texas, like some sick joke the world played on me, put me right back in front of you. I left you in that hotel room because I thought I was protecting you. Look what good that did. My stupidity tied us together forever. Don't you see? I never had the strength to stay away. And now I don't know if I saved you or destroyed you worse than anyone else ever could."

I was shaking so hard I could barely stand. My throat ripped with words. "You think I had choices? You think Texas was freedom? I carried you like a ghost in my veins. Every man I looked at, every bed I tried to sleep in, you were there. No one else could ever touch me without me wishing it were you. Do you get that? I couldn't cut free. I didn't want to. You ruined me, and I still wanted you to ruin me again."

His laugh was savage, broken. "Then you're sicker than me. Because at least I know what I am. At least I can say it out loud. You keep dressing me up as your salvation when I'm the bullet in your chest." He pointed at himself, eyes wild. "I am not your safe place. I am not your cure. I am the reason you'll never breathe easy again."

I screamed back, raw and shaking. "Then kill me, Elijah. Because I can't undo you. I don't want to. You're in my bones. You are the infection and the medicine all at once, and I would rather die from you than live without you."

552

He froze, chest heaving, tears cutting through ash still clinging to his skin. For a moment, we just stared at each other, hysterical, ruined, and tethered by something so violent it felt holy.

Finally, his jaw clenched so tightly I thought it might crack. His hands dropped, knuckles white, and his words ripped through his teeth. "I can't hold all of this for both of us anymore. If we're going to survive it, we tear apart together or not at all."

I staggered forward, tears burning down my face. "Then break with me. Stop acting like you're the only one who bleeds. You think I wanted this? You think I wanted a life where my daughter's father is a man who can't sleep at night? Where I dream about blood on my hands every time I close my eyes? I am chained to you because I love you, not because I'm too broken to leave. Don't you dare reduce me to that."

He shouted back, voice raw, "And don't you dare make me your redemption. I am not your hero, Victoria. I am the villain you keep choosing, and maybe that says more about you than it does me."

The room spun, both of us ragged and heaving, not willing to surrender.

He reached for my wrists, not to hurt, but to keep me from tearing away, and I shoved back against his chest hard enough that he stumbled. His teeth bared, eyes wet and furious. We collided again, hands grabbing, pushing, clinging like drowning people. Words tore out between the contact, accusations and confessions that could not be unsaid. We were not calming each other, not saving each other. We burned every lie down to the bone, daring the other to run or stay in the fire.

A glass tipped in the sink and broke with a clean sound. Water spread across the counter and down our forearms.

Elijah's breath rasped. "Say it."

"What?"

"That you wanted me to ruin you."

"I wanted you to love me," I said. "You did it like ruin."

He blinked once. It looked like pain. His jaw worked. "Then say you hate me."

"I will not."

"Then say you will stay."

"I will."

My knees went soft. I held the counter like it could keep me upright. If we kept talking, we would say the thing that could not be taken back. I wanted him to stop. I wanted him to keep going until there was nothing left between us but the truth.

He stepped in so close that our foreheads nearly touched. His jaw tightened. "We break together, or we don't make it at all."

I stood there shaking, the weight of his words cutting deeper than the fire ever could. He had finally cracked, not in pieces, but in flame. And in that fire, I saw the truth. He wasn't unbreakable. He was breakable in all the ways that made him mine.

In the sink, a broken rim of glass gleamed under the light.

CHAPTER SEVENTY-SEVEN

The morning after felt like walking barefoot across glass. Every sound was too sharp—the spoon against the mug, Isla's feet dragging her doll across the floor.

Elijah sat across from me, eyes bloodshot, arms braced on the wood as if he moved the whole room might collapse. We had screamed ourselves hoarse. We had bled words we couldn't take back. But now there was only silence, thick enough to choke on.

I tried to butter the toast. My hand shook too much to spread it clean. Isla hummed to herself, obliviously, asking for more jelly on her toast. Elijah picked up the knife and spread it for her, his hand steady when mine wasn't. He didn't look at me. Not once.

By the time I was at work, I could still feel the vibration of our fight in my bones. The office chatter was needles in my ears. People laughed too loudly at nothing. A printer jammed, and I nearly flinched.

I shut myself in the restroom and pressed my forehead against the stall wall, breathing shallow. The tile smelled like bleach, but not the kind we had scrubbed into Sarah's blood. The partition was cold against my forehead. I took three slow breaths, and none of them helped. My chest felt too small. My ribs locked around my heart like iron bars.

I texted Elijah.

Me: Is she okay?

Minutes ticked. My pulse thundered in my throat. Finally—

Elijah: Fine.

One word. Like that was supposed to hold me together. I stared at the four letters until they felt like a door closing.

I typed, deleted, typed again. Did she eat lunch? Delete. Did she nap? Delete. My fingers itched to call him, to hear his voice, even if it was flat, even if it was cruel. But I refused. I kept quiet and only sent one more.

Me: Tell her I love her.

The read receipt lit, and nothing followed.

That night, when I dragged myself home, the condo was quiet but alive in the wrong way. The sink dripped, slow and steady, the sound too loud in the silence. Garbage truck brakes sighed two streets over, thin as a wheeze.

A dish towel had slipped to the floor, damp at the corner. Elijah's boots sat by the door, lined up neat, like he needed order to hold himself together. Even that small sight split my chest open.

I gripped the counter like it might steady me. The world tilted and spun. We were looping. Cycles. Summer to summer. Wire on the beach. Hotel rooms in Texas. Now this. Playing house on the bones of the girl I killed. A family blooming from rot.

My stomach lurched.

I locked myself in the bathroom and pressed my fist to my mouth so Isla wouldn't hear me sob.

Why was Elijah so calm? How could he keep moving forward when I was unraveling every time I closed my eyes? Wasn't he afraid of me? Shouldn't he be?

Maybe he would be better for her than I was. He didn't snap like a live wire when the world pressed too hard. He didn't look at a child and wonder if one day she'd flinch from him.

I pressed my back to the door, sliding down until the tile caught me. Tears blurred the edges of everything.

Why me, Elijah? Why come back? Was it love or just convenience, the wreck drawn back to the wreck because chaos felt like home? Maybe I was still the mistake everyone warned me I'd become.

The towel lay just outside the bathroom door where I had dropped it, dark with water. Proof that he could live in the mess, even if I couldn't.

My throat ached with the scream I couldn't let out. My heart beat hard, wild, too many beats at once. Three heartbeats. One mine. One his. One more we had made.

My hands shook as I tore open the cabinet beneath the sink. The box was buried under cotton balls and cough syrup. I bought it weeks ago and prayed I would never need it.

My breath came shallow as I peeled the plastic, as if the sound alone might wake Isla in the other room. The test felt too heavy in my palm. I counted the grout lines to sixty. The dye crept like a slow bruise. It bloomed through the paper, cruel and certain.

Minutes stretched into forever. The little window was filled, slow and merciless.

Two lines. Clear as blood on tile.

The second one didn't ask who we were. It only asked what we had done.

I pressed both hands to my stomach and curled forward until my forehead hit my knees. A sob tore out of me, silent and violent. Not just fear. Not just grief. Something bigger. Something I couldn't name.

The door creaked. His shadow filled the crack of light.

"Victoria." His voice was raw.

I couldn't look at him. My fingers trembled as I shoved the test across the tile toward him. It clattered once, stopping at his socks.

For a second, I almost hoped it would vanish if he didn't look.

Silence swallowed us.

Only the sound of my breath breaking. Only the sound of the world tilting for good this time.

His hand came down slowly, steadily. He lifted the test, stared, jaw set. His thumb tapped twice against the plastic, then went still. For the first time since the fire, since the fight, his knees bent. He sank down to the floor across from me. His eyes found mine, sharp and undone.

Three heartbeats between us. His. Mine. And the one we had made.

CHAPTER SEVENTY-EIGHT

He didn't speak at first. He just sat on the cold tile, the test clutched in his hand like a verdict waiting for a jury. His jaw worked, grinding, as if he could chew the truth into something smaller, easier to swallow. His eyes flicked from the lines to me, back again, like he kept hoping the result would blur away if he looked hard enough.

Finally, he exhaled, a sound that was more growl than breath. His eyes narrowed, jaw tight. "You weren't…" He stopped, shook his head once, then bit it out. "I thought you were on birth control."

The tile was cold through my knees. I kept my spine against the cabinet to stay upright.

Heat flared up my neck. "Obviously, I was. Obviously, I have been. But I have also been cleaning blood out of my head every night and trying to keep us alive. I missed a pill. Maybe once. Maybe more. I don't know. I have been stressed and preoccupied since you came back, and you know it."

His mouth flattened. "So, this just happened."

"This didn't just happen," I snapped. "This is what happens when two people who can barely breathe still find a way to find each other. Don't make it sound like I planned this. I didn't trap you."

He stared at me, eyes hard. "Then say you didn't."

My mouth went dry, but I gave him the only truth I had. "I didn't," I said, voice shaking. "I didn't trap you. I wouldn't do that to you. Or to me."

Silence pressed in. His grip on the test eased a fraction, like the words had taken a little weight from it.

"Don't." His voice was sharp. "Don't say you didn't mean it. We don't get to pretend. We burned the world down together, Victoria. And now…" He lifted the test, shook his head, and dropped it onto the floor between us. "Now there's no way out."

My head snapped up. "No way out of what? We already have Isla. There was already no way out. So, say what you actually mean."

He swallowed, voice rough. "Well, fuck. I thought I was going to struggle being any kind of father to one kid. And now you want me to try with more?"

Tears blurred my vision. "Then tell me what you want. Tell me if you want to leave. Tell me you can't do this. Just don't sit there and make me feel like I'm trapping you."

His eyes snapped up to mine, vicious with hurt. "You think that's what this is?" He leaned in, forearms braced on his knees. "I stayed when I could have walked. When I should have walked to protect you both from me. I stayed for you. For Isla. And now." His voice broke, ragged. "Now it's not just the three of us anymore." He stared like the room had lost its corners.

I covered my mouth, a sob ripping free. "I don't know how to survive this, Elijah."

He reached out, caught my wrist, not gentle, not cruel. Just holding me in place. "We survive it the only way we know. We fight through. We tear down what's left and we build again. But we don't run."

I shook my head, frantic. "We can't raise another baby in this place. Not in this condo. Not with ghosts in every corner."

His grip tightened. "Then we don't." He shifted closer until his forehead pressed to mine, his voice low, steady, final. "We find somewhere else. Somewhere no one knows our names. We start over. I don't care if it's a hole in the wall or a shack by the water. We will make it ours."

I searched his face, desperate, broken. "You swear?"

His mouth curved, not a smile, but something like a promise. "I swear. Maps and promises, that is all we have. But it will be enough. We will make it enough."

He stood and hauled me up with him. We moved like old people, careful with the ground. He opened the junk drawer and pulled out a beat-up road atlas with a torn cover and a coffee ring stain. We took it to the floor. He flattened the creases with his palms.

Coffee ringed Florida like a bruise.

"How did you pick Texas?" he asked, eyes on the paper.

"I did not," I said. "It picked me." I caught his hand. "Close your eyes. Hold your finger in the air."

He obeyed. I closed my eyes too and wrapped my hand around his wrist. Together we brought his hand down, blind, the paper crackling under our skin. His fingertip landed on a cluster of lines and green. A river name we could not pronounce curved like a promise.

He opened his eyes. "Tennessee."

My chest pulled tight and then loosened. "Tennessee."

"We will make it ours," he said. "Mountains, trees, quiet. No one who knows us."

He tapped the map twice over the dot like a signature.

"We will make it ours," I repeated.

The test lay forgotten on the tile, a fragile line between ruin and rebirth. His arms came around me, and for the first time since Sarah, since the fire, since the fight, I let myself believe we could crawl out of the wreckage. Not clean. Not whole. But together.

Elijah lowered a hand to my stomach, hesitant, almost reverent. His thumb brushed the thin line below my navel without thinking.

"Another heartbeat," he said, the words catching in his throat. "I never thought I could be a father to one. Now…" He shook his head, eyes burning. "Now I will be damned if I do not try to be a father to the next one."

I covered his hand with mine, the weight of it steady and impossible. Tennessee stared back from the map, promise inked in roads and ridges.

Florida had been ruin.

Texas had been running.

Tennessee would be rebirth.

"All the pieces we broke," I whispered, my voice shaking but sure. "We will carry them with us. And we will rebuild anyway."

He bent until his forehead touched mine, the smell of ash and salt between us. "Then that is what we will do," he said. "Piece by piece."

"Then we'll go," I said.

And this time, we don't look back.

EPILOGUE

The road to the rental wound through trees that looked like they had been standing watch since before anyone learned our names. Pines. Oaks. A low creek you could hear before you saw it.

The place was a small cedar cabin, one story, weathered boards and a tin roof, a narrow porch with rough-hewn posts. A rusted stovepipe cut the sky. A neat stack of split logs leaned by the steps. The screen door squeaked when it opened and sighed when it shut. It was ours by key and by want.

Boxes lined the wall. Isla wore socks and slid across the wood like it was a game she had been waiting to play. Elijah set a toolbox on the counter and ran his palm along a crooked cabinet door as if it had a pulse. The air smelled like old lemon cleaner and new beginnings. It did not smell like smoke. Cold iron waited in the corner where a woodstove would live when winter came. A line of flat creek stones sat on the porch rail like small moons.

We put the ultrasound photo on the fridge with a chipped magnet. Two shadows in a gray sea. Proof that a line on a stick had turned into sound. At the appointment, the tech had turned the screen, and there it was. A gallop. Fast. Sure. I cried without looking at Elijah. I did not have to. His hand found mine on the paper sheet and held.

Outside, a neighbor waved and kept walking. No one knew us here.

The quiet did not look at me like it knew my past.

Elijah hauled a headboard down the hall and did not swear when it scraped the paint. He only steadied it and tried again. He

564

measured a window for a curtain and wrote the numbers on his palm. He carried the crib box to the bedroom and sat on the floor to read the instructions. He did not throw them away. He did not pretend he could do it alone. He set out the screws in rows like a prayer.

Isla climbed into the empty closet and made it a fort. She asked if the bears would find us here. Elijah told her there were no bears in this house. He said it with a straight face. She believed him. So did I.

I stood in the doorway and watched them and thought about Florida. Heat that never let up. Streets that knew my footsteps. I thought about Texas. A room that smelled like cleaner and fear and the sound of a door closing when it should have stayed open. I put my palm on my stomach, and the baby moved like a fish turning.

"Tomorrow," Elijah said from the floor, a screw between his fingers. "We take her to the creek."

"Tomorrow," I said. "And the day after."

He looked up at me. The light through the blinds cut across his eyes. He did not look like the boy who had learned to make a fist before he learned to ask. He did not look like a man who needed to burn to stay warm.

He looked tired. He looked alive.

He set the screw down and came to stand in front of me. His hand settled on my stomach. He did not say anything at first. He did not have to. The house filled with simple sounds. A bird. Water on stone. Isla counting to ten for no reason.

"We keep the promise," he said. "We start here."

I nodded, my throat full. "Piece by piece."

He smiled, small and real. "Until we have all the pieces."

Later, after the crib stood straight and the sheets were smooth and the tools were back in the box, we sat on the porch steps and watched the last of the light turn the trees the color of copper. A moth bumped the screen and kept trying. Fireflies stitched the yard with slow light. The air cooled and did not bite.

Isla fell asleep sideways across my lap. Elijah tucked a blanket around her and left his hand there a moment longer than he needed to.

He rested his hand on my stomach. His thumb found the thin line below my navel, a quiet vow.

"Home," he said. He said it like a test, like a prayer.

I said it back, quieter.

I looked up at the Tennessee sky, a clean field of stars above the little cabin and the dark line of the hills and the road that had led us here. Every road we took taught us how to leave, and still, they bent back to each other. We were the point the map kept circling. I thought of the map on the floor and the way our hands had moved together without looking.

He looked at me like a man done running. "I love you," he almost whispered.

"Say it again," I said, closing the space between us. He framed my face in his hands and kissed me, slowly and certain.

"I love you," he said against my mouth.

We did not need it easy.

We became the home we needed.

Together.

Rebecca Davis writes the kind of stories that bleed, dark, romantic, obsessive tales about broken people who find each other when the world least expects it. She does not shy away from trauma, rage, or love that hurts, because she believes those are the moments that carve us into who we are meant to be.

Rebecca's love for writing started in childhood. She filled notebooks with stories, poems, and worlds no one else could see, eventually winning a high school writing award that convinced her she was meant to do this. She graduated with honors, carrying that passion forward even when life demanded other roles from her.

By day, Rebecca is a Personal Injury Paralegal, wrangling real-world chaos and fighting for people's stories to be heard. By night, she pours that same grit into fiction, creating characters who refuse to be silenced. All the Pieces is her debut novel, born out of years of collecting memories, scars, and what-ifs.

A lifelong book addict, Rebecca has a collection of over 1,700 books, ranging from vampire romance to classic history texts. Her shelves are as eclectic as her stories, proof that sometimes obsession builds into destiny. She calls herself a book nerd, a history collector, and a dreamer with too much caffeine in her system and too many plots in her head.

When she isn't writing, she's home in Florida with her husband and their three daughters. Family is her anchor, messy, wild, and beautiful. Her daughters inspire her daily with their wit and resilience, and her husband has been her fiercest champion, the love story behind every word.

Rebecca is also a passionate advocate for autism awareness and support, inspired by her own family, and she proudly supports veterans, honoring their resilience and sacrifices.

She believes love is the bravest choice we can make, no matter how much it hurts. That belief threads through everything she writes because broken things can still be beautiful.

Coming Soon from Rebecca Davis:

🔥 All the Fire

Some ghosts don't die.

Some of them live in the mirror.

I used to think I could outrun what we did.

But you can't bury love and sin in the same grave and expect

one to stay quiet.

Florida was supposed to burn behind me.

But the universe doesn't do mercy, it does reminders.

And hers found me again.

Victoria Drayton.

The girl who taught me how to bleed and call it survival.

The girl who killed to keep me alive.

She says we were kids. That we didn't know any better.

But I still see her face every time I close my eyes.

Every scream. Every lie. Every kiss.

It all smells like smoke.

And when I find her again, it's not fate.

It's punishment.

Because some loves aren't meant to heal you.

They're meant to finish what the fire started.

I told her love was dangerous. I forgot to mention so was I.